Blush

ALSO BY JAMIE BRENNER

Summer Longing
Drawing Home
The Husband Hour
The Forever Summer
The Wedding Sisters

A Novel

JAMIE BRENNER

G. P. PUTNAM'S SONS

New York

PUTNAM
— EST. 1838 —

G. P. Putnam's Sons
Publishers Since 1838
An imprint of Penguin Random House LLC
penguinrandomhouse.com

Hardcover ISBN: 9780593085752
Ebook ISBN: 9780593085769

Printed in the United States of America
1st Printing

Book design by Elke Sigal

Dedicated to Jackie Collins and Judith Krantz

To make a great wine, a winemaker has to put all at risk,
and walk a fine line between complexity and spoilage.

—LOUISA THOMAS HARGRAVE, *THE VINEYARD*

Blush

Prologue—1985

Cutchogue, New York
Spring

It was the time of year known as bud break, that late-spring moment when the entire vineyard turned green.

She looked out at the orderly rows of plants as far as the eye could see. The knotty wood trunk of the vines gave way to a lush canopy of leaves that her father tamed with wire, and little nubs of the fruit poked through with the promise of abundance. It was Leah's favorite season, the moment before everything changed.

The sun began to set, but her father showed no sign of slowing down. Her older brother had lost interest and wandered off long ago. Her father patted her head, saying, "At least one of my children is paying attention to what's important." The praise thrilled her. "See here, Leah—we don't need all these shoots," he said, indicating where he had clipped away at the plant tied to the trellis wire. "This is the primary shoot, and we can't have others competing for the plant's resources."

Her father had been bringing her out into the fields from the time she could walk. The winery was her home, and the acres of surrounding fields were her secret garden. This made her feel special; it made her feel like she had a destiny, and no matter what happened at school or with her friends, she had something bigger to hold on to. Here, she belonged.

A young man emerged from the row of Syrah plants. Javier was her father's most trusted field hand.

"Javier, tomorrow we'll start at five thirty," her father called out to him.

"Yes, Senõr Hollander."

Javier had black hair and black eyes and long limbs that made her watch his every move with fascination. When he disappeared into the distance, the fields suddenly felt a little less alive. She was twelve years old, Javier was her first crush, and her feelings made the vineyard seem even more magical.

At dusk, she and her father walked silently back toward the sprawling eighteenth-century farmhouse that her parents had converted into a winery. She heard laughter from the back deck, an assembly of women in which her mother held center court.

It was the last Tuesday of the month, and that meant book club.

Her father walked past the group with a small wave to Leah's mother, following a path around to the front of the building. Leah lingered, hoping to remain unnoticed for even just a few moments so she could watch them. The women all looked glamorous, in their dresses by Halston, Nolan Miller, and Escada, their hair teased and sprayed into style, their lips bright with gloss. But the standout in any crowd was always her mother, with her ash blond hair, blue eyes, and sharp cheekbones. She looked like the actress who played Krystle Carrington on their favorite television show, *Dynasty*.

Their glasses bubbled with the sparkling version of Hollander Estates Winery's pale pink wine, the one called blush. Leah's brother, Asher, had snuck a sample for them both one day when they were helping out in the bottling room. It was sweeter than she'd expected, better than she'd expected—especially since her father dismissed it as "swill."

"Then why do you make it?" she'd asked him. Her father was the winemaker, and if it was swill, it was swill he had created on purpose. He was a third-generation vintner, a family tradition that had begun in 1910, when her great-grandfather was gifted a winery in Mendoza, Argentina, as payment for a debt. Her father had told her the story many times.

"Because it sells," her father said.

It was a calm, windless evening, and a honey-like scent hung in the air, a promise of the summer to come. The women took seats around one of the cherrywood tables, carrying their wine and books. They were already flipping through pages, whispering and pointing at certain passages. Occasionally, one of the women would glance over to make sure Leah didn't hear what they were saying.

"Leah, time to run along," her mother said. "We're going to begin."

Leah did not want to run along. She yearned to be included in the group, to get dressed up and sit by her mother's side and talk about books.

"When you're older," her mother had said when Leah shared this with her. What she hadn't confessed was that she'd been reading the books with them all along, sneaking her mother's copy when she wasn't around. The pages were filled with sex.

Leah had been tempted to admit her secret to the winery's sales rep, Delphine, who had recently joined the book club. She'd spotted Delphine reading *Scruples* in the tasting room just a few days earlier. Delphine herself seemed to Leah like the heroine of a novel: beautiful, exotic, and endlessly knowledgeable about wine in a way Leah hoped to be when she grew up. Delphine was French. Leah's parents constantly had to remind Delphine not to smoke in the winery because it would "blunt the palate."

Now, looking around the veranda, it seemed the entire book club was assembled except for Delphine. She lingered until her mother placed a cool hand on her back.

"Leah, you *must* go," her mother said, consulting her diamond Ebel watch. "And where is Delphine? I have half a mind to start without her."

She looked around, but the only new arrival was Leah's father, breathless and red in the face.

"Vivian, I need to speak to you," he said.

"Can't it wait, Leonard? We're about to begin."

"Absolutely not."

What could this be about? Her father never went anywhere near the book club, and Leah knew that that was exactly how her mother liked it.

Vivian excused herself from her friends, patted her perfectly coiffed hair in irritation, and followed her husband down the stairs a discreet distance from the deck. Leah followed them and ducked behind a flowering shrub.

"Delphine is hysterically crying in the office. I need your help dealing with this."

"What happened?"

"What happened is—she's been sleeping with our accounts, and now one of our biggest is dropping us."

"Dropping us? Why?"

"Because Delphine broke up with him. This is why women shouldn't work at a winery!"

He stormed off, leaving her mother clutching the Bulgari necklace at her throat. She spotted Leah, who tried to slink away. "For the last time, get to the house, young lady," her mother said. "You don't belong out here."

Of course she did. No matter what was happening, Leah knew it was the only place she'd ever belong.

Part One

⁓

Bud Break

Girls may start out smart, but not all girls
stay so damned smart.

—JUDITH KRANTZ, *LOVERS*

One

New York City

"I'm looking for something decadent," the woman said, leaning over the counter and squinting at the menu board. "Something to impress."

She was not one of Leah's regular customers, the ones who stopped in every week to buy cheese for their weekend charcuterie boards or just to stock their fridge. Those people Leah had come to know over the years, as they debated the merits of tossing a good Castelrosso into salad instead of feta.

"Are you looking for a soft or hard cheese?" Leah asked. Typically, she would ask for more information: What other food would be served? If wine would be part of the meal, what varietal? But lately, she was distracted.

"Either one," the woman said. She had brown hair shimmering with gold highlights and wore a chic, lightweight trench coat.

"I'm a big fan of the Kunik," Leah said. "It's a triple cream cheese. Very silky texture and truly delicious. Try this—like butter," she said, passing the woman a sample of the soft white cheese.

The woman tasted it, and her eyes widened. "You know what you're talking about."

Yes, she did. Leah had opened the cheese shop eighteen years earlier, when her daughter was just three years old. The small space on the corner of Seventy-Ninth Street and First Avenue had stood vacant for a long time. Every day, passing it on her way to buy groceries at Agata & Valentina, she fantasized about turning it into a cheese shop. She even had a name for it: Bailey's Blue, an ode to her love of blue cheese.

The door opened, and this time it was a regular, a party planner named Roya Lout who had talked more than one hostess into using Bailey's Blue instead of a larger purveyor. "I like your style," she had declared, and Leah knew she wasn't talking about her clothes. Years earlier, before it was popular, Leah had made a commitment to feature locally produced cheese, and her shop consistently showcased northeastern artisanal varieties.

There had been a time when she thought about expanding her space to include the location next door if it became available. She taught wine and cheese classes in the cramped back room of the shop, and she could use a dedicated space for that. At just around eight hundred square feet, Bailey's Blue had one long counter, and one display case filled with wheels of creamy Brie, Camembert, Comte, and Gruyère. She also had one case for her beloved blues: Roquefort, Stilton, Gorgonzola, a few wedges of the classic Maytag, Pur Chèvre Bleu from Illinois, and Bergère Bleue from upstate. The shelves behind the counter brimmed with jars of assorted olives, figs, chocolate-covered almonds, artisanal crackers, and jam—the accoutrements to tease out the nuanced flavors of fine cheese. Her husband had recently added a mounted display of cheese knives and serving boards for sale.

"It's getting cluttered in here," she'd said. But Steven, recently retired and now working beside her in the shop, was eager to make his mark.

As it turned out, there would be no expanding next door: the landlord was selling the entire lot to developers, and they would be losing their lease in six months. It was happening all over the Upper East Side neighborhood known as Yorkville, once a haven of mom-and-pop bakeries, hardware stores, boutique pharmacies, and beauty shops. Now entire city blocks were being razed to build high-rises, the small businesses replaced by CVS and Citibank.

Steven saw it as an opportunity to start fresh with a bigger, better space.

"Change can be a good thing," he said.

Leah, who had been in business for nearly two decades, felt like maybe she needed a moment to catch her breath.

"Congrats," Roya Lout said. "I read your daughter's story. To be published in *The New Yorker* before she even graduates college? She's a genius."

A genius who had not answered any of Leah's texts or calls for the past few days.

"Thank you," Leah said, brushing the concern about Sadie out of her mind. "And I think you'll love this Hudson River Valley blue. It's mellow, but you'll notice a bit of tanginess."

Roya slipped the sample into her mouth. "Mmmm," she said. "There are some tropical fruit notes in here. Right?"

Steven walked in, his arms laden with shopping bags. He gave the customers a nod of greeting before joining Leah behind the counter.

"Mission accomplished," he said, unpacking the special cheese wrapping paper and bags from Formaticum she'd run out of. Her delivery wasn't due until tomorrow, so Steven had made a trip to Brooklyn. She smiled at him.

Steven Bailey was tall and lean, his thick dark hair threaded with silver. His intense eyes appeared green-gray, except in the sun, when she could see they were, in fact, blue. He was as handsome as he had been the day she first saw him. She had been fresh out of college, working behind the counter at the legendary shop Murray's Cheese in the Village, where Steven was the assistant manager. It was supposed to be just a summer job, a last hurrah in the city before she returned to the Hollander winery to take her place in the family business alongside her father.

It hadn't worked out that way.

Another customer appeared in the doorway, and Roya and the trench coat woman had to squeeze in to make room.

"Good morning, Mrs. Fryer," Leah said. The woman had lived in the neighborhood for sixty years and had been widowed for half of that time. She kept busy with her four Dachshunds and local gossip.

"Tell me it isn't true," Mrs. Fryer said.

"What isn't true?" Roya asked.

"I'm going to take the Kunik and the Brie," said the trench coat woman.

Leah nudged Steven out of the way so she could reach into the cheese case. The place really was not big enough for the two of them.

"She's closing the shop," Mrs. Fryer announced to the whole store.

"No one's closing anything," Steven said.

"Who're you?" Mrs. Fryer asked.

Steven and Leah exchanged a look. She shrugged.

"I'm Leah's husband, Steven. We met last week."

"Well, you can't fool me, *husband*. The landlord sold to developers. This entire block is going! They're putting up a big condo."

Outside, Mrs. Fryer's leashed dogs began to bark. "I'll be back this afternoon for my Gouda." The door stuck as she left, and warm air wafted in. The trench coat woman reached to close it. When she paid for her cheese, she handed Leah a business card.

"My name's Anouk Jansen—I'm a real estate agent."

"Anouk. What a lovely name. Swedish?" Leah said.

"Dutch. If you're looking for a new retail space, feel free to be in touch."

"We're definitely looking for a new space," Steven said, taking the card from Leah.

"At *some* point," Leah said, shooting him a look.

Everything was moving way too fast.

A few months earlier, in a corporate restructuring, Steven's company had offered senior management—including members of the in-house legal team—the option to take a package and retire early. Steven had jumped at the chance. He'd never enjoyed being an attorney. It had always been a means to an end: supporting his family. But now that Sadie had only one year left of college, the pressure was off.

Leah had fully supported his decision. The truth was, she was ready for a change, too. She'd become tired of running the shop. She'd lost the spark. Yes, she still loved cheese, and maybe she would still try to teach. But she'd had enough of the day-to-day running of the business: the payroll for her part-timers, the politics of the New York City Department of Health, the vendors, her landlord.

But when she admitted to Steven that she wasn't planning on reopening, he had other ideas.

"I'll help you. I'll have so much free time. We can run it together. It can be *our* cheese shop."

Leah had been shocked by the suggestion. And not in a good way. Growing up, she'd seen her parents navigate working together, and it had been fraught. "Someone has to be the boss," her mother had once said to her.

Maybe she could discuss it with her mother next week; she and Steven would be vacationing at the vineyard where Leah had grown up.

Steven opened the register and folded in some receipts.

"Do you need help with the class tonight?" he said.

"No, thanks—I've got it."

He turned to the shelves, rearranging jars that were already exactly how she wanted them. She looked away, willing herself not to ask him to stop. She loved her husband. But all of this togetherness was an adjustment.

It would get easier—she hoped.

Two

Upstate New York

"I can't believe you didn't even pack yet," Sadie Bailey's boyfriend said. He sat at the small wooden desk next to her bed, waiting for her to finish halfheartedly tossing clothes into an overnight bag.

He had every reason to be impatient. After all, they were supposed to already be on the road to his parents' beach house on Cape Cod.

"Almost done," she said, glancing up but avoiding eye contact. Behind him was a poster of Sadie's favorite Virginia Woolf quote: "Who shall measure the heat and violence of the poet's heart when caught and tangled in a woman's body?" *What does that even mean?* Holden had once asked.

They had so little in common. And yet she'd found Holden Dillworth irresistible, with his golden-boy good looks and boundless energy. By day he was captain of the crew team; by night he was a beer-chugging partier. Sadie had been smitten the moment she spotted him at the dining hall.

Holden had blond hair and brown eyes. He had flawless skin and teeth that had never needed braces. He very much resembled Kristoff from *Frozen*, though a tad less burly.

Sadie, on the other hand, did not resemble a Disney princess. She might be cast in a movie about a family's perilous flight from the Ukraine in the 1800s, which was something that had actually occurred in her ancestry. Sadie had curly dark hair and brown eyes and was not tall. She did, however, have her mother's dramatic eyelashes and a version of her father's high cheekbones, as well as an aquiline nose that she felt gave her face a certain strength of character.

Holden initially found her seriousness and intellectualism intriguing. But now reality was catching up to them. Holden complained about how much time she spent reading and writing. He complained that Sadie was never willing to be "spontaneous."

Things had worked when crew was in season; they made time for each other in the margins of their first priorities. This always felt like an appropriate balance to Sadie. She never considered it a sacrifice to write instead of hanging out with Holden. And she thought Holden felt the same way about her own schedule, until crew ended, finals finished, and he announced that they finally had time to "really hang out."

It wasn't that she didn't want to spend time with him. But apparently the only thing Sadie knew how to be truly devoted to was her writing.

Sadie closed the overnight bag. "I need to talk to you." She beckoned Holden over to the twin bed in the corner. They sat facing each other. He shook a lock of hair out of his eyes, even blonder now after a month or so of sunshine. "Look, I'm sorry I'm distracted. I just met with Dr. Moore."

"Can we not—for one weekend—talk about Dr. Moore or your thesis?"

Sadie immediately felt defensive. The only reason she was at that particular school was Dr. Moore.

Sadie had applied to only one college. It was a decision that mystified her parents and high school advisors alike. It was not the most prominent school—certainly not as prominent as, say, Harvard or

Princeton. It was not the most beautiful campus—certainly not as beautiful as, say, Vassar. But the college had one thing that no other school had: English professor Rohita Moore.

Sadie had first met Dr. Moore when she was a junior in high school and had won a spot at YoungArts, a prestigious national arts competition. The essay she'd written had been part poetry, part treatise on the objectification of adolescent girls in popular culture. YoungArts flew her down to Miami, where she had room and board for a week to spend with other high school artists—writers, ballet dancers, playwrights, actors—and to study under mentors who were professionals in their field of interest. One of Sadie's mentors had been Dr. Moore, a groundbreaking music journalist who had also published several volumes of award-winning short fiction. Now she was her academic advisor, and Sadie had planned to spend the summer working as her research assistant.

She'd never been more excited about anything in her life. The fact that she had just been published in *The New Yorker*—the magazine that published her literary idol Susan Sontag—paled when compared to the anticipation of working with Dr. Moore for the next few months.

Holden would never understand, but there was no place she would rather be, even on a flawless spring afternoon, than inside the redbrick Colonial building that was home to the English department. Somehow it smelled of musty library books even though it didn't actually house a book collection.

An hour earlier, Dr. Moore had welcomed her into her office looking uncharacteristically somber. In hindsight, Sadie should have known something was up by the lack of Dr. Moore's usual warm smile.

Dr. Moore stood and closed the office door. She wore one of her signature jewel-toned dresses that complemented her dark skin and large brown eyes. She had close-cropped hair, and the only jewelry she wore was medium-size gold hoop earrings. A striking woman, she wore her beauty effortlessly because she knew her looks were only her second-best asset.

The thing Sadie liked the most about college was the way it felt to be surrounded by brilliant women. In high school, she'd read the book *Steal Like an Artist*, and it said if you were the smartest person in the room, you were in the wrong room. Well, for the first time in a long time, she felt like she was in the right room.

Dr. Moore resumed her seat and leaned forward at her desk, looking at Sadie with a direct gaze. "Sadie, you continue to miss all the key deadlines for your thesis."

"Um, well, not all of them. Exactly."

She had been admitted to the university's honors English program, a track that would enable her to take masters-level classes during her senior year. To graduate with the honors degree, she would spend her senior year writing her thesis. The outline had been due the week before finals, and she still had not handed it in. The shameful truth was, she still couldn't quite home in on the right angle for her paper.

It should have been easy. The subject of her thesis was her favorite writer, Susan Sontag. She'd originally intended to examine two works: Sontag's *Illness as Metaphor* and her seminal 1964 essay "Notes on 'Camp.'"

She had thought her passion for Sontag's work would be enough to sustain her through the rigors of developing a thesis.

Apparently, it wasn't.

"I'm a little behind, but I have my topic now," Sadie said. "Detachment as methodology in the works of Susan Sontag."

"You were supposed to have finalized your topic months ago. You should have an outline already."

"I can catch up."

Dr. Moore clasped her hands together and leaned forward on the desk. "Sadie, I can't in good conscience keep you on as my research assistant. Even if I wanted to overlook the fact that your status in the honors program is in jeopardy—a prerequisite for the research position—you need to focus on your academics."

Sadie crossed her arms, hugging herself. "I just need a little more time. Can we talk after the weekend?"

"Sadie, this isn't something that can be figured out in one weekend. Nor should it be. I want you to give this some thought."

Some thought? All she'd been doing was thinking about it! She was exhausted.

"I don't know what's wrong with me," she said quietly.

"Nothing's wrong with you. This is exactly how you should feel."

"I'm supposed to feel like I'm failing?"

"No. But this is meant to be a challenge. Have you ever felt challenged before?"

"Of course," she said. But inside, the answer was a stunning no. She'd never thought of it that way before. She'd always worked hard, but writing short stories felt natural to her—like flexing a muscle that ached to be stretched. Writing this paper, based on research and a sort of rigid academic logic she wasn't accustomed to, was like she was asking her body to lift two tons.

"Sadie, the purpose of this time of your life is to push yourself. Get out of your comfort zone. Dig deep."

Dig deep? Sadie's ideas were subterranean. There was nowhere *deeper* to go.

So no—she wasn't in the mood to spend the weekend at the beach meeting Holden's family.

She looked up at him.

"The truth is, Dr. Moore fired me from my research position. I have to get back on track. I mean, maybe I wouldn't be offtrack if I wasn't going out all the time."

"Going out all the time? You're a twenty-one-year-old hermit."

What was he talking about? She went out. Sometimes. Not everyone could keep up with his drinking.

"Look, I'm not outdoorsy like you. I didn't grow up in Connecticut."

"What's that supposed to mean?" Holden said.

Sadie was not a beach person. She didn't want to lie down in glorified dirt. She didn't want to walk barefoot and step on creatures. She didn't want to deal with plastic bags packed with moldering food.

Holden didn't wait for her response. "Sadie, I'm sorry about the gig with Dr. Moore. But you have all summer to figure this out. Let's get on the road." He walked over to her dresser and pulled out some clothes, tossing them into the half-packed bag. "No more excuses. We're going to have a great time. My parents and sisters can't wait to meet you."

Sadie wanted to meet them, too. She wanted to meet his mother, Catherine. His dad, Douglas. And his sisters, Lily and June. She wished she were the type of person who could run around with the sunny blond Dillworth family, clamming and sailing and doing whatever it was normal people did on a summer weekend.

But she had to work. Surely, Holden would understand that.

"You're asking me to choose between you and my work."

Holden tossed his car keys from hand to hand, impatient. "Are you coming or not?"

When Sadie didn't move, Holden kicked the desk chair. She flinched.

"So that's it?" Holden said. "You know, it's one thing to work all the time, to never be spontaneous . . ." There it was again. She wasn't "spontaneous" enough. "But now you're just bailing for no reason. It's bullshit."

"I'm sorry," Sadie said.

"This is over." Holden headed for the door but then stopped and turned around. "One more thing: don't be sorry for me. I feel sorry for *you*. You think you're living some big 'life of the mind.' But you're not living at all."

Three

Sometimes Vivian Hollander wondered if her husband was testing her. At the very least, he was trying her patience. But after fifty years together, she could never stay angry for long. And at that particular moment, she couldn't let her irritation show at all.

She was surrounded by customers on the vineyard's back deck, a four-thousand-square-foot space the family called "the veranda." Lots of groups of women in sundresses, open-toed shoes, jumpsuits, aviator sunglasses. Men in cargo shorts and baseball hats. People were out to have a good time. Her employees, wearing dark blue T-shirts that read *Hollander Estates Vineyard* on the front and *Family owned since 1971* on the back, poured glasses of wine at the long bar.

The veranda offered a perfect view of the vineyard. From her vantage point it was just endless green fields. Not a single house could be seen in the distance and never would be; decades earlier, her husband had sold the development rights of all their acreage to the county as protected farmland.

The sun was shining, and a breeze blew off the nearby Peconic Bay. The North Fork of Long Island had roughly thirty-four thousand acres of active farmland but was also a peninsula framed by the Long Island Sound, the Peconic, and Gardiners Bay. The terrain and climate offered unique—and uniquely challenging—conditions for founding a winery. And no one had done it before Vivian and her husband, Leonard.

In recent decades, dozens of new wineries had followed the path she and Leonard had forged. Today, other North Fork wineries might have flashier ads or trendier packaging, but one thing Hollander Estates had was legendary status. They were the first, they were the original, and plenty of customers—not all, but enough—knew that a conversation with Vivian Hollander was worth every penny they paid for their glass of Chardonnay or case of Cabernet Franc. Vivian made daily appearances in the tasting room and on the veranda. Her primary role had become that of the winery's glamorous figurehead.

But she still had opinions, and that was why, when one of their employees made a beeline for her, explaining that, "There was no one in the office to sign for the new labels," she was disconcerted. New labels?

"I tried to find Mr. Hollander," the employee said. "But he's not answering his phone."

Vivian didn't bother asking why he didn't try to find Asher. No doubt their son—the vice president of Hollander Estates—was on one of his endless lunch breaks.

She looked out at the vineyard and spotted her husband walking among the vines in the distance.

"If there's no one to sign for the labels, just let them be returned," she said. The employee shuffled back to the office, and she made her way down the veranda steps to the grass. Shielding her face from the sun with her hand, she walked through the rows and rows of leafy plants tied with trellis wire, just the smallest green berries beginning to appear.

Leonard, as always, was lost in his own world. His love of the vines perhaps rivaled even his love for her.

When he finally noticed her, his hooded dark eyes lit up. Okay, so maybe his love of the vines didn't compare to his feelings for her. No, she could never stay angry for long.

And yet.

"Leonard, you aren't changing the labels on any of the bottles, are you?"

Vivian hadn't been involved with the day-to-day running of the business for many years now. In the early days, she'd done everything from weeding the crops to knocking on restaurant doors to, yes, designing the labels. They were eggshell colored with a parchment edge and midnight blue lettering—elegant and timeless. Why mess with them? It had to be their son's misguided idea.

"Asher suggested it was time for a change. I'm giving it a try," Leonard said.

"Why on earth would you do that?"

"To encourage his involvement, Vivian. You know I've been asking him to contribute more."

"Well, let him contribute in some other way," Vivian said, distracted by a text from her head of housekeeping: *There's a problem with one of the guest suites.*

Vivian could not imagine what that problem might be, but with her daughter arriving in two days for a long-overdue visit, she couldn't take any chances. Every summer, she counted the days until her daughter arrived with her family. She wished Leah visited more often—really, she wished she'd never left. But she couldn't blame her for creating a new life for herself in Manhattan. Not after the way Leonard had handled things.

"I need to get back to the house. Leonard, promise me—don't change the labels."

He leaned forward and kissed her on the cheek. He smelled like fresh-cut grass and the sweet apple shampoo he used of hers while complaining it was too "girly."

The trellised stone path from the winery to the main house was worn and familiar to Vivian. She had walked back and forth under the pergola, with its winding vines of roses and wisteria, for nearly fifty years.

The sight of the mansion still surprised her sometimes. When she had first set eyes on the house as a young newlywed, it had been a humble, rambling three-hundred-year-old farmhouse befitting the potato fields it had once stood upon. Over the decades, as the winery flourished, the house had evolved to the châteauesque wonder that had landed it on the cover of more than one architectural magazine. But in her mind's eye, it was still the home of her early marriage, the days when she woke at six in the morning to start pruning vines. It was the land that had created their fortune, but lately, it was the house that made her feel rooted in her own life.

Vivian took a shortcut to one of the side entrances. The red Italian slate was hot under her feet; she could feel it through the thin soles of her ballerina slippers. She still wasn't used to wearing flats, but she had finally made peace with the fact that at her age, she could no longer spend every day in heels. It didn't matter that some customers somehow felt no hesitation in showing up to the tasting room wearing shorts and sneakers; Vivian still valued decorum.

As soon as the house came into view, she saw a flash of movement, a figure walking toward the hedgerow and disappearing from sight. If it weren't for the hair, she might have missed it. But that hair.

Bridget Muldoon had first appeared in her son's life last August, the latest in a seemingly endless parade of vacuous young women, none of whom he ever seemed inclined to settle down with—not that Vivian wanted him to settle down with any of them. Admittedly, since Asher was almost fifty, this did not reflect positively on his judgment or life choices. But he was her son, and Vivian worried about him.

Bridget was twenty-eight years old, with long auburn hair the shade of a purebred Irish Setter. Asher marveled over the color as if it were a miracle of nature, despite the brown roots that appeared once a month.

She took the winding back stairs to the third floor, where the guest suites—formerly her children's bedrooms—were located. Only one of them was still occupied: Asher's. He'd never moved out, and Leonard didn't mind because he was always on call to help with the business.

She passed a sitting room, a decorative ottoman, a reading room, and continued down a long hallway to the bedrooms.

"In here, Mrs. Hollander," the housekeeper said, leading her to the en suite bathroom of Leah's childhood bedroom. Vivian and Leonard entertained a few times a year, and during some of their more extravagant weekends, their visitors stayed overnight. But Leah's room had not been occupied since their New Year's weekend celebration, when the governor of New York stayed with his wife.

"Oh, my good lord," Vivian said.

The bathroom was all white marble and custom millwork, with an antique cherrywood-framed mirror mounted above the vanity. The white monogrammed towels hanging on the nickel bars were the first hint that something was amiss: they were all smudged with lipstick and streaked with peachy beige face makeup. The vanity was covered with jars of moisturizer, lipsticks, bottles of nail polish. A hair dryer was left plugged into the wall; the trash bin overflowed with tissues and round cotton discs also bright with makeup. Dirty clothes were piled in one corner.

What on earth was Bridget doing in this bathroom? If she was sleeping in Asher's room, why not use that bathroom? Clearly, she'd decided to use this room as her dressing space.

"Please, just throw all of this away," Vivian said. "Salvage whatever towels you can clean, and the rest—just dispose of those as well."

"Throw it away? The makeup and hair dryer, too?"

"Yes! This is a trespass. Total disrespect for this home. And lock the door behind you."

She took a deep breath. In just a few short days, Leah would be in this space. For now, Vivian would forget about Asher and his ill-mannered girlfriend. She wouldn't worry about labels, or changes, or anything else. She wanted to focus on the positive.

Her daughter was coming home.

Four

Leah spotted the distinctive turrets of her childhood home rising in the distance and felt a flutter of excitement. As Steven navigated the road, she opened the passenger window, inhaling the briny air as though it were the first time she'd breathed in months.

The winding drive leading to the house was lined with towering, densely leafed European hornbeam trees. The surrounding acreage was abundant with wild lavender, an apple orchard, and formal English flower gardens. Vivian, with her affinity for English gardens, spent years planting flower beds and trees to cultivate a showcase garden. The apple trees had also been a pet project; it had taken six years for the first Cortland apple tree to bear fruit, and that first apple was treated like gold.

A familiar face greeted them inside the house. Leah embraced the family chef, Peternelle, hugging her fiercely.

"Dinner's on the veranda—you're late. Hurry, hurry . . ."

Peternelle had been with the family for as long as Leah could remember. She was British, round-faced, with pink skin that barely seemed to age and pale blue eyes. The only sign that Peternelle was older now than she was in Leah's memory was her hair, which was white instead of its former brown. Some of Leah's most vivid memories were of Peternelle cooking her breakfast, a special concoction she'd called "eggy toast"—French bread with a hole torn in the middle, an egg cracked in the center and cooked in a frying pan.

By the next day, they would be on winery time: awake with the chirping of the birds, early-morning strolls out in the fields, late-afternoon Chardonnay in the tasting room, followed by dinner on the veranda. Only eighty miles from Manhattan, but a world away.

"We're barely ten minutes later than we told them we'd be. I built in time," Steven said.

Still, they rushed to the winery's back deck, which overlooked the vineyard. During the day, it served as an extension of the tasting room. On weekends, it was often reserved for weddings. At night, it was one of the family's favorite spots for dinner, overlooking the endless greenery of the vineyard.

"There she is!" her mother called out, standing from her seat at one end of the table long enough to seat twenty. It was their "picnic" table, made of plank cherrywood. Tonight, it was set for six, with a crisp white runner down the center, cobalt blue wine goblets, and bunches of blue hydrangeas and coral tea roses in short Murano glass vases. Leah knew that inside the house she would find every room filled with flowers.

As a girl, Leah had taken the simple elegance of life at the estate for granted. During the week, there were three formal meals a day. Vivian maintained a chef's garden, and every morning after breakfast Peternelle would pick vegetables and thyme, basil, rosemary, or mint for that evening's dinner preparation.

Her parents had hosted lavish parties nearly every weekend. She would watch them plunk fresh strawberries from the garden into flutes of sparkling white wine, her mother dressed in Halston or Ungaro, with a wildflower tucked behind one ear.

Tonight, her mother looked beautiful as always, her carefully maintained silver-blond hair coiffed and just reaching her shoulders. She wore a white linen dress and ropes of black pearls around her neck. Her manicured nails, kept short enough to be functional, were a glossy coral that matched her lipstick.

Beside her, her father poured a glass of red wine. He wore a powder blue polo shirt and his usual khakis, his white hair striking against his tan. While he had once been handsome in a young-Marlon-Brando sort of way, now his features appeared blunt and almost brutish in his creased face. But his intense dark eyes flashed with brilliant intensity, and when he gave a rare smile of approval, it had the force of a stadium light.

He waved them over, and Leah could tell by the set of his jaw that he was annoyed by their late arrival. Leah had learned, by following her mother's example, not to get caught up in her father's moods.

Across from them, on the opposite side of the table, was her brother, Asher. Looking at Asher was like looking at a male version of herself; she and Asher had their father's dark coloring. In the summer, they tanned no matter how much they hid under hats and used sunblock. It was their Sephardic roots—Argentina via Ukraine via someplace long forgotten. Now in his late forties, Asher still had the youthful appearance of a much younger man. They had their shared forebears to thank for good skin and thick hair.

Next to him, a pretty redhead wearing a low-cut halter top. Ah, yes—the girlfriend du jour, Bridget.

"I'm so sorry we're late. The traffic . . . ," Leah said, kissing her mother and father and taking a seat next to her brother. Asher raised his hand for her to high-five him hello.

Steven shook her father's hand and kissed her mother on the cheek, gestures that reflected relationships that had mellowed into mutual respect after some rocky early years.

"I was just telling your mother to start without you, but she wouldn't hear of it," her father said, summoning one of the food servers, who appeared with trays of cucumber cups stuffed with crab meat and seared scallops.

"Do we have salad? Bridget's not eating fish," Asher said.

"I thought you're pescatarian," Vivian said. Then, to Leah, "Have you met Bridget?"

"No, I haven't." Leah smiled at the young woman. The very young woman. When would her brother grow up?

Her father stood and uncorked a fresh bottle of wine. "We're having steak for the main course, so I'm going to recommend the Cabernet." Cabernet Sauvignon was one of the grapes her parents had their earliest success growing. The fruit had thick skins and the vines were hardy, so the climate was not an issue. It was one of the first grapes her father taught her about when she was a girl. It was the world's most widely planted grape, but it hadn't even existed before the 1600s, when it was produced by a cross between Cabernet Franc and Sauvignon Blanc.

"Nothing against the Cabernet, Dad, but a glass of rosé would be perfect right now," Leah said. Like a lot of their friends, she and Steven had fallen into the habit of drinking the crisp, pale wine all summer.

"This winery will make rosé over my dead body," her father said. "You know how I feel about trendy wine. Fads come and fads go, but quality is forever."

She knew, and yet she couldn't help but prod him to change his mind. "Dad, come on. Rosé isn't a fad. Last summer the Hamptons literally ran out of it, people were drinking so much."

"That's a red flag. One year the vineyards can't produce enough, then the next year you get stuck with stock you can't move. I've seen it happen."

She let the subject drop. It wasn't her business. It wasn't her problem. He'd made that clear a long time ago.

Growing up, she believed the winery would be her life's work. After graduating Barnard with a business degree, she'd been prepared to return to Hollander Estates and work alongside her father. With her brother disinterested in the winery, she was the heir apparent.

Apparent, that was, to everyone but Leonard. The wine industry was rife with sexism. Her father, a vintner who learned how to cultivate grapes from his immigrant father, believed that a winery was a man's world. When Leah realized the full implications of this, it had been painful—so painful it had taken her a few years before she could visit the vineyard. By that time, she had met Steven and had a demanding job in Manhattan working for the legendary cheese purveyor Murray's. She rationalized that things had happened for a reason: if she had stayed on the North Fork, she wouldn't have met Steven.

"Fine. I'll have the Viognier," she said.

She would never understand her father. He refused to produce rosé, and yet he devoted time and energy to Viognier, a very old, difficult varietal to grow. He'd told her once that the rough translation of Viognier was "the road to hell." But oh, how it paid off. Every season, Hollander's light white wine, with its notes of jasmine and white peach, was her favorite. When the vintage was most fresh, it was so clear it almost looked like water. As the months passed, the color deepened and the flavor changed. That was the amazing thing about wine: It was never one thing. It had a life cycle.

"The Viognier is too light to pair with the meat," her father said.

"Leonard, indulge us. We're philistines," Steven said. There was the slightest edge to his voice—just enough for Leah to notice. To be fair, she had no one to blame but herself for his cynicism about her parents. When she and Steven first met, her feeling of betrayal at being turned away from the family business had still been fresh. As they began dating, the portrait she'd painted of her family over long walks and dinners had not been flattering. Stung by her father's refusal to bring her into the family business, she told Steven how she had been turned away unfairly—disregarded because she was a woman.

By the time Steven finally got to know her parents, it was too late for him to form objective opinions about them. He saw them as selfish people who had turned away the woman he loved from her birthright. When they married, one of his vows had been "I promise to put you first. To create a family where you never feel shut out or second place. You will always be my priority, Leah."

When the wine was poured, Leonard stood and raised his glass. "A toast: to the start of the summer season."

It was his traditional toast every year at that time. "To the start of the summer season," everyone echoed. Leah sipped her wine, relishing the familiar notes. She might have left the wine business, but, as she often told the customers who crowded in the back room of Bailey's Blue for her classes, cheese and wine had one very important thing in common: both were made with the philosophy of terroir, or the taste of a place. And this wine tasted like home.

Vivian launched into an anecdote from the previous weekend about a limo full of bachelorettes who showed up for a wine-tasting already drunk.

"We need to ban limos," her father said.

"Aww, that's no fun," said Bridget. Leah looked at her and smiled. She had a vivacious energy about her, and it was clear she wasn't at all intimidated by Leonard and Vivian.

"It's getting out of control," said Vivian, ignoring her. "These young kids. Speaking of kids—where is my granddaughter?"

"Mom, I told you. She has a job at school. As a research assistant."

"She couldn't take a few days off?"

"It's a prestigious position," Leah said. "You know how seriously she takes everything."

"Her grandparents would like a visit. That's something to take seriously," Leonard said.

Leah and Steven exchanged a glance. Her father had always been gruff, and he certainly wasn't mellowing with age. But Leonard, like a lot of brilliant, successful men, was given a lot of latitude. He commanded respect. Even when she was irritated by him, she had to admit she also worshipped him. He had been her first teacher in life, and her most important one. Nothing she learned in college or in running her own business could overshadow the lessons learned growing up with Leonard Hollander.

"So how's the cheese biz?" Asher said.

"Business is booming," Steven said.

"Oh, yeah—you two are working together now," Asher said. "I forgot."

"How wonderful," Vivian said, smiling first at Leah and Steven and then at her husband. "Working together has been such a rewarding part of our life together."

Leah shifted uncomfortably. She turned to her brother.

"So—how did you two meet?"

Asher and Bridget exchanged a look, that intimate look between a new couple, as if they were the only two people in the world who had ever met and fallen in love. Leah remembered bringing Steven to the estate for the first time, sitting in that very spot.

"I was sailing with my buddies out of Sag Harbor," Asher said.

"I was working on the boat," Bridget added, smiling at him.

"It was this epic, sixty-three-foot catamaran. My friends and I were kicking back, having some drinks. I asked for a bottle of champagne. And then this vision appears holding an ice bucket. I said to myself, *Before we reach dry land, I'm getting her number.*"

"Before we reached land? You got my number before I even uncorked the bottle."

Someone's phone beeped, then beeped again.

"Whose phone is that? No phones at the table," Leonard said. It was a policy he adhered to himself, even though running the winery was a twenty-four/seven job.

"Sorry. My bad," Bridget said. Then, to Asher, "I posted that thing, and my phone is, like, blowing up."

Leah glanced across the table at her mother, her face framed by the verdant greenery in the background. But Vivian was distracted, looking in the direction of the house. Her face broke into a smile.

"Oh, Leah. You fooled me. Sadie is here after all!"

Five

~e~

The bedroom furniture had been replaced since the days of Leah's childhood: a king-size bed instead of a queen, muted wallpaper instead of the lavender she'd insisted on as a teenager, museum-quality paintings on the walls instead of her Madonna posters. But while the décor had been updated long ago, in her mind's eye, it was still 1988.

Steven turned on the TV, a news channel. She slipped into the bathroom, brushed her teeth, and changed into a well-worn tank top and loose cotton night shorts. When she was growing up, her mother had always worn fancy nightgowns—"peignoirs," she called them. Vivian Hollander would never dream of wearing a T-shirt to bed. Leah didn't hold herself to that kind of standard, but in the summer she did like to find cute things at the GapBody store on lower Fifth Avenue.

She returned to the bedroom, where Steven was unpacking his clothes.

"What do you think about Sadie showing up like that?" he said.

"I'm thrilled, obviously. But I have to wonder if something's going on with her."

It was so unlike Sadie to be spontaneous; when she explained her sudden appearance by saying that she just couldn't miss the family vacation, Vivian had nodded approvingly. But Leah and Steven had exchanged a look: Sadie had been too busy to answer their calls for days, and suddenly she felt compelled to run out to the vineyard?

"Your mother kept asking me if you and Sadie planned the surprise all along," Steven said, closing a set of drawers and putting his empty suitcase into a closet. Leah was one of the few among her friends who didn't have reason to complain about her husband being a slob.

She climbed into bed. "Why would we do that?"

He shrugged. "You know your mother loves to make things dramatic."

"Oh, she doesn't. Come on."

"Did you notice that she barely spoke to your brother's girlfriend the entire dinner?"

Leah sighed. "Yeah. I'm sure she'll have plenty to say to me about her tomorrow when we're alone."

Steven slipped into his side of the bed. Leah gave him a smile before he turned out his light. She felt a slight pang—very slight—when she thought about how their first night of vacation used to end. The tank top she'd just put on would quickly be coming off. But it had been a while since "going to bed" together meant anything more than going to sleep. The worst part of this was that she didn't mind.

There had been a time when Steven's touch could have made the entire world recede. Her love for Steven had been so strong it had overwhelmed her at times. Their attraction had been like a force, a storm that overtook her, and she hadn't had to think about responding to him any more than she had to think about breathing.

The first night she gave in to her feelings for Steven, it had been a co-worker's birthday. After the last shift at Murray's Cheese, a bunch of them went to a bar on West Fourteenth Street. This was before the Meatpacking District had been turned into a glittering outdoor mall. The streets were desolate, some of the butcher shops still in operation by day but dark and secured with pulldown grates at night. Rumor had it that the bar they were going to, the Cooler, had until just recently been a meat storage facility.

The Cooler was dark and crowded, with raucous live music and a red cast to the lighting that gave her a headache. She sipped her beer and stayed longer than she otherwise would have because she happened to have a huge crush on the cheese shop's assistant manager, Steven Bailey. She had a weakness for men with light eyes and dark hair, that striking combination known as "black Irish." Steven was reserved and kind, even when someone messed up by not letting the cheese rise to room temperature or missed a shift. Plus, he was working his way through Columbia Law, so she had a lot of respect for him.

Or maybe it was just the eyes.

Either way, by midnight, even the pull of Steven Bailey's charms couldn't keep her at the loud bar another minute. She said her goodbyes, and surprisingly, he offered to walk her out.

Standing on the corner of Ninth Avenue, she said, "Okay, well—see you Monday."

He just stood there, looking at her in a way that made her stomach do a little flip.

"I'll walk you to the subway. It's pretty late," he said after a moment. A group walked by, laughing and debating the merits of two nearby bars. Steven watched them pass and said, "Look at the type of shady characters this neighborhood attracts. It's really not safe."

She laughed. "I'm not taking the subway. I live on Bank Street."

After she'd graduated college and discovered that she wouldn't be returning to the North Fork after all, she'd rented an apartment in a West Village brownstone, a fifth-floor walk-up that she shared with a roommate she'd found through a service. It was run by a man working out of a shoe box of an office in Chelsea. He had chain-smoked and shuffled through three-by-five cards like a matchmaker from the old country, but he did find her someone compatible. Keira worked in fashion and traveled constantly. She and Leah had barely exchanged more than a few sentences in the entire year they lived together. They kept track of whose turn it was to buy toilet paper or clean the kitchen by a magnetic whiteboard on the refrigerator. Sometimes

Keira's exclamation points could feel a little passive-aggressive, and Leah looked forward to being able to afford her own place. Her parents had offered to help with her rent, but out of pride she'd refused.

"I'm taking the Six, so Bank is on my way," Steven said. "Unless you really don't want company."

Again, their eyes met.

"Company would be great," she said softly.

To this day she remembered the details of that walk: stopping at the Korean deli on the corner of Fourteenth and Eighth (now the site of a high-rise condo) for a bottle of water, and the way it smelled like grease from the hot buffet (if she'd been alone she would have gotten a container of fried rice). When they reached her building, a long-haired tabby cat occupied the top step, and when they walked up it jumped to the adjacent garbage bins.

She couldn't recall what they talked about, but she could still feel the tension as she turned the key in the front door. The brownstone had double doors, the first a heavyweight wrought iron. Steven helped her pull it open, and in the time it took for her to unlock the second door she'd decided to invite him in.

Still, she made a show of acting like this was in no way a romantic overture, trying to act casual as she stopped in the mail room and collected her bills out of the small square door in the row of a dozen other square metal doors. She had closed and locked the door with her tiny mail key when she felt his hand on her back—gentle, an almost imperceptible touch. When she turned, the intensity in his eyes gave her butterflies. *He's going to kiss me*, she thought. But he hesitated, and so she took one step forward, tilting her face toward him. He pressed against her, moving her back flat against the wall of mailboxes, his mouth meeting hers. In the morning, she would look in the mirror and find marks where the metal had bit into her shoulder blades. But in the moment, all she felt was the soft pressure of his lips, the coolness of his hands slipping under her light jacket, the hammering of her own heart.

Somehow, they made their way upstairs, into her bed. A little voice in her head asked her if she really wanted to sleep with someone she worked with—on the first date. Not even a date! But that voice was no match for the overwhelming drive she felt to be naked and against him and touched by him.

He peeled off her clothes so slowly, it was as if he was giving himself a chance to reconsider. In fact, he murmured at one point, "Is this a good idea?"

Her answer was tugging off her underwear and unzipping his jeans. His body was chiseled and taut, and she ran her hands over it with unabashed admiration. She had slept with only two other men, and neither had inspired such fervor. After a short while, a switch seemed to flip within Steven, and any hint of hesitation was gone. His mouth was on her neck, her breasts, and when he touched her between her legs, her stomach fluttered like she was looking over a ledge. When he moved inside her, she felt, *Yes, this is it*. She was twenty-three years old and finally experiencing the delirious heights of sexual ecstasy. Her body had a mind of its own, and that night, it spoke in a language she'd never heard before but in which she became fluent over the decades.

But lately, for the past year or so, it seemed they'd somehow fallen into the "friend zone." They still enjoyed each other's company; they talked and laughed and kissed and hugged. But sex? She had no interest. And he barely seemed to have more than she did. Or maybe it was her own lack of enthusiasm that had dampened his. Either way, it was concerning.

Steven gave her a peck on the cheek and was snoring lightly before she'd even adjusted her pillow.

Leah turned off her bedside light. She would be awake for hours.

Six

In a house full of extraordinary rooms, the library was possibly the most extraordinary. It had captured Sadie's imagination as a young girl and never lost its grip.

This past winter, toiling away in the college library, trying desperately to make something workable out of her thesis, she thought about her grandparents' vast book collection. Now, her first morning at Hollander Estates, she hoped the library of her childhood would jumpstart her work. That it would justify her impulsive decision to run out to the vineyard after she'd told her parents she wouldn't be there.

Don't be sorry for me. I feel sorry for you. *You think you're living some big "life of the mind." But you're not living at all.*

Holden was wrong, of course. She was fine. She didn't have a problem. And to prove it, she was going to enjoy a few days of vacation with her family. *And* make progress on her thesis.

If only she wasn't so distracted by their breakup.

Holden, an avid bird watcher, would have loved to have seen the European starling perched on one of the vineyard posts yesterday afternoon. Sadie snapped a photo but held back from sending it. The night before, when the sun set with a streak of purple across the sky, she thought of him again.

She knew, deep down, that it wasn't necessarily Holden she was missing, but more the idea of him. The idea of a partner. She was twenty-one years old and had never been in love.

Maybe this was just supposed to be a time of work. So what if half her friends were coupled up? So what if her mother had met her father when she was just two years older, and her grandmother had already been married at her age? Those were different times.

She sipped her coffee, the early-morning sun streaming into the vast room. The library had double-height ceilings and rows and rows of walnut bookshelves spanning two floors, the second of which was reachable by an interior spiral staircase. The space was filled with late-nineteenth-century walnut furniture covered in red silk damask, Oriental rugs, and walls decorated with French tapestry in baroque frames. The centerpiece of the room was a white marble fireplace. Silk damask curtains covered the windows. When they were pulled closed, the room felt like nighttime even on a bright summer day.

Sadie settled at one end of the long table closest to the fireplace. She cued up her laptop and opened her copy of "Notes on 'Camp.'"

She'd first read the essay when she was in middle school and discovered Sontag's *Against Interpretation*. She'd been with her mother at the Strand bookstore.

"You're lucky to have so many books for your age group to choose from," her mother had said, emerging from the labyrinth of shelves with a bundle of books in her arms and presenting one to Sadie. The title was in pink letters, the cover showcasing a long-haired blonde lounging on her bed as she stared at her phone. "When I was growing up I only had Judy Blume, Norma Klein, and Paula Danziger."

"I already found a book," Sadie had said, waving the thin paperback in Leah's direction. Her mother had squinted at the cover, taking it from her hand and examining it with confusion.

"You want to read *that*?"

Sadie loved her mother, would not trade her for any other mother in the world. But there had been many times while growing up that she saw with stunning clarity how little her mother understood her. And yes, she knew—even without reading mainstream teen fiction—that parents typically did not understand their teenage children. But Sadie felt certain that the difference between herself and her mother was a gap that might never be fully bridged. She knew that her parents were proud of her—*so* proud of her. And yet sometimes her accomplishments left them looking a little bewildered—stunned, even. She had seen them share more than one glance that seemed to say, "Where did this creature come from?"

That was why the idea of camp fascinated her. Her taste in books and film and music was so different not only from that of her parents but also that of her friends. It was reassuring to read an examination of taste as a consistent worldview—an essay that said that experiencing the world uniquely was a strength and not a shortcoming.

The essay had always been not only precious to her, but private. It felt, absolutely, like it had been written just for her. But then "Notes on 'Camp'" came into broad view in the most surprising—and somewhat appalling—way: it had been selected as the theme for the Metropolitan Museum's splashy, celebrity-studded costume gala. Suddenly, everyone from Kim Kardashian to Cardi B was talking about camp.

Sadie knew it would be a perfect topic for her thesis. But what could she say about camp that hadn't already been said by Lady Gaga?

Sadie flipped through her notes, her fingers poised above the keyboard. Nothing came to her. Her mind drifted, images of Holden's angry face the day he left. What if Sadie had handled things differently? What if she'd been more honest? *I don't like the beach, and the thought of meeting your family in that setting makes me incredibly anxious.* But it was hard to admit weakness, quirks. It was so . . . messy. Now she realized she should have said, *Compromise: I have to work this week, but let's go to my family's vineyard at some point this summer.* Why was that so impossible for her?

She wasn't cut out for relationships. She should stick to no-commitment hookups and work. That was where she was most comfortable.

Except the work was not working.

"Damn it." In an act of surrender, Sadie pushed back from the table. She looked up, up at the ceiling, her gaze drifting to the tall spiral staircase leading to the upper stacks. When was the last time she'd been up there?

While the first floor was filled with only leather-bound tomes ranging from medieval literature to American and British twentieth-century classics, the second floor offered more contemporary reading. Sadie climbed the stairs to the collection of modern fiction: John Updike. John Irving. Philip Roth.

All white men, Sadie couldn't help but notice. Disinterested, she kept browsing, moving on to a shelf of thick maroon and hunter green volumes engraved with dates on the spines. She opened one dated 1982 and found that it was a photo album, each page a glossy, professional photograph of her mother's family posing in various locations around the estate: On the veranda. In the vineyard. In front of the family home. Her grandmother was dressed in the vibrant colors and poufy sleeves of the day, her makeup bright, her hair golden blond, a heavy Bulgari necklace at her throat. Grandpa Leonard wore a suit with a wide, paisley-patterned tie. Her mother was in a miniature version of the dress her grandmother wore. Uncle Asher wore a powder-blue button-down shirt. They all smiled stiffly into the camera, page after glossy page.

She pulled out another album, and then another, until they were scattered all around her. Only then did she think about how badly she was procrastinating and that she had to return everything to its proper place. She peered inside to determine how best to fit them back and noticed a seam in the wall between the shelf ledge and the one above it. Multiple seams that formed a square. She bent down lower, bracing herself with one hand on the shelf. Toward one side of the square she saw metal. Was it a small keyhole? She reached inside the shelf space and traced it with her fingertips. Yes, there was a small hole in the center. She pulled her phone out of her pocket, got onto her knees, and shined the light into the space.

It seemed to be a cubbyhole. She pressed on it, then felt around for a latch or way to open it. It was locked.

Did she dare try to unlock it? *You're being ridiculous,* she told herself. *This is taking procrastination to a whole new level.*

She looked around the floor for any small key that might have been dislodged along with the photo albums but didn't find anything. She sat back on her heels, thinking. What could she use to try to spring the lock? She needed something small and pointed, like a hairpin.

She took the stairs back down to the table where her work was spread out and grabbed one of her plastic mechanical pencils.

So much for the library helping her get some work done.

Back on the upper level, clearing a space among the clutter of photo albums, she knelt back down again and shined the phone light on the lock. She leaned in, again bracing herself with one hand on the shelf ledge. She pressed the pointed feeder tip of the pencil into the lock and jiggled it around.

The cubbyhole door sprung open. It was filled with . . . albums and books.

Well, what had she expected? The crown jewels?

Sadie pulled a leather-bound album onto her lap. This one didn't have a year engraved on the spine. Opening it, she discovered it didn't have any photos, either. It was not, in fact, an album but instead some sort of journal filled with lined pages, the first one reading: "Book Club meeting: December 12, 1984." Sadie recognized her grandmother's tight cursive script.

It was Delphine's idea to start the book club. She is the only one who understands how frustrated I feel sometimes . . . so underutilized here in the vineyard I helped build. She said when women gather, there is power . . .

The library door slammed closed, making her jump with guilt. She stood and peered over the balustrade. Her grandfather had walked into the room. He moved slowly, almost trancelike, to the window and stared out.

Sadie cleared her throat.

"Hi, Grandpa," she called down.

He looked up, startled and clearly displeased. "What are you doing up there, Sadie?"

"I'm working on my thesis."

His brow creased even more than it usually did. Her grandfather always seemed mildly irritated. He'd been that way for as long as she could remember. She'd been almost afraid of him as a child, but she'd learned that his bark was worse than his bite. He'd been the one to teach her to ride a bicycle. He taught her about the grape plants and the flowers in her grandmother's garden. He was just impatient and didn't suffer fools. Which made it inexplicable that he seemed to favor Uncle Asher over her mother. She had to chalk this up to good old-fashioned sexism. Toxic patriarchy.

"I'm glad you're making use of the library, but I need this room for a meeting," he said. "You'll have to come back later."

Flustered, she looked around at the pile of books on the floor.

"Okay. I'll be down in a minute."

She shoved the journal back into the cubbyhole, closed it up, and then jammed all the photo albums back in as orderly a fashion as she could manage. Surveying her cleanup, she felt confident there was no hint that anything had been disturbed. It was as if she had imagined the hidden compartment. But she hadn't.

And she would be back.

Seven

Leah followed her mother to a spot in the field just off the veranda so Vivian could show her the new varietal they were planting, Auxerrois Blanc.

"Why didn't Sadie join us? There's no use sitting in the library all day. She could do that back at school," Vivian said, putting on her trademark oversize sunglasses. Growing up, Leah never saw her mother without three things: big sunglasses, usually Chanel; high heels; and her gold Bulgari necklace featuring a panther head with emerald eyes.

It was just after nine in the morning, a gentle breeze blowing through the vineyard. In the distance, an owl hooted. Aside from that, silence. The winery would open in two hours, and her mother had suggested they spend quality time together before the day got started.

"Mother, please. Just be happy that she's here."

"Don't get me wrong—I'm delighted. But, Leah dear, if you have to preface something with 'just be happy that,' it means you're settling. And one should never settle."

Leah chose not to take that bait. She wasn't sure what her mother was implying she'd settled for: Her life in Manhattan? Running a cheese shop instead of working at the vineyard? As if she'd had a choice.

She spotted a familiar face a few yards away: Javier Argueta was tending to an unruly row of plants.

"Hi, Javier," she said, giving him a wave. In his fifties now, Javier had a thick head of silver hair and sun-weathered skin. His eyes were still the same deep black pools that never failed to remind Leah of her girlhood infatuation with him.

Javier was from Guatemala, a place that seemed impossibly far away and unknowable to her as a teenager. He spoke Spanish. And it had been his idea to use only indigenous, native yeast to ferment the Hollander wines. This began Leah's favorite vineyard tradition: on the first day of harvest, they asked each employee to bring something from home—an apple from a tree in the backyard or a seashell from the beach—and they added it to a sample of the first press of juice off the vines. They mixed it all up, and within twenty-four hours they'd have active fermentation—kind of like a sourdough bread starter. The resulting yeast was used to create all the wine that year. Leah had loved dropping in a dandelion or a pebble from the front yard, a small gesture that gave her a connection to that season's vintage.

For a time, everything Javier said or did made her feel lit up inside. She could blush now just thinking about the very vivid fantasy she used to have about the two of them in the barn—a rustic building at the edge of the fields that had long ago been converted into the vineyard management office. But back then, it was just storage for field equipment.

She walks into the barn late on a hot summer afternoon. Her father has sent her there to fetch something—a pair of shears. Javier is there, wearing a tight T-shirt, his muscled arms glistening with a fine sheen of sweat. His brow is smudged with dirt. His dark eyes flash at her.

"What are you doing in here?" he sneers, contemptuous of her privileged life.

"I'm just trying to find something," she says. "Can you help me look?"

He doesn't want to help her but feels obligated. They hunt around for the shears, and their hands accidentally brush each other's. They both freeze, the electricity between them as shocking as it is undeniable. Even though it's wrong—so wrong—they can't resist. They kiss . . .

"Welcome home," Javier said with a smile, jolting her back into reality.

"Thanks," she said. It had been a long time since Hollander Estates had been "home" to her. She was a different person than the young woman who had left all those years earlier. "So tell me about the Auxerrois Blanc," Leah said.

"It's a cousin of Chardonnay. We're the only ones growing it on the North Fork. Your father hasn't lost one ounce of his ambition," Javier told her.

"Speaking of ambition," Vivian said to Leah, adjusting her oversize straw sun hat, "we solved our vineyard management problem thanks to Mateo. And he's doing an excellent job."

Vivian had told her months earlier that their previous vineyard manager had been caught sampling a little too much of the product he was making. Javier's son, Mateo, stepped up to fill the position. It was a big job, one that involved crop cultivation, thinning, pruning, tying, suckering, managing the canopy, planting and replanting, irrigating and harvesting. At most vineyards, the position would also entail making recommendations related to crop planting and fruit quality. But Leonard had never delegated those duties.

Javier hadn't wanted the job; after nearly forty years at the winery, he was ready to pass the torch. At the end of each day he retired to the three-bedroom house at the entrance to the winery, a place called Field House. The property dated back to 1710 and was part of the historic registry; Vivian and Leonard had learned this the hard way when they tried to renovate it back in the 1980s. When they learned they couldn't tear it down or integrate it into the winery building, Leonard decided to give it to the young Argueta family so Javier didn't have to travel after his long workdays.

"Thank you, Señora Vivian," Javier said. "I need to go speak to him now. Leah, wonderful to see you."

Leah watched him head farther into the field, wondering how it was possible that Javier had a twenty-seven-year-old son. But then, she had her own grown child. They were no longer young. Time was passing too quickly.

"It's great that Mateo got promoted," Leah said.

"I only wish your brother put in half the work that Javier's son puts in. Now he's distracted with that nightmare girlfriend."

"Oh, she seems nice enough," Leah said.

Her mother shot her a look. "Don't get me started."

"Why do you still let his girlfriends bother you? Asher is never going to change, but on the plus side, he's also never going to settle down. Next summer it will be some other Bridget."

Her mother smiled at her. "Enough about that. Tell me what's new with you."

Now was the chance to discuss how difficult she was finding it to have Steven in the cheese shop alongside her every day. Having navigated the family business all these years with her own husband, maybe Vivian would have some advice. Still, she didn't want to be overly negative. She didn't want her mother to get the wrong idea—her marriage was fine.

While she searched for the right words, her mother's phone rang.

"It's your father," she said to Leah. Then, into the phone, "Leonard, I'm showing Leah the new vines . . . What? Now?"

She ended the call, put her phone back in her bag, and sighed.

"I'm needed at the house." She kissed Leah on the cheek. "You stay. Relax. I'm so happy you're home."

Eight

V ivian couldn't imagine why her husband was calling her back to the house for a meeting. She wasn't usually consulted on business matters.

To be fair to Leonard, this hadn't entirely been his decision. When they first bought the winery in 1971 and before they had their winery license, a federal ordinance allowed only a "head of household"—a man—to make wine for private use.

"That's absurd," Vivian had said at the time. She hadn't left everything behind in Manhattan and followed Leonard to the middle of nowhere to be relegated to the sidelines. But winemaking was a man's world. When she complained to her mother about this, her mother admonished her to "support your husband." Even though her parents hadn't approved of Leonard, that hadn't meant they hadn't raised Vivian to be a proper wife.

And so she turned her attention to the house. Even before the renovation of the 1980s, she had been filling the house with antique furniture. It began with her fascination with nineteenth-century hunting prints, a way to bring horse imagery into her home décor since she didn't have time to ride anymore. Working with the architects to design the expansion, she'd requested they build stables; they remained empty to that day.

When her parents died, she inherited some wonderful pieces: a

Tiffany grandfather clock that held a place of honor in the entrance hall. A mahogany George II bowfront desk from the 1700s. A Federal gilt mirror that hung in her bedroom. The treasures of her home had, over the decades, come to tell a narrative about her life, her family origins, the things that made her happy. If the winery was Leonard's achievement, the house was her own success story.

The second odd thing about that day's summons was that meetings were held in the office at the winery, not in their home. Long ago, Vivian and Leonard had made the deliberate decision to establish boundaries between their family and work lives. The walk between the main house and the winery might be only three minutes, but the emotional distance was invaluable.

Vivian climbed the stairs to the library on the second floor. As far as she was concerned, there was no decorative touch that could compete with the beauty of shelves lined with books. But she had made sure all the room's fixtures were museum quality.

"I certainly hope there's a good reason for—" She stopped short.

Seated around the table were Leonard, their attorney Harold Feld, their accountant Marty Pritchard, Asher . . . and Bridget. It took all of Vivian's self-control and generations of good breeding not to say exactly what she was thinking, which was "What is *she* doing here?"

Instead, she took the seat next to Leonard without another word.

"Thanks for joining us, Vivian," said Marty. "It's important to Leonard that we all be on the same page here."

"I'm sorry," Vivian said, glancing at Bridget and then at Leonard. "If this is a business meeting, it's family only."

No one said anything. Asher reached for Bridget's hand.

"Mom, we haven't had a chance to tell you yet, but Bridget *is* family: we got engaged late last night."

Vivian's eyes moved to Bridget's left hand. Sure enough, a two-carat diamond in a platinum art deco setting decorated her left ring finger. She recognized it from her late mother-in-law's collection.

"Engaged?" Vivian said.

"In the vineyard," Bridget said, smiling. "Asher got down on one knee right there in the dirt."

Soil, Vivian thought, her jaw tightening. *It's soil, not dirt.*

She again looked at her husband, and he seemed to shrug, as if this were all news to him. But someone had made that ring possible.

Vivian could barely breathe for the feeling of betrayal. How could Leonard know about this and not tell her? But she knew how. He'd always indulged their only son, granting him far more latitude than he did anyone else. She didn't think it was necessarily kindness that made him view Asher through rose-colored glasses; it was wishful thinking. Sometimes even delusional thinking. Oh, she loved Asher. But that didn't make her oblivious to the fact that he was lazy, and entitled, and had been born far too handsome for his own good.

"Well, then I suppose congratulations are in order," Vivian said evenly. "But if this is why you called me up here, I need to excuse myself."

"Please sit down, Vivian," Leonard said. "That's not what this is about."

"Well, what then?" She was impatient. Irritated. She'd been having such a lovely time with Leah, and she wanted to get back to her. Her time with her daughter was fleeting. She didn't want to waste a second of it. And the sooner she got out of that room, the sooner she could try to stop thinking about the disastrous step her son was taking.

"Decisions have to be made," Marty said. "Difficult decisions."

"Yes, well, that's often the case in this business," Vivian said, glancing at Leonard.

"This is different. The winery is hemorrhaging money," Marty said.

Hemorrhaging money? She resisted the impulse to roll her eyes. Vivian didn't appreciate hyperbole.

"We know how to deal with ups and downs," she said. "Right, Leonard?"

Together, they had overcome countless problems over the decades. The August when the yellow finches destroyed their entire crop of Pinot Noir. Losing power for a week after Hurricane Gloria. The seasons when they'd gotten caught up in trendy varietals and failed to antic-ipate them falling out of favor. The year mold consumed their top-tier Chardonnay grapes.

Every challenge had proven, in the end, to be a learning experience. Every failure had made them stronger. All except for one: the cata-strophic, short-lived partnership that changed her family forever.

"I'd like to speak to my wife alone for a minute," Leonard said.

Vivian followed him out of the room, the sight of the diamond burned into the backs of her eyelids like a sunspot. She stood near the stairwell banister, rubbing her forehead.

"I can't think about the winery when *that woman* is sitting there. How could you not tell me about this absurd engagement?" she said.

"I have more important things on my mind than Asher and that girl."

Vivian was about to get indignant, to ask what could be more im-portant than their son marrying a gold digger. Good lord, she could only hope the woman wasn't pregnant yet. But something in Leonard's voice silenced her. She had known Leonard Hollander since she was a teenager and had only one other time heard him speak so low in volume but at the same time trembling with the effort of restraint.

"Leonard, we'll figure out whatever it is. If you saw how full the veranda was yesterday instead of sitting in here holed up letting Marty get to you . . ."

"We're going broke, Vivian." His face flushed with stress.

Okay, that got her attention.

"So we'll tighten our belt. We've done that before."

"It's different this time," he said.

Vivian knew things were changing in the wine industry. Global competition made it difficult for a small family winery to hold its own. Leonard had been complaining for years that the big corporations could sell at a lower price point because they made their money by volume. Hollander Estates couldn't increase production—they had a finite amount of land.

"Okay. So what can we do?" she said.

"We've been going over our options," he said. By "we," she knew he meant Marty, Harold, and Asher. Asher, the heir apparent, even though the only hoe he'd ever picked up was the type who latched on to wealthy young men. She loved her son. They both did. But sometimes it felt like she was the only one who saw his weaknesses.

"I should have been included in those conversations," she said. After all these decades, it was still frustrating that while Leonard respected her completely as the matriarch of the family, she had become a second-class citizen when it came to the business. She'd built the vineyard by his side, with her bare hands—literally. And yet she'd made one bad hiring decision years earlier and he'd never let it go—despite the fact that he'd made plenty of mistakes of his own.

"I'm including you now," he said. "I waited as long as I could because I didn't want to needlessly upset you. But, Vivian, we have to sell."

She froze. "Sell the winery? That's not happening."

"Vivian, listen to me. It *is* happening. Our sales have been flat for years. We're losing money. The best we can hope for this summer is to make the winery seem as appealing as possible to buyers."

What? That didn't make sense.

"If someone else can buy it and turn things around, why can't we just fix whatever isn't working ourselves?"

"Because any fix will take time. The money has run out. What we need is a buyer who is in a position to lose money for a few years. Who wants the winery for the fun of it, for the cachet. We don't have that luxury."

"So we find someone to buy the winery while we just sit around the house watching our legacy from afar? That doesn't sound realistic."

His expression softened as he looked at her. "No, I'm afraid it's not. I'm sorry, Vivian, but we're selling this house, too."

Nine

The first thing Sadie always noticed when she walked into the winery was the smell of sugar and alcohol. It was as if the aroma had seeped into the pores of the wood, and the building breathed it out.

It was a wide-open and welcoming space, with vaulted ceilings, shelves and shelves of bottles, and plenty of room for customers to relax and enjoy themselves. Jazz music played on the sound system. In the tasting room, couples sipped glasses of the new Hollander vintage while sitting at the steel-topped bar. Ceiling fans whirled gently overhead, and the sound of popping corks filled the air.

One of the quirkiest things about the Hollander estate was the aesthetic difference between the winery and her grandparents' home. The winery building was a simple, elegant farmhouse—functional and subtly chic. But their house was like something out of Versailles. She'd never known which style truly represented her grandparents. Maybe the hidden journal she'd discovered would give her some insight into her grandmother.

She'd been trying to work in the library again, thinking about the journal and whether she had any reasonable right to read more of it, when her mother called her to come help with bottling.

"Gran invited us to label the new Cabernet," Leah said. Sadie was relieved for the excuse to abandon the pretense of writing. She could use a distraction. She'd considered, briefly, telling her mother about her discovery of the book club journal, but she hesitated to admit her snooping.

She was happy to help in the bottling room. At this point, she needed a distraction from her distraction!

Sadie passed stairs that led to the second-floor mezzanine—a comfy space with armchairs, a fireplace, and wide windows with views of the vineyard—and headed to a door marked *Do Not Enter*. She opened it, walking into a cavernous space that held three hundred oak barrels, all imported from France. The bottling room, just off to one side of the barrels, had floor-to-ceiling windows so the elaborate machinery could be viewed in action. She remembered when her grandparents had traveled to Italy to learn how to use the equipment that enabled them to pack a thousand cases a day.

Her mother was already inside wearing protective goggles.

"We're just waiting for Gran," she said.

One of the assistant winemakers waved them into the room.

"Mrs. Hollander sent a message to start without her." He handed them both a pair of sound-canceling, protective headphones. "We're doing the Petit Verdot today."

The bottling machinery took up most of the space in the glass-enclosed room. It was a conveyer belt that filled, labeled, and corked the bottles of wine. The area around the machine was cluttered with giant plastic bags filled with corks, reams of labels, boxes of empty wine bottles, and white cardboard cases that would be filled with the finished bottles and taken out the back door by forklift. It was a mostly automated process, but it still took a few people on the line to feed those items through the system.

"Sadie, I'm putting you in charge of corks," the man said, motioning for her to stand near the cluster of bags.

"Okay," she said, dutifully putting on her headphones. The senior winemaker, Chris Kessler, materialized next to her and jotted something down in a marble notebook. Sadie glanced at the pages, reading

Chris's notes about pH levels and other numerical calculations she didn't understand, with a few comments like "no sugar addition" and "topped everything in house." There was something uniquely compelling about winemaking. It was the magical combination of art and science. She had conveyed her appreciation once to her mother, and her mother had responded, "It's in your blood."

"So why did you decide not to work at the winery?" Sadie had asked. The question had been posed many years earlier. She was still waiting for an answer.

Her mother positioned herself at the end of the line, helping with the cardboard boxes. The booming apparatus was turned on, and Sadie began feeding the corks into the machine. Each bottle closure was accompanied by suction and a loud sealing sound. It was rhythmic and, now that she was committed to the activity, almost relaxing.

"Stop, stop, stop whatever you are doing!"

Her grandmother rushed into the room, waving her arms wildly. Someone hit the switch, and the machinery ground to a halt. Sadie removed her ear protectors to find out what was going on.

"Is there a problem, Mrs. Hollander?" the winemaker asked.

"Who approved these labels?" Vivian said.

The labels featured swathes of red, green, yellow, and black, like an abstract expressionist painting. The winemakers looked at one another.

"Asher," said Chris.

Vivian marched over to the rear of the room, where a shelf was filled with empty bottles that represented each of the winery's varietals, each marked "height standard" in black Sharpie to make sure they were filled uniformly. She grabbed the Petit Verdot bottle with the classic Hollander label in soft eggshell with simple blue lettering and walked it over to the winemaker, waving it.

"This is the label. This has *always* been the label."

"I think the idea was to . . . liven things up?"

"Why doesn't anyone listen to me?" Vivian marched back to the doorway. "Don't do any more bottles until you hear from me. No one touch a thing!"

Sadie turned to Leah, who simply shrugged.

So much for a calm, pleasant distraction.

Vivian, still reeling from the news that the winery was in dire straits, could barely process the flagrant disregard for her opinion about the labels. Heart thumping with indignation, she fired off another text to her son. Again, no response from Asher. She searched the winery and vineyard for him. When she still failed to locate him, she went to her last resort: calling Bridget.

"Oh, hi, Vivian. He's here with me—at the pool!" Bridget said.

Vivian somehow refrained from correcting her with "Mrs. Hollander." It drove her crazy that the woman had never hesitated in being familiar with her. Now that there was an engagement, it was too late to course-correct.

How, oh how, had everything fallen so far out of control?

She opened the gate to let herself onto the pool deck. Sure enough, Asher was lounging on a chair, his hair and swim trunks wet, headphones over his ears. As if there was no work to be done. As if they weren't fighting for Hollander Estates' survival.

Bridget sat beside him in an obscene white bikini, displaying her various tattoos.

"Taking the day off?" Vivian said, walking toward them, suddenly very hot in her white blouse and skirt.

Asher pulled the headphones from his ears.

"Hey, Mom. Just an early break. What's up?"

"A very early break, I'd say. I can see how an hour of work might be exhausting." Sarcasm was never ideal, but neither was expressing her frustration through shouting. "I was just in the bottling room and got some surprising news about new labels. Do you know anything about that?"

Bridget, perhaps sensing the tension, jumped up and pulled on a pair of turquoise terry-cloth shorts so tiny Vivian failed to see the point. "I'm going to get iced coffee," she announced. "Anyone else want anything?"

"No, thanks, babe," Asher said, reaching out to squeeze her hand before they parted. He watched her walk into the house with his tongue practically hanging out of his mouth.

Vivian crossed her arms. "Asher. The labels?"

"Oh, yeah. John asked for the switch."

"John?"

Asher nodded. "I ran it by Dad, and he okayed it."

John Beaman was their head of wholesale. It was one of the company's most important positions, and a very demanding one at that. They had a high turnover rate, but John had been with them for over a decade.

Leonard had recognized from the beginning that the job of their wholesale reps would be different than those in other places because of their proximity to Manhattan, the restaurant capital of the world. "We are the only wine region in the world that can send people to sell who work on the farm, too. That's an advantage. People like to have contact with the farmer or person who helped make it," he'd told her on more than one occasion. At the same time, no one in Manhattan had any interest in New York State wines. Their sales reps had their work cut out for them.

John and his team of reps—all men—walked into restaurants and liquor stores with bags full of samples and asked the person in charge of buying to give Hollander Estates a try. She remembered from her own days of knocking on doors that it was a job that never ended. You might get on the wine list of the best restaurant in the country and they'd be pouring your wine by the glass for a month, only to suddenly replace it with a wine from France. It was rare to have a wine stay on a list for even one full year. So when John got feedback from the field, Leonard listened. It was one of the few instances where he did.

"Last week your father told me that changing the labels was your idea."

Asher squinted against the sun. "Yeah. But it was John who said something about needing them to be modernized."

"We never had a problem before now."

"I guess it's time to try anything we can to, I don't know, maximize revenue."

Vivian sat on the chair Bridget had vacated. She instantly realized her mistake when water seeped into the back of her skirt. She jumped up, but she wasn't ready to leave. She had one more question for him, one that had been burning her up since Leonard told her about the sale.

"How long have you known about the decision to sell the company?" she said. The tension in her gut told her she'd avoided asking him thus far because she didn't want to know the answer.

Asher sighed. "A few weeks?"

The answer stung. Leonard liked autonomy when it came to the business, but she had helped build the winery. She was his wife. There was no justification for Asher knowing about this before she did.

"Why didn't you tell me?"

"Mom, come on. It's not my place. Dad was still working things out—he told me he'd tell you as soon as the decision was final."

"It never crossed your mind that I might want some say in what happens to the business I helped create?"

Asher adjusted the towel behind his back and reached for his sunglasses. When he turned back to her, she marveled at how handsome he was. She just wished his looks weren't his only asset.

"Mom, is this really about the engagement? I'm sorry I didn't tell you ahead of time. But I know how you feel about Bridget, and I didn't want to argue with you."

"The engagement is the least of your mistakes lately," she said, patting down her hair. She could feel that the flurry of activity all day had set it askew. "But then, dealing with conflict has never been your strong suit."

But it *was* hers. She walked off in search of her husband.

Ten

Standing at the window of the master bedroom, Vivian had always felt like a queen looking out from her castle. Now, with her kingdom at risk, she had to remember that there had been other hard times and they had gotten through them.

"I'm not ready to give up," Vivian said, turning back to look at Leonard, who was reading *The Wall Street Journal* in bed. "And I can't believe that you are."

"It's not giving up," he said, not even glancing at her. "It's being smart."

She walked over to the bed and pulled his paper away. "We were under pressure in 2012, and look what happened the following year—a glorious vintage."

The 2013 season had started late after Superstorm Sandy and a rough winter. But then the fall came, and the area went without rain for fifty-seven days. The grapes were able to reach optimum levels of ripeness in the dry climate, with no threat of mildew and rot. It was like a miracle.

Their entire life together felt like a miracle sometimes.

In the beginning, the vineyard had been a giant leap, a gamble. Or, as her father had put it, pure folly. Vivian had been born to live a gilded life in Manhattan, not to till the soil out in the country. Her grandparents, Avigdor Freudenberg and his wife, Ida, had been German Jews from Bavaria who created a department store empire before dying in each other's arms on the *Titanic*.

Vivian's father was the sole male heir, and he passed the business down to Vivian's brother, who remained at the helm until a hostile takeover in the mid-1980s. If there was one lesson Vivian had learned early in life, it was that business was a man's world.

All her parents wanted for her was to make a "good" marriage. Wedding at the Plaza, followed by moving into a town house on Fifth Avenue and, eventually, a winter home in Palm Beach.

Growing up, her experience of Long Island had been summers in East Hampton and weekends at riding stables to train as a competitive equestrian. Nowhere in that picture was there an imagined future that landed her on a defunct potato farm in Cutchogue. But she had fallen in love with Leonard Hollander.

"There won't be anything to save us this time, Vivian," Leonard said. "Not even the most perfect harvest in the world."

"You're just letting Marty get to you. He's very conservative. You know that."

Leonard shook his head.

She felt a chill. In the hours since the meeting in the library, Vivian's one consolation had been her certainty that ultimately, this was much ado about nothing. Earlier, when she confronted Leonard about looping in Asher before telling her, he'd said, "I didn't want to worry you unnecessarily." Leonard, for all his faults, had always been her protector. When he'd proposed, after he said, "Will you marry me?" he'd said, "Let me take care of you for the rest of your life." It was as if he'd read her mind, as if he'd seen into her soul and understood how, despite the material comforts of her childhood, she had never felt truly cared for. She had never felt loved.

So she could accept that he kept the problems of the winery from her because he didn't want to upset her. But she also knew that on some level, he didn't believe—had never believed—she could possibly have a solution where he could not find one. She didn't fault him for this thinking; she might have married into the wine business, but it was in his blood.

The name "Hollander" was not from Holland but from a town in Lithuania settled by the Dutch. In the late nineteenth century, Ashkenazi immigrants fleeing the pogroms in Russia and Eastern Europe settled in Argentina because of its open-door immigration policy. In 1910, Leonard's grandfather Mordecai Hollander was given a Mendoza winery as payment for a debt. Thirty-five years later, his son, Samuel, would go on to create the first branded Argentine wine, a Malbec he named *gema de la tierra*—gem of the earth.

But after World War II, the rise of Nazi sympathizer Juan Perón worried the Jewish population. Samuel Hollander moved his family— his wife, Gelleh; his eight-year-old-son, Leonard; and his six-year-old daughter, Rose—to the United States and settled on the Lower East Side of New York City. There he worked as a merchant, never reaching the success he'd had as a winemaker in his native country. Gelleh, no longer recognizing the depressed man who was her husband, suggested they try to find a way to reproduce their old life in America. Samuel moved his family again, this time to California, where he created a successful winery he named after his supportive wife. Leonard had grown up on Gelleh Estates Vineyard, where he had learned everything he knew.

So yes, Leonard—a third-generation winemaker—was the authority, and he never failed to remind her of this. It didn't mean he didn't love her. After all, he'd created Hollander Estates just so they could be together.

She slipped into bed next to him.

"I know we can think of something. We always do. You simply can't allow this to happen."

Leonard narrowed his dark eyes, then gathered up his pillows and headed for the bedroom door. "I've had enough talking for one night. I'm going to sleep in one of the guest rooms."

Vivian was taken aback; it wasn't like him to be so sensitive.

"Leonard, stop. Nothing will be solved by you leaving. I'm not trying to aggravate you. I'm trying to help."

He walked back to the foot of the bed. "The most helpful thing would be for you not to question me. I need your support. It's the only way to get through this."

"Okay. Please—come back to bed." The problem wouldn't be solved overnight. She didn't want to sleep apart.

He hesitated just a moment before settling back next to her.

She reached out and touched his arm. "I'll be supportive," she said to placate him. "But we have to tell Leah what's going on."

"Why ruin her vacation?"

"This doesn't just affect the two of us, Leonard. We always planned to pass the vineyard on to our family. We have two children and a grand-daughter. You're contemplating a move that would take the business away from all of them permanently. Leah has a right to know."

"Asher is the only one working at the business."

"And whose fault is that?" Vivian said, crossing her arms. "I thought that what we were doing here meant something. That our grand-children would walk the same fields as their father and grandfather. It wasn't just about making money. I could have stayed in New York City with my parents for that."

"Vivian, I don't think you understand: I'm not selling to be rich. I'm selling to survive. To walk away with *anything*."

What was he talking about?

"You're exaggerating. That isn't what Marty said in the meeting."

"I told him not to discuss how bad things are in front of Asher. I don't want Asher to know. If he finds out there's no fortune left, he's going to run off. It doesn't look good to prospective buyers if my vice president quits. This summer is about keeping up appearances at all costs."

"Leonard, don't be ridiculous. All this land? It's valuable."

He shot her a look. "Are you needling me?"

For a minute, she was confused. What had she said? And then she realized the true problem. They were not in a bind just because the winery wasn't making enough profit; their hands were tied thanks to a business decision made thirty years earlier. In need of an influx of cash, Leonard sold the development rights to all of their land to Suffolk County. At the time, the sum the county had paid seemed enormous. But it was an infinity deal: the property went into a land trust that would prevent it from ever being used for anything other than winemaking or farming. It could never be developed for commercial use. So while their neighbors in the Hamptons were getting millions and millions for a tract of land, their property on the North Fork was a money pit.

"The company balance sheet determines the value of the sale—not our property," he told her.

She felt a ripple of fear. Could that be true? They were losing everything?

"You should have told me," she said, her voice almost a whisper. "You should have told me sooner."

"What good would it have done?" His face was tight with frustration.

She stood up and gathered her own pillows.

"I think *I'll* sleep in one of the guest rooms tonight," she said.

Eleven

B reakfasts were a big deal year-round at Hollander Estates, but the summers made for a particularly abundant first meal of the day. Peternelle set out bowls of fresh berries with cream straight from a local dairy farm, peach scones baked with fruit from their own trees, homemade granola, croissants, and custom omelets upon request. It always took Leah a day or two to adjust since her only breakfast in Manhattan was a quick cup of coffee on her way out the door. But now she was fully on winery time.

The kitchen invited a leisurely appreciation of food. With its open shelving, hanging copper pots, and large central island, it was warm and elegant. The island was made from a walnut English table that had been expanded and topped with green Connemara marble. Leah remembered when her mother had discovered the marble from the west coast of Ireland and became obsessed with its palette of hunter green, gray, and eggshell. Leonard had been appalled by the cost, but he'd been spared by the fact that the marble was a limited quantity. Vivian had only been able to acquire enough to use it for the island and the wall behind the stove.

Leah scooped some berries onto a plate and pulled a stool up to the island.

"You're up early," Asher said, strolling in, tapping away at his phone. He was dressed in khakis and a button-down shirt.

"Right back at you. And dressed up. What's the occasion?"

"A meeting," he said, opening the refrigerator. "What are all these flowers doing in here?"

"I told you before," Peternelle said. "I put the hydrangeas in overnight to stay crisp and then by noon, voila, they open."

Asher asked her to "whip me up a quick omelet" and slid onto the stool beside Leah.

"Missed you at dinner last night," she said. "Did you two go out?"

He nodded. "We took the boat to Sag Harbor to celebrate," he said.

"Celebrate what?" Leah said.

"Mom didn't tell you?"

"Tell me what?" Her mother had been strangely quiet the past day.

"I proposed to Bridget. We're engaged. I can't believe Mom didn't mention it."

Leah smiled, trying not to look as surprised as she felt. She never thought she'd see her playboy brother settle down. She loved Asher, but she didn't understand how he could be so infantile. He only dated much younger women, he lived in the house they grew up in, and he certainly did little to earn his position at Hollander. Maybe that was his response to their father's overbearing personality. It was a form of retreat.

"Ash, congratulations. So . . . she's the one."

He nodded, grinning. "It seems that way."

It was strange that her mother hadn't mentioned it. She wasn't happy with this turn of events, of that Leah was certain. But still. What was going on with her?

"Do you have a wedding date?"

"We're working on it," he said. His phone buzzed with a text. She looked over his shoulder and saw that it was from her father.

"Busy day in the winemaking world?" she asked lightly.

"Ah, yeah. You could say that."

"Anything new?"

He slid his phone into his pants pocket. "Nothing worth talking about."

In other words, none of her business. Leah sipped her coffee, trying to quell the prickly feeling rising inside of her. Some things never changed. Case in point: to this day, the only female employees at Hollander Estates were Peternelle and the housekeepers.

"I gotta run," Asher said, even as Peternelle set a perfectly cooked omelet in front of him.

Leah slid the plate toward herself.

"Thanks, Peternelle," she said. "This looks delicious."

Sadie pulled open the heavy library curtains, sun streaking through the room. She could see dust motes in the air, and she felt a lusty romanticism toward her surroundings that filled her with curiosity about her grandmother's journal.

She shouldn't. And yet . . .

Sadie pushed her chair back. The journal was from thirty-five years ago—it wasn't like Sadie was reading something out of her bedroom, something current. Her grandmother had probably forgotten it even existed.

She again climbed the narrow spiral stairs and headed right for the shelves of photo albums. This time, she pulled out just enough to give her access to the hidden compartment and she placed them neatly next to her in a pile. Her hands perspired as she pressed the pencil point into the lock. It took a few seconds to give, and she had a moment of panic that it had been a fluke that it had worked last time. Only then did she realize how badly she wanted to continue reading her grandmother's words.

December 12, 1984

It was Delphine's idea to start the book club. She is the only one who understands how frustrated I feel sometimes . . . so underutilized here in the vineyard I helped build. She said when women gather, there is power.

We're meeting once a month—there's eight of us, including Bess Winnel, even though she says she barely has time to think, let alone breathe, now that her twins are toddling around. I, on the other hand, have more time than I care to think about.

Friends have told me to try keeping a journal, but I always give up after a few weeks. Maybe writing about the book club will give me something to focus on, so I'll stick with it.

*Delphine chose the first book—*Lace *by Shirley Conran. She said it was an amazing miniseries earlier in the year, but I missed it. The book kept me turning the pages, but parts were shocking and I'm afraid I'll blush talking about them tonight. At the same time, all of the mistakes and bad behavior of these characters make me feel better about my own.*

What mistakes and bad behavior? Sadie flipped through the pages. It seemed the book club had lasted just half a year—ending in May of 1985. Out of just six books read, two were written by the same author, Judith Krantz. Sadie had never heard of her. She hadn't heard of any of the writers except for Jackie Collins, although she might have been confusing her with an actress. All she knew was that the page of notes about the first book, *Lace*, included mention of a porn star, a secret adoption, and . . . sex with a goldfish.

Did her grandmother still have a copy of the book stashed away in the library? She must have saved it. Putting the journal aside, Sadie made her way back to the contemporary fiction section of the shelves.

"Conran . . . Conran," she said, passing by the "B" last names and brushing her fingertips over the mid-alphabet "C" names.

Her phone buzzed with a text from her mother.

Mateo is going to give us a tour of the grapes planted for this season. Meet me on the veranda.

Mateo Argueta was a few years older. He'd grown up at the winery and started working with his father when he was a teenager. Sadie barely knew him; he always seemed quiet. Not just quiet, but like he was thinking something important and didn't want to be disturbed.

She'd go on the tour. Better to risk being bored in the present than entertained by snooping around in the past.

Twelve

V ivian stood at the edge of the veranda, framing her eyes against the sun. In the distance, Leah and Sadie walked the fields with Mateo Argueta.

If not for the current crisis, the sight of her daughter and granddaughter enjoying the literal fruit of their family's decades of labor would have been gratifying. She still couldn't believe they might lose it all.

When she and Leonard made the giant leap to start their own vineyard, neither set of their parents had faith in them. The Hollanders wanted him to continue working at Gelleh Estates in Napa. Her family wanted their new son-in-law to have a proper career, and that meant joining the Freudenberg department store empire. Leonard had his own ideas.

"We'll make our own dynasty," Leonard said to her at the time. "It's you and me against the world." Madly in love, she made the leap, and they set out for the North Fork. Her parents, appalled, cut her off financially.

What she hadn't known at the time was that conventional wisdom said that wine grapes would not grow on the North Fork. Yes, Long Island was full of grape trees—native American grape trees, *vitis riparia*. They had too little sugar and too much acidity to produce good wine. In order for Leonard to produce wine to match the success of his father's West Coast vineyard, he needed to cultivate *vitis vinifera*. The *vitis vinifera* had first been planted in Persia. The Greeks brought vinifera vines from the Middle East back home, and then the imperial Romans took the vines to France, Spain, and Germany. People had been trying to grow the grapes in New York State, but the plants were simply too fragile for the climate.

Vivian and Leonard were determined; Leonard to prove to his father that he could be a winemaker out on his own, and Vivian to follow her heart and show her parents that she was not throwing her life away.

That first season, they planted descendants of the grapes that had grown in Bordeaux—Cabernet Sauvignon, Merlot, and Sauvignon Blanc—and also the varietals planted in Burgundy: Pinot Noir and Chardonnay.

They did exhaustive research, and Leonard called on everything he'd learned at his father's knee. There was no inherent problem with the land: the mix of sand and organic material made it loamy and drain well. The climate was variable but not unlike that of one of the world's great wine regions, Bordeaux. Leonard was confident that the Napa Valley was not the only place in the country where great wines could be produced.

They used grafted vines and picked out the weak ones before planting. Leonard knew how to recognize the weeds early—dandelion, pepperweed, redweed—and to remove them quickly so they did not compete with the vines for moisture and nutrients. Eventually, Leonard's father, impressed with their determination, came out to help with the delicate art of pruning. The plants took root, and so did their life together.

It was backbreaking work. Gone were weekends of horseback riding and brunch. Vivian fell into bed each night so exhausted she couldn't bother to turn out the light. Her legs and arms were covered with bruises and insect bites. But progress was made.

And now this.

Vivian had meant what she'd said to Leonard the night before: Leah had a right to know that the winery was in trouble. And she wanted to tell her now, in person, not after Leah was back in New York City. Leah should know that this summer might be her last at the vineyard so that she could experience it accordingly.

Vivian walked over to the group standing among the blooming Cabernet Franc. Mateo noticed her first and greeted her with a hearty wave.

"Hey there, Mrs. Hollander," he called out.

"Mateo, these plants are looking wonderful. I haven't been out since you put up the catch wire."

Mateo was a big improvement over their previous vineyard manager, Joe Gable. Joe had not only been drinking from the stockroom, he had failed to treat their entire Chardonnay crop for insect control and they'd lost it all. Still, Leonard waited weeks to give Mateo the position. It was as if he couldn't believe the best candidate for the job was right there under his nose. Vivian had hoped he would hire him but didn't push, knowing he would say something along the lines of "Do I need to remind you what happened the last time you told me to hire someone? And what happens if it doesn't work out? I can't fire Javier's son. It would be a disaster."

In the end, his need for a strong right hand in the field won out over his concerns. Now they had the best vineyard manager since the one who worked for them in the seventies and eighties. But apparently, that was not going to solve their problems.

"Hi, Gran," Sadie said.

"Mom, I'm glad you're here. I called but kept getting your voicemail," Leah said.

Vivian barely heard her. Sadie, wearing gardening gloves and holding a pair of pruning shears, was a sight to behold. Her granddaughter's dark hair and dark eyes resembled the Hollanders more than herself, yet seeing her stand in the same spot where she had stood at that age—a newlywed, a hopeful pioneer—brought the past rushing back. The thought of losing it all felt like a physical blow.

"Sadie, dear, you look very professional. I hope Mateo is teaching you all the tricks of the trade. And in the meantime, I must borrow your mother for a moment," Vivian said.

Vivian motioned for Leah to follow her, and they walked to the lawn just beyond the veranda. She sat at a picnic bench under a patch of dogwood trees, surrounded by lush foliage: tall grassy stalks of salt-meadow rush, a blaze of orange-red trumpet vines, delicate wild geraniums in pink and white, and the New England asters that always reminded her of purple dandelions.

Leah slid onto the bench across from her, her back to the veranda. Vivian eyed the winery, making sure no one was close enough to overhear them.

"Mom, what's going on?"

Vivian hesitated. No need to tell her how bad their money problems might be. She would spare her at least that. She contemplated, for a moment, how to ease into the news. The more she thought about it, the more anxious she felt. Best to just rip off the Band-Aid.

"Your father is selling the winery," Vivian said.

"What? Why?" Leah looked stricken.

"It's time."

"Time? It's our family business. Dad *lives* for this place."

Vivian shifted uncomfortably. "Well, things change."

"Dad always says winemaking is in his blood. That's not something that changes. Is he sick?"

"No! He's healthy as a horse."

"Are *you* sick?"

"Leah, stop. Your father is fine, I'm fine. It's just . . . this is for the best."

"What does Asher say about this?"

"Asher supports this decision."

Leah jumped up from the bench. "Well, I don't."

Surprised by the vehemence of her response, Vivian said, "I know it's a big change."

Leah stepped forward and grabbed her hands. "Mom, are you really okay with this? You built this place, too. It's just as much your business as it is Dad's."

Vivian took a moment before saying, "I trust your father."

She wondered if her daughter noticed the break in her voice.

⁓

Leah marched into her father's office and found Asher sitting on the worn leather couch. His feet were up as he scrolled through his phone.

The walls of the office were filled with framed press clippings about the vineyard and her parents, including her favorite, her mother on the cover of *Town & Country* magazine in the spring of 1990. She had been photographed in the vineyard, dressed in Escada. The cover read "Earth Mother: Vivian Hollander and the Rise of the Modern Matriarch."

"Oh, hey, Lee," Asher said, not looking up.

"How could you not tell me about selling the winery?" she said.

Asher looked up. His expression seemed puzzled. "Tell you? I thought you knew."

"How would I know?"

He shrugged. "Mom? Dad? Why would I be the one to tell you?"

"I saw you this morning at breakfast. You never thought to mention what's going on?"

Asher sighed. "Okay, look—I didn't tell you because I knew it would start a whole big thing and I didn't want to talk about it."

"Yeah, I'd say it's a whole big thing. A very big thing!"

"Why are you getting hysterical? You don't live here. You don't work here."

"Are you joking? You think just because I don't live here anymore I'm not upset to lose this place?"

"Leah, come on. This had to happen at some point. Dad's getting old."

She sat next to him. "I thought that was what you're here for. You're supposed to be helping him—take some of the pressure off."

Asher pulled a stress ball out of the pocket of his cargo shorts and tossed it into the air, catching it. "This is what Dad wants. I guess nothing lasts forever."

"This winery could have lasted a long time. I'm sure Grandpa Samuel would agree with me if he were still here."

"Why? Gelleh Estates doesn't exist anymore."

"But Hollander does—his son's winery. We're still a winemaking family."

"You're getting all emotional about it. And then you wonder why Dad doesn't hire more women."

"Oh, my god, you didn't really just say that."

"Say what?" Bridget appeared in the doorway. She wore cutoff denim shorts and a bikini top, her brassy red hair loose and wet, evidently from the swimming pool. Leah glanced at her ring finger.

"Bridget, hi. Congrats on the engagement," she said, trying to smile.

"Thanks . . . *sis*." Bridget winked. "Are you having a fun vacay?" She took a seat in the chair behind Leonard's desk, her hair dripping onto it. Leah felt her breath catch in her throat. She wouldn't dare sit at the desk, and she was his daughter.

She exhaled. "I am. But Asher and I are just in the middle of something. Can you excuse us for a few minutes?"

"Sure. No prob," Bridget said, jumping up. She leaned over and gave Asher a kiss before strolling out of the office.

"Was that necessary?" he said.

"Yes. Unless you want me to say, in front of your new fiancée, that I think you're dropping the ball."

He threw the stress ball into the air again and this time caught it with an exaggerated flourish.

"Very funny," she said. "Asher, you should be fighting to keep the winery in the family."

"And again, I ask, what do you care?"

"Fine, forget about me. Think about Mom. Whether she admits it or not, I can tell she's devastated."

His hand stilled, no longer tossing the ball. For a moment, he said nothing. And then: "She'll come around. Selling is the right thing to do."

"What about Javier and Mateo? Have you told them?"

"No. Not yet. I advised Dad to wait until the sale is finalized. We can't risk losing them when it could take a while for this to go through. Why are you looking at me like that?"

"They have a right to know."

"Well, Dad agreed with me. Do you really doubt that Dad knows what he's doing?"

"I doubt that *you* know what you're doing. Have you even tried talking him out of this?"

"No," Asher said. "Because I have no intention of spending the rest of my life with Dad standing over my shoulder, barking orders."

"So you're encouraging Dad to sell this place so you can sail off into the sunset with Bridget?"

"Something like that."

"And what are you going to do for work?"

"Why will I have to worry about work? Do you think he's selling the winery for peanuts?"

Leah thought about that for a minute. Was her father selling to cash out or selling because the winery was in trouble? If he was in trouble, there might not be money after the sale. Was Asher too dense to realize that?

She thought of the way her mother's voice had broken when relaying the news. Vivian tried to put up a good front, but Leah knew better.

"Well then," Leah said, standing up and heading for the door. "Sounds like you've got this under control."

"Always," he said, grinning. "Really, you should be thanking me."

"Thanks, big brother." She knew that her sarcasm was lost on him. Like everything else she had just tried to say.

Thirteen

The swimming pool had been built during a burst of extravagance in the early 1980s, a time when Vivian and Leonard had remodeled their modest farmhouse home into one of the grandest homes on the North Fork. Vivian had been too busy to use it during those years, except as a backdrop to their famous parties, which were written about in newspapers and magazines.

She started swimming in her fifties, when her doctor advised her to start exercising. After a summer spent doing daily laps, she'd had an indoor pool installed in the lower level of the house to sustain herself during the winter months. As much of a luxury as the indoor pool was, Vivian always counted the days until she could return to the outdoor, Roman-end-shaped pool, with landscaped planters around the perimeter, the entire deck laid with hand-crafted limestone.

After her conversation with Leah, she'd needed the water as much for her mental state as her physical workout. She glided through it, arching her arms to be mindful of her form while going fast enough to clear her head. Her heart beat steadily, her eyes open behind her goggles. She felt herself grow tired and knew the timer on her waterproof watch would soon go off. When it didn't, when she began to wonder if she could keep going, she swam over to the ladder in the deep end and grabbed hold of the rail. She checked her watch: she still had five minutes to go. Was the stress affecting her stamina?

"I've been looking all over for you," Leonard called from the opposite end of the pool, walking toward her.

"Well, you found me," she said, climbing out and taking off her goggles and unstrapping her bathing cap.

"It's late in the day for you to be taking your swim," he said.

"Yes, well, it's not the only thing that's a bit off today."

He ignored the pointed comment, as she knew he would.

"The veranda is full. People are asking for you."

Vivian reached for the towel she'd left on one of the lounge chairs and wrapped it around her waist. She sat down.

"I'm in no mood to be the charming hostess today," she said.

Leonard sat in the chair next to hers. His thick white hair was covered by a Hollander Estates baseball cap, and from underneath the brim his dark eyes focused on her. He was deeply tanned, and if she hadn't been so upset she would have allowed herself to be softened by how handsome she still found him to be. Through all the ups and downs, no matter how difficult Leonard could be, Vivian had always been in love with her husband. And he had always been devoted to her. She knew those were the important things in life. And yet . . .

"Leonard, we cannot lose this home."

"I know it's difficult," Leonard said, his eyes filled with empathy.

"Difficult? It's unthinkable!"

She'd never imagined it would come to this, and that was perhaps no one's fault but her own. Maybe it had always been inevitable that she would pay for the naive choice to walk away from the financial security of her family. It had been a decision one would make only when very young or madly in love, and she had been both.

She had met Leonard during her first year at Barnard. Her parents had only allowed her to apply to women's colleges, and when she was accepted to Barnard, they insisted she live at home, not in the dorm.

She was serious about her studies, and between her parents' strictness and her desire to get high marks, she rarely socialized. The night she met Leonard, she'd been dining with her parents at a fancy steak house on Lexington Avenue just blocks from the family's department store. She hadn't wanted to go out that night, but her parents said she was "moping" and insisted. It was true that she'd been in a bit of a funk; when your entire life has been planned for you, when it seems clear that there will be no surprises, a numbing stillness sets in that is as terrifying as rootless uncertainty.

The maître d' knew her family; he called her Miss Freudenberg. They were seated at a prime table near the window. While her parents sipped martinis, she stared dreamily out at the foot traffic on Lexington. A young man with dark good looks walked past, focused on a slip of paper. She wondered who he was, where he was going—and idly had the thought that it was sad she would never see him again. Minutes later, while she picked through the bread basket, he walked into the room. The paper he'd been staring at must have been the address; he'd been searching for the restaurant.

He was tall and lean, with dark hair. He had prominent brows, and his nose was slightly too wide to afford him a classically handsome face. But there was an energy about him, a surefooted confidence.

The man turned in her direction, catching her eye. She was embarrassed to have been caught staring but couldn't look away. He smiled, and her insides fluttered. Those bedroom eyes! The sight of him was almost embarrassing. His date was a very lucky woman. But then, there didn't seem to be any date; he sat at the long wooden bar and began animatedly chatting up the bartender until he was joined by the sharply dressed restaurant manager.

Midway through the meal, Vivian excused herself to go downstairs to the ladies' lounge. The restroom was a large suite with its own coatroom, sitting area, and white-gloved attendants. Her father handed her a few bills for tips. When she crossed the room, she again made eye contact with the stranger. Closer now, she could see his eyes were as dark as his velvety hair.

Her heart pounded as she walked down the stairs. She said a silent thank-you to whatever god in heaven had given her the thrill of this man, a hint that maybe she would someday meet someone who changed things after all.

The ladies' lounge had a counter filled with supplies: combs, hair spray, face powder, cotton balls, and breath mints. She spent some time fixing her already pristine ponytail, humming to herself. When she climbed the stairs to return to the table, feeling fortified to withstand the rest of the dull meal with her parents, she had to step aside to let someone else descend into the lounge.

It was him.

They faced each other in the dim light of the corridor, the music from upstairs providing a backdrop to the moment.

"I don't make a habit of visiting the ladies' lounge," he said, smiling.

"I should hope not." She could feel herself blushing.

"I'm Leonard Hollander," he said, his expression changing to a more serious set of his jaw, his eyes bright with something that made her feel like she was glowing. He held out his hand, and without a moment's hesitation, she placed hers in it. His touch was cool, and his fingers closed around hers firmly. She wanted to press herself against him, to breathe in the wool of his jacket, to reach her hand behind his neck and feel the feathery touch of his hair. It was overwhelming.

"I'm Vivian," she said, pulling her hand away. "I should get back to my table."

"Wait—before you go: I don't live in the city, but I'm here for work a lot."

"What do you do, Leonard Hollander?"

"I'm in the wine business," he said. This sounded very glamorous to her. "The vineyard is on the West Coast, but all the important restaurants are here. Next time I'm in town I'd like to take you out to dinner."

Vivian simply nodded, too thrilled to put energy into more banter. He wrote her phone number on a matchbook.

It would be a few months before they saw each other again, but after finally meeting for a first date, they were never apart. They married a year later.

Dropping out of school, losing the support of her parents, leaving Manhattan for life on a farm—she'd never second-guessed any of it. She still didn't.

"You should have seen the look on Leah's face when I told her what's going on," Vivian said.

"I asked you not to do that."

"I didn't admit how dire things are financially. But she had a right to know about the decision to sell."

Leonard sighed, reaching for her hand. "I'm sorry. I know this is hard, but we need to stick together. Fighting with each other is not going to help. It's you and me against the world. Remember?"

Yes, she remembered.

She remembered it all. That only made it harder.

Fourteen

Steven returned to the house just in time for dinner after taking Sadie scallop fishing late that afternoon in nearby Corey Creek. He kissed Leah on the forehead, and she inhaled the familiar scent of him, woodsy and male and, today, with a hint of saltwater. It was summertime Steven.

She patiently let him download all about the great time he had with Sadie—and she was happy to hear it. But really, all she could think about was the sale of the winery.

She didn't know what she'd expected when she told him. Maybe some acknowledgment of the loss? Instead, he was maddeningly philosophical.

"Look, people sell businesses," he said. "Or businesses close. We have our own business to worry about. Your parents will be fine."

"I opened the cheese shop almost twenty years ago. The Hollanders have been vintners since my father's *grandfather* began it in Argentina. Don't you see the difference?"

"Of course. And one of the main differences is that the cheese shop is *ours* and Hollander Estates is not. Your father turned you away from the company. It was hard for you at the time, but now you're in a position where the fate of the winery really has nothing to do with you. So be thankful for that."

"I grew up here," she reminded him.

"I understand that. Look, I loved the house in Maine where I grew up. But when my parents retired and sold it, I had to let them do what was best for themselves and move on."

"But your parents decided together to sell that house. My mother doesn't want this. She's putting on a show of a united front, but I know she's upset."

"Vivian is a strong woman. She'll be fine."

Then he had to get in the shower. The conversation was over.

Steven emerged from the bathroom with a towel wrapped around his waist. He had some color from the past few days in the sun, though he had to be careful about that because he burned. The blue in his eyes was particularly vivid; he looked, in that moment, as he had the first time they visited her parents, six months after the night of the Cooler. They had already said "I love you." And the sex—good lord, the sex.

They had been late for dinner that first visit, too—but for entirely different reasons. After an early-evening swim, she'd gone into the bathroom to shower, but before she could peel off her wet bikini, Steven followed her in and closed the door.

She smiled at him in the mirror. "What are you doing?"

He didn't answer her, but stepped forward, kissing her neck. A shiver ran through her, a combination of her damp skin and the thrill of anticipation. She protested feebly, murmuring about her parents expecting them. But he slid her bathing suit bottom to the floor, along with his own. She didn't move—barely breathed—still facing the mirror. She leaned forward just enough to reach out and brace herself against the vanity, and when he was inside her, their eyes met in the reflection. It was the most thrilling moment she'd ever experienced.

Now, standing in front of the full-length Chippendale mirror in the bedroom, she wondered if he was thinking about that first visit, too.

"Can you zip me up?" Leah asked. As his fingers brushed the bare skin of her back, she wondered if he would try to take her dress off instead of getting it on. And if so, would she be able to respond?

"There you go," he said, closing the seam with one swift motion before crossing the room to retrieve his pants and shirt from the armoire. "I'll be ready in five," he added, his back to her.

Okay. It was just as well.

They wouldn't be late to dinner after all.

Sadie looked around the dinner table. The tension was thicker than the humidity. No one except her uncle Asher and his girlfriend was talking. There were long silent gaps, the only sound the uncorking of more wine bottles.

The picnic table was set with a spread of farro salad, corn, roasted chicken, French bread, and tomato and mozzarella drizzled with olive oil. Sadie had worked up a huge appetite spending the entire day outdoors, but the introvert in her was screaming for relief. Not only that, it was clear that something was *up*.

She poured herself a glass of Sauvignon Blanc. Sadie had been sipping wine with her family since she was an older teenager. They were very European in that way. Still, she had always been careful to temper her consumption. But now she was twenty-one and no longer had to act like a kid invited to the grown-ups' table. And so, after perhaps one glass too many, she blurted out, "Why is everyone so quiet?"

"Weelll," her mother said, and Sadie could tell by the looseness with which she dragged out the word that she, too, was a little tipsy. "Since I know what it feels like to be left out of *important family news*, I'll tell you."

Vivian leaned forward. "Leah, please—"

"Your grandparents are selling the winery," Leah blurted out.

Sadie's jaw dropped. Selling the winery? What a buzzkill. She'd been busy the past few years and probably hadn't visited as often as she should have. But she never even considered the thought that someday it would be gone. She hadn't considered a lot of things: like the fact that Mateo Argueta was incredibly hot.

They'd never hung out that much before. Still, how had she not noticed? Maybe she hadn't lifted her face out of her books long enough to take in his intense dark eyes and the five-o'clock shadow that made her want to run her fingers along his jaw. He had leading-man bone structure and lips that belonged on a Kardashian. Plus, he knew things.

"When grapevines flower it's called an inflorescence," he'd told Sadie. "Microscopically, it was formed the previous year in the bud."

Inflorescence. Sadie loved the word. She would use it in her fiction writing someday.

"This type of trellising is VSP—vertical shoot positioning," Mateo had added, adjusting the metal wire holding the vines in place. His hands moved with certainty, twisting the metal and adjusting the leaves, speaking the fluid and foreign language of the grapes. "We tie the plants down so that when the new shoots come up with fruit, the foliage is standing straight up. That way the fruit has optimal sun exposure."

The previous vineyard manager, a grizzled old dude, had always seemed pestered by Sadie's presence in the field. And while her mother told her stories about how her father, Grandpa Leonard, had taught her everything she knew, Sadie found that hard to reconcile with her aloof grandfather. So this tour with Mateo Argueta was, remarkably, her first real tour from a viticulture standpoint. Sadie was fascinated, though she didn't know if it was the wonders of the grape growing that had her so captivated or the wonder of Mateo Argueta's fine body poured into those jeans.

It was a nice distraction from the fact that Holden still hadn't texted or messaged her. Breakup or not, she had been sure that time apart would show him how irrational he was being.

"But in happier news, we're engaged," Bridget said, beaming.

Sadie turned to her uncle. "Wow—congratulations."

"So, Sadie, do you have a boyfriend?" Bridget asked as Asher murmured his thanks. "I still remember my college boyfriends."

"Babe, please. You're almost a married woman," Asher teased.

"I would imagine you do remember," Vivian said mildly. "That was just a few years ago."

Meow, Sadie thought. "Um, no. I don't have a boyfriend."

"Wait—what happened with Holden?" her mother said.

"I bet it's because of all those books," Leonard said. "Men don't like women who read too much. It gives them ideas."

"What kind of ideas?" Leah said.

"Ideas about how terrible men are."

"Dad, you don't really believe that!" Leah said, aghast. But Sadie could tell by the faint smile on her grandfather's face that he was just being provocative. Vivian clearly knew it, too, because she just shook her head and rolled her eyes. Still, for Sadie, it hit a nerve.

"Yeah, well, you're right, Grandpa," Sadie said. "My boyfriend broke up with me because I work too much."

She downed her glass of wine and wondered how long before she could reasonably retreat to the library.

Fifteen

Midafternoon, the sound of merriment, of clinking glasses and champagne corks popping, reached Vivian before she climbed the stairs to the veranda. She felt, as she always did, the electric energy of people noticing her. Of people whispering, *That's Vivian Hollander.*

After saying some hellos and agreeing to a few selfies—heavens, how she hated that cultural development—she noticed Asher and Bridget in the corner talking to a woman holding a clipboard. She had salt-and-pepper hair and was dressed in a pantsuit. Asher waved Vivian over.

"Mom, you know Patricia Curtis," Asher said. Now that Vivian had a good look at her face, she realized she was familiar. And then the tired synapses in her brain made the connection: She was a wedding planner. She'd worked with many couples who had their ceremony at the winery.

"Nice to see you, Mrs. Hollander," Patricia said.

Vivian smiled and looked around the veranda. "Meeting clients here today?"

Bridget emitted a small, inappropriate laugh.

"Mom," Asher said, reaching for Bridget's hand. "*We're* the clients. We're getting married here."

"Oh—of course." Somehow, it hadn't crossed Vivian's mind that Asher would get married at the winery. A vineyard wedding was something she had dreamed about for Leah, but she had chosen to elope. Vivian had resigned herself to seeing only strangers wed in the spectacular setting she and Leonard had created.

"It was actually Bridget's idea," Asher said.

"Have you set a date?" Vivian said, her mind racing. How much time would he need to come to his senses and realize this was a mistake?

"We're thinking Labor Day weekend."

"Lovely. That gives us more than a year to plan."

"No, Mom—this Labor Day."

"So soon?" Vivian said, all veneer of pleasantry gone. "What on earth is your rush? You just got engaged!" Good lord, maybe Bridget truly *was* pregnant.

Asher and Bridget exchanged a look. Clearly sensing the tension, Patricia Curtis pretended to have an incoming phone call and wandered off.

"I mean, who knows how long we'll have the winery," Bridget said, her voice low. "With selling it and all."

Vivian had no doubt this little fortune hunter expected quite a windfall from "selling it and all." Maybe getting rid of her would be as simple as telling her the truth: the gravy train was out of gas.

"How sentimental of you, Bridget. But let me reassure you, it could take months to get an offer, and months beyond that until a closing," Vivian said. She looked out at the green fields, confident there was no way this wedding was happening.

"Mom," Asher said. "I met with Dad this morning. There's already an offer on the table."

⁓

Sadie pulled her messenger bag off her shoulder and unpacked her work onto the library table. In the stillness of the room, surrounded by all the great volumes of fiction, poetry, biography, the implications of her grandparents selling the property hit her more fully. She could imagine the vineyard going. She could imagine the winery in new hands. But this house? This library? She shuddered to think of every book in the room sold to the highest bidder.

Did her grandmother remember that her old book club journal was tucked away in here? And what about the books themselves? She hadn't found *Lace*.

She climbed the stairs, painfully aware now that her time in this special place was finite. She returned to the alphabetically shelved contemporary fiction. Again, she looked through the books by authors with last names beginning with the letter "C": John le Carré, Raymond Carver, Raymond Chandler, Paulo Coelho . . . and then she spotted it: Shirley Conran.

Sadie pulled the copy of *Lace* onto her lap, studying the pink satin nightgown and silver serving tray that adorned the book's cover. It evoked expensive hotel rooms and cheap perfume. She cracked the book open and read the inside jacket: *Four elegant, successful, sophisticated women in their forties have been called to the Pierre Hotel in New York to meet Lili, the world-famous movie actress.*

A porn star, from what Sadie could glean from her grandmother's journal.

Already a legend despite her youth, Lili is beautiful, passionate, notoriously temperamental . . .

And also, people really liked adjectives back in the eighties.

Each of the four has reason to hate Lili. And each of them is astonished to see the others; for they are old friends who first met in school, old friends who share a guilty secret—old friends whose lives are changed when Lili confronts them and asks: "Which one of you bitches is my mother?"

Oh, you have got to be kidding me, Sadie thought. This was what her regal, high-bred grandmother and her friends had been reading? Total trash. Probably not worth the paper it was printed on.

She wondered if it would fit in her messenger bag.

Sixteen

Vivian paced the bedroom, walking back and forth in front of an antique Georgian mahogany sideboard covered with framed family photos. She felt the eyes of her children following her as she contemplated the end of the wine dynasty she had once imagined for them.

An offer to buy Hollander Estates. As if there was any price that would be worth giving up her home. And yet, because of the amount of money the winery was losing, the offer wouldn't even be enough to buy a more modest house. It was a failure on a magnitude Vivian never imagined.

She heard the bedroom door click open.

"Vivian," Leonard said. "You've been hiding in here all day."

"I'm not hiding! I'm thinking," she said.

"Well, it's dinnertime," he said. "Everyone's going to be at the table in twenty minutes."

"How can you expect me to eat at a time like this?"

All her energy was going to her racing mind. Could she have done something to prevent this? Why had she let Leonard handle everything?

Because she'd always believed in him.

Oh, there had been moments of doubt. Cutchogue in 1970 had not been a welcoming place; eighty miles from Manhattan, it might as well have been on Mars. The town had a population of just under three thousand. There was a small stretch of stores, including a post office, a pharmacy, and a tiny grocery store.

Leonard's father, taking pity on the dreamy newlyweds who had bitten off more than they could chew, flew out to help with the pruning to make sure they struck the balance of not too much, not too little.

Their first crop was the summer of 1971. How had they succeeded where so many others failed? A trial-and-error system of grafting, weeding out the weakest vines before planting, and expert pruning. Though there were ordinances against women running a vineyard, winemaking was, at its heart, farming. And there were no laws against women working in the fields. From day one, Vivian helped hand-hoe the vines and pick the first harvest.

They worked outdoors year-round. One winter brought three-foot snowdrifts into the vineyard and they had to literally roll themselves from plant to plant. In the summer, they were dodging lightning and thunder. It became so dangerous that Vivian begged Leonard to ask his parents for money so they could afford to install lightning rods. That was the one and only time he accepted financial help from his father.

August brought the birds, a menace attracted by the increase in sugar in the crops. They required a netting system: more money.

In 1976, Hurricane Belle destroyed their 1974 crop, and that was another tough recovery.

Labor, cash infusion, labor, cash infusion. And so it went until, like a child on a bike with training wheels, one day, the winery took off.

She never imagined it hitting a wall like this.

"You can't stay up here and miss dinner," Leonard said.

That was true. No matter how much she was hurting, no matter how afraid she felt, she couldn't let it show. It was the only thing she could control. Keeping up appearances was her superpower.

Leah was under the covers by nine. It was barely dark out. Still, Steven followed her lead, turning off the TV and then the bedroom light. He knew she was upset and put his arm around her.

"Your parents will figure it out," Steven said. "Don't worry about them so much."

He kissed her. She kissed him back in an "okay, goodnight" sort of way, but then he kissed her neck. She was surprised by the overture and willed herself to go with it even though she wasn't in the mood. She pressed her body against his, hoping to feel something catch inside of herself. When she didn't, she told herself just to do what she would do if she *had* felt something. She reached down and began stroking him over his boxer shorts and immediately realized that although she wasn't feeling anything, he certainly was. She should have been happy about that. Instead, it made her feel terribly alone.

He gently tugged down her underwear. From the first time Steven ever touched her, it was like he knew her body intuitively. But now the practiced stroke of his hand felt clinical.

"I'm going to get on top," she murmured, wanting to keep things moving, not wanting to get so much in her own head she couldn't continue.

"Everything okay?" Steven said after a minute.

"Yes," she said, opening her eyes. "Are you close?"

His movement beneath her stopped, his body still except for his heavy breathing.

"What's wrong?" she asked.

"I don't know, Leah. You tell me. It's like you're not even in the room."

She moved off him and lay down by his side, staring up at the ceiling. Her heart beat with equal parts guilt for feeling so detached and defensiveness that he picked up on it.

He sat up, running his hand through his hair and looking at her. "What is it?"

She clutched the sheets to her chest. "I think I'm just upset about the winery."

When she was a younger woman, sex could offer escape—just like drinking or running off to the beach or taking an aimless drive with the music blasting. Nothing was ever so bad that sensory pleasure couldn't fix it at least temporarily. But now that she was older, whatever was bothering her was always primary. And she had to be in a perfect frame of mind to have sex.

"Leah, I know it's a loss. And of course you need to be supportive of your parents. But you can't let this consume you. You have a life waiting for you back in the city."

She was thankful for her life in Manhattan. She'd run a successful business of her own while raising her daughter and sustaining a loving marriage. But the cheese shop, as much as she'd wanted it to, never filled the void that had been created when she left the winery. In the way that music and books and movies you see later in life can never compare to the ones you experienced as a child, so it was with a place.

Just like wine and cheese had a terroir, so did people. And this vineyard was her terroir. It was unthinkable that she was losing it, and yet there was nothing she could do about it. Her father had made sure of that.

But there was something she could do, and that was be there for her mother. Oh, she'd put up a good front at the dinner table. But Leah knew it was just that: a front. The dark glasses stayed on, and while she smiled and made conversation, she drank more than she ate. And when Sadie said something about being sad to leave, she hadn't responded in her typical way, which would have been, "So don't." She was a strained, superficial version of herself. "I don't think I can leave tomorrow," Leah said. "I need to stay."

"What do you mean, stay? For how long?"

"I don't know. A week or so?"

"To do what?"

"Give my mother some moral support."

"It's not your job to fix this, Leah. You weren't needed in boom times, so they can do without you during the bust," he said. "Besides, we have to get back to work."

"Just for a week," Leah repeated.

"So you want me to go back to the city and deal with Bailey's Blue?"

"Can you?"

He hesitated, and she could tell his mind was racing with images of long customer lines at the counter during the day and the hours of bookkeeping and placing orders at night . . . all things she had managed with an occasional part-timer, but things he was relatively new to handling—and never all alone. Still, she knew he could do it. It was just a matter of whether he was willing. And that was what she knew he was truly grappling with. When he ultimately nodded, Leah reached for his hand. "But, Leah," he said, "don't get overly caught up in all this. Your parents make the decisions about Hollander Estates. They made that clear a long time ago." He got out of bed and walked to the bathroom.

Leah knew he was trying to be protective of her, but it felt like criticism. And the truth was, she had been a Hollander before she was a Bailey. But this, like her disconnection from their sex life, was something she couldn't express to her husband. And with a few days apart, she wouldn't have to try.

For now.

Seventeen

Sadie awoke on her last morning at the vineyard in no hurry to leave.

She also wasn't in a hurry for breakfast; an hour after opening her eyes, she remained huddled under the covers, furtively turning the pages of *Lace*. Every time she felt a hunger pang, she told herself: just one more chapter.

Sometimes, on formal occasions Charles would make Maxine gasp or blush or even forget what she meant to say. He could manage this by directing one meaningful look at her.

A knock on the bedroom door made Sadie jump. She shoved the novel under her pillow.

"Uh, come in," she said.

"Just want to make sure you're packed," her father said.

"Yeah, yeah. All set."

"I'm going to grab a quick bite downstairs and then we'll hit the road."

"This early?"

"I want to beat the traffic."

Traffic heading *into* Manhattan? It was probably just an excuse. Her father was itching to leave.

He closed the door. She sat up and pulled the book onto her lap.

One night, shortly after they were married, Charles had murmured, "I don't want you to wear any underwear to the de la Fresange ball tonight. I want to know that if I care to feel you at any time, you will be ready for me."

Appalling. And, she had to admit, intriguing. Sadie got out of bed and tucked the novel into her suitcase. She doubted anyone would miss it. Especially once the library was all packed up into boxes and stored away somewhere.

With a quick check in the mirror to tame her hair, wild from sleep, she changed into cutoff jeans and a fresh T-shirt. She tossed a few last things into her suitcase and zipped it shut.

Another knock on the door.

"Come in."

This time it was her mother. Leah's hair was in a messy knot, and she had shadows underneath her eyes. Sadie couldn't tell if the rumpled yoga pants and T-shirt she was wearing were her night clothes or day clothes.

"Your father wants to leave earlier than planned," she said.

"I know, Mom. He was just in here. You okay?"

Leah sat on the edge of the bed. "I've decided to stay a few more days. Maybe a week. I'm concerned about your grandmother."

"Is there anything I can do?"

"No, no. You have a job to get back to. Just say goodbye before you head out to the car."

Sadie felt a pang of guilt. She hadn't exactly lied to her parents about her job—she just hadn't told them she lost it.

Leah leaned over and kissed her on the cheek before leaving. When she was gone, Sadie sat and looked at her suitcase, thinking about the copy of *Lace* stashed inside. Maybe she should have found some time to ask her grandmother about the book. What she really wanted to ask her about was the book club, but that would mean admitting she'd snooped around and found the journal. Now it felt too late to talk about anything; Vivian had more important things on her mind. And Sadie needed to get her own head back where it belonged: with her thesis paper.

She headed down the hall and saw that the door to her grandparents' bedroom was closed. She knocked. No response. She knocked again.

"Gran? It's me, Sadie. I want to say goodbye before I go."

Her grandfather opened the door.

"Hello, Sadie," he said. "Maybe come back in a little bit? Gran is tired."

"I'm leaving soon. My dad wants to get going." Sadie looked past him. The room was dark, the curtains still closed against the bright morning sun. From the hallway, she could feel the frostiness of the room's air-conditioned climate.

He reached out and patted her head. "Give her a call when you get back to the city. Wonderful having you this week. Good luck with your studies."

He closed the door, but she didn't move. That was it? Even for her brusque grandfather, it felt a little abrupt.

She couldn't leave without saying goodbye to Vivian. In the past few days she'd discovered another dimension to her grandmother: beyond the elegant, manicured façade, she was also a woman who had a secret trashy novel book club. A club she recorded in a journal she'd subsequently hidden in the wall.

Sadie wondered if Grandpa Leonard had known what was in those novels his wife was reading. Had Vivian sat there beside him in bed at night, furtively turning the pages while Leonard watched the eleven o'clock news? The thought made her smile.

Her grandmother was a spirited, interesting woman. Fine, she wasn't exactly a feminist. But in that book club, in those secret stashes of books, Sadie detected a hint of rebellion. Where was that spirit now that the winery was on the line? Her grandmother had loved stories of outrageous women, but she had played it safe in her own life. Sadie didn't want to see her grandmother's story end like this.

She didn't want to see her own story end like this, either—back on campus for the summer, with a failed thesis and a breakup and no job. What, exactly, was she rushing back to?

Leah walked to the driveway where Steven was packing up the car.

"You weren't even going to say goodbye?" she said.

He slammed the trunk closed. "Don't start, Leah," he said.

"I'll probably be home as early as next weekend," she said.

"What's going to change with your mother between now and next weekend?"

"I don't know. Maybe nothing. Don't lawyer me, Steven."

"I'm not 'lawyering' you—that's a legitimate question. I just get the feeling you're looking for an excuse to spend time apart."

"I'm not." But was she? Alone at the vineyard, she wouldn't have to make decisions about the cheese shop. She wouldn't have to deal with her flagging sex life. At the vineyard, she actually felt younger: spending most of the day outdoors, surrounded by the sights and sounds of her childhood. Nature changed with the seasons, but it always rejuvenated. Some plants even got better with age; an older grapevine produced less fruit, but what it did produce was higher quality than the fruit of young vines.

Her love and attachment to the vineyard, something she had tried to forget about for so long, had boomeranged back to her. That was the oddest thing about middle age: the past could sometimes feel more potent, more relevant, than the present. Life was like tossing a ball into the ocean. She thought the past was the past, but then it came riding back on a wave and lying at her feet.

The truth was that she wasn't just staying for her mother. She was staying because she wasn't ready to say goodbye for good. Why did she think this would be so difficult to admit to her husband? Sometimes in marriage you didn't have to have total understanding, just acceptance. Still, something held her back.

"You know, it's not the worst thing in the world for you to drive back with Sadie," she said. "Have some father-daughter time."

Steven's expression brightened. "That's true." He checked his phone. "Where is she? I told her to be out here by now."

The front door opened, and Sadie walked out, sunglasses on but without her travel bag.

"Hey," she said, jogging over to the car. "Sorry I'm late. I was trying to say goodbye to Gran."

Trying?

"All right, let's get on the road," Steven said, opening the passenger-side door.

Sadie made no move toward the car. "Actually, Dad, I've decided to stay."

Part Two

Bloom

I have known more than one woman living in
an imaginary dream world, rather than
face the reality of her own life.

—SHIRLEY CONRAN

Eighteen

⁓

The photograph was the last thing Vivian looked at before she went to sleep every night, and the first thing she saw when her eyes opened in the morning.

The image on her nightstand, framed in sterling silver, was of her children in the 1970s, sitting on the steps of the veranda, the lush green of the vineyard in the background. Asher wore a lightweight summer blazer, and Leah wore a madras plaid dress, her long dark hair in a braid. She'd had more than one photographer tell her that her family looked as perfect as a Ralph Lauren ad. From the outside, her entire *life* looked as perfect as a Ralph Lauren ad. But things were never truly as they appeared.

She sat up with a sudden realization: the photo by her bedside was just one of hundreds like it in albums shelved in the library. With the potential buyers coming to poke around the property today, who knew what they would get their grubby hands on? She would have to start taking inventory of the house and hiding anything personal. She might not be able to protect her winery, but she could still guard her privacy.

The bedroom door opened.

"Mom? It's Leah."

"I'm sleeping."

"No, you're not."

Leah walked to the windows and slid the curtains over half an inch. Vivian, having seen so little natural light over the past few days, saw spots.

"It's a beautiful morning," Leah said. "Come on. I know you're upset. But I'm here and Sadie decided to stay and we want to spend time with you."

She could barely experience the good news. She felt like nothing would be okay ever again. At the same time, she didn't want Leah and Sadie to see her like this.

"I am entitled to take to my room if I wish."

"The tasting room is full, and people are asking for you. They want to see the glamorous Vivian Hollander. And I know you enjoy being that person."

She did enjoy being that person. She would be that person until the new owner dragged her off the property kicking and screaming.

But first, the photo albums.

∿

The crowd of customers trickling out from the tasting room to the veranda made it hard to believe the winery was failing. Leah walked among the tables, surrounded by groups of women laughing and taking photos and pouring bottle after bottle of wine. One table had tall balloons shaped in the number "21" tied to the chairs. The women looked like teenagers, and they were clearly well into their second or third bottle.

It was strange to witness a dual reality: the happy customers, and the stress and strain behind the scenes.

In the distance, Mateo pulled leaves from the vines. Leah wondered if the winery's new owners would keep the Arguetas employed. The possibility that they might not made her shudder.

Mateo clearly shared his father's passion for the land. Just a few days earlier, he had shown Leah and Sadie a clonal stock of new Chardonnay and explained that the older the grape variety, the more cloning took place. Mateo had started talking about something else that she just remembered. Something about Hollander being a forty-eight-year-old winery, and therefore . . . therefore what?

A cork popped, distracting her. Jazz music played from the high speakers tucked into the four corners of the vaulted ceiling. Leah inhaled one of the customers' sweet perfume. It struck her, amid the merriment, that the customers on the veranda were mostly women.

And then her father, along with four men in suits, emerged through the winery's door. The potential buyers.

Leah turned away, took the stairs down to the lawn, and walked toward the field. She felt compelled, for some reason, to talk to Mateo a little further. What *about* the vineyard being forty-eight years old? Leah knew she was being ridiculous, as if she could ask enough questions to solve the problem that her father, in all his years of experience, could not.

The sun was bright and strong. Leah wished she'd worn a hat. She wouldn't burn, but it still wasn't great for her skin. The photos of her grandmother Gelleh reminded her what too much sun could do. The woman's face, dominated by wide dark eyes, had been like a raisin. As a child, Leah had found her terrifying.

"Hey," Leah called out.

Mateo turned around. "Oh, hi, Leah."

"How's it going?"

"Just shoot thinning the Chardonnay. We have lots of it."

Chardonnay, a white grape from Burgundy, was thick-skinned and versatile and because of that was possibly the most widely grown grape in the world. The flip side of that was that it was responsible for some very mediocre wine. Hollander Estates had always been able to tease something miraculous out of it.

"Mateo, I know my father can be very set in his ways. You said something the other day about this being a forty-eight-year-old winery; I know that's a winery in its infancy in some parts of the world, but for the North Fork of Long Island, it's a long time. I'm just wondering if there's anything that maybe has become . . . habit? Rote? Any opportunities that might have been overlooked just by the sheer longevity of this operation?" It was a question that nagged at her.

Mateo looked out into the field, wiping his brow with the back of his hand. "Your father did an incredible thing. He was a pioneer out here."

"I know, I know. I'm not trying to suggest otherwise. I was just wondering: If you *had* to do something different, what would it be?"

Mateo shrugged. "I'd probably rip out some of the existing fields and put new varietals in. We're top-heavy in Merlot."

In 1995, *Wine Spectator* had hailed Leonard Hollander as the "Long Island Master of Merlot." Of course he grew a lot of that particular grape. It was his calling card. He'd never rip out any of those plants.

Mateo looked around, then took a step closer.

"Can I ask you something?" he said, dropping his clippers to the ground.

"Sure."

"Are the rumors true? Is your father selling?"

Leah could have kicked herself for opening herself up to the question—and she definitely wanted to kick her father and brother for putting her in this position in the first place. She believed what she told Asher: the Arguetas had a right to know what was going on. And yet her respect for her father simply ran too deep for her to go rogue on this. Mateo looked her in the eye, and she glanced away.

"Um, my father doesn't really loop me in on business decisions."

Maybe it was time for that to change.

Nineteen

~⚬~

Sadie couldn't put the book down, and she kinda hated herself for it.

Reading *Lace* in the library surrounded by so many other, more worthy reading options—including "Notes on 'Camp'" sitting on the table just waiting to be explored in her nonexistent thesis—made her focus on the trashy novel all the more shameful.

On a flawless summer day, she was huddled indoors, racing through six hundred pages of outrageous drama and even more outrageous sex.

If she had any intellectual integrity, she would have stopped reading at the prelude, a graphic scene of a thirteen-year-old-girl getting an illegal abortion at the hands of an indifferent doctor. But then the book jumped ahead a few decades to four successful women—Maxine, Judy, Pagan, and Kate—who had been summoned to the Pierre Hotel. They'd been called to meet with an international film star named Lili, who Maxine thought of as "that gold-digging slut." Maxine, in her forties, had already had a face-lift, justifying that it was sensible to have it done when you were still young so that nobody noticed. *Now, there's some life advice*, Sadie thought. Judy, at least, had some more useful words of wisdom: the idea that you became an adult when you stopped caring about what other people thought about you and instead started caring about what you thought of them.

The four women were old friends from a Swiss boarding school.

When they were all assembled for the surprise reunion, Lili appeared and said: "Which one of you bitches is my mother?"

Sadie had to admit: that was an opening. And the writing was serviceable, even if its primary service was detailing the women's glamorous and privileged lives.

The book flashed back for long sections of the characters as teens at their boarding school. The pages were filled with "flesh throbbing" and various scenarios of consensual and nonconsensual sex. Just when Sadie thought she'd had enough, that it was an insult to her intelligence to be reading the book even as a guilty pleasure, one of the characters would do or say something that made her rethink the book. For example, despite the retro gender roles, Maxine called out the sexual double standard, noting that it was accepted that a boy could get carried away by passion but it was always the girl's responsibility to set the sexual limit. Why was it *her* job to control *his* lust?

Right on, sister, Sadie thought.

What had her grandmother thought of all this? Her friends? She'd resisted the urge to delve further into the book club journal because she didn't want any spoilers. But as soon as she was finished with the novel she was going back to the journal.

She could see the appeal of book clubs for the first time; she'd never understood the point before—maybe because her need for group intellectual discussion was fulfilled by her classes. But now? *Now* she would have loved to hash out this crazy story with someone. Like Holden. If they were still together, they probably could have gotten off together over some of the sex scenes.

"I thought I'd find you here," Leah said, surprising her from the doorway. "I could use some company."

Sadie tried to hide *Lace* under her laptop, but she was too slow. Leah grabbed it.

"Are you reading this?"

"No," Sadie said quickly. "I just found it on the shelf." Well, searched it out and found it. But no need to go into all of that.

Her mother examined the cover. "My god. I think this is the original edition. I *remember* this book."

"You read it?"

Her mother smiled. "I wasn't supposed to. But Gran used to have a book club. She and her friends would get all dressed up and sip wine on the veranda—it all seemed very glamorous to me at the time. My parents had lots of parties, but this was different. It was exclusive, and certainly exclusionary to me."

Sadie couldn't help but glance up at the stairs. Should she tell her mother about the book club journal? Did she already know about it?

"Anyway, the book you're reading was one of their selections," Leah said. "I snuck Gran's copy when she wasn't around."

"Mom. You rebel."

Leah flipped through the pages and laughed. "No wonder you're not getting any work done."

Sadie felt herself blush. No, she wasn't getting any work done. But only partly because of the book. How much longer could she pretend that she was making progress on her paper? She hated to admit her failure—even to herself. It was definitely not something she wanted to share with Leah, but at the same time, she didn't want to lie. Her parents believed she had a job to get back to. "I wasn't getting work done before."

Leah put the book down and focused on her. "Hon, then maybe you shouldn't have stayed out here. Get back to school. I don't want this stuff to distract you."

Sadie shook her head. "No, that's not it. I wasn't getting any work done at school, either. I seriously hate to say this but . . . I'm a little frozen on my thesis."

"Since when?"

Sadie hesitated. "Months."

"What's wrong?"

The distressed look on her mother's face was exactly what she'd wanted to avoid.

"I don't know," Sadie said. "I kept thinking it was just temporary.

But for the first time, I just can't get a handle on what I'm supposed to be writing."

"Why don't you take the summer off and focus on your work for Dr. Moore?"

"Well, that's another thing: since I've missed deadlines for my thesis, my status in the honors program is in jeopardy. Dr. Moore . . ." Sadie swallowed. "She fired me."

"*Fired* you?"

"Not in a punitive way. But she doesn't want me spending time working for her when I should be focused on my academics."

Leah frowned. "Why didn't you tell me?"

"I guess I didn't want to let you down."

"You could never let me down."

"I thought the change in scenery out here would help. But for the past few days I've just been reading this crazy novel. I can't believe that Gran—"

"You can't believe Gran what?" Vivian said from behind them.

Sadie and her mother turned to find Vivian standing in the doorway along with Peternelle, who held cardboard boxes. Sadie slipped the copy of *Lace* back into her bag.

"Mom!" Leah said. "I'm so happy to see you out and about."

"Not a moment too soon, from what I just heard in here," Vivian said. "What are you two gossiping about?"

"Nothing," Sadie said quickly. "Just . . . it's such a great collection here."

"Yes, well, I'm glad you're enjoying it while you still can. Those awful buyers are here today. I suggest you both lock your bedroom doors. I can't prevent them from traipsing through here, unfortunately, so Peternelle is going to help me gather a few things."

"We can help, too," Leah said.

"Fine. I need the family photo albums from the upper level. That staircase is treacherous, so I'm hoping you more agile beings can get the job done. Peternelle and I will start down here."

Sadie followed her mother up the stairs, feeling paranoid. Was her grandmother really collecting the photo albums because of people visiting the winery, or did she suspect Sadie had been snooping around? Did Vivian even remember that the journal was up there?

Her mother bent down and began piling albums into her arms. "I'll get this row. If we can each pack up half a shelf, I think we can make it in just a few trips."

What if her grandmother had forgotten about the journal and mistakenly left it behind for the new owners to discover? She had to confide in her mother; Leah would know what to do.

"Mom," Sadie whispered. "Did you know that Gran had a book club journal?"

"What do you mean, a journal?"

"She wrote down all this stuff about starting a book club. How she'd tried to keep a journal before but didn't stick with it, so instead she was going to write about this one specific thing: the books they read, who was there . . . that kind of thing."

"How do you know?"

"I found it hidden away in a compartment behind this shelf."

Sadie, one arm full of photo albums, pointed to the spot at the back of the shelf. Her mother crouched down on her knees to get a better look.

"It's locked," Leah whispered.

"It's not—I sprung the lock last time. We can pull it open."

"Do you need another set of hands?" Vivian called from below. "Should I summon Asher?"

"No, Mom—we've got it," Leah yelled back. She turned to Sadie. "We really shouldn't invade her privacy."

"I know," Sadie said.

"But I have to admit, I'm curious," Leah said. "I never knew her to keep any kind of journal."

"She wrote stuff in there about feeling pushed aside, not having a lot to do. This was, like, *her* thing. A project."

"Pushed aside? I always saw her as so busy and in control of her domain." Leah bent lower, peering again into the shelf. "Well, I don't want to snoop."

They sat in silence. Sadie, trying to justify her own behavior, said, "If you just read, like, the first page it wouldn't be so bad."

"Maybe just a few sentences?"

Sadie glanced nervously at the stairs, hoping no one was walking up to bust them. Then she pulled open the compartment door and retrieved the journal, passing it to her mother.

"What in heaven's name is taking you so long? At this rate we'll be here all day!" Vivian called out.

"Coming down now," Leah said, tucking the journal in her arms behind the photo albums. They reached the first floor and unloaded their armfuls of books onto the table.

"Wonderful," Vivian said. "Peternelle, please hand me a box."

Leah began organizing piles. Sadie looked around for the journal but had lost track of it. She had to trust that her mother would take care of it.

Vivian walked around the room, directing Peternelle to pull certain books, and then they all pitched in to seal them in boxes. The efficient operation ended with her mother calling for staffers to help carry out the boxes. Vivian trailed behind them, muttering about the indignity of having to pack up her personal belongings to keep them safe.

When she was alone with her mother, Sadie said, "Do you have the journal?"

"No," Leah said. "I slipped it under your Susan Sontag book."

They glanced back at the table, completely empty. "Notes on 'Camp'" was gone.

And so was the journal.

Twenty

Leah took her place at the dinner table. A light breeze blew off the nearby bay. The veranda was pleasant except for the buzz of mosquitos. Peternelle lit citronella candles.

"To good health," Leonard said, raising his glass of Pinot Noir. If he was fazed by the impending sale, he didn't let it show. Her mother, on the other hand, was in a mood and refused to take off her sunglasses even as daylight began to fade.

"Sounds great, Dad," Asher said.

"Would you mind if I had vodka tonight?" Bridget said. "I'm trying to cut carbs. We can't have a puffy bride."

"Young lady, at my table we drink wine," Leonard said.

Leah wouldn't have minded some hard liquor herself. Before dinner, she'd had a conversation with her father that left her frustrated and more anxious than ever. He'd been on the phone in his office, and she stood in the doorway, waiting for him to finish so she could talk to him. He waved her in, and she sat in the threadbare armchair across from his desk. Despite the many renovations and upgrades of the main house and other parts of the winery over the years, her father had had the same office furniture since the day he moved in.

She waited, feeling inexplicably nervous. She had a right to an opinion, didn't she?

"What's on your mind?" he'd said when he finished the call.

"I wanted to talk to you about the winery, Dad. Are you sure selling is the only thing to do? It seems so . . . permanent."

Leonard leaned back in his chair, smoothing one of his brows. "Did your mother put you up to this?"

"What? No. I'm concerned. Maybe I can help you—"

He waved the comment aside. "I know you run a little shop in the city, but this is a different ball game, my dear."

"A little shop? Dad, I've had a successful business for almost two decades in one of the most competitive retail environments in the country."

"Leah, no need to get defensive. I'm not trying to diminish your accomplishments with the shop." He leaned forward. "But it's not a winery."

Leah knew there was no sense debating her merits as a businessperson. Her father was stubborn, and he existed within a world of his own logic, and that logic included the idea that winemaking was a man's business.

Sometimes she'd wondered why he spent so much time with her out in the fields as a girl if he never intended for her to help run the place. She'd decided it was both love and ego: As a father, he enjoyed seeing her delight in discovery of the vines. He couldn't imagine any of his offspring not having a deep knowledge of wine. But as a winemaker, neither of these could overcome the fact that he couldn't imagine having a daughter as a business partner.

"I can think of some ways to increase revenue," she said.

"Leah, I'm sorry you're having a hard time with what's happening, and I'm willing to hear you out so you can get your feelings off your chest. But ultimately, you need to let it go. And please don't start getting your mother's hopes up. The sale is as good as done."

"If it's as good as done, then why haven't you told Javier yet?"

He began to say something, then stopped. "I don't need to explain myself to you, Leah. Please extend to me at least that degree of respect." After that, he seemed considerably less open to conversation.

Across the table, Bridget reached for the wine. Leah noticed that her engagement ring was different; the antique had been replaced with a small, heart-shaped diamond set in a simple platinum band.

"Oh, you changed your ring?"

"This one's just a little more modern," Bridget said, extending her hand and admiring it.

Why was Asher spending money on jewelry when it was clear money must be an issue? Sometimes the family dysfunction was too much to take. No wonder Steven rushed back to the city.

"What? So where's my mother's ring?" Leonard said.

"I'll give it back to you, Dad," said Asher.

"Damn right you will."

"No offense, Mr. Hollander. It's just that these days, girls want to have a say in their engagement rings. It's, like, a reflection of their personality, you know?"

"Why even wear rings?" Sadie said. "If you want to be modern about it, don't let yourself be marked as someone else's property."

"Sadie, please," Leah said.

"Oh, I think rings are so romantic! I would never not wear one," Bridget said. "Also, Leah, I wanted to know if you would be my maid of honor at the wedding."

"Matron," Vivian corrected. "She's a matron."

"So you settled on a date?" Leah asked, stalling. Surely Bridget had a friend or a relative who could do the honors. They barely knew each other.

Leah checked her phone, trying not to feel bothered by Steven's empty seat next to her. Her husband had not abandoned her. She was the one who had decided to stay behind. They'd had a perfectly amiable text conversation before dinner. Everything was fine.

"Labor Day weekend," Asher said. "We want to get married here before the new owners take over."

Leah nodded. That made sense. Now that she thought about it, she hadn't seen a wedding at the winery her entire visit. During past summers, she had seen several over the course of a weekend.

"Speaking of weddings," she said to her father, "did you book any for this summer? I'm surprised I haven't walked into the middle of one yet." She smiled to show she was just making light conversation, not questioning how the winery was being run. Although she was starting to have questions. The bulk of their on-site retail business was done through weddings and organized tastings on weekends, and she had the sense they weren't booking enough of them. Plus, there had to be something they could host during weekdays or evenings.

"Of course we have weddings booked," he said.

Peternelle brought out littlenecks and hand-shucked oysters.

"This is the mignonette sauce, and this is spicy cocktail," she said. "The zucchini cups are coming."

"You guys should do more with social media. I could shoot short videos of the weddings for Insta," Bridget said.

"That's a good idea," Leah said, aware of the fact that she hadn't yet accepted the matron of honor position. But it seemed Bridget had either already forgotten her request, or just assumed the answer was yes.

"Yeah, Dad," Asher said. "Companies pay Bridget to post their products."

"That's very cool," Sadie said. "One of my dormmates is an influencer. She makes a lot of money. I told you about her, Mom. The one who gave us all the freebie furniture to decorate with?"

Leah nodded, distracted. "You know what I noticed on the veranda today? It was mostly women. I feel like there used to be more couples."

"Maybe they *were* couples, Mom," Sadie said.

Leah shot her a look. "What I mean is, there seem to be fewer men."

"Oh, yeah. You're right about that," Asher said. "A beer distillery opened down the road. So now women come here for wine and their boyfriends and husbands bro-out over a few beers."

"So you've lost half your customers?" Leah said, shocked.

"I told Dad we should start serving beer, right, Dad?" Asher said.

"Over my dead body," said Leonard.

"I think it's fun that it's mostly women," Bridget said.

"Children, I'd like to relax over a nice meal. Enough with the shop talk," Leonard said.

Leah finished her wine. It was excellent: rich, full-bodied, complex. Her father knew how to make exceptional wine. Her parents had been pioneers. They'd had a good run. They had started it, and now they would have to finish it. Why was she letting this bother her so much? Was it just empathy for her mother? Or had she believed, on some level, that there would be a time when someone—her father, her mother, maybe even Asher—realized that she belonged there?

If she had been waiting for that day, clearly she'd waited too long.

Twenty-one

Vivian pushed through the warm water, then turned over onto her back to see the stars. *Make a wish*, she thought, the magical thinking of her girlhood.

She had always loved night swimming and wondered now why she didn't do it more often. Probably because her husband didn't like swimming after dinner, and she had always adapted her habits to accommodate him.

But tonight, with their entire world turned upside down, a shift in their routine was a luxury she allowed herself. Even if that also meant risking nostalgia, something she found herself indulging in more and more lately.

Although there was no sense in looking back too much. What had her old book club notebook been doing mixed in with the photo albums? Had she mistakenly forgotten to put it away at some point? She couldn't remember the last time she'd looked at it. She couldn't remember the last time she'd thought about the club, though she did think about the young woman who'd encouraged her to start the group in the first place.

Enough. She didn't want to think about that time. Not now. There was too much to worry about in the present.

Vivian moved her arms with disciplined strokes, pushing the water away from her body to propel her back and forth. She blinked, the view of the stars blurring from water splashed into her eyes. Oh, how she'd hated getting water in her eyes when she was little. She'd create a huge fuss and her mother got very frustrated.

As a girl, Vivian spent her summers at her family's cottage in East Hampton. Aside from horseback riding, the biggest treat was an evening swim, when her parents entertained guests in the dining room or on the lawn and Vivian and her brother had the pool all to themselves with only their nanny watching over them.

The Freudenbergs were Jews, and as such were not welcome at the Maidstone Club or any of the other social institutions in town. Her mother, Lillian, determined to give her husband the social life a man of his stature deserved, made certain that their oceanfront mansion functioned like a club. The house, called Woodlawn, offered three formal meals a day, evening cocktails, tennis matches, swimming, and parties all season long. On the Fourth of July, Woodlawn even had its own fireworks show.

When Vivian and Leonard started the winery, she anticipated that her life would be very different from that of her parents. It was hard to imagine during those early years of fieldwork that she would ever have a moment of luxury again. She didn't mind; the financial end of things and decision-making was her husband's business, her husband's family money. But out in the field, they were equals. Then even that changed. They were able to hire people to do the labor-intensive, day-to-day work. Leonard could focus on the big picture and management, business instead of farming. And, of course, they wanted to start a family.

When Asher was a few years old, she researched schools in the area and found her favorite was in Bridgehampton.

"You're going to drive him back and forth an hour each way?" Leonard had said. She knew he thought it was crazy, but he also wasn't going to give her a hard time about it any more than she gave him a hard time about his decisions in the vineyard. Their division of labor had been set.

She became a full-time mother, carpooling her two children, managing their field trips and doctor's appointments and playdates, leaving the business to her husband. But by the early 1980s, Leonard needed her help. It seemed that a great winery was made not just in the field, but in the marketplace. They had proven they could produce great wines. They attracted customers to the tasting room and sold their wine by the caseload. But if they were going to truly succeed, they needed their wine in restaurants. The most celebrated wines in the country were produced on the West Coast, but it was the New York City restaurant market that could make or break a brand. And New York City restaurants wanted nothing to do with Long Island wines.

"You know what our greatest asset is, Vivian?" Leonard had said one night. "It's not out in that field. It's right here, in front of me. It's you."

Suddenly, the decision to send their children to school in the Hamptons wasn't so crazy. The Hamptons were filled with influential Manhattanites.

"I need you to network," he told her.

It sounded simple enough, but she soon found that the Hamptons social scene was, in the 1980s, as closed to her as it had been to her parents in the 1950s—not because she was Jewish but because she was an outsider. The Freudenbergs were long gone from the Hamptons; they had sold Woodlawn and their townhouse on Fifth Avenue and moved to Palm Beach. Any remaining connections from her parents' generation were too old to help her. The parents of her children's friends were cordial but clannish. If Leonard and Vivian were going to make inroads socially, she'd need to follow her parents' model with Woodlawn.

"Okay," she said. "I can do that. But we need to start entertaining. And that means renovating this house."

The pool had been built during that remodeling. As Vivian oversaw the house renovation, making countless decisions large and small, she remembered her love of night swimming as a child. And so one of the design elements of the pool was dozens of fiber-optic lights that looked like the reflection of the stars at night. Looking at them now, she wished she could transport herself back to the optimism of the 1980s. She hadn't appreciated it at the time, but they were the happiest years of her life. She had her children, the winery was flourishing, she was young and beautiful and in love. She believed their family and business would continue to flourish. She had no idea what was just around the corner.

Vivian heeded Leonard's request that she make inroads in the Hamptons social scene. Invitations came their way sporadically, but none had brought them any closer to connections that might help them crack the Manhattan restaurant market.

And then one night, the mother of one of Asher's classmates invited them to a dinner party she was hosting in East Hampton along with her husband, an investment banker. Vivian's expectations for the evening were low; by that time, they'd been to a few such parties, driving down dark streets lined with hedgerows so tall you could only imagine what was hidden behind them. The evenings were pleasant, full of fine food and small talk. But nothing had ever come out of them.

Vivian felt out of place at the parties. A decade of working in the field pulling leaves and setting out bird netting and pruning vines had left her more comfortable running around with her kids barefoot in the backyard than slipping on heels and a Norma Kamali dress for cocktails at a waterfront mansion. Ironically, if she had followed the path her parents had wanted for her, she would be living in a house just like the ones she visited as a guest, hosting parties all summer long instead of worrying about sour rot.

Security greeted them at the foot of the drive and directed them to another gate at the side of the sprawling front lawn. They followed a stone path to the poolside terrace. A bar was set up on the terrace, and another on the lawn. The entire area was strung with small, decorative lights. Beyond the pool, a long table set for forty with arrangements of roses and lilies and twinkling with countless votive candles. Music played from outdoor speakers, Elton John's hit "Little Jeannie."

Their hostess wore a cream-colored, flowy knee-length dress, a silk flower in her upswept hair. She smelled faintly of marijuana, and it was hard to reconcile her with the plain mom Vivian mostly knew from drop-offs and pickups and bake sales. She took Vivian by the arm and said, "I'm glad you're here. Someone wants to meet you."

"Meet me?" Vivian echoed, turning to look at Leonard. But he'd already made his way to the crowd of men smoking cigars poolside. Vivian followed her hostess to the terrace, where she immediately noticed a pretty blonde, a Cheryl Ladd look-alike who stood out from the crowd in a ruby-red tunic dress that reached the ground.

"Vivian Hollander, meet Baroness de Villard. Baroness, this is the friend I was telling you about—with the winery."

The woman stood from her seat and extended her hand. The name de Villard sounded familiar, but Vivian was certain she'd never met the woman before.

"*Alors,*" the woman said. "Please—call me Natasha."

"A pleasure to meet you," Vivian said.

"The pleasure is all mine, Mrs. Hollander. I've heard so much about you." The woman was clearly not French, but American. And not just American, but—judging from her accent—from Brooklyn or Queens.

"Natasha's husband, the Baron de Villard, owns a winery in France," their hostess said.

"Oh, lovely," Vivian said, trying to get her bearings in the conversation as she realized why she recognized the name. The de Villard family was a famous name in wine. Their vineyard in Bordeaux was *grand cru classé*—the highest classification in France.

"I'm from New York," Natasha said. "But I can't imagine growing grapes here. I understand that you and your husband were the first."

"That's right," Vivian said. "We came out here over a decade ago. It was just potato farms."

"How impressive," Natasha said. "I'd love to see your vineyard sometime. And of course, you must come to France and meet my husband. He doesn't like visiting the States. The only thing he likes about America is that it produced me," she added with a wink.

And then she drifted away. Vivian couldn't recall if she'd spoken another word to her the entire evening. Certainly, by the end of the summer, the particulars of that party had faded to a dim memory. So she was surprised when, in September, she received an invitation to Château de Villard in the mail—along with two first-class plane tickets to France.

There had been no question that they would go. It was a decision they would both come to regret.

Vivian's limbs became heavy with the last few strokes, and she swam to the side of the pool and grabbed hold of the ledge. How long had she been out there? She wasn't ready to go inside, but then Leonard appeared. He was dressed in his robe and looked tired.

"I've been looking all over for you," he said. "What are you doing out here at this hour?"

"I'm trying to tire myself out so I can sleep."

Leonard walked to the pool's edge.

"Things went well with the buyers today," he said. "They increased their offer."

"Is that my cue to be happy?"

"We're going to walk away with something. Not a lot, but something."

Vivian had been sad when her parents sold Woodlawn and the Manhattan apartment she'd grown up in. But she had her own life by that time, and she knew that if she wanted a forever home, she'd have to create one with her husband.

"I know we built the house to advance socially—for the business. But deep down, I was doing it for our children. I imagined them bringing their children here, and their children's children here. You know, Jews are a wandering people. To me, success meant not wandering anymore. I wanted to put down roots, literally and figuratively."

"Vivian," Leonard said, "we can't indulge in sentimentality. This deal is going to save us. In the morning, I'm telling Asher I've accepted the offer."

"How long will it take to close?"

"A few months."

"So we'll have the summer here. And then what? What about Peternelle? The Arguetas?"

Leonard walked toward the house, calling back to her, "It's late, Vivian. Come to bed."

She submerged herself underwater, swimming toward the fake stars.

⁓

The library felt different at night. It was as if the spirits of all the authors whose works were collected there were speaking to one another. Or maybe it was just the silence of the grand house at midnight. Or maybe, Leah thought, it was all the wine she'd had at dinner.

Her buzz had worn off, leaving her anxious. And the phone call with Steven after dinner hadn't helped. He'd seemed eager to get off the call. Or maybe they just didn't have that much to talk about aside from the cheese shop, and every mention of that included the unpleasant subtext that she was shirking her responsibilities.

She turned on one panel of lights, illuminating the middle section of the vast room while keeping the perimeter of shelves in shadow. She walked up to the second level, where she and Sadie had gathered up the photo albums, now packed away. Where Sadie had discovered her mother's old book club journal.

She remembered those racy books with the glamorous women on the covers, with their big eighties hair and bright makeup. But more, she remembered Vivian in her prime, holding court on the veranda, surrounded by her friends, delighting in the fictional misadventures in the pages of the novels.

"Mom?"

Leah looked over the ledge of the landing to see Sadie.

"What are you doing here so late?" Leah said.

"What are *you* doing here so late?" Sadie closed the door behind her.

"I can't sleep," Leah said. "I need something to read."

Sadie climbed the stairs, holding a copy of *Lace*. She slipped it back onto the "C" shelf.

"You finished it?" Leah said.

Sadie smiled sheepishly. "Yeah. All six hundred pages. I wish I could read what Gran wrote about it. Did she ever mention the book club journal to you? She must have it. It couldn't have just disappeared."

"She didn't mention it to me," Leah said. "It's possible Peternelle just packed it up along with your book. You could just ask her what she thought about it."

"Um, no. The last thing I want is to talk about Gran's hot take on all the sex. I just thought *reading* the discussion notes might be interesting. From a sociological perspective, of course."

"Of course," Leah said, smiling. "You should get some sleep, sweetheart."

"Yeah. I'm going to try." She kissed Leah on the cheek. "'Night, Mom."

Leah waited until her daughter left, then turned back to the shelf where she'd placed *Lace*. She thought she'd spotted something.

She pulled out another thick novel, the cover featuring a beautiful brunette, dressed in a black evening gown, her dark eyes staring directly into the camera lens. Above her head, in big gold embossed letters, the title: *Chances*.

With a thrilling sense of anticipation, Leah tucked the Jackie Collins novel under her arm and headed back to her bedroom.

Twenty-two

The vintage black Jaguar was arguably a ridiculous car. It was not something Sadie would ever dream of driving in New York City or even up at school. But it was what she found available in her grandparents' garage. And it made her feel like one of the characters in *Lace*.

Sadie needed some space. A three-hundred-guest wedding had taken over the winery, and she didn't want to spend another day holed up in the house worrying about her paper. A quick search on her phone suggested a restaurant in Southold called the Fish Market.

She felt strange behind the wheel, as if she were playing a role in a film from a glamorous bygone era. It was a moment of absurdity she would have liked to have shared with Holden.

Holden. Another reason to get on the road, distract herself. Every time she looked at her phone or computer, she couldn't help stalking him on social media.

She turned left off the property onto Main Road. Peconic Bay Boulevard ran parallel to it, and she'd overheard winery guests saying the other day that it was the smarter route to take when a little tipsy. Sadie knew her grandmother would have a fit if she'd heard that; they were very careful not to let guests drink and drive.

Sadie took a detour on Indian Neck Lane to see the water. She didn't get out of the car, but just turned off the engine and stared out at the Peconic. On a whim, she reached for her phone, and this time instead of taking the easy way out with a text, she dialed. The phone rang and rang, and she could imagine Holden looking at the incoming call, debating whether to answer, his fair brows knit together with irritation.

The call went to voicemail.

Sadie tossed her phone back into her bag. So much for that.

The Southold Fish Market was a simple clapboard building across the road from the water. The outdoor tables were full. Inside, walls were lined with chalkboard menus of the day's shellfish and whole fish, and ice-packed fish was on display throughout the room. She ordered fish and chips and paid for it at the counter.

"We'll call your number, hon," the cashier said.

A couple cleared a table just in time for Sadie to take their spot, a window seat. She checked her phone, still hoping for a response. Nothing. Before she could get worked up about that, she noticed Mateo Argueta across the room.

He was deep in conversation with an older man whose back was facing Sadie. She tried not to stare, but she'd found herself thinking about Mateo, hoping she'd run into him during her brief outings in the vineyard. With the change of scenery, his dark good looks were even more striking. Clearly, she wasn't alone in her feeling on this; the two women at the table next to her were stealing their own glances.

Mateo and his lunch companion stood and shook hands. The older man left. Mateo, still standing and looking toward the door, noticed her and gave a nod. Sadie wondered if she was supposed to go over and say hello, cursing her social awkwardness. Yes, she probably should.

Crossing the room seemed to take an extraordinary number of steps.

"Hi, Sadie. What brings you out here?" he said, his black eyes sharp.

Before she could answer, her name was called for her food order.

"I'll be right back," she said. Now, this was awkward. She had to return with her food, essentially inviting herself to eat with him. But whatever—they basically worked together. Or he worked for her grandfather, so it was like a business lunch.

When she returned with her fish and chips, he pointed out the window.

"A table opened up outside," he said. "Do you want to grab it?"

Sadie never understood the appeal of outdoor eating. She was sure this feeling was the product of growing up in Manhattan. The outdoor restaurant tables always seemed to be on a bus route or jutting out onto the sidewalk, and all the people walking by looked at you and your food. It was different out here, with the view of the water and the fresh air. But she was a creature of habit.

"No, thanks. I'm good."

"Those outdoor tables are prime. I've never seen one passed up."

"I'm more of an indoors person," Sadie said.

"That's interesting."

"Why is that interesting?"

"Because your grandparents are farmers," Mateo said. "You can't get more outdoors than that."

Sadie shrugged and sipped her Diet Coke.

"You shouldn't drink that," Mateo said. "It's poison."

"It's not the healthiest, but . . ."

"No, it's poison."

"That's a little judgmental coming from someone who works at a winery."

"You think wine is poison?"

"I mean, alcohol isn't *good* for you. That's not exactly breaking news."

"Everything in moderation," Mateo said. "Except toxic chemicals." He smiled.

"Fair enough," Sadie said.

Was Mateo flirting with her? Or was he just extremely opinionated about soda? It was hard to say.

"So," Mateo said. "You're going into your senior year?"

Sadie nodded. Hmm. Asking about her age was a possible sign of interest.

"What's your major?" Mateo asked.

"English. I'm working on my thesis this summer. Did you, um, go to college?"

"Stanford," Mateo said.

"Really?"

"You don't have to look so surprised."

"I'm not surprised." She was shocked. "It's just, why did you come back to the vineyard?"

"I thought about moving to the city after school but decided to return to the North Fork. It seemed there was no better place than a vineyard to put my degree in sustainable development to use."

Sadie found that incredibly hot. Mateo was flexing. Mateo was *definitely* flirting with her.

"Listen," Mateo said, leaning closer, "I'd rather you not mention seeing me here today."

Sadie found her pulse racing. Clandestine. She was into it. "Totally. I get it."

"I don't want your family to know I'm already interviewing."

"Wait—what?"

"The man I was talking to. It was about a job."

"You're quitting?"

"I have to start looking before I get laid off. I have my father to think about. He doesn't just work at Hollander, he's lived there my entire life."

Oh. The sale.

Mateo stood up. "For now, though, it's back to work," he said.

"Yeah, um—okay. See you back at the winery."

He smiled. "Remember: stay off the poison."

"Right," she said. "No soda for me."

Sadie watched him leave with just the subtlest sinking feeling. The entire room seemed to dim. Mateo had that kind of energy about him. When he was out of sight, she reached for her Diet Coke.

Twenty-three

ᷟᷤ

The bride posing for photos on the veranda steps reminded Vivian of her younger self, a hopeful, bright-eyed blonde adorned in lace and duchess satin.

"Can I get a photo with you, Mrs. Hollander?" the bride asked.

"Oh, I'm not dressed for the occasion," Vivian demurred. The truth was, she happened to be wearing a fabulous lavender ribbon tweed knit dress by St. John. She always dressed for the weddings. She'd witnessed hundreds at the winery, and the power of them never faded. Two young people—or, in some cases, older people—beginning a life together. Optimistic. Passionate. Surrounded by loving friends and family.

Her own wedding had been a source of strain and anxiety. Her parents disapproved of her engagement—not because she was too young, or because she might not finish college, but because of Leonard. Her intended betrothed was not from a "good" family, meaning one of the several dozen highly affluent German-Jewish families on the East Coast. Vivian's parents weren't impressed that the Hollanders owned a successful vineyard in Napa; Samuel and Gelleh might as well have been field hands.

Vivian had considered eloping, but ultimately her parents threw them a lavish wedding with a ceremony at Temple Emanu-El on Fifth Avenue followed by a reception for four hundred at the Plaza. Vivian had worn a custom Yves Saint Laurent gown in white damask cotton and white elbow gloves, and the wedding photographer told her over and over that she was a more beautiful bride than Grace Kelly. Yes, she certainly looked the part. But inside, she was a wreck. If her parents were already unhappy about her marriage, they would have a fit when they learned of the couple's plans for the future.

Leonard had no illusions about how challenging it would be to start the first winery on the North Fork of Long Island. He'd been prepared to work hard. And he had. They both had.

She watched the groom pull his bride into his arms, dancing her around the veranda to the song "Lady in Red."

Vivian felt tears in her eyes and blinked them back. She couldn't pretend any longer that it was the loss of the business, the loss of the fortune, that was what really devastated her. After all, she had married Leonard Hollander for better or for worse, for richer or poorer, in sickness and in health.

It was the creeping sense of guilt.

She rushed away from the veranda, under the shady pergola, to the house. She felt weak with the unshakable certainty that this was karma, that she herself was responsible for the vineyard's ruin.

⌇

Leah turned the pages of *Chances*, settled in a lounge chair by the pool. In the distance, she heard the wedding band playing "I Gotta Feeling" by the Black Eyed Peas. The sun moved directly overhead.

The book was sprawling, over eight hundred pages, moving back and forth in time between the present-day 1970s and the characters' early lives in the 1920s through the 1960s. It was taking her longer to read than she'd anticipated even though the characters jumped off the page: Gino Santangelo, a gangster with a heart of gold but a happy trigger finger; an African-American prostitute-turned-socialite named Carrie; and Gino's gorgeous and rebellious daughter, Lucky. The supporting characters were an assorted band of blackmailers, lovers, petty thieves, and social climbers. The sex scenes were graphic, the dialogue blunt and profane. Jackie Collins wrote with an energy that left Leah, as a reader, nearly breathless. But what really got to her was the relationship between Lucky and her father—the way she refused to let Gino's limited view of her define her life: *She had no intention of following the route he had planned for her. School. College. Marriage. No way. She wanted to be like him. Rich. Powerful. Respected. She wanted people to jump when she gave the orders—just the way she always had for him.*

Leah put the book down with a sigh. Lucky was the ultimate heroine: beautiful, ballsy . . . and respected. When she was young and her father was teaching her the ins and outs of his empire, it came with the caveat: "Of course, you're only a figurehead. You'll never be called upon to get involved." And then as soon as he was temporarily exiled from the country, running from legal problems, she seized the moment to take the helm. By the time he returned, Lucky was the boss.

She couldn't help but think of how she'd handled her own difficult father: scuttling off like a scared little rabbit.

"Hey," Asher said, appearing at the edge of her chair. He was dressed in a white button-down shirt with the sleeves rolled up, and powder blue pinstriped shorts. His thick head of Hollander hair, just starting to silver at the temples, was tucked under a winery baseball cap. His tan had deepened in the past few days. He was slightly stockier than their father, and moved without Leonard's air of authority. Still, anyone looking at him would see success—a guy who didn't have a care in the world. And, considering his attitude about the sale, maybe he didn't.

Leah took off her reading glasses, shielded her eyes from the sun, and looked up at him. "Hey."

The wedding band had shifted to a slower gear, now playing that eighties song "Lady in Red." Leah remembered dancing to it at her senior prom. She also remembered sitting in this very spot a few days before her prom with her friends, all working on their tans. All her friends had had crushes on Asher, and Leah had looked up to him.

"I need to talk to you," Asher said.

"What's up?"

"Dad just told me he formally accepted the offer for the winery."

Now, all of a sudden, Asher was confiding in her?

"Well, I guess we knew that was coming. Do you think the new owners will keep the staff?"

"I can't worry about the staff right now," Asher said. He sat down at the edge of her chair and lowered his voice. "Leah, there's going to be very little money after the sale."

"What do you mean?"

"It means we've been operating with huge losses for a long time. Losses I didn't realize."

"How could you not know? You're a VP."

"I'm not a finance guy . . ."

"You're not a finance guy, you're not a winemaker, you're not a sales-person. What exactly do you do, Asher?"

He shook his head. "After all this time, you're still jealous."

"Jealous? Okay, Asher. Whatever. Sorry your plan to cash out isn't looking so good."

He took off his baseball cap and ran his hand through his hair, looking like a movie star. Leah felt so annoyed she wanted to slap some sense into him.

"I'll deal with it. But I'm afraid Bridget is going to freak out."

"Yeah. She might even have to sell her second engagement ring."

"Low blow."

"You're right: I shouldn't attack Bridget for your shortcomings."

"Just . . . don't say anything to her about all of this."

"I think she'll notice when the moving trucks arrive," Leah said dryly.

"The sale will take months to close."

And by then, they'd be married. Asher, like most people headed to the altar, thought the wedding was the finish line. They had to learn for themselves it was just the starting mark.

Keeping this secret was not a good way to start.

Leah stood at her bedroom window, watching the sky turn from gold to pink to purple. The natural beauty of the North Fork always astonished her. And tonight, it made her miss her husband. That, and some of the steamy love scenes in *Chances*.

As much as the book offered in action and plot twists, it had a surprisingly tender love story between Gino and his second wife. Reading the scene of them making love for the first time gave her an actual twinge deep inside, a flickering reminder that she was still a woman with her own desire, however latent it might be. And she knew that if her libido was showing signs of life, she should be at home with Steven. Maybe staying behind had been a mistake.

A knock at the door, and then Sadie poked her head in. "Do you have a sec?"

"Of course. What's up?"

Sadie sat in the armchair. "So I don't know if I should tell you this, but then I thought maybe I should: I found out that Mateo is interviewing for a new job."

Leah sighed. "Not surprising. I would be doing the same thing. How did you hear?"

"I ran into him when I went to Southold for lunch. Has Grandpa announced the sale?"

"I think he's going to this week."

Sadie picked up the copy of *Chances* on Leah's bed. "What's this?"

"An old book of Gran's. I'm rereading it—indulging in a little nostalgia. I was in eighth grade the first time I snuck this out of the library."

Sadie opened the book, scanning a page. Her eyes widened. "Wow. Even as a member of the internet porn generation, I find this shocking.

Is Dad aware of your precocious reading habits? It seems like something that should have been disclosed."

"Very funny."

"I just can't believe Gran and her friends were into this stuff."

"Okay, Ms. Literary Fiction. 'Which one of you bitches is my mother?'"

Sadie rolled her eyes. "My reading is purely anthropological. I'm in college. It's a time of experimentation. In fact, Dr. Moore told me to expand my horizons."

"In Gran's defense—and mine—these were very popular books at the time. The one you were reading was also a television miniseries. I'll never forget watching it in my pajamas. The actress who played Lili—Phoebe Cates—seemed like the most beautiful woman in the world to me. Most of the actresses and models at the time—not to mention all the Barbie Dolls—were blond, wholesome, girl-next-door types. Phoebe Cates was the first actress I really noticed who looked a little different."

"Did Gran know you watched that? Because you didn't even want me watching *Gossip Girl*."

"No. She definitely did not," Leah said. "But I wished I could have talked to my mother about the books. I would watch the ladies on the veranda, drinking their wine, all dressed up. My mother loved the book club." Leah took *Chances* from Sadie's hands. "Maybe she'd enjoy re-reading this as much as I am."

"No offense, Mom, but I think it's going to take more than a book to lift Gran's spirits."

"Sadie, I'm surprised at you. You love books. Books are your thing."

It didn't matter what Sadie thought. Leah remembered her mother's book club, she remembered a time when the vineyard was thriving, her mother was in her prime, and anything seemed possible. It wasn't just the rosy hue of her memory: the Vivian of her childhood would not give up on the winery. Leah was certain of that.

Maybe the book would help her mother remember, too.

Twenty-four

"Don't be ridiculous," Vivian said. "I have no interest in reading this."

She'd been watching the sunset on the veranda when Leah appeared and handed over the old book. Leah, dressed in leggings and a T-shirt with long sleeves that almost covered her hands, looked like a teenager.

"Why not? Don't you remember it?"

Of course she remembered it. The sight of the cover, the woman in the black evening dress, with big hair and heavy brows like Brooke Shields, brought her right back to the eighties. One thing she loved the most about books was that they never changed, and when you picked one off the shelf after years, it brought you back to the moment you first held it. Vivian cracked it open, inhaling that old-book smell.

"Where did you get this?"

"I found it in the library. You know, I used to sneak these books when you weren't around. All I wanted was to be part of that book club."

The book club had been, in the words of Virginia Woolf, a room of her own. It didn't matter how big and luxurious the house was because that house was an extension of her marriage to Leonard. And she treasured their partnership. But the assembly of women who gathered once a month on the veranda? That was hers. There was a special joy in dressing up when it wasn't to impress anyone, when it wasn't for work or any special occasion but her own mood. And there was a catharsis in discussing love and life—and, yes, sex—through the lens of a novel. It was one part of her life that was lived completely on her own terms.

Until Leonard fired Delphine and any illusion of control—even over the book club—was shattered.

"Of course I remember it," she said. "I'm surprised you do."

"Are you kidding? You and your friends looked so glamorous to me. All I wanted was to be part of the conversation, but you never let me stay."

"Oh, Leah. The books weren't appropriate for you." They had been, however, perfect for her. The stories of outrageous love affairs and kinky sex and beautiful people had been just what she and her circle of friends needed. She'd even started a journal, chronicling their get-togethers and the books that kept them entertained.

"Yeah, I'm realizing that. I'm an adult, and this one is making me blush."

Vivian hadn't thought about the book club and her journal in years. But then the other day, packing up the family albums to protect them from the prying eyes of the new buyers, the journal appeared. She moved it to the back of her bedroom closet without reading it. Looking back was painful.

But how had it gotten mixed up with the stack of photo albums and books?

Had Leah been snooping?

She handed the copy of *Chances* back to Leah. "Well, you can put this back where you found it. Since you clearly know your way around the library."

Leah averted her eyes. So she was snooping!

Decades earlier, when Vivian oversaw the expansion and reno-vation of their house, she asked their architect to model library shelves after the walls in a celebrated French estate. He had taken her direction literally, down to every last design quirk, including hidden locked compartments. This was where she'd hidden the journal. She couldn't imagine how Leah had found it. If she'd found it.

"Mom, it might be fun if we read it together. I just started it and, I don't know, it brings me back to a simpler time."

"I have no interest in old books. There's too much going on right now."

But Leah wasn't listening. The sight of something in the distance distracted her.

"That's Javier. I need to talk to him." She kissed her on the cheek. "Think about what I said."

Leah rushed off. Only after she disappeared into the darkness did Vivian realize she'd left behind the copy of *Chances*. She reached for it, opening to the first page.

Bitch. Child. Liberated lady. Temptress. Costa knew her as all of those things.

"So you see"—she fumbled in an oversized Gucci bag and produced a pack of cigarettes—"no way is it the right time for my father to come back into the country. No way. You must stop him."

A simpler time, Leah had said. Well, simpler for her. She had just been a young girl. Vivian, however, had been an adult. An adult making adult mistakes.

She stood and began to pace in the darkness. The mention of cigarettes on the page made her yearn for one now. Decades after quitting, she still dreamed of smoking.

Yes, the book brought her back. She'd read it on the flight to France to see Natasha de Villard's grand cru vineyard.

She could envision the Bordeaux countryside like it was yesterday even though it had been nearly forty years since her visit. Natasha sent a car to pick them up from the airport, and it had been from the back seat of that sleek Mercedes that she first caught sight of Château de Villard, rising in the distance like something out of a dream. When Vivian had embarked on renovating their own home, she had imagined something grand in French Renaissance tradition. But Château de Villard was the real deal, and her wildest imagination had failed to equal it. The château's steeply pitched roof seemed to go on forever. With its gables and spires and turrets, it was like the skyline of a small city.

The driver whisked them up through an allée of linden trees, and closer proximity to the house only heightened its grandeur. The limestone building featured an entrance tower and several prominent wings. To the right of the entrance, an open loggia with pillars and topped with stone gargoyles.

Staff emerged from the house to take their luggage, and they were shown into a marble entrance hall. Glasses of champagne were pressed into their hands before a uniformed housekeeper led them up a spiral staircase. Vivian's jaw dropped as she realized the stairs wrapped around a four-story chandelier.

The third-floor hallway was lined with paintings by Sargent and Boldini. They passed several rooms before the woman stopped and opened a door to a baroque extravaganza.

"Please, make yourself at home. The baron and baroness look forward to seeing you at dinner. I will return to bring you to the dining room at eight."

Alone in the bedroom, Leonard walked around, silently admiring the walnut paneling, sixteenth-century tapestry, and Louis XV–style furniture. He finally turned to her and said, "What do you think all of this is about?"

"I have no idea," Vivian said. "But I can't wait for our luggage to get here so I can figure out what to wear when we find out."

The housekeeper returned, as promised, to escort them down to the dining hall, a cavernous room with a seventy-foot-high ceiling and an oak table that could seat over sixty people. A triple fireplace spanned one end of the room, more antique tapestries on the walls.

Natasha de Villard rose to greet them. She was even prettier than Vivian remembered, the grand surroundings serving to heighten her beauty instead of dwarfing it. Dressed in a Chantilly lace suit with ribbon appliqué, she looked like she belonged in the pages of *Vogue*. She greeted Leonard and Vivian with a kiss on both cheeks.

"This is so much fun!" she said.

The baron rose from his seat at the head of the table. He was tall and lean, with sandy-colored hair, slate blue eyes under thick brows, and a long nose.

"Welcome, welcome," he said, approaching them. His smile was tight, but his voice was warm. He opened his arms to Vivian, and she dutifully stepped in for an embrace. As he kissed her once on each cheek, she felt an odd shiver.

"Thank you for the generous invitation," Leonard said.

"My pleasure," the baron replied. "I'm only sorry it took this long. We travel all summer, but as soon as we were back in residence, we were delighted to reach out."

He wasn't necessarily handsome—not with those cold eyes. But he had undeniable charisma, a sort of palpable energy that signaled he had power and ambition running through his veins.

It felt strange to sit at one end of a long, mostly empty table. Leah was certain they must have had a dining room that was more appropriately scaled. Later, Leonard would point out that it had been a power move. As if summoning them to the château weren't enough of one.

The truth was, they could have dined in the stables. The wine was so extraordinary, it rendered the backdrop for the meal irrelevant. The highlight was a grand cru white Burgundy Montrachet that made Vivian gasp.

The conversation was surprisingly easy. The baron's English was flawless, and although Natasha had lived in France for several years, she remained obsessed with American pop culture, leaving her eager to discuss *Dallas* and the new TV phenomenon *Dynasty*. Vivian glanced at Leonard from time to time, and his exchange with the baron seemed equally congenial.

"Your husband tells me you're a rider," the baron said.

"Well, not for quite some time," Vivian said.

"Tomorrow I'll show you our stables."

After dessert, the baron stood. "If you ladies will excuse us, we're going to the billiards room to have a few cigars."

Natasha took her on a tour of the formal gardens, all five of them, breathtakingly lovely even in the dark of night. But the travel and the wine caught up with Vivian, and she had to sit on one of the stone benches for a break.

"I'm sorry! Of course you must be exhausted. I'm just so excited to have a new friend. Come—let's get you back to your room."

Vivian was disappointed to find Leonard was still downstairs. She changed into her nightgown and waited for him.

By the time he showed up, reeking of cognac and cigars, she'd fallen asleep. The click of the bedroom door woke her.

"What on earth have you two been doing all this time?" she asked, propping herself up on her elbows.

"Celebrating," he told her. "We're going into business with the baron."

Natasha, the baron had apparently informed Leonard, "is very sentimental about her home state. Now that she has seen the wine country there, it seems a New York winery is simply not something she can live without. And I like to make sure my wife is happy."

The baron, not being a patient man, determined that the fastest and most efficient way to get his wife a winery would be to pair up with an established vineyard. His proposal was thus: a joint venture with Leonard, fifty-fifty, with small production of just five thousand cases. Both the Hollander and the de Villard names would be on the label. They would look for a parcel of land to start a new vineyard, but in the meantime, Hollander Estates would provide the grapes and make the wine for the joint venture until the new winery could provide for itself.

Now, all these years later, Vivian could still remember the sense of excitement on that trip, the belief that finally, after all the years of struggling to get their vineyard off the ground, things were going to change.

And change they did.

Vivian looked out at the field, but there was no sign of Leah. She picked up the copy of *Chances* and carried it back to the house. Maybe reading a few pages before bed wasn't the worst idea in the world.

⁓

Leah followed Javier as he traversed the property heading toward Field House.

If Mateo was looking for another job, Javier had to know about the sale. She just hoped her father had ultimately done the right thing and told him directly—that Javier hadn't found out from someone else first. Either way, she owed him an apology.

"Javier—do you have a minute?" she called out.

He stopped walking and waited for her to catch up with him.

"Has my father spoken to you about what's going on?" she said.

"Yes. Your mother must be very sad."

Her stomach churned. How very typical of Javier to be thinking of others even when his own livelihood and home were in jeopardy.

"It's a shock," Leah said. "But she'll adjust. I'm concerned about you, though. And I have to apologize: Mateo asked me the other day if my father was selling the winery and . . . I lied. I said I didn't know. I'm sorry."

Javier shook his head. "He shouldn't have asked you. It's not your place to tell."

"No—no. He had every right to ask. I just wish there was something I could do. But I can't imagine that the new owners wouldn't keep you on. Aside from my father, you're the backbone of this place. And now with Mateo managing operations . . ."

"Your father said not to count on it."

Leah felt stricken. As for Javier, she didn't know if it was the evening darkness—shadows falling across his brow—or just end-of-the-day fatigue, but he looked years older than the man she had greeted in the field when she first arrived. It was hard to reconcile the man standing before her with the boy of her girlhood dreams.

"I'm sorry," she said again.

He glanced back toward Field House.

"It's late," he said.

"Of course—I don't mean to keep you."

"Leah, if there's anything you can do," he said. She looked into his troubled dark eyes, the eyes that used to light up her day when she was a girl. She was painfully aware that he'd been at the vineyard for nearly her entire life.

"I'm going to try. I promise."

She watched him disappear into the night, but she couldn't bring herself to turn around and go back to the house. She didn't want to face her empty bedroom—nor did she want to face the fact that Steven was right: although she'd stayed behind to "help," she was powerless.

Twenty-five

It was the first darkly overcast day since she arrived at the vineyard. Sadie settled on the veranda, waiting for the rain to come. Watching a storm shower the vines was always dramatic and lovely, even at the expense of a summer day.

She opened her phone and cued up the reading app she'd down-loaded the night before. She'd never owned an e-reader and generally thought it was crazy to read on a phone, but she was curious about the book her mother was so obsessed with. And she didn't want to be seen reading it. So far, *Chances* was the saga of an oversexed gangster with an empire in jeopardy and a rebellious daughter named Lucky.

"That's the problem with your generation: you're always staring at a screen," Leonard said, appearing behind her.

She immediately put down her phone.

Her grandfather had always been an almost unreal figure to her, the stuff of legend. The living room was filled with framed photos of her grandfather with statesmen and celebrities. Her mother had told her, many different times, in different ways, the story of how Leonard Hollander, the son of immigrants, had built his fortune. People looked at the winery now, when the North Fork had over fifty robust wineries, and it seemed like Hollander Estates was a no-brainer. But back in the day, Leonard had been a visionary.

He placed a hand on her shoulder. "When your grandmother was your age, she was knee-deep in soil, out in the fields, every day starting at dawn."

Sadie nodded, unsure what point he was making. Was she supposed to be working in the vineyard? Maybe there was no point. Maybe he was just a grumpy old man. She loved him, but she didn't understand him. She was pretty sure her mother felt the same way.

"That's impressive," Sadie said.

"We've worked very hard," he said. "I should hope that sets an example for you."

"Absolutely," Sadie replied. He looked at her expectantly, showing no sign of leaving.

"You're right, Grandpa," she said, standing up and putting her phone in her bag. "I'm going to go find the vineyard crew and see if I can help out."

"Now, that's what I like to hear! Onward. Be productive."

She walked out to the field with purpose in her stride. It just wasn't the purpose her grandfather thought she had.

Reading *Chances* was making her think about sex. And thinking about sex was making her think about Mateo.

The air was heavy with moisture, and she inhaled. In the distance, Mateo was busy tending to the vines. She walked faster, the humidity creating a sheen of moisture all along her body.

Mateo, dressed in jeans, a gray T-shirt, and a black Hollander Estates baseball cap, crouched down low, his gloved hands tugging at the grapevines. Alongside him, all down the row, workers did the same. Everyone was so intent on the task at hand that not a single person noticed her.

"Hey," Sadie said when she'd gotten close enough. "Need any help?"

Mateo pulled some leaves from a plant and looked up at her. At the eye contact, Sadie felt a little jolt.

"You want to help?" He looked skeptical.

"Um, yeah."

He waved her over. "See this? These are baby Syrah berries. We need to clear away the leaves so they get exposure."

Thunder sounded in the distance. Normally, this would send Sadie running. She hated lightning, especially out in the country. But her interest in hanging around with Mateo trumped her survival instinct.

"Don't the leaves protect the fruit?" Sadie said.

"No, it's the opposite. It's going to rain the rest of the week. This is an extremely wet growing climate for grapes. We get fifty inches of rain a year, compared to California, where they might only get five inches. So we need the sunlight and breeze off the bay to reach the vines and dry out the clusters after the rain. That prevents mildew and mold from growing."

The clouds rolled in faster, so dark and heavy that day became night. Drops began to fall. A streak of lightning split the sky.

"We gotta clear the field," Mateo called out to the workers.

They made a mad dash for the small farmhouse adjacent to the field, a utilitarian building with a wide-open, garage-like space for storing field equipment and a few small offices that everyone called "the barn." Once they were inside, the rain pelting the roof sounded like pennies on tin.

"You can wait out the storm in here if you want," Mateo said, shaking water from his hands and unlocking his office door. "I think this will blow over soon enough."

Mateo's hair was soaked, his tan skin dewy with rain. A drop of water glistened on his upper lip, and Sadie wanted nothing more than to reach out and wipe it away.

"There's a foldup chair behind the door," he said, eyeing her. She was suddenly very aware of her soaked T-shirt and shorts clinging to her body.

The office smelled damp and faintly of fresh-cut grass. A few pairs of work boots were lined up in the corner of the room. A large mounted whiteboard took up most of one wall. On the other wall, two framed photographs. One was a closeup of what appeared to be fruit and flowers in a jug of white wine. The other was of a man drawing vertical lines in white chalk on the side of an orange building.

The room was so small that when Sadie unfolded the chair and sat, she could reach out and touch both the door and Mateo's desk. The desktop was spare, with just a few pens stuck in a Hollander Estates mug and a laptop.

He sat behind his desk, facing her. Their eyes met, and for Sadie it was every bit as electric as the lightning flashing outside the window. She suddenly regretted breaking his confidence to tell her mother about his job search. She couldn't take it back, but she could at least come clean.

"I have a confession to make," Sadie said. Mateo leaned forward, folding his hands together. She hesitated for a moment. What if she didn't tell him about her slight indiscretion? What if she confided, instead, that he'd been on her mind? They were closed up in that small space, the storm raging outside. It was so romantic, like the scene from *Chances* where Lucky was trapped on an elevator with a hot guy during a blackout. But she wasn't a ballsy gangster's daughter; she was a neurotic Jewish girl from Manhattan who needed to assuage her guilt.

"I told my mother that you're interviewing," she blurted out.

Either she imagined it, or Mateo physically shrank away from her.

"Didn't I ask you not to tell anyone?"

"Yeah, but it's my family. You put me in a bad position," Sadie said.

"So what did she say?"

"Um . . . that she would do the same thing."

Mateo shook his head. "Well, next time, learn to keep a secret."

"I'm sorry," Sadie said.

Mateo moved his laptop out of the way and leaned forward on his elbows. Sadie felt herself beginning to perspire.

"So what brought you into the field today? Since you're not an outdoors person," Mateo said.

Not an outdoors person? Oh—right. Their conversation at the seafood restaurant.

"My grandfather basically implied that I'm useless," Sadie said.

"He can be tough."

A clap of thunder made her jump. It was as if the universe were punctuating his observation.

"Yeah. But it's hard not to respect someone who's so accomplished."

"Your grandfather grows excellent grapes," Mateo said, seeming to choose his words carefully. "But a successful vineyard is not just about growing great grapes. It's also about growing the *right* grape for the time."

"And my grandfather doesn't?"

"Well, I don't know if I'd say that," Mateo said. "After all, you might repeat it."

Ouch.

He turned to look out the window.

"It looks like the rain is slowing," he said. Was that Sadie's cue to leave?

She shouldn't have opened her big mouth. She always said the wrong thing. Had she been too honest? Was there such a thing as too honest? Oh, relationships—even just casual interpersonal dynamics—were exhausting. This was why she was better off just reading or writing. Even if lately, the only thing she was managing to read were selections from her grandmother's trashy book club.

Now Leah needed to find a bookstore. The night before, somewhere between talking to her mother and talking to Javier, she'd misplaced her copy of *Chances*.

"Are you sure you haven't seen it?" she asked Vivian at breakfast.

"No," her mother said.

Leah drove to town, fully aware there wasn't a bookstore on Love Lane. There was, however, a great cheese shop.

The Village Cheese Shop was usually one of Leah's first stops on the North Fork. This summer, she'd gotten distracted. But the cloudy day and her missing book inspired a visit.

Vivian had bemoaned the shop's opening. "You've lost your chance!" For years, she'd been hinting that Leah should expand Bailey's Blue to the North Fork. Leah knew it wasn't so much a business suggestion as it was her mother's way of saying that she missed her.

The shop was so spacious, it made Bailey's Blue look like a closet. It had cheerful yellow walls, a black-and-white-checked floor, and a dine-in café. She walked the length of the display case and spotted a gorgeous wheel of English Wensleydale, heavily marbled with cranberry. It looked like a cake. She would bring some back to the house.

Before she could place an order, her phone rang with a call from Steven. She'd left him a message earlier; he was expecting her home the next day. After her conversation with Javier the night before, that simply wasn't possible. She dreaded telling Steven, but the longer she waited, the worse the conversation would be.

"Hey," she said, walking over to a display of Harney & Sons tea. "How's it going there?"

"Busy," he said. "I'm managing, but I miss you."

He missed her. That was a good sign. He wasn't still upset with her for staying behind. But that didn't mean he was going to be thrilled with what she had to say next.

"I miss you, too," she said, swallowing hard. "The thing is, I can't come home yet." Silence. She picked up a tin of peppermint herbal, then put it back. "Steven?"

"Why not?" he said, his voice tight.

"It's just . . . the implications of the sale are really hitting everyone. I'm worried about Javier, Peternelle . . . I can't leave in good conscience until I'm sure I've tried everything I can to maybe stop the sale. Or at least make sure that our people are taken care of if it does happen."

She heard the buzz of Bailey's Blue customers in the background and the distinct screeching sound the front door to the shop made when it swelled with the humidity.

"I can't talk about this now," he said, before ending the call.

Leah stood staring at the phone for a few seconds before slowly making her way through the other shoppers and back outside. When she pulled out her keys to unlock the car, her hand was shaking.

Steven didn't understand why she was getting involved. Was she being ridiculous? What was she *doing*?

She was halfway back to the winery before she remembered she'd forgotten all about the English Wensleydale.

Twenty-six

The rain left the vineyard smelling fresh and alive. If Vivian ever lost sight of what they were doing there—growing fruit, creating life—the calm after a storm always reminded her.

Vivian pulled on her mud boots and walked through the rows of Syrah. She still took pleasure in the blooming vines. There was no amount of external stress that could diminish that for her. She especially loved seeing the red varietals, the Syrah and Merlot, when they were little green berries. It felt like glimpsing a secret of nature. It amazed her how many people didn't know that red grapes always started out green. Living at a winery, she found that the world of nature was like a second language she'd needed to learn. And then, once understood—never mastered—making a living off the land felt like belonging to a private club. After that first vintage, she never saw the world the same again.

Her phone rang. She sighed, missing the days when a walk in the fields meant she was unreachable. She should have left the damn thing back in the room.

"This is Vivian," she said. The incoming number was from the winery landline.

"It's me," Leonard said. "Can you bring a stack of invoices from my desk to the loading dock? I've got a situation here and I can't get back to the office."

"Oh, for heaven's sake. Okay. If I can find it." For all of his meticulous care of the grape plants, Leonard's desk was a bit of a mess.

She trudged back to the winery. Leonard's office was stuffy and hot. She opened a window before shuffling a few things around, looking for the invoices. Something else caught her eye, a slim booklet printed on cream-colored paper. The front cover read "Hollander Estates Vineyard, North Fork, Long Island." She flipped it open and realized immediately it was a sales brochure. Their home, their life's work, on the chopping block. She felt a flash of anger toward her husband.

The stonework around the property is imported European red slate. The landscaping of both the winery and the private residence reflects rustic North Fork authenticity; the house evokes the sophistication and elegance of the great châteaux of Bordeaux, France.

Who had written this? "Evokes Bordeaux" indeed. No one who had spent time at a grand cru vineyard would ever make that comparison. Sometimes, when the weather was cool and misty, she was pulled back to that long-ago visit to the château. As hard as she'd tried to forget, it still snuck up on her. The first morning, she had woken up to moody skies and a dampness that permeated the walls of the château. She had wrapped herself in cashmere before making her way downstairs for breakfast. Leonard, shivering in his wool blazer, said, "Have the French ever heard of heating?"

At breakfast, the baron made good on his promise to show her the horse stables; he announced they would be going riding.

"Oh! I didn't pack any clothes . . ."

He waved away her concern. "Natasha has everything you could possibly need."

Vivian borrowed breeches and boots but was disappointed to find that Natasha wouldn't be joining them.

"I'm recovering from tennis elbow," she said. "I haven't been able to ride in weeks. Henri is ready to kill me."

Despite the convivial evening the night before, Vivian wasn't comfortable around the baron. She couldn't put her finger on it, but something about him set her on edge. Back upstairs in their room, when she was supposed to be changing for the outing, she shared her misgivings with Leonard.

"If you don't go, he'll be insulted," Leonard said.

"So come along."

"I don't ride, and it will make me look weak. Please—just be a sport."

Leonard was so excited about the potential partnership he would have offered up their firstborn to seal the deal.

"Fine," she said.

Vivian knew that once she was in the saddle she would feel in her element—possibly the only scenario at the estate that would let her feel in control.

A servant led her to the stables, where two horses, a bay mare with beautiful coronet bands and a smaller palomino, were dressed in English saddle. The baron stood next to the mare, patting her shoulder. He smiled when he saw Vivian, and this time, it seemed to actually reach his eyes.

"I'm happy to have company for my ride today. Natasha injured herself over the summer during a much less refined sporting activity."

"Yes, she told me. Well, I'm always happy for the chance to ride. I don't have time for it back home."

He looked at her with a raised eyebrow. "One must always make time. Do you have stables?"

She smiled. "We just renovated our house, so we have stables. But they're empty."

"You must fix that. Come." He beckoned her toward the palomino. "He's a very gentle soul."

She approached the horse's left side, patting his neck. She looked around for a mounting block, and the baron said, "I'll help you up."

"Oh no—that's fine. I've got it," she said. But he moved close to her as if she hadn't said anything. His eyes, which had seemed gray the night before, were now the same blue as the sky. He smelled faintly of tobacco and something she couldn't identify, but the combination made her feel weak in her riding boots. In his nearness, she realized why he made her so uncomfortable: she was desperately attracted to him.

He bent down, linking his gloved hands together to offer her a platform for mounting the horse. Only when she was firmly in the saddle, the reins in her hand, did her breathing steady. She knew that no matter how fast she galloped, it wouldn't be nearly as fast as her racing heart.

It was the only time they were alone together that trip. And for the remainder of their stay at Château de Villard, she found herself mentally returning to that moment again and again.

She eagerly anticipated dinner, longing for him from across the table. Every time she looked at him, especially on the rare occasion when their eyes met, she felt a shameful heat deep inside. She was a married woman, a mother of two, and yet she was experiencing the first true "crush" of her life. With Leonard, there had been no painful yearning, no wondering if he thought about her. They'd met, and he'd made his interest instantly clear. His courtship of her had been immediate and dogged. She wanted him, but at the same time she felt their union was an inevitability. With the baron, she looked at him and thought, *I will never know the feeling of his touch.*

Except, one day, she did.

Vivian set the brochure back down on the desk and looked around for the invoices. There was no sense being angry at Leonard about losing the winery. There was plenty of blame to go around.

⁓

Leah found her father wandering among the Syrah grapes. She made her way out toward him, following the dirt path carved between the rows of plants, adjusting her hat against the bright midday sun.

She experienced a moment of déjà vu, of being a young girl in that very spot, of her father teaching her about bud break, about veraison, about canopy maintenance. How he had always loved his vineyard.

And he had seemed to love sharing all his wisdom and experience with her.

He looked so entirely at peace, so utterly at home among the flourishing vines, she almost didn't want to disturb him.

Almost.

"Dad," she called out, drawing closer to him.

He looked up in surprise. "I'm thinking we need to drop more fruit." He glanced at her. "What do you think?"

"Maybe just from the short shoots," she said.

He looked back at the plant, kneeling down and touching the soil. "It's been dry and sunny so far. We'll see what happens next month. We had a wet August last year and Botrytis was a problem with the whites." He pulled off some fruit. "These grapes will turn in a few weeks."

Oh, she knew the rhythm of the vineyard. She had tried to forget, but it was a part of her, just like the breath of her own body.

Her father busied himself clipping away at the plants. She stood, the sun hot on her back, summoning the nerve to say what she had to say. Her father did not take kindly to "suggestions," but he had at least listened to her about telling Javier. Or maybe he would have done it anyway. But she couldn't stop with that conversation, as much as she hated being the object of his wrath.

"Dad," she said. "I understand you have to sell. I know you wouldn't do it except as a last resort. But you need to do something to protect your employees. Can you make it part of the deal that the buyers keep them on? At least for a few years?"

He stood, dropping the clippers to the ground. "You're a lawyer now? You want to negotiate the contract for me?"

"No, I'm just saying . . ."

He put his hands on her shoulders. "Leah, I know your heart is in the right place. But you need to let me handle my business. I want things to work out—for everyone involved."

"What if you're handling it wrong?" she said, her heart pounding.

"You would do things differently?"

He seemed more amused than angry, and that made her furious. She looked up at the sky, a bird circling overhead. In a few weeks, the fruit would be ripe enough to attract them.

Her father was waiting for a response. His question hadn't been rhetorical. She said the first thing that came to mind.

"Well, for one thing, I would have produced a rosé," she said. "Not that that solves the problem at hand. But it might have bolstered sales over the past few years."

He nodded, rubbing his chin as if contemplating this. When he spoke, it was very slowly. "Do you know what the French do with their rosé?"

"Um, no. Not exactly."

"I didn't think so. We are in a global market. Rosé is the only wine with an annual expiration date."

"Rosé doesn't go bad in one year."

"No, of course, the wine itself can last a long time. But the French, the Provençal rosé people, flood the American market every February with that year's vintage of rosé. They buy back old vintages of rosé from Manhattan restaurants because they only want the current rosé available. And because they are so powerful and because they control the market around the world, every other winery now does that."

"Okay, so—"

"So if you have leftover rosé, restaurants won't buy it. You're stuck holding the bag. I'm not playing that game. You hear me?"

"Yes," she said. "I hear you."

How could she not? His voice was raised. But she would not be shouted down. She would not be shut out.

Not this time.

Twenty-seven

Leah tried to luxuriate in the natural beauty of her surroundings, to find peace in the moment. Sitting poolside, she turned the pages of the paperback copy of *Chances* she'd bought to replace the copy she couldn't find. Up above, the evening sky was streaked with pink and gold. It looked like a painting, like something Leah had conjured by sheer force of longing. Next to her, Sadie curled up in a chair, staring at her phone.

As much as the book kept her turning the pages, she found herself underlining passages that got under her skin.

Gino was just going to have to realize the fact that he was no longer boss. No sirree. She wasn't about to give it all up. Power—the ultimate aphrodisiac. She was in control. She planned to stay in control. And he was just going to have to accept that fact.

Reading this, Leah couldn't help but think that she was no Lucky Santangelo. She wasn't going to usurp her father. She couldn't even get him to take her seriously in a conversation. She should just go home to her husband. Her husband, who was freezing her out. Or maybe he was just busy. Either way, it had been almost twenty-four hours since she and Steven had talked.

"I was wondering where you two were." Vivian walked out carrying a glass of wine and . . . the copy of *Chances* that Leah had been looking for.

"Mom, is that my book?"

"No. It's *my* book," Vivian said.

"Yeah, but I asked you if you'd seen it . . . Oh, never mind." She was just happy her mother took her suggestion to heart. "Mom, I forgot to ask you before: Was the book club your idea?"

"No," Vivian said. "If you must know, it was Delphine's."

Leah hadn't heard that name in a long time. Delphine Fabron was the niece of her father's former business partner. She'd come from France to live with them for a while when Leah was in middle school. She'd worshipped the woman—it was like having a beautiful and slightly naughty big sister. Now that she thought about it, she did remember Delphine at the book club. But then her father fired Delphine. Her parents argued about it. And it was around that time that the book club seemed to end.

"Did you stop hosting the book club because she left?" Leah said.

"Oh, who remembers," Vivian said, suddenly very busy examining the book cover.

"That's what the journal was for—to keep track of things," Sadie said. "Right?"

Leah shot her a warning look. Vivian turned to them both.

"Okay, you two: Who went through my things? You had no business invading my privacy like that!"

Sadie bit her lip. "I'm sorry. It's my fault. I was just looking for more photo albums."

"How did you even get the compartment open?"

"I picked the lock with a mechanical pencil," Sadie said, glancing at her.

Vivian glared in her direction.

Leah held up her hands. "Yes, I knew about it. Guilty as charged. But in my defense, I only read a few lines of the journal. In fact, we lost track of it. I only saw it once."

"And that's the last you will see of it; I have it now, safe from you savages," Vivian said. Leah could tell from the relaxed set of her mouth that she wasn't truly angry—just mildly annoyed.

"Gran, I'm sorry for going through your stuff. But the truth is I'm really interested in your thoughts on the books," Sadie said.

"Whatever I thought of the books was a lifetime ago. It hardly matters."

"Well, there's just a lot of stuff in here that's sketchy to me," Sadie pressed. "All that violence against women . . ."

Leah leaned forward. "You're reading *Chances*, too?"

"Sort of. On my phone. I was curious about what had you so excited," she said sheepishly. "It's pretty bad."

"Bad? The story is ambitious—Gino's entire life," Vivian said.

"I thought you said you didn't remember what you thought," Leah said.

"Well," Vivian said, "I might have reread a page or two after you practically forced the book on me. Okay, maybe more than a page," she added primly at Leah's knowing look. "And the sweeping nature of it . . . it's like that Donna Tartt novel. The one with the bird painting."

"*The Goldfinch*? Gran, you're comparing *Chances* to the Pulitzer Prize–winning novel *The Goldfinch*?" Leah could practically see her high-minded daughter's head exploding.

"I'm just saying, it's epic in its own right."

"It's *long*, but I don't know if I'd call it *epic*. And I have no empathy for Gino, and so much of the book is from his point of view," Sadie said.

"He's an antihero. But he means well," Leah said. Except when his son was born, a year after his daughter, and he thought, *A son was a direct extension of himself. A daughter could never be that.* It was just a novel, but the words stung.

"I love the flashbacks to the 1920s and the 1970s. She really brings the drama of those eras to life," Vivian said, abandoning all pretense of disinterest. "And as for violence against women . . . that's a reflection of the world, my dear."

"But I think this book glorifies it, in a way. Especially the sex scenes. A lot of it's nonconsensual," Sadie said.

"There is a lot of sex," Vivian conceded. "I didn't remember so much of it being nonconsensual. Or so graphic."

Neither had Leah.

Ironically, now that she was apart from her husband, she found herself thinking about sex. Maybe even wanting sex. It couldn't be a coincidence that she was also now reading these books. Still, she was afraid that the minute she returned to the city, she'd go right back to forgetting all about it.

"The thing that strikes me about the sex scenes is that sometimes they don't seem written by a woman," Sadie said. "It's more like female sexuality as written by a man's fantasy. And all the gay characters are villains. Or at least devious. Did you talk about that at your book club?"

"I can't recall it coming up for discussion. Readers weren't as sensitive back in the day," Vivian said.

"I don't think it's a matter of sensitivity." Sadie crossed her arms. "It's just common decency."

"Okay, I think we can all agree the book wouldn't be written that way today," Leah said to defuse the tension. *Talk about a generation gap . . .*

Vivian looked at Sadie. "So you don't like the book?"

"I didn't say that," Sadie said. "But it's not exactly great writing."

"Isn't it, though? Look at how all the plotlines came together. The way Leonora's daughter came back into the story? Brilliant," Leah said.

"That was amazing," Sadie conceded.

"I will admit the author went a little far with all the abuse on poor Carrie," Vivian said. "That final turn as a prostitute was perhaps too much."

"Oh, my god, that scene where Whitejack pimps her out again? My heart just broke." Leah paged through the book to find the scene and read aloud.

"I gasped at that," Sadie said. "Like, I literally gasped. But that's what I mean. So much of this book is just abuse heaped on women."

"Well, not all the women. Clementine Duke is sexually powerful—maybe even sexually predatory," Leah said.

"But as soon as she sleeps with Gino, he has the power. He always has the power," Sadie said.

"Except when it comes to his daughter," Vivian pointed out.

"Lucky doesn't always challenge his power. What about the scene where he's forcing her into an arranged marriage? And then he hits her."

"It's terrible, of course," Vivian said. "Inexcusable. But for the whole book, she's the one person who makes him feel completely out of control. And it's also fear—the fear all parents feel for their children."

It was also, Leah realized, the fear all children eventually had for their parents. She'd long heard about the role reversal that took place later in life, when the children became the caretakers. Her parents, thankfully, still had their health. But they were losing their life's work, and that was going to be a tough transition. It was for her, too.

She'd suggested the book to distract her mother from the impending sale of the winery. And maybe it was helping. But reading it herself was making her own powerlessness that much more apparent.

Sadie. With those questions about her old journal! As if Vivian would ever admit to her feminist granddaughter that she'd been so desperate to feel productive, to have something of her own to manage and perfect, that she'd turned the casual book club into a project.

There had been years when she'd forgotten how to have something of her own—something that wasn't about pleasing someone else. And then Delphine reminded her.

Delphine had been grateful that Vivian believed in her enough to give her an important job within Hollander. She said it changed her entire outlook and that she wished she could return the favor.

"I have everything I need," Vivian had said.

"You need to have more fun," Delphine had said. "It's work and kids, work and kids. Where I grew up, women know how to play." Her own mother, she said, spent weeks and weeks every year island-hopping. Delphine knew that Vivian didn't want to actually get away from her family or the vineyard. But she needed to do *something*.

"What do you do just for yourself?" she'd asked her.

"I like taking the kids to the beach. I love harvest, when it's so busy everyone is included in the work. Making apple cider in the fall . . ."

"Vivian, something aside from all that."

"I like to shop. And I like to read." She especially liked to read books about women who did a lot of shopping.

And so the book club was born.

Ultimately, it had all been short-lived. She didn't have the heart to continue the book club after Leonard fired Delphine. And the journal languished, locked away where she didn't have to think about it and no one would discover it. Or so she believed.

"Mom, are you still with us?" Leah said. She and Sadie looked at her expectantly.

"Sorry. I was just thinking," Vivian said.

"I asked who your favorite character is," Leah said. "Mine is Lucky. Since I'm also a woman whose father never saw her as an equal—who was marginalized from the family business."

"Is that true?" Sadie said, snapping to attention.

"Yes."

"Oh, Leah," Vivian said. It hurt to hear her daughter express the sentiment. Even if it was the truth.

"What happened? You wanted to work here?" Sadie said.

"I think this is a conversation for another time," Vivian said, shooting Leah a look. The last thing she wanted was the conversation to devolve into a prolonged attack on Leonard. Even if he deserved it. She still felt protective of him. And, perhaps, she felt her own sense of culpability in letting Leah be pushed aside.

"Well, I didn't identify with anyone in this book," said Sadie. "And honestly, I find it shocking that this book was a *New York Times* bestseller."

Vivian sipped her wine. "Why wouldn't this book be a bestseller? It has it all: passion, a business empire, love. This is what storytelling should be. Personally, I liked Clementine Duke. She had fabulous parties."

Clementine Duke, a high-society dame who had a penchant for lovers of a different class, summoned Gino Santangelo to her mansion. Vivian couldn't help but think about the summons to a mansion that had completely altered the course of her own life.

For weeks after their trip to Château de Villard, she'd thought about the baron. Ironically, once she wanted to be around him, he all but disappeared. The remainder of the weekend was segregated, with Leonard and the baron walking the fields and discussing their new business venture while Vivian and Natasha lounged around the estate, drinking wine and talking about the royal wedding. They both had been obsessively following every bit of news about Princess Diana (whom they both still called "Lady Di") and both agreed her wedding gown was a bit busy. Vivian felt they might very well become friends. By the time the chauffeured Mercedes whisked them back to the airport, she could almost pretend the surge of nearly violent desire for the baron had never happened.

But back on Long Island, tucked away in her own bed, alone with the thoughts roaming free in the secret corners of her mind, her feelings for the baron were more vivid than they had been in the moment. In her fantasy, the weekend unfolded differently: the horseback riding had not seen them innocently cantering through the fields of Bordeaux, but instead ended with him ravishing her in the stables. Every time she imagined the scenario, she became so worked up she was in a sweat. She lost sleep at night and during the day was plagued by an unease and guilt for betraying her husband even in her imagination. For the first time in a long time, she was the one to initiate sex, and through intimacy with Leonard she was ultimately able to excise his new business partner from her thoughts.

In the days that followed, Vivian thought long and hard about the way she was raised. She thought about her marriage vows. She thought about her children. She asked Leonard to go with her on a "date" to see the movie *The Four Seasons*.

By the time the holidays rolled around, she got her emotional equilibrium back. She could pretend the baron didn't even exist. Until the day Leonard announced that the baron's niece, Delphine Fabron, was coming to live with them.

"We are an ocean apart," the baron said. "And I'm not inclined to spend much time in your country. This is a gift for my American wife, you understand. So having a member of my family on the ground will give me peace of mind. I'm sure you understand."

Leonard did not understand. And he certainly did not want one of the baron's representatives "on the ground" with him. But he knew it was a small price to pay; their association with the hundred-year-old Château de Villard gave their fledgling vineyard an instant boost in credibility. The request that they welcome his niece to Hollander was not irrational. And it would have to be accommodated. He would simply have to do his best to keep her from interfering with the way he managed Hollander.

When the baron's chosen representative arrived on that freezing day in February, it became clear Leonard didn't have anything to worry about: Delphine was twenty-one years old and, curiously, seemed to have absolutely no interest in the business of winemaking.

Delphine Fabron was a beautiful girl, with long, lustrous dark hair and big blue eyes that were unmistakably sad. The only thing that seemed to lighten her mood was spending time with nine-year-old Leah.

Leah, who was always squabbling with Asher and wanted a sister, was equally as delighted with their exotic new guest.

"She's so pretty," Leah kept saying to her mother. "And her accent! Do you think she could teach me French?"

That seemed doubtful; that girl appeared to struggle just to get through each day. Vivian felt badly that their guest was so unhappy, but she and Leonard had their own problems: while they were selling strong on-site and in liquor stores, they were still making very few inroads with New York City restaurants.

Their wholesale rep quit. He was burned out. The obstacles were insurmountable: Sommeliers didn't know that New York State produced wine, and when they did learn, they were skeptical. Some buyers had tried early vintages and had not been impressed. Part of this was Leonard and Vivian's fault: they had rushed to market in the early years, their learning curve creating a barrier to quality. Their first season, birds attacked the budding vines, so they picked early to preserve the fruit, but they didn't allow the sugar content to get high enough.

They made errors with grape varietals: Zinfandel grew wonderfully in California—where Leonard had learned everything he knew—but it did not like the climate on the East Coast. Instead, they needed to focus on wines like Malbec.

Meanwhile, after a month of Delphine hiding in her room or listlessly wandering the house, Vivian finally insisted she accompany her on a trip to town to run errands. The girl slumped silently in the car's passenger seat, staring out the window like a convict being transported to prison.

"I thought you'd like to see the market and main street," Vivian said. "When we first moved here—"

"Did you invite me out today so you could break the news that you're sending me away, too?"

"Sending you away? No. Why would you think that?"

It all came out with a burst of sobs: Delphine's love affair with her father's friend, a member of French Parliament. The newspaper article. The press camped out on her parents' front lawn. Leah realized Delphine had not been sent as the baron's representative on the ground. She had been exiled.

Vivian immediately felt empathy for her. Since her marriage to Leonard, her parents had cut her off financially and barely been in touch except to see their grandchildren. It didn't feel good to be punished by the people who were supposed to love you just because of your choices—good or bad.

"Delphine, we're happy to have you here," she said. "For as long as you'd like to stay."

When Vivian relayed the information to Leonard, he just shook his head.

"We have to give her something productive to do," Vivian said.

"She can help Joe out in the field," Leonard said. "I don't see what else she could possibly do except get in my way."

But the more time Vivian spent with Delphine, the more she realized the girl had a surprisingly deep knowledge of wine. Her mother, the baron's sister, Marie-Élise, had married into another wine family, and Delphine had been raised at her knee, walking the fields and hanging around the tasting room, absorbing every nuance of the art and science of producing great wine.

When she confided in Delphine about the problem with the New York wine market, Delphine said, "The wine managers at these places are all men, right?"

"Of course," Vivian said.

"Let me try to sell your wine. In my experience, men have a very difficult time saying no to me."

Delphine had made good on her promise that men could not say no to her; she began visiting Manhattan's top restaurants in the spring of 1982. With her pedigree and beauty, there were few doors that would not open for her. Within a month she had landed accounts with the Four Seasons, the 21 Club, the Rainbow Room, and Delmonico's. Only Lutèce said no.

With each Manhattan restaurant account she landed, Delphine's ethereal glow radiated more strongly, her blue eyes bright and jewel-like in her porcelain face. She always wore her thick curtain of dark hair loose, and she never cut it.

Even Leonard, who had balked at the imposition of the baron's niece, who had resisted letting her work in sales, was impressed with their rising star. Leah, an impressionable preteen, followed her around like a puppy, insisting on growing out her hair, asking to straighten her curls. She gave up her brightly colored Ocean Pacific shorts and tube socks in favor of pale linen dresses. While most girls her age were tying bandanas around their heads, trying to look like Madonna, Leah was trying to look like a sophisticated French girl. Vivian had found it adorable.

By the spring of 1985, the girl the baron had sent to them as a depressed wallflower had blossomed into a confident, vivacious young woman.

But then, the evening when all hell broke loose. Vivian had been on the veranda with her friends for their book club discussion. It was a night eagerly anticipated all month long. She'd just been about to begin when Leonard came running out of the winery in a tizzy after finding a slew of messages from their restaurant reps. Apparently, Delphine had not only been knocking on doors in Manhattan, she'd been breaking hearts. She'd slept with several wine buyers, and with the New York City restaurant world being small, word got out. The bruised egos got together and called Leonard, canceling their orders.

"I always told you women don't belong in the business," he said to Vivian. "This is what happens!"

Vivian made the point that their restaurant accounts were up ninety percent since Delphine started working for them. Fine, the accounts were dropping them—but she was the one who'd brought them on in the first place. Leonard could not be reasoned with. He felt she had brought shame upon Hollander Estates and couldn't be trusted to work for them any longer.

Leonard fired her, and that triggered a visit from the baron.

Vivian moved *Chances* off her lap, onto the table and facedown. It had been a bad idea to revisit the old book. She didn't want those memories. Not now.

The door to the house slid open, and Bridget emerged, her wild auburn hair loose around her shoulders, the strap of her tank top falling off one shoulder. She carried a glass of white wine in one hand and a vape pen in the other.

"Oh!" she said. "I didn't know you were all out here." Her expression shifted, as if she realized she had been excluded from something.

"Where's Asher?" said Vivian.

"He's in Amagansett. But he's coming back soon. I was just going for a swim." She looked around the table. "You're all reading the same book?"

"Sort of," Leah said.

An awkward silence fell over the group.

"Well, I'm off to bed," Vivian said, standing up and tucking her copy of *Chances* under her arm.

She'd had enough togetherness for one evening.

Twenty-eight

⌒

The library was bright with sunshine. Sadie blamed the brightness, the reminder of the beautiful day outside, for distracting her. An hour at the library table, immersed in Susan Sontag essays, and no progress on her thesis.

She stood up, crossed the room, and closed the heavy curtains, knowing all the while the light had nothing to do with it. It was that damn book.

No matter how much her mother tried to frame *Chances* as a story about a woman finding her own power, or how much her grandmother waxed nostalgic for the days when casinos were glamorous and women wore Halston, Sadie knew the book was all about sex.

It annoyed her. She read books to expand her mind, to grow as an intellectual. She didn't want reading to remind her that her life of the mind had led her to neglect her life of the body. She didn't want to think about her breakup with Holden or her inconvenient attraction to Mateo.

Maybe the women in the book had it right. Sex could be just sex, and there didn't have to be a messy relationship, an intimacy doomed to failure. It didn't have to be all or nothing. This was good news for Sadie, who had failed at her only serious relationship.

There was one element of the book that Sadie *did* appreciate: the heroine, Lucky, was fueled by rage. And female rage was a topic that no feminist reader could ignore, regardless of the package it came in. The heroine of *Lace*, Lili, was also full of anger and vengeance. Sadie wondered if other books of the era had a similar message. Was that what had attracted women to read them in droves?

She tucked the book back into her tote and carried the bag up the stairs to the second level to see what other 1980s novels were in her grandmother's collection. She passed the section where the photo albums had been stored, the shelves now empty. In the absence of all those books, she noticed a collection of marble notebooks in the farthest corner of the bottom shelving. She reached for one, sitting on the floor and opening it.

The pages were penciled notes, mathematical equations like $2.46 \times 16 = 39.36$. Records of pH balance. Dates with annotations like "topped everything in house." Page after page of numbers and phrases that meant nothing to her—a foreign language: "1984 white wine kegs & CB racked into 1 SS drum. Topped Amphora with CC Viognier drum, balance went to blue drum."

The notebooks were like the one she'd seen in the bottling room a few weeks earlier, the one where the senior winemaker, Chris, had kept his notes. Except the bottom of these pages were initialed with "LH."

They were her grandfather's wine ledgers. The playbook for his creations.

"Sadie, are you in here?"

Her grandfather's voice boomed from below. What was he doing here? It was as if she had conjured him with her snooping.

"Um, yeah, Grandpa. I'm up here."

"Well, come down," he said, his voice echoing off the high ceiling. "There's work to be done."

Why was he so interested lately in making sure she was busy working in the vineyard? When she first got there, he barely seemed to notice her. That was how it always was with her grandfather; he was always working or thinking about work. So what changed that he would, in the middle of the morning, have it on his radar to check on

Sadie? Was it the impending sale? Did he suddenly realize he couldn't take their time in the vineyard for granted? Maybe there were things he'd always planned to show her and never got around to it.

"Leave those books and the computer here."

Or maybe he just didn't respect her life choices.

She followed him outside, along the dusty, stone-lined path to the barn. Everywhere she looked, grapevines; the plants had transformed in just the month that she'd been at the winery. The horizontal branches that had sported hard little green berries had spawned grapes hanging in full bunches under the canopy of leaves.

"A vineyard is a communal place," Leonard said as they walked. "If this is our last summer with the winery, I want to at least know that my children and grandchild have learned how to be part of something larger than themselves."

Up ahead, workers moved field equipment into the barn. She and her grandfather passed them, stepping around machinery and bins. Leonard didn't talk to anyone but headed straight for Mateo's office.

This was going to be awkward.

Mateo's door was open, and he was busy typing on his laptop.

"I've got a helper for you," Leonard said.

Mateo looked up from the computer. "Oh—hello, there, Mr. Hollander." He barely glanced her way.

"What's on the agenda for today?"

"The Malbec; dropping some fruit."

"Take Sadie with you. Show her how it's done, eh?" Leonard patted Sadie on the shoulder. "Put in a solid day's work and you'll forget all about screens and other nonsense."

Sadie watched him walk off. When she turned to Mateo, she thought about making a joke, something like: *Thought he'd never leave* . . . wink wink. But she refrained.

"So, you're here to help out?" Mateo said, stepping out from behind his desk. He wore a gray T-shirt, jeans, and work boots.

"That's my grandfather's big idea. I'll probably just slow you down."

"Don't sell yourself short," Mateo said casually. If there was any leftover tension from the fact that she told her mother about his job search, he was clearly willing to let it go.

"Okay, I'll give it a try," she said.

They walked outside, and Mateo climbed behind the wheel of a dilapidated golf cart.

"Hop in," he said, his dark eyes shining with a hint of mischief. He really was so hot. The T-shirt pulled tight against his biceps, his big, callused hands on the steering wheel.

They took off in the cart, the motor rumbling loudly. A breeze whipped up her hair, and they bumped through the borders of grass between the rows of grapevines. The cart picked up speed, and Sadie felt a lightness of spirit she hadn't experienced in a long time.

Mateo steered down a path next to a wooden post marked with an "M."

"And here we have the Merlot," Mateo said, cutting the engine. They disembarked from the cart. The sun was so strong Sadie felt like she could reach out and touch it. Mateo pulled a Hollander Estates baseball hat from the back and put it on. "I think I have another one in here somewhere . . ."

"It's fine," Sadie said.

"Are you sure? You'll be able to see better with some shade."

Sadie dutifully accepted a battered cap and pulled it on.

Mateo handed her a pair of shears that had a springing mechanism in the middle. "I just happen to have an extra pair of snips."

"Why are you cutting grapes now?" She knew the harvest wasn't until fall.

"The vines are growing rapidly this month. We need to thin the clusters to just the right amount that the winemaker needs for bottling and also to keep the vines in balance. The vine's natural tendency is to produce hundreds of clusters, but we can't let them do that or they'll all be weak, insipid flavors and stunted growth. When we thin the clusters, the remaining ones ripen with better flavors."

"I guess no one wants insipid flavors and stunted growth," Sadie said.

"No," Mateo said. "They don't." They shared a smile, and Sadie felt another wave of powerful attraction.

"I'm sorry—what was that?" She realized Mateo was explaining something, and she'd completely zoned out.

"We're cutting in two types of areas: big clumps, where it's all jammed up with fruit—like here—or short shoots."

"What's a short shoot?"

Mateo pulled out a wispy branch. "See the size of this compared to the others? There aren't any leaves, and this section won't grow good fruit, so we might as well cut it off now." He pulled a bunch of grapes away from the vine and lopped it off. She felt herself leaning toward him like a plant toward the sun.

"I thought you didn't want too many leaves," she said. "The last time we were out here you were thinning leaves."

"It's all about balance. Too many leaves, the fruit has reduced sunlight and airflow and you're more likely to get disease. But if you pull too much, there's no canopy and you need some leaves because photosynthesis helps create the sugar in the fruit. So you just cut like this." He lopped off a bunch, and it dropped to the ground.

"And then you just leave all these grapes on the ground? Isn't that a waste of food?"

"They aren't ripe. They're inedible. Here—squeeze this." It was hard, like a plastic grape. "If we had pigs around, maybe we could use them. But it's fine—they'll fertilize the field."

They worked methodically, side by side. Sadie consulted with Mateo whenever she felt uncertain whether to cut. Mateo had a laser-like focus. He worked quickly and made a point of telling Sadie not to rush to keep up with him. He talked and talked, casually explaining the life of the vines.

"The plants will stop producing next month. At that point, we just have to let the sugars accumulate." There was something immensely satisfying about the crunch of the metal against the plant, the sound of the fruit hitting the grass. The results were so tangible compared to writing.

After a while, Mateo became quiet. He pointed to indicate where Sadie should work. Sadie admired his intensity, the way he seemed impervious to the heat and the insects and the dirt. She wondered what Mateo thought of Susan Sontag. The answer was: he didn't.

She wondered what Mateo would be like in bed. The answer was: hot.

"Is something wrong?" Mateo said.

She had stopped clipping. She was staring at him.

"No," she said.

After a moment—a long moment, a moment in which Sadie felt she barely breathed—Mateo said, "This can't happen. You know that, right?"

Twenty-nine

Vivian came up for air in the deep end. Through the fog of her goggles, she spotted ridiculously high heels and crimson toenails. Bridget, teetering at the edge of the pool, peered down at her.

"Can I help you?" Vivian said.

"Sorry to interrupt your swim, but Leonard asked me to find you. There's a meeting at the vineyard office."

The charms on Bridget's gold anklet made noise when she moved her feet. How on earth did that not drive her crazy?

"Please tell my husband I'll be there in five minutes. No, make that ten."

She waited for Bridget to trot off before pulling herself out of the pool. Why hadn't Leonard thought to tell her himself? Then she checked her phone and saw she had several missed texts and calls.

She took a quick rinse in the pool house shower and ran a comb through her hair before changing into a linen dress and a pair of ballerina flats, all the while her stomach in knots. She was all but certain she was being summoned for official news about the closing. The day she was dreading—the day she was cast out from her home—was one step closer.

"Oh, hey, Mom. I didn't know you were out here." Leah had settled on a lounge chair with her book. Her skin was sun-burnished, her hair still lustrous and dark even as she approached her late forties. Those deep-set Hollander eyes. She looked so very much like Leonard.

Vivian decided right then and there that if she was going to the meeting, so was Leah. Why should Bridget be at the meeting and not her own daughter?

"I need you to throw some clothes on and come with me."

"Where?"

"I'll explain on the way."

Leah tugged shorts and a T-shirt out of her canvas bag, pulled them over her bathing suit, and followed Vivian down the path to the vineyard.

"Your father called a meeting, and I want you there."

They circumnavigated the veranda—already filling with visitors— and cut through the loading dock behind the oak room. The office door was closed. Vivian knocked once before opening it. Inside, she found the usual suspects: Marty Pritchard, Harold Feld, Leonard, and Asher. Surprisingly, Bridget wasn't there. Maybe Asher had asked her to sit this one out. Her son might not be the brightest bulb, but he was smart enough to know to keep the family problems within the family—at least until after the wedding.

The wedding. She'd been so preoccupied with thoughts of losing the winery, she'd barely had time to think about it. Or maybe she was just trying to forget.

Leonard looked up when she walked into the room, doing a double take when he saw Leah. Before he could say anything about it, Vivian said, "Leah is part of this family. She has a right to be part of this conversation." In the past, she never would have made such a move. Maybe rereading *Chances* had had an effect on her. Whatever the reason, she couldn't afford to sit on the sidelines any longer.

"Mother," Asher said.

Leonard started to say something and then stopped, perhaps deciding he was embattled enough; he didn't need to fight with her. "We have a problem," he said instead. Marty Pritchard shuffled a few papers.

Harold Feld steepled his fingers and looked at him intently. Asher checked his phone.

"Obviously," Vivian said. "Our estate is for sale."

"The buyer backed out," Leonard continued, his jaw tense. The hand gripping his pen was white with the pressure of his grasp.

"The offer fell through?"

"Yes." Leonard looked stricken, but Vivian couldn't help but feel relieved. A stay of execution.

"What happened?" Vivian asked.

"They bought the brewery down the road," Leonard said.

"See, Dad," Asher said. "I told you we should serve beer—"

"Shut up!" Leonard snapped.

The stress was getting to him. As infuriated as she was by this whole situation, she felt a rush of empathy for her husband. She had not always agreed with him, but she knew he'd always tried his best. It was all she could ask of him.

"So now what?" Vivian asked.

"So we're back to square one," said Marty.

"We need to focus on whatever we can do to make this vineyard appealing to buyers. Which we're already doing," Leonard said.

"Are we?"

Everyone looked at Leah in surprise.

"Yes, we certainly are," Leonard said, his voice gravelly and low. It was his "I'm barely keeping my temper under control" voice. "So let's just keep that tasting room full all summer and focus on having a strong harvest. And in the meantime, considering this setback, I don't want any talk of the sale around our staff. We don't want to scare off valuable members of the team when we need them the most. John Beaman is already asking me questions. The last thing we need is to lose our sales rep."

Did Leonard look pointedly at her when he said this? No, it was Vivian's imagination.

And yet it was difficult not to think that she had been the one to insist they hire Delphine as their wholesale rep. She was their first female employee at the winery—and it had ended disastrously.

Until Leonard fired Delphine, the baron's aversion to the United States had kept him on the other side of the Atlantic. After nearly four years without seeing him, she could pretend her attraction to him had never existed. And yet, the morning of his arrival on a bright day in late May, she found herself dressing with particular care. With fumbling fingers and a shiver of guilt, she tied a navy-and-gold equestrian-patterned Hermès scarf around her neck.

Leonard apologized for firing Delphine, explaining that he had tried his best to employ her but it hadn't worked out.

"I need a man in that position, as you can surely understand," Leonard said. The baron had responded convivially, and both Vivian and Leonard felt a crisis had been averted. Together, she and Leonard took the baron on a tour of the vineyard. She was relieved to find herself feeling calm and professional. Until the baron turned to her and said, "I'd like to see your stables."

"What?" She thought for a moment that she'd heard him wrong.

"Back when you visited the château, you mentioned you had horse stables."

She couldn't believe he recalled the offhand comment.

"Did I? Well then, I must have also mentioned we don't have horses," she said, touching the scarf around her neck.

Leonard, who was uncharacteristically insecure while hosting the baron, jumped on their guest's show of enthusiasm.

"Well, we might someday," he said, just as Peternelle appeared to tell Leonard the tasting room manager needed him. "Vivian, why don't you two go take a look at the grounds and then meet me back at the winery."

The baron was silent for their walk to the rear of the house. He was taller, broader, more kinetically present than she had remembered. She suspected it was the change in scenery, the relatively humble Long Island estate rather than the sweeping backdrop of Bordeaux. They strolled with half a foot between them, and yet she felt like they were touching.

"It's a shame Natasha couldn't make the trip," she said, desperate to normalize her breathing. Willing herself to forget the way she'd imagined his hands on her body.

"Natasha and I are no longer together," he said. He stopped walking, looking at her in a way that felt searing, like he could see through her clothes. And then it rushed back, the old attraction, as fierce and unwelcome as it had been four years earlier.

"Oh." She swallowed hard. "I'm sorry to hear that."

Why did she have such a reaction to this man? She didn't know him and probably wouldn't like him if she did. Whatever pull she felt toward him was clearly just chemical, a trick of the body. And yet she was thirty-seven years old and had never experienced anything like it.

Inside the stable, he politely admired the stone masonry and woodwork. Still, she knew he had to be underwhelmed by the modesty of it all. They had spent very little of their renovation budget on building the stables, and now she wished they had been able to be more ambitious. But the simple, barnlike structure did have a lovely brick interior with stalls of southern yellow pine.

"We really built this on a whim," she said, turning to face him. "I can't imagine when I'll have time for horses again. And my daughter shows no interest—"

He touched her elbow and, in a movement that took her by surprise even as it seemed to happen in slow motion, kissed her. She felt enveloped by that faint tobacco scent she'd first experienced in France, and the warmth of his mouth sent waves of pleasure through her entire body. Her response kissing him back—immediate, ardent, instinctive—encouraged him to pull her close, to press his body against hers in a way that gave a thrilling suggestion of what lay beyond the kiss. She wanted him more than she'd ever wanted anything physically in her life. Everything else was forgotten: The vineyard. Delphine. Leonard. The kids. Even, in a sense, her very self. There was only, in that moment, need. His touch thrilled her and scared her in its absolute authority over her senses. He untied her scarf, his fingers brushing her neck as the whisper of silk fell to the ground. Then he kissed her collarbone and unbuttoned her dress, his hands on her body as no one but Leonard had ever touched her.

It had been so long since she had been anything other than a dutiful wife, a grape farmer, a mother. And maybe she'd never been what she was under the soft pressure of the baron's lips—just a woman in the heat of a moment that would burn bright, then disappear, like the flash of a camera. What was so wrong in that? She could almost convince herself that there wasn't anything wrong with it. She wanted so badly to allow herself this. But then they were down on the ground, their naked bodies entwined but not yet one. She looked up at the vaulted ceiling of the stable Leonard had built for her, despite the impracticality of having horses at the vineyard. The thought was like a splash of cold water. Her husband loved her. She loved him.

Vivian pulled away from the baron.

"I'm sorry. I can't," she said.

"Can't? We *are*," he said.

She stood up, pulling her dress in front of herself.

"You and my husband are business partners."

"Maybe not," the baron said. "He just fired my niece."

"What? You just said you understood—that you would have done the same thing."

"My mind could change. Besides, this whole venture had been to please Natasha. Clearly, that's no longer a priority. So now I have to wonder: What's in it for me?"

He couldn't be serious. "Is that a threat?"

The baron's steely gaze was all the answer she needed. She dressed quickly and fled the stable. She hoped that would be the end of it. But it wasn't.

Now, sitting in the crisis meeting, she felt a crushing sense of culpability.

"So what can we do?" Vivian said, her mouth dry.

"It's all hands on deck," said Leonard. "And that includes Sadie. I want that granddaughter of mine to help out around here. There's too much work to be done to have her drifting around with her nose in a book all summer." He turned to Leah. "You were in the field at her age."

Yes, Vivian thought. *And a year later, you cast her out.*

But Leonard was not entirely to blame. She couldn't help but wonder if they would be in a different situation today if that afternoon in the stables hadn't happened.

She'd never know.

Thirty

Leah wasn't a big proponent of day drinking, but after that meeting, she was willing to bend the rules. She sat at the bar in the tasting room, alongside three couples. A cork popped, and the tasting room manager poured a flight of reds.

"This is the first red we make every year," he said. "This is your Monday through Thursday red, your training wheels red."

"I can taste the pepper in this one."

"Goes well with barbecue," said the tasting room manager. "And this is our Malbec: note its deep purple color. It has a great mouthfeel, great finish."

He was good at his job; all of the winery and vineyard staff were. While her mother was clearly relieved about the buyers backing out of the deal, Leah knew it was just delaying the inevitable. Leonard would not change his mind about selling.

Still, it was only July. What if they had the best summer of all time—a summer to make Leonard believe in the ability to turn things around? They might still be losing money, but if things at least started to head in the right direction, it could give him hope. The question was, what could she do quickly, in the short term, to increase revenue?

"Well, that was fun," Asher said, sliding onto the stool next to her.

"What a nightmare," Leah said.

"You ran off pretty fast." Asher signaled for a glass of wine.

"I mean, what was there left to say?" Leah said.

The manager made his way to their end of the bar, already opening a bottle of Asher's favorite Cabernet. He set out two glasses.

"Don't you have work to do?" she said. "It's not even lunchtime."

"Sure. Nothing like moving deck chairs around on the *Titanic*."

"Considering Mom's ancestry, that's in poor taste," she said. "Asher, come on. We can't just give up."

"Do you have any better ideas?"

"I'm not the one who's been working here my entire life. What should we do?"

"Nothing. You can just accept, like I have, that this is *fucked*."

"Does Bridget know the sale fell through?"

He shook his head. "I don't want to worry her."

"You mean, you don't want to scare her off."

"No, that's not what I mean. And speaking of Bridget, she said you and Mom have some sort of book club?"

"Book club?"

"Yeah. Around the pool the other night?"

"Oh—that wasn't a book club. We were just talking about a book."

"Yeah . . . a book that you all read. That's called a book club. Can you invite Bridget to join in? I want her to feel like part of the family."

"We all have dinner together every night. Isn't that more a family-bonding activity than a book club?" Leah said. As soon as the sentence was out of her mouth, the words "bonding activity" reverberated in her mind. *Bonding activity*. Was there any bigger bonding activity for groups of women than book clubs? Hollander Estates had always done a lot of business with bachelorette parties. Why not book clubs, too? And what better setting for a book club than a vineyard, as her mother had proven all those years earlier?

She knew she was on to something.

"I hope you'll at least consider inviting Bridget." Asher finished his wine and set the glass down hard. "You of all people should know how it feels to be excluded."

✧

"I'm not too happy about that stunt you pulled today," Leonard said, slipping into his side of the bed. Their room was cool, a breeze blowing through the open window. The curtain billowed, and Vivian let it catch her eye.

"I assume you're referring to bringing Leah to the meeting?" she said, taking off her reading glasses.

"We have enough going on without you muddying the waters."

"Muddying the . . . Leonard, I'm just about losing my patience," she said, turning to him. "Leah is here to be supportive. Maybe you could let her try to help."

Leonard sighed, reaching for her hand. "I wish it were that simple. But losing that offer . . . it's a bad sign. I'm worried, Vivian."

In all of their ups and downs, Leonard had never uttered those words to her. Leonard prided himself in being a fixer, in having the answers. She felt a shiver of fear.

"Have you considered reaching out to another winemaker? Maybe partner with someone else around here?"

Leonard pulled his hand away. "You can't be serious."

It had been years, so many years, since either of them had so much as acknowledged the disastrous partnership with the baron. And she was the only one who knew the abrupt end of it had been her fault.

In the weeks and months following their encounter in the stable, the baron continued to contact her. First it was phone calls to the winery office; he'd ask for Leonard, and if Leonard wasn't available, he'd ask for her.

"I understand your hesitation at your own home," he said. "But I'll meet you anywhere in the world. Fly you anywhere in the world."

She told him no, begged him to never speak of it again. Then the letters began arriving, sometimes two a week. Vivian existed in a state of panic that Leonard would somehow get to the mail before she did. She intercepted the letters, finding creative ways to dispose of them or hide them so they weren't discovered in the trash even by one of the household staff.

One day, the letters stopped. And the baron pulled out of his partnership with Hollander Estates.

Thirty-one

The sea grass, tall around the perimeter of the veranda, was loud with the clicking and humming of nocturnal insects. Above, the moon was electrically bright and nearly full. The air smelled damp and of the soil. Leah inhaled deeply, looking out at the vineyard.

The idea of reaching out to book clubs was taking shape. She would start by using her own mailing list from the cheese shop. She could ask Bridget to help promote it on social media. Wine and cheese, wine and books . . . some things just went together. It was a no-brainer.

She noticed movement across the grass and the glow of a phone.

"Sadie?" Where was her daughter going at that hour? She stopped walking, and Leah waved her over.

"Hey," Sadie said.

"What's up?"

"Just . . . going for a drive."

Leah's maternal antennae went up. "Everything okay?"

"Yes—all good," Sadie said, leaning over and kissing her on the cheek. "See you in the morning."

Leah's phone rang—Steven.

"It's your father," Leah said. But Sadie was already walking away. "Hey," she said into the phone.

"Hey," he said. "A customer has a special order and I think it's from that farm that doesn't have email?"

Okay. All business.

"I can take care of it tomorrow. Just text me what she wants. How's it going otherwise?"

"Fine. How about you?"

"Oh, the drama continues. Did you get my text earlier? The buyer backed out. I think my mother sees it as a reprieve. But in reality, the longer this stretches out—"

"Leah, it's going to be a long haul. I know you have good intentions, but you can't see this through to the end. Come home. I miss you."

She looked up at the quarter moon, thinking that he was under the same moon. They weren't that far apart. A firefly alighted in the distance. Could she leave, knowing she could maybe do something to help? She was torn. All she knew was that she wanted both—to stay at the winery and to make Steven happy. But she couldn't have both. She couldn't have it all. Life, especially midlife, was all about understanding that.

"I'll come home soon," she said.

"How about this weekend? I'll come out and pick you up."

This weekend? That was so soon. But Steven was probably at his limit. Past his limit.

She nodded, then remembered he couldn't see her. "Okay. Great. Sounds like a plan."

When she hung up, she felt a rush of anxiety.

The truth was, it didn't matter what kind of ideas she had. Her father would never change. He'd never once asked about Bailey's Blue beyond a cursory "How's that little store of yours?" As if she were selling trinkets. Never mind that cheese was arguably as complex as wine. That maintaining a business in New York City was one of the biggest retail challenges imaginable. That she was as knowledgeable in her field as he was in his own. Okay, she didn't create cheese. But she knew it, she knew it in a way that let her find the perfect variety for each customer. She had inspired more happy pairings than Match.com! And more, she understood the symbiotic relationship between cheese and wine. She doubted her father knew Kunik from Cottage.

Leah stood and began to pace. She thought about the English Wensleydale from the shop in town and wondered why her parents didn't offer cheese boards at the winery.

In *Chances*, Lucky had waited for an opening, for a moment of her father's weakness. Then she stepped in and made it her business to learn everything about his business. She made decisions. In some cases she completed his vision; in other areas she had her own. She didn't wait for permission. She didn't apologize.

Leah grabbed her phone and scheduled a reminder to herself to make a run back to Village Cheese the next day. She still had a few more days before Steven arrived.

She wasn't done yet.

⁓

Walking over to Field House at that hour of the night was a crazy thing to do. Sadie knew this, but still she went.

There was no guarantee that if she knocked on the door of the Arguetas' home, Mateo would be the one to answer. Even if he did, what was she going to say? But if she didn't do something, she would be up all night. She couldn't stop thinking about the jolt when they'd looked at each other in the field. Mateo had felt it, too. That was why he'd said, *This can't happen.*

That was it, that was what she would say: "Why can't this happen?"

Did he have a girlfriend? Was it the age difference? She needed to know. She had to understand the stumbling block before she could get it out of their way.

The winery was linked to Field House by a slate path framed by a white wooden pergola filled with winding greenery and purple wisteria. She'd walked by it her whole life, but she'd never walked through; she didn't have reason to visit Field House. So what she didn't know was that at the end of the path, just before the house, was a locked gate.

"So annoying," she said, reaching over the door to see if she could unlatch it. No luck. She could backtrack and go all the way around, but it was so dark out.

Really, the gate was mostly ornamental. She could scale it. Sadie grabbed hold of a pergola beam and climbed onto one of the gateposts. She balanced atop the post, holding on to the beam, gauging the jump onto the other side of the gate. It was so dark, she couldn't see what was on the ground. She reached into her pocket for her phone, trying to turn on the flashlight with one hand.

The phone fell onto the other side of the fence.

"Damn it!"

Now she had no choice but to jump. She let go of the beam and landed on something hard, then bounced onto the grass. Whatever she'd fallen into kept moving until it made a shattering sound on nearby concrete.

An external house light turned on. Now she'd done it. She scrambled to her feet. The back door opened, and a flashlight shined on her—a strong beam, not a little phone light.

"Sadie?" Mateo said, incredulous.

"Um, yeah."

"What are you doing here?"

"I got lost."

"Lost? Oh, man. Did you knock over this potted plant?"

"I might have, um, bumped into it."

He walked around the small patio adjacent to the lawn, surveying the damage. "This thing shattered."

"I'm sorry," she said, mortified. She wanted to just slink off into the night. But her phone. "Um, can you help me find my phone? I dropped it."

"Where?"

"I'm not sure. Somewhere around here."

He moved closer, shining the flashlight on the grass. They walked in circles, but the phone was nowhere to be seen.

"Wait, try over here," she said, reaching for the light to point it closer to the gate. Their hands touched, and her phone was instantly forgotten. She experienced the slight contact as a shiver through her entire body.

Sadie pulled the flashlight from his hand and turned it off.

"What are you doing?" he said.

"I didn't get lost. I came here to see you."

"Sadie . . ."

"Look, if you tell me you don't feel it, too, then I'll go. But I have to know."

He was quiet. An animal scurried around in the bushes. She felt herself holding her breath. After what felt like *forever*, he said, "I feel it. But it's impossible."

She stepped closer to him. "Why do you say that?"

"Because I work for your grandparents. My father would kill me."

"Kill you? Why?"

"It's disrespectful."

"Oh, come on. What year is this, 1950?"

The truth was, Mateo's employment never even crossed her mind. She thought of Javier, not Mateo, as the one who worked for the winery. When she was growing up, Mateo was just an older kid hanging around, keeping his distance.

Now that she thought about it, since he worked for her family, was this sexual harassment?

"I don't mean to put you in a bad position," she said. "I'm sorry. But the thing is, you're already interviewing to leave. The winery is sold. I mean, you're worried about what my grandfather would think—or your dad would be worried—but it doesn't seem he's worried about you."

"You studying to be a lawyer?" he said, stepping closer to her. Her heart pounded. The porch light cast his face in shadows, enough for her to make out the angles of his chiseled features, but not enough to see the intensity of his black eyes. She wanted to reach out and touch him so badly.

"No," she breathed.

He took the flashlight from her, his fingers grazing the back of her hand in a way that had to be deliberate. Once more, she felt it through her entire body. But to her disappointment, he turned the light back on and resumed the search.

"There it is," he said, following the beam to a spot a few feet away. He handed her the phone. She'd never been less happy to see it.

"Great. Thanks." She didn't move. "Look," she said. "I get that there's weirdness with the whole work thing. But we could still hang out as friends, right? I mean, there's only so much time I can spend with my mother and grandmother."

He hesitated, just long enough that she knew he was at least considering it.

"Goodnight, Sadie," he said.

Thirty-two

Leonard's desk was covered with spreadsheets and maps of the various crops throughout the vineyard. He was already thinking about the harvest coming in mid-September.

"I need you to stop shutting me out of the decision-making around here," Vivian said. "There has to be something more we can do."

He looked up at her. "Don't you think I wish there was? All we can do is sell a lot of wine this month, pray for a dry August, and head into the fall strong. And if we do that, the next offer we get just might be enough for us to walk away with a little something to live on."

Vivian swallowed hard. If it rained a lot in August, the grapes would not ripen very well. Their future was literally riding on which way the wind blew. Oh, how could this have happened?

Someone knocked. Before she could tell them to come back later, Leonard said, "Come in." John Beaman, their head of wholesale operations, strode in and closed the door behind himself.

"Good morning. Leonard, I need to talk with you. If now isn't a good time, let's set a meeting—"

"Now's fine," Leonard assured him. "What's on your mind?"

John glanced uneasily at Vivian. "My guys are having a tough time in Manhattan," he said.

"Well, it's a competitive market," Leonard said. "If it was easy, everyone would be doing it."

"Yes. So competitive that even you're having a rough time," John said pointedly. "Maybe it's time—past time—to consider the one thing I've been asking for."

"Don't start with this again," Leonard said.

"With what?" Vivian said.

John turned to her. "Mrs. Hollander, we need a rosé."

"Leave her out of it," Leonard snapped.

Oh dear. This was a battle she was not going to get into. Not even if John Beaman was right. Not after the disaster in the 1980s, the last time Leonard had put his faith—and resources—into a trendy wine.

It had been at the bequest of Delphine.

"It's all about blush right now," she'd told Vivian, who relayed the input to Leonard. "Blush" was the name of the pale, peachy-pink red that had begun in California and was quickly becoming a phenomenon. Winemaker Bob Trinchero, of Sutter Home Winery in Napa, had been trying to improve his red Zinfandel. In the process, he pressed out some of the white juice and bottled it. This wine evolved, become increasingly sweet thanks to an accident caused by stuck fermentation leaving residual sugar. The wine took off, and other vineyards copied it. Because of the pink color, winemakers soon gave it the name "blush."

Leonard ordered a case from Sutter and declared it "swill."

"It's swill that sells," Vivian had said. "And we need revenue."

Leonard resisted listening to them. What did they know about business? Yes, Delphine made inroads—because of her pretty face, not her business acumen.

Vivian agreed with the strategy and had asked Leonard to just humor her this one time. Marriage was about compromise, she said. "This is business," he'd said.

"Well, when I left my home and followed you out here, it became about marriage, too," she'd countered.

It was decided that in the fall, a portion of their red grapes would be devoted to producing their first vintage of blush.

The wine sold like crazy.

They amped up production. In three years' time, ninety percent of their red grapes were devoted to the production of blush. The pale pink, sweet wine sold as fast as they could bottle it. They produced as many cases of blush as the vineyard was capable of producing. They considered buying grapes from other vineyards to increase production even more, but that would mean losing their "estates" winery designation, a line Leonard was not willing to cross. They would devote all of their reds to the production of blush, but no more than that. Everyone considered it a compromise.

That fateful little accident of a wine became their cash cow. Until the market bottomed out. In the summer of 1986, sweet wine fell out of favor for more sophisticated, dryer whites and full-bodied reds. They were left holding hundreds of unsold cases of blush. This, when they were still reeling from the failed partnership with the baron.

Now Leonard was stuck in old thinking because of that loss. But in reality, while rosé looked like blush, it was a different wine entirely. It was less sweet and more sophisticated. What Leah had said the first night at dinner was true: the Hamptons had sold out of rosé the previous season. Leonard saw this as a warning sign, not reason to change his stance: "They sold out because even the wineries that are producing it are being cautious. It's musical chairs, Vivian. And the music is going to stop. I'm not going to be left without a seat this time. We started this vineyard with the mission statement of producing classic wine on the North Fork. We need to be faithful to that vision."

John Beaman turned to Vivian. "If you want someone to buy this winery, they're going to expect a rosé."

Now John knew about the sale? So much for quietly shopping it.

Vivian's phone buzzed with a text: Leah, asking her to meet in the library.

"When someone else hangs a sign with their name above the door, they can produce whatever they damn well please," Leonard said. "But as long as it's my name on this vineyard, we sell classic varietals. That's what sets us apart. That's worth investing in."

John shook his head. "I need to assure our accounts that you're committing some grapes for rosé for the next vintage or they're going to stop taking my calls entirely."

"I am giving you excellent wine to sell," Leonard said. "If you can't sell on quality, then that's your failure, not mine."

"Fine," John said. "Then I quit."

⁓

Leah arranged a collection of her mother's old hardcovers on the library table. Many of them were familiar, especially the one with the black jacket featuring a photo of a woman with high cheekbones and long red nails, waring red lipstick and a black turban-like hat with face netting. The epitome of 1980s glamour. The title was emblazoned across the center in white script: *Scruples*.

She turned to the inside flap description: "The story of love, desire, and the triumph of one woman who dared to reach out for everything she needed." Women in these books were always daring to do *something*. The least she could do was make one small suggestion to her own mother. So why did she feel so anxious?

"I hope this is important," Vivian said, breezing into the room. "There's a lot going on at the office . . ." Her mother's diaphanous silk wrap trailed behind her. Her face was hidden behind her usual sunglasses, but there was a tension around her mouth that suggested her morning was off to less than a good start.

"I have an idea," Leah said. "What if we reached out to book clubs to host them here? The groups could sit on the veranda, have bottles of wine—leave with a few cases if they're so inclined—and have their book discussions overlooking the fields where the wine was grown. What could be better? You and your friends loved it. Other women will feel the same."

Vivian sat at the table, picking up one of the novels. Closer now, Leah could see the sheen of sweat over her immaculate application of makeup.

"Why did you put all of these books out like this?" she asked.

"I wanted to remind you how much you enjoyed them."

"Oh, Leah. I was reminded of that the other night at the pool, talking with you and Sadie about *Chances*."

"So then you get my idea."

Vivian took off her glasses. Her eyes were bloodshot, with either fatigue or distress. Maybe both. "John Beaman just quit," she said.

"Why? What happened?"

"I don't want to get into it," Vivian said.

Their sales rep was gone. Their vineyard manager had one foot out the door. The buyer had pulled out.

"We need to do everything we can to make money," Leah said. "I'll help you with the marketing for book clubs. You just have to do your thing: charm them when they get here, make them fall in love with the place, sell the wine."

Vivian reached for the copy of *Scruples*, flipping through the opening pages.

"I've lost the spark," she said. "This whole situation is so disheartening."

"I know, Mom. I get it. But we can't give up."

"Fine," she said, looking at her. "I'll back you on the book club idea. But there's something I want in return."

"Sure. Whatever you need."

"I want to have our own book club: you, me, and Sadie. Reading this." She handed her the copy of *Scruples*.

Leah felt a surge of satisfaction—she'd known it was a good idea to show her mother the copy of *Chances*! In the midst of all the turmoil, it gave Vivian something positive to focus on. She wished so much she could just shut out the demands of her own life and indulge in the idea of a multigenerational book club. There was nothing she'd rather do.

"Mom, it's a great idea. But realistically, I can't stay much longer. Steven is losing his patience. He's coming this weekend, and I said I'd go back with him."

The door opened, and Sadie walked in carrying her laptop and a book bag. She looked surprised to see them.

"Good morning," Leah said, remembering that Sadie had left the house the night before and wondering, again, where she'd gone. She didn't want to pry, and she definitely didn't want to pry in front of Vivian.

"What are you two doing in here?" Sadie said, setting her bag on the table.

"Just chatting," Leah said.

"Actually, I was telling your mother I want to start a book club with the three of us, but I've been informed you're leaving after the weekend."

"Leaving?" Sadie said, looking at Leah.

"Dad's coming, and I'm going back with him." Leah looked at the two disappointed faces staring blankly at her. Her mother's, she understood. But what was going on with Sadie? "We've been here over a month. We can't stay here forever. I have work, you have your thesis—"

"I like the idea of the book club," Sadie said, turning to her grandmother as if Leah hadn't said a word. "I'm in."

Thirty-three

"Come in," Mateo said from inside the closed door of his office.

The barn was hot and humid, and Sadie pulled a rubber band from her wrist to lift her heavy curls from the back of her neck. After the sting of the previous night's debacle, she had planned to keep her distance from Mateo for a few days. Why push it? She probably already seemed like a psycho. But now time was running out.

With her father coming this weekend and her mother ready to pack her bags, there was absolutely no justification for staying any longer herself. It was true: she needed to either get her thesis going or find a summer job, or both. She had to get back to real life. The book club excuse was pretty flimsy. But in the moment, she would have agreed to anything just to stall.

What did she expect to happen with Mateo? Nothing, probably. All she knew was that she wanted to spend time with him. She felt pulled to him, an itch she had to scratch. Leaving the vineyard was probably the only way to get rid of it. But as long as she was still there, she would indulge herself.

"You lost again?" he said, but with a smile. Hot *and* a sense of humor. Who could blame her for acting a little crazy?

"No," she said, pushing her sunglasses on top of her head. "And I left my phone back at the house."

"With your track record, that's probably smart."

"Funny." She pulled a chair up to the front of his desk. "Am I bothering you, or can you take a break?"

"Do I have a choice?" But again, the warmth in his tone, the light in his eyes, belied the edge to his words.

She looked at the photographs hanging on the wall.

"I meant to ask you about these," she said. "What are they from?" She had no doubt the framed pictures were Mateo's and not a relic from the days when old Joe Gable occupied the space.

Mateo leaned back in his seat and looked at the frame closest to him, the one of the man with gray hair, dressed in a blue vest and blue pants, drawing vertical lines in a long row along the side of an orange building. He glanced at Sadie, as if considering what he was going to say—or if he was going to say anything.

"What do you know about Guatemala?" he said.

"Not that much," she admitted. "I know about the Mayan ruins. I know about the civil war. But if you want to make me feel uneducated and uninformed, I can guarantee it will be very easy."

He shook his head. "I'm not trying to make you feel uneducated, though most people are when it comes to my parents' country. Like you said, they either know it for its tourist attractions or for its violent history. But there is so much more to it. Like beautiful art."

She nodded. "So this is a Guatemalan artist?"

"This photo is by Francisco Morales Santos from a piece of 2008 performance art by Isabel Ruiz. The performance is called *Matematica sustractiva—Subtractive Math*. Ruiz drew forty-five thousand lines to represent the number of people who 'disappeared' during the three-and-a-half-decade civil war. He dedicated the performance to the disappeared Guatemalan writer Luis de Lión."

Sadie knew so much about literature but very little about visual art, especially from other cultures. She tried to think of something to add to the conversation, something indicative of her intellect, but came up short. Then she was saved by the proverbial bell when his office phone rang.

"Hey, man," Mateo said into the receiver. "How's that Chenin Blanc looking?"

Sadie watched his long, tapered fingers drum his desktop. He swiveled his chair to look out the window, and it was all she could do not to leap over the desk and touch the back of his lustrous hair.

"I'd love to but I can't," he said. "Hollander doesn't do that. We had a big offer to buy some reds and he nearly took my head off when I asked him, so I don't think he'd let your boss buy any of our Chard. I can shoot you an email with some people to call, but I've got someone in my office right now . . ."

Sadie couldn't help but overhear. She was sitting right there, and besides, she wanted to know everything about him. Everything he did, everyone he knew, what his days were like.

What his nights were like.

"Hollander doesn't do what?" she asked when he was done with the call.

"Sell his grapes to other wineries. My buddy needs some whites." He stood and closed his computer. "It's time for me to get out there. Want to help?"

Did she.

They took the golf cart out to the farthest field, where the Petit Verdot was planted. She thought about the photography, and the pathos in his voice when he explained it to her. It struck her that she'd never had a serious conversation with Holden. When she tried to talk about art, or the lives of great artists like Sylvia Plath or Virginia Woolf, his eyes glazed over.

"I'm going to do a visual survey of the fruit growth so far. At the end of the summer, Leonard will give me a target date of what he wants for tonnage. I'll weigh the fruit and count clusters, and if out of two acres he wants six tons, my father and I will go out and determine how much fruit we have out there and figure, for example, okay, we need to leave two clusters per shoot."

He parked the cart next to the row marker and cut the engine.

"Can you hand me that clipboard near your feet?" he said.

She leaned forward and retrieved it. When she passed it to him, she said, "I'm leaving this weekend."

"And you're telling me this because . . . ?"

Oh, so that was how he was going to play it?

"Just FYI," she said.

"Noted."

She followed him into the field, where he stopped in front of the vines just a few feet in from the marker. He counted the clusters of buds on one of the plants. "These little guys are late bloomers."

A cloud passed in front of the sun, granting merciful shade. Sadie's skin was already a deep tan, and a smattering of faint freckles had appeared on the bridge of her nose. She didn't have her mother's olive skin tone, and that seemed to confirm that she was not meant for a life outdoors.

She and Mateo had absolutely nothing in common. This was pointless.

"You didn't tell me about the other photo in your office," she said.

He glanced at her. "You didn't recognize what that was?"

"No. Should I?"

He shrugged. "It's your winery."

"It's not mine. It's my grandparents'." And apparently, not even theirs for very much longer.

"It's a photo from the Harvest Circle ceremony years ago."

Sadie didn't want to admit that although she had a vague recollection of her mother mentioning the Harvest Circle to her, she couldn't remember exactly what it was. The blank look on her face must have given her away, because Mateo said, "Hollander Estates doesn't use industrial yeast to ferment wine."

Sadie knew that without yeast, wine was just grape juice. It was the yeast that converted the grape sugars into alcohol.

"My mother suggested to your grandfather that he try using natural flora. He liked the idea, so now on the first day of harvest every year, Leonard has Chardonnay juice pressed and puts it in a big jug. All the employees are invited to drop something in: a flower from their backyard, a shell from the beach—whatever."

"That works?"

"Yeasts are everywhere. In the air, in plants, fruit, flowers, leaves, and rocks. So it works, but the process is very risky—we have to monitor it closely. The upside is more interesting biodiversity and no additives. Plus, the wine is, in a sense, produced from a piece of us all."

Why did everything about the vineyard sound noble and romantic when Mateo explained it to her? It was him. *He* was noble and romantic.

And gorgeous. With her sunglasses covering her eyes, she could stare at him all she wanted and he wouldn't know what she was looking at. Like the fact that she could stare endlessly at the fullness of his lower lip. Or the dimple in his right cheek when he gave her a hard-won smile.

She couldn't take it another minute. She leaned forward and kissed him. After a split second of hesitation, he cupped her face with his hands, kissing her back hard. She tasted the salt from his sweat and, pressing herself against him, felt his heart beating against hers. But then he broke away.

"Sadie."

"What?" she said, breathless.

He smiled and shook his head. She stared at his mouth, those lips, incredulous that she had just tasted them. Her wanting was obscene.

"That was very forward."

She felt a flash of irritation. She thought of the part in *Lace* where Maxine calls out the sexual double standard: a guy could get carried away by his passion, but a woman was always supposed to control herself.

"What does that mean? Why do I need permission to express my wants? Men never do!"

He took her hand and tugged her down gently to sit on the ground. The grass tickled the backs of her thighs. The sun beat down stronger again, but she felt impervious.

"My mother took the photo of the flowers and wine in the jar. She's the one who taught my father how to do it. She has a feminist heart, too." With that, he gave her hand just the smallest squeeze.

Well, that was her answer: No, she didn't need permission to express her wants. Or maybe he was saying that he wanted her, too.

They locked eyes, and Sadie knew there was no way she was leaving with her parents this weekend.

Thirty-four

⁓

Leah and Sadie waited for Steven in front of the house. As soon as Leah spotted him pulling into the driveway she felt a ripple of happiness. She'd missed him.

"Hey," he said, smiling as he got out of the car. "How are my girls?"

He reached for Leah. She inhaled his scent, pressing her face against his stubble. How could she have willingly spent so much time apart? It suddenly seemed like a sort of madness.

"Sadie, look at you! You've actually gotten a little sun," he said.

"Ugh, don't remind me." Sadie put her hand up to shade her face.

"It looks healthy," he said.

"She doesn't like healthy. She likes the 'I don't need air or light, only books' pallor," Leah teased.

"Okay, on that note"—Sadie leaned forward and kissed Steven on the cheek—"I'll see you two at dinner. I'm going to get some writing done."

They watched her leave, bonded in the emotional shorthand of loving their daughter.

"I'm so glad you came," she said.

"Me too. So you and Sadie had some quality time together?"

"Yes," Leah said, and she could feel herself beaming. "It's been wonderful."

"I'm happy about that," he said. "I really am. And now maybe you and I can have some quality time together."

They looked into each other's eyes, the tension of the past few weeks evaporating. She felt herself exhale.

"Can I show you the Chardonnay berries?" she said. "I love this time of year. All the fruit has come out. No matter how many times I experience bloom, it still amazes me."

He smiled. "Sure. Let's go see those berries."

They walked hand in hand around the perimeter of the winery to the crop of Chardonnay. Crows called out in the distance. The sound of laughter drifted from the veranda. The day before, they'd had six hundred reservations for the tasting room. Leah examined the end-of-day receipts and noted that while every guest bought wine by the glass, only a fraction left with cases. She thought again about the book club. And her other idea—the one she would present at dinner, with a little help from Village Cheese.

Leah wanted to share all of this with Steven, but he would just hear it as lobbying to stay longer. That wasn't what she was doing; she'd committed to leaving that weekend, and she would go. These suggestions were just her final effort to make a difference.

She bent down in front of the first row and indicated the baby green grapes sprouting from a shoot.

"That's a lot of growth since I left," Steven said.

"It's amazing," she said. The sun was strong, but a breeze rustled though the vineyard. If conditions stayed like this through August, they would have an exceptional vintage. If that even mattered anymore. She shook the thoughts away. This moment, at least, she should enjoy without worrying about the winery.

"You know what that tells me?" he said.

"What?"

"We've been apart too long."

Well, she walked right into that one.

Steven pulled her into his arms and kissed her. She kissed him back, the sun warm on her neck and shoulders.

"I'm sorry. I really wanted to do something to help. I wanted to fix things."

"Leah, you always do your best. This isn't yours to fix." He reached for her hand, squeezing it. "So come home to what *is* yours."

Hundreds of people filled the veranda. It was perhaps not the best day to be meeting with the party planner about using the space for Asher and Bridget's wedding, but then Vivian hadn't been consulted on the matter.

Bridget and Patricia Curtis stood at the base of the steps, next to the hedge of sea grass. Patricia spotted her and waved.

Vivian waved back, trying to smile. She pulled her sunglasses down over her eyes. No, she had not been consulted about the timing of the appointment, but Asher had made it clear that he wanted her to be more involved with the wedding planning—not for her actual help or input, but to make Bridget feel welcomed into the family. "I don't want this business stuff to put a dark cloud over the most special time in her life. And mine," he said.

This business stuff? She had been sorely tempted to tell him what she was really thinking: Why waste time planning a wedding when Bridget would soon realize her sugar daddy was sugar-free? Frankly, she was surprised the girl hadn't already headed for the hills. But then, the "optics"—as Asher would say—still looked good. It was hard, even for her, to reconcile the life they were living today with what might lay in store for tomorrow. If she could still experience moments of denial, surely Asher's fiancée could labor under similar delusions.

Trying to look on the positive side, Vivian *had* always wanted to throw a family wedding at the vineyard. She'd thought certainly that would happen with Leah, but her daughter had eloped. Vivian had been terribly disappointed by that decision, and while Leah insisted it had nothing to do with her anger at her father for excluding her from the family business, Vivian felt certain that it did.

So while planning a wedding for the woman standing in front of her was not exactly what she had dreamed of, it was at the very least her chance to plan a family celebration. And it gave her a way to fill her time, to be constructive instead of sitting around wringing her hands. Vivian hadn't had a big project in a long time. She needed this.

"Just to get you up to speed," said Patricia, "the last time I met with Bridget and Asher, we discussed a configuration of ten round tables of ten guests, with the family table and the bride and groom's table on the veranda and the rest of the space used as the dance floor."

Vivian shook her head. "When I entertain out here, we do fewer tables, rectangular but long, and perhaps in this instance we'd plan seating on just one side so everyone is facing the veranda. No tables *on* the veranda. The back will still function as the bar, so we want a clear path for the guests."

Bridget played with a lock of her hair. The roots were coming in dark, so many inches it could not be an oversight but rather a deliberate aesthetic choice.

"Actually," Bridget said, "Asher and I are thinking differently now."

Vivian and Patricia looked at her expectantly.

"I knew it," Patricia said. "Your guest list has expanded." She winked at Vivian. *Those crazy kids.*

The guest list. Vivian had lost sleep over it. The cost of throwing a proper wedding was the last thing they needed right now. She had discussed this with Leonard, asking how best to cut corners to keep things going as long as possible.

"Canceling the wedding would be a Band-Aid over a bullet wound," he'd said. "Might as well bleed it out."

So it would be a last hurrah, the final celebration at the estate they had built from nothing. It would also be a way to save face with the industry, the press, and their friends: they were selling the winery, but they were not down, and they certainly were not out.

"Bridget, my husband and I have our own guest list to add. So it will certainly be well over the hundred people you're already planning on. That's factoring into my thoughts about the tables."

"Well, what I was going to say is that Asher and I just decided we're not having any guests aside from immediate family."

Vivian and Patricia exchanged a look.

"Just immediate family? You mean . . ." Vivian was confused.

"Um, yeah. Just, you know—Leah, Steven, and Sadie. My parents. And you and Leonard, obvi."

"Why would you do that?" Vivian said.

"To be practical," Bridget said. "Like, with everything that's going on."

Patricia could smell gossip. Her ears practically moved forward— like a dog on high alert.

"Can you excuse us for a moment?" Vivian said, taking Bridget by the arm and leading her off to the side, out of earshot. "What are you thinking?"

"I thought you'd be happy," Bridget said. "This will save money."

"Why didn't you talk to me about it privately? I don't need you broadcasting our problems to the world! If you're going to be part of this family, start acting like it."

She was surprised to see tears spring into the other woman's eyes. She forgot sometimes how young she was. What was Asher even doing?

"I'm sorry," Vivian said, softening her tone. "This is a difficult time."

"A difficult time? From the minute I met you you've acted like I'm some gold digger who got her claws into your son. Well, guess what: I don't need Asher. He needs me."

Vivian's jaw dropped. "What's that supposed to mean? Is that some sort of threat?"

"No, it's just reality. I make him happy. And I want to keep making him happy—for the rest of his life. And also, we don't need a wedding.

We're happy to sail off and get married at sea. We were doing this for you. But I don't see the point anymore. No offense, but if you keep this up, you'll not only lose your winery, you'll lose your son, too."

Vivian whirled around and marched away. How dare Bridget speak to her like that? All she was trying to do was help. Her indignation was too much of a burden to bear alone. She knocked on Leonard's closed office door.

"Can it wait?" he barked.

"Leonard, it's me."

She turned the knob, but it was locked. Unusual. She waited impatiently for the click from the other side of the door.

"Why are you locked in here?" she said, stepping into the office and closing the door behind her.

"Because I don't want to be disturbed," he said, returning to his seat behind the desk, which was covered in spreadsheets.

He looked tired, the bags under his eyes tinged with blue. Or maybe it was just the artificial light. She walked to the window and opened the shades.

"What in heaven's name are you doing that for, Vivian?" he said.

"Why do you think? I'm worried about you."

"I'm fine. Is that why you stopped by?"

"No. I want to discuss the wedding."

He drummed his fingers on his desk with impatience. "I'm busy here, Vivian."

"This is our son's wedding. The only wedding we're ever going to host as parents. Doesn't that mean something to you?"

"At the moment, no."

"Why? Did something happen?"

He sat back in his seat, moving papers around absently while looking at her. "Another offer came in."

"They made the offer sight unseen?"

He didn't look up. "Not exactly. But it's a decent offer. Not great, not what I'd hoped for. But it's enough to get us out of this mess."

"How much?" she said.

"We're still negotiating."

"Okay, well, I'd think you'd be happy about that."

His eyes met hers.

"Vivian," he said. "The offer is from the baron."

Thirty-five

The sun slipped lower in the sky as the family took their places around the dinner table. Vivian hid again behind her Chanel sunglasses.

She couldn't face her husband and her children. How, oh how, had fate brought the baron back into their lives? If she could have retreated to her room for the night without raising alarm, she would have gladly. She needed time to absorb this news.

The guilt over cheating on Leonard had not faded over the years. If anything it had grown sharper. As time passed, it was difficult to remember the passion—so ephemeral. But she could not forget the physical transgression itself.

There was no hiding from her past, and there was no avoiding the present: Leah wanted a festive dinner for Steven's arrival. And so they gathered at one of the picnic tables out in the field adjacent to the winery. They would dine under the stars, their meal framed by baby Syrah and Merlot plants, an orchestra of crickets serenading them. Vivian remembered eating in just that spot on a picnic blanket, a summer night before a single grape had grown. Did Leonard remember it, too?

He opened bottles of Cab and Riesling. Red and white wineglasses were set before each plate. Her hand shook as she reached for one.

Asher leaned over and whispered something to Bridget, who

laughed. Leah and Steven held hands and smiled as Sadie arrived at the table.

"Sorry I'm late," Sadie said.

"You're just in time," Leah said.

"Sadie, I notice you've been out in the field. I'm glad to see you're getting your hands dirty for a change," Leonard said. If Vivian wasn't mistaken, the praise made her granddaughter blush.

Leonard stood at the head of the table, raising a glass.

"To the future," he said, looking pointedly at Vivian. She'd gasped when he told her about the baron, unable to hide her distress. Leonard assumed it was just her surprise at selling to a man who had spurned him in business before. He had no idea there were other reasons—bigger reasons—for her to be upset by the reappearance of the baron.

And she hoped to heaven she could keep it that way.

How could they be in this situation? Yes, she blamed herself for betraying Leonard with the baron. But she couldn't help but feel angry at him for betraying them all by letting the family business slip away. She looked around the table at the happy faces of her children, knowing they were still hopeful that there would be a solution to this problem as there had been to every other challenge in the history of Hollander Estates.

He asked her not to say anything about the sale until things were further along. No sense getting everyone worked up for nothing like last time. And Vivian hoped beyond hope that this offer would end like the last one: rescinded.

Peternelle set out cheese boards.

"What's this?" Leonard said, looking at Vivian. He only liked salad before dinner. Cheese, if it was served at all, came before dessert.

"It's my idea, Dad," Leah said. "I thought we could do a wine and cheese pairing before the main course."

"Ooh, I'm not doing dairy this month," Bridget said.

"It's not mandatory," said Leah.

Peternelle set out three more bottles of wine, a Merlot, the Viognier, and a sparkling white. Steven stood to help her uncork them.

"Leah, you're upsetting the whole rhythm of the meal," Leonard said.

Vivian looked at him sharply. "I love the idea," she said. "Go ahead, Leah. This will be fun."

Leah stood, her face flushed.

"The first cheese on the board is Kunik, one of my favorites. I tell my students it's a gateway cheese—even people who have only enjoyed American cheese before my class fall in love with Kunik and become more adventurous. It's a mixed-milk cheese, just so buttery and decadent. I've paired it with the Viognier to balance it out with some acidity."

Vivian scooped some of the creamy cheese onto her knife and tasted it, washing it down with a sip of the white wine. Truly, there were few pleasures in life that could compete with wine and cheese.

She noticed Steven beaming at Leah with pride. It was gratifying to see Leah's husband take such joy in her work. She wished Leonard had paid more attention to her own contributions to the winery. Maybe it was this deep-seated feeling of being overlooked that had left her vulnerable to the baron's attention. Not that she was making excuses for her actions. It was just that all these years later, she was still trying to understand it.

"Next we have the Castelrosso. It's an Italian cheese from the Piedmont region. You'll see that the cream line is visible, and it will progress as the cheese ages," Leah said.

"It's kinda like feta," Asher said.

Leah nodded.

"I feel like I should break my diet," Bridget said, fidgeting with her hair.

"Babe," Asher said, putting an arm around her. "You should eat what you want. You're perfect."

Vivian rolled her eyes and reached for more wine. Bridget, perhaps resisting temptation, took out her phone and began snapping photos of the cheese instead of eating it.

"Finally," Leah said, gesturing to the third cheese on her plate. "Classic cheddar. This particular one is Stockinghall, named after a building at Cornell University. I've paired it with our Merlot."

"Do you really get paid to explain to people what cheddar cheese is?" Leonard said. "Don't people in the city know that?"

"Leonard, please!" Vivian said. The stress was making him unbearable. She could only imagine what would happen as negotiations continued with the baron.

"Dad, it's not about what cheddar cheese *is*," Leah said. "It's how to appreciate it, how to bring out the sweet and savory complexity of the flavor with the right wine pairing. And it's about learning how the process informs the flavor and texture. Did you know that in making cheddar, the curds are cut into tiny pieces to pull out the moisture and create a dry, firm cheese?"

"No," Leonard said. "But I do know that I'm hungry and want to get to the main course."

Vivian kicked him lightly under the table. "Delightful, Leah," she said. "Thank you.

Leah sat back down as the table was cleared. "I was thinking," she said slowly. "You could host wine and cheese classes in the tasting room during the week. I know the weekends are always busy, but this could—"

"We don't do that sort of thing," Leonard said.

"Well, you could try it," Leah said. "When I teach them in the city people tend to buy all the wines that get introduced along with the cheese."

Vivian looked at Asher, who was busy on his phone. Maybe if he'd been thinking a little more like his sister, they wouldn't be in this situation.

"I think it's a marvelous idea," Vivian said. "How soon can you do it?"

It could be months before the winery was actually sold. And in the meantime, she wanted her daughter involved.

"Oh, I didn't mean I would teach it. You could find—"

"Leah, who could be better than you?" Vivian said.

Leah glanced at Steven, who shook his head.

"Vivian," Leonard said. "Now's not the time."

"Why not? There's no downside to this. You said yourself the one thing we could do this summer is make the winery more appealing to buyers."

Vivian smiled at her daughter, her daughter who was trying to help save them.

In the books she had read and loved all those years earlier, the books she was revisiting now, there was always a moment in the heroine's life when she had nothing left to lose.

Maybe this was their moment.

⁓

"I know I said I'd go back to the city with you," Leah said, changing into her sleep shirt, "but you don't need to be this angry about it."

She hadn't planned on running the cheese classes herself. She just wanted to show her parents the possibilities—the appeal of it. But standing in the vineyard, flush with her own hard-earned knowledge and expertise, she felt how far she had come from the little girl who had followed her father around, his dutiful pupil. She should have come back with this idea a long time ago—not for the winery, but for herself.

"I'm angry because an hour before dinner, we were lying in this bed together talking about how it was time for you to come home."

Yes, they'd been cuddling after a failed attempt to have sex. It had been an awkward dance of both of them thinking, *We've been apart, therefore we should be eager to jump into bed.* Leah had gamely gone through the motions, knowing her body wasn't cooperating with her mind but still determined. Steven, perhaps sensing her lack of enthusiasm, had his own physical issues. They kissed and decided they would pick up where they'd left off after dinner, when they could really relax.

Now it was after dinner, and they were about to get into an argument.

"I know I agreed it was time for me to come home. I want it to be that simple, but it's not," she said. "Being here feels like something I have to do."

He shook his head. "It took you a long time to get over this place. But you did it. You made a life for yourself away from here."

"Yes, but maybe now's the chance to finally have what should have been mine."

"You think a wine and cheese class is going to save a money pit of a winery? Leah, that doesn't make any sense."

"Of course not. There isn't a silver bullet, but I think there are a lot of little things—missed opportunities, bad decision-making—that could be corrected. And even if it's not enough to make the place viable for my parents to sustain, at least it can put them in a position to negotiate the best possible sales price. Maybe they could have something positive to show a buyer, instead of having a fire sale. Dad's too set in his ways, Mom's given up trying to convince him to do things her way—that power dynamic is just bad. Asher is clueless. If not me, who?"

"I thought you'd let all of this go a long time ago."

"So did I," she said. "But I guess not. Why can't you just be open to where this leads?"

He shook his head. "Because it seems to be leading us apart. We just started working together."

"Steven, you retired. You put in a lot of years, you had a great career, but law was your day job. It wasn't your ultimate passion."

"So? What's your point?"

"The cheese shop is *my* day job."

"How can you say that? You love cheese. It was your dream to have a cheese shop."

"No," she said. "My dream was the winery."

Thirty-six

Sadie was in a fever. She'd never experienced anything like the physical longing she felt for Mateo Argueta. She had no appetite, she couldn't sleep. Her thesis work was nonexistent.

All she could think about was sex. Everything she looked at seemed erotic: the fruit on the vine, the flowers unfolding to the bees, even the shape of the wine bottles at dinner the night before was suggestive of the curve of a body.

It was Sadie's nature to try to understand and master anything that was taking up space in her head, and this consuming lust was no exception. Why had she never felt this way before?

She theorized that the intensity of her attraction to Mateo was partly because they were strangers and partly because they were opposites. When you met someone at college, you had enough in common that you both chose the same school. With Holden, there was nothing unexpected or clandestine about their hooking up, and that precluded the dangerous, sharp-edged feeling that she got from Mateo.

The night before, she'd barely been able to function at dinner. It seemed incredible that no one noticed the change in her. She felt sure it showed on her face, in her voice. How could the molten lust she felt inside not reveal itself to the world? Fine, it was just one kiss. But it was something. It was an opening. It was the beginning of something—she could feel it. He might still have issues with getting involved with her, but she knew they could get over them. She was going to do her best to at least try. How could she not?

The novel she'd downloaded onto her phone didn't help; *Scruples* was just as erotic as *Lace* and *Chances*. Maybe more so. How was she going to discuss them with her mother and grandmother?

"There you are," her father said, appearing out of nowhere.

Sadie closed her reading app. "Oh, hey, Dad. What's up?"

"I wanted to talk to you before I left."

"You're leaving? I thought you were here for the weekend?"

He sat on the edge of her chair. "Yes, well, your mom is busy, and I don't want to be in her way."

Sadie felt a flicker of concern, but only briefly; it couldn't compete with her own self-absorption.

"Do you want a ride back?" he said.

"Um, no thanks, Dad. I'm going to stay a little longer."

"Sadie, you don't have to babysit your mother."

"That's not what I'm doing."

"I don't want you getting distracted from your own work. What happened to the research position with Dr. Moore? I thought that was going to be all summer."

"Yeah, well . . ." She was surprised her mother hadn't told him about her thesis problem. She'd asked her not to say anything, but her parents talked about everything. Or at least they usually did. "I'm taking a little break. What's going on? Are you and Mom not getting along?"

"We're fine," he said in a way that told her they were anything but. "What do you mean, you're taking a break? I've never seen you take a 'break' from writing since you were old enough to hold a pen." He squeezed her arm.

She sighed. "I don't know. I guess writer's block isn't a myth."

"That doesn't sound good. You *are* getting distracted. Come on— pack up. It's time to get back to reality."

"No, Dad. I was stalled on my thesis before I came out here. I missed deadlines, and now Dr. Moore won't let me be her assistant because I have to be in good standing with my honors work for the research position. So honestly, I came out here to regroup. Dr. Moore told me I had to 'get out of my comfort zone.'"

He rubbed the stubble around his jawline. "I'm sorry you're having a rough time. I know it's important to take a breather sometimes. I just want to make sure you're out here for you and not because you feel like you can't leave Mom."

"You don't have to worry." She smiled to reassure him.

"What happens if you don't get back on track with your deadlines?" As a lawyer, her father was a big proponent of deadlines. He felt meeting deadlines—like being on time in general—was not only a practical issue but also a reflection of character.

"I mean, worst-case scenario is I lose my spot in the honors program."

His brow creased. "But that was the whole reason you chose that school. To study under those professors."

"I know," she said, trying to feel the urgency she was supposed to feel. "Dad, it's going to be fine."

He stood up. "I don't want to push you. But think about coming back to the city."

She nodded, knowing she had zero intention of leaving anytime soon. A month earlier, she woke up in the morning thinking only about Susan Sontag.

Now she woke up thinking only about Mateo Argueta.

⁓

The winery's oak room was a place where Leah used to feel like she could get lost as a young girl. Filled with hundreds of oak barrels that her father imported from France, row after row, it was like a forest of aging wine. The smell of the room hadn't changed a bit, the magical alchemy of sugar and yeast permeating the air. Beyond the oak room, the tanks where the wines fermented and processed. She tried to let herself feel lost in the room once again, to forget the way Steven had looked at her before driving away a few hours earlier.

Leah had some questions for Chris, the senior winemaker working under her father. The day before, while she was planning the wine and cheese pairings, the absence of rosé had been glaring. And it was going to be a big hole in her class. She knew if she brought it up with her father, he wouldn't take it seriously. But surely, Chris had to realize it was long overdue to have a Hollander rosé. She just didn't know if they had enough red grape crop to spare, and if so, when the decisions about what to do with the reds had to be finalized. Despite a common misconception, rosé was made completely from red grapes, not from red and white combined.

"Do we have enough reds for rosé?" Chris said. "And still produce our Malbec and Syrah, etcetera?" He looked around the room and made a sweeping gesture with his arm. "It's doubtful. But then, half these barrels are empty."

"*What?* Why?"

"We only have a finite capacity to grow grapes. If we wanted more, we could buy them for production, but your father would never do that. We'd lose the estates designation."

"But the winery would be able to increase revenue."

"Red wine still requires at least a year in the barrel. If you want to increase revenue quickly, you need something you can bottle in a few months. Get it on the shelves. So that would mean bringing in white."

Or making rosé, which could also be bottled and on the shelves in a matter of months. With red wine, you spent a lot of money and then had to wait for your return on that investment. Not so with rosé.

Chris excused himself and walked off to the loading dock. Leah stared after him, then looked back at the barrels. She was distracted by a noise coming from the tank area. Something that sounded like sobs.

She rounded the corner and found Bridget, who was perched on a small wooden bench, a loose hose and small puddle of water at her feet.

"Bridget? What are you doing in here?"

The woman practically jumped out of her skin. She quickly wiped her tear-streaked face.

"Oh. I was just . . . I wanted to be alone," she said, standing and brushing off her denim skirt.

"Is everything okay?"

Bridget bit her lip. She looked so young, with her dyed red hair in a messy ponytail, her smeared mascara, her bra-strap tan lines. Leah felt oddly maternal. Yes, she was technically old enough to be the mother of the woman her big brother was marrying. Why didn't he ever date women his own age? Was a mature woman that undesirable? Conversely, she never had to question why these young women dated Asher. At forty-eight, he was still an extremely handsome man. Men didn't get old—they became distinguished-looking. And he was wealthy. Well, used to be wealthy. It wouldn't be long before that little secret was public knowledge. She was surprised it had stayed out of the press this long. Her father's controlling nature did have its upside.

"No, everything is not okay," Bridget said. "And you know it's not."

Leah was confused. Had Asher told her what was going on? He'd sworn Leah to secrecy until after the wedding.

"Okay," Leah said slowly.

"I went down to the kitchen after dinner last night," Bridget said, pulling a clump of wet mascara from her lashes. "I overheard your parents arguing."

"About what?"

"Your father doesn't want you getting involved with the winery— the wine and cheese class. He hates the whole idea. And your mother said since they're losing it all anyway, why not try something new for a change." Bridget began sobbing again. "So I went back upstairs to tell Asher, and he told me how with the winery sale they'll probably be lucky just to break even. How they've been operating at a loss for years."

Leah nodded. So now Bridget knew she hadn't struck gold.

"I'm sorry that you had to find out this way. But better to know now, right? I mean, before this whole wedding thing went any further."

Bridget looked at her like she'd lost her mind. "What do you mean?"

"That it's understandable if you don't want to get married now. Considering . . ."

"Why wouldn't I want to marry Asher? You mean, because of the money problems? I love him. I'm upset *for him*. Oh, forget it."

"I'm sorry," Leah said. "I just meant—"

"You know, Asher never wanted to work here. But he felt so much pressure. Your father forced him into this business, and now he's going to be left with nothing. If they'd just let him choose his own path, he probably would have found something else to do a long time ago. He's a Gemini, you know. What's he supposed to do now?"

Leah blinked, stunned at the outburst.

For all these years, she'd resented Asher for being handed the job she'd wanted to have while he never seemed to care about it at all. Now, for the first time, she realized he was just as much a victim of their father's stubborn, controlling ways as she was.

Her brother was suffering. Bridget was suffering. Her mother was suffering. And there was nothing Leah could do to change any of it. Well, maybe there was one thing she could do.

"Bridget," she said, "would you like to join our book club?"

Part Three

***

Fruit Set

My biggest critics are the
people who've never read me.

—JACKIE COLLINS

Thirty-seven

In a scene straight out of Leah's childhood memories, the book club assembled on the veranda as the day faded into twilight. Except this time, instead of standing on the sidelines and dreamily watching her mother and her friends, she was a part of it—along with her own daughter.

The air was damp with a fine mist, the sky streaked with gold. All around them, the click and hum of hidden insects, evidence that the vineyard was vibrantly alive.

All of Leah's senses were heightened. She tasted the acidity of the wine, she smelled the nearby honeysuckle, she saw the sky changing color, and she was aware of every breath rising in her chest. She was reminded of when she was young and in love, the way that every moment was heavy with importance. In recent years, mindfulness had become a thing. But there had been a time when she didn't have to *try* to be present; the present had claimed her, mind and body.

She missed feeling passion. In the two weeks since Steven again returned to the city, all of their conversations centered around the logistics of Bailey's Blue. Still, she couldn't complain; he was covering all the classes she'd scheduled before she knew she'd be away for the summer.

"We could cancel them," she said. But that would be bad business. So she talked him through the itinerary.

Also, he was still pushing to find a new location, something she couldn't deal with while she was preoccupied with the vineyard. They ended their calls with "I love you," but the words felt rote. She meant them, and she knew he meant them, so why did they feel so hollow?

"I'm very pleased you two indulged me," Vivian said, lighting citronella candles on the table. "So much to discuss," she said, pulling a list of questions from her handbag.

"Wait, Mom. We have one more person joining us."

In a prime example of the adage "It's better to beg forgiveness than ask permission," she had not told her mother about inviting Bridget.

"Who?" Vivian said, just as Bridget appeared at the stairs.

"Did I miss anything?" she said, clopping over to the table in high heels. She wore a tank top with a bikini strap tied around her neck and tiny cutoff shorts. Sunglasses were perched on the top of her head, holding back her bright hair. It was clear she'd taken her preparation seriously: her copy of *Scruples* was heavily dog-eared, with neon-colored Post-its sticking out from a quarter of the pages.

Vivian pursed her lips. Sadie stared at her phone.

"Sadie, no phones," Leah said.

"The *book* is on my phone," she said.

"Well, then—unless you have any more surprises for us, Leah, shall we get started?" Vivian said.

"I'm ready," she said.

Vivian adjusted the silk scarf around her shoulders, then consulted the monogrammed notepad in front of her.

"What do we think of the heroine's transformation early in the story?" Vivian said.

Scruples, the story of an ugly-duckling-turned-swan, unfolded in a torrent of sex, scheming, and shopping, to show Billy Ikehorn Orsini evolve from an overweight wallflower to a powerful beauty.

"I think all women experience their early twenties as transformative," Leah said. "Maybe not as dramatically as in this book, but there is that intense post-adolescent moment that defines who we will be for the rest of our lives."

"That was certainly true for me, getting married and moving out here," Vivian said.

"I feel like my twenties are still my teens, but at the same time, like my thirties. Does that make sense?" Bridget said.

"No," said Vivian.

Leah saw Sadie bite her lip to keep from laughing.

"One thing that strikes me after rereading a book I'd first read as a teen is that it seems like a different story entirely now," Leah said. "If you'd asked me a month ago what *Scruples* was about, I'd have said it was a novel about sex and shopping. Now it's clear it's a story of a woman overcoming the wounds of her childhood to become her own person.

"What do you think, Sadie?" she said.

"I thought a lot of the stuff in the Paris section was fat-shaming," she said.

"What does that mean?" Vivian said.

"One of the characters refers to Billy as a hippo. Or thinks of her as a hippo? Either way it was offensive."

Leah nodded. "It's clearly not the way we talk about women's bodies today. But we have to give the author some latitude. It was a very different time."

"I liked the fact that Billy changed because of a trip to a new place, not because of a man. That's usually how these types of books go," Bridget said.

"What types of book?" Leah said.

"Romance novels."

"This isn't a romance novel. Romance novels are about falling in love. This book is about a woman finding herself." Leah wouldn't have been able to enjoy a traditional romance novel—not with her own relationship feeling so stale.

"But her power comes only after she's beautiful. And it comes through sex. And it comes through marrying a rich man," Sadie said.

"That's how things worked," Vivian said. "You girls don't know what it was like fifty years ago. You take so much for granted."

"She didn't marry Ellis Ikehorn for money," Bridget added. "She loved him."

"Yeah, she loved him so much she started sleeping with all the male nurses she employed to take care of him. Which—by the way—is sexual harassment," said Sadie.

"I can't take all of this political correctness," said Vivian. "Bridget is right: she loved her husband. She was grieving even before he died. The sex was a distraction."

Leah looked at her mother and thought, *Bridget is right? I think hell just froze over.*

She flipped through her book. "It seems to me that the author was clear about her intent with Billy's journey. I'm going to read a line I highlighted: *The fact that Scruples represented the smallest part of her fortune didn't make it any less important to her, because, of all the sources of her income, Scruples was the only one she had been personally responsible for establishing.*"

"I don't think it's a bad thing that she becomes happy when she turns beautiful," Bridget said. "How we look on the outside can affect how we feel on the inside."

Leah saw her mother look at Bridget as if seeing her for the first time.

Footsteps on the stairs interrupted them. Mateo appeared, carrying a bin full of vine trimmings.

"Apologies," he said. "I just need to drop these off inside."

Leah felt, even before she saw, the immediate change in Sadie's demeanor. She sat up straighter in her chair and turned toward Mateo, the intensity of her focus like a plant leaning toward the sun. In turn, he glanced at her with a look that could only be described as . . . intimate.

Could it be? And if so, how long had this been going on?

It was amazing what one could learn at book club.

⁓

Vivian should have known by her age that life was full of surprises. That had never been more evident than the past hour or so with Bridget at the book club. Apparently, there were some serious thoughts inside that head of dyed red hair—and those thoughts resonated with Vivian. Out of everyone at the table, her experience in reading the book was most closely aligned with Bridget's.

She'd been thinking a lot about Bridget since the shakeup over the wedding planning. It had been shortsighted of her to feel deprived of throwing a big party. She recognized the change in plans for what it was: a gesture to say, *We're not doing this for the extravaganza. We just want to be married.*

Of course, marriage was still just an idyll to Bridget. Something ephemeral, dreamy, flawless in the way that only the as-of-yet unexperienced could be.

She wondered if Leah had noticed the line in the book, one of the many nuggets of truth buried in the fantastical story: *Every woman's husband is hopelessly irredeemable in one way or another.* The same could be said of a marriage.

She hadn't focused on the line the first time she read the book. She'd barely noticed it because she hadn't yet grappled with her husband's flaws. Nor, to be fair, had she dealt with her own.

Vivian brought her wineglass to her lips. The baron would be arriving later in the week to spend time at the winery and "take a look at the operation." Leah still had no idea about the new offer; Vivian had kept her promise to Leonard about keeping it a secret until the deal was more solid. But now, sitting across the table from her daughter and granddaughter, talking and laughing and mulling over the vagaries of life and love, staying silent felt impossible.

She was going to crack.

Thirty-eight

Once Mateo showed up, Sadie didn't hear another word anyone said. When he looked at her she felt a jolt. For real. After that, she was done. It seemed the height of irony to sit around talking about love and sex instead of, well, actually having sex.

Besides, after reading six-hundred-plus pages about people hooking up in every possible place for every imaginable reason, how could she let a technicality like Mateo's job get in their way? That was why fiction was romantic and real life wasn't.

"I have to run to the bathroom," she said, standing up.

Her mother and grandmother, distracted with their conversation about a vineyard in the novel, barely noticed her slip away.

At eight thirty in the evening, the winery was mostly shut down except for a few people working late in their offices. Of them, the only one Mateo was likely to be seeing was the senior winemaker, Chris.

Chris's office was next to her grandfather's, and to reach that area she had to cut through the oak room.

It was eerie to walk through the rows and rows of barrels in the stillness of night. The pervasive smell of wine was even more noticeable. She thought of the juice sequestered away in the individual mini-caves, changing day by day. Like writing fiction, there was no absolute formula for great wine, and like writing a book, a wine was never truly "finished." In this sense, she found it fascinating, a noble pursuit. Mateo thought it was odd that she didn't like the outdoors since her grandfather was a grape farmer, but maybe she'd inherited her creative drive from him.

Leonard's office was dark, the only light shining out from under Chris Kessler's door. Was Mateo inside, or had he already left? A door in the back of the oak room led to the loading dock. She checked it, but it was locked. No, if Mateo left, he'd probably just go out the way he'd walked in and she would have run into him. So she waited. After what seemed like forever but was actually just a few minutes, the office door clicked open and Mateo appeared.

"Hey," she said.

He didn't seem particularly surprised to see her. With a glance behind him, he gestured for her to follow him to the back of the oak room. He unlocked the door to the loading dock, and they walked out into the field, his flashlight guiding their path.

"What are you doing back here?" he asked.

"Following you," she said.

"Sadie . . ."

"What? I'm an adult, you're an adult. My grandfather is selling this place. Who cares?"

"It's not that simple," Mateo said.

"It could be. Mark Twain said, 'You'll be more disappointed by the things you didn't do than by the things you did.' Or something like that."

"Are you seriously quoting Mark Twain right now?"

She could hear the teasing in his voice, and it emboldened her. She moved closer to him.

He turned off the flashlight. In complete darkness, he took her hand. Her heart raced like it was going to explode. And then his mouth was on hers, kissing her like he'd never get enough. It was as if a switch had flipped—in Mateo, and within herself.

If anyone had asked Sadie before that moment what made her tick, she would have said, without hesitation, the creativity and intellectual curiosity she'd felt for as long as she could remember. Now, for the first time, her mind was blank. She was all body.

They tumbled to the ground between two rows of grapevines. When her clothes were off, the grass tickled her skin. She turned over, the soil soft under her fingers as she moved on top of him. She wished it weren't so dark, that she could look down and see that lush mouth she'd been fixated on for weeks, now hers for the taking. But it was the darkness that gave them cover, that allowed them this spontaneity. She couldn't see, but she could feel.

And she felt turned inside out.

Mateo gently pulled her down beside him, switching their position so her back was now against the grass. As they moved together, his cheek against hers, murmuring things she heard but did not hear, all of her senses muted except for touch. Deep inside, a spark was ignited and she felt like she could burst.

When they were finally still, they lay entwined, looking up at the stars, framed by the vines. She wondered, idly, if they had consummated their feelings among reds or whites. She would check the next day, and when those grapes were turned into wine and bottled, she would know it was "theirs."

"Your family is going to wonder where you are," he said quietly, stroking her hair. "What will you tell them?"

She wished she could tell them the truth: like three generations of farmers before her, she had finally gotten her hands down in the dirt.

⚜

Leah and her mother were in no rush to go to bed, even long after Sadie and Bridget had said their goodnights. Back at the house, they lingered in the kitchen.

"We forgot to pick a book for our next meeting," Vivian said, setting the teakettle on the stove. "Should we ask Sadie and Bridget, or just decide among ourselves?"

"Mom, as much as I'd love to do this again next month, I can't stay out here indefinitely. And neither can Sadie."

"Speaking of Sadie: Where do you think she ran off to in the middle of our discussion?"

Leah sat at the marble island in the center of the room and avoided her mother's eyes. She had a very good idea where Sadie ran off to, but she wasn't about to share it.

"She went to the bathroom. Maybe she took a phone call. I'm sure she misses her friends."

It was just as well Sadie had left for a half hour or so. The conversation had turned to Billy the heroine's second marriage, and Leah couldn't help but feel that she was pulled into a thinly veiled expression of her own marital woes—not a topic she wanted to explore in front of her daughter.

Reading Judith Krantz, it was tempting to get caught up in the more frothy, salacious elements. They were the parts that had come to define the book over time. And yet the latter chapters of the novel offered a deeper truth. Billy's marriage turned her from a fantastical heroine to an everywoman. This was where the novel snuck up on Leah, the mindless escapism suddenly turning a mirror toward herself: *Who can teach you about the times when the well of love seems to run almost dry and you just have to keep going on faith?*

She asked the group, "Why do you think Billy struggled with her marriage to the movie producer?"

"It forced her to change. At the beginning of the book she's so solitary, and by the end she has her tribe," Bridget had said.

"But she ultimately concludes that a woman is always alone in the truth of her own marriage," Vivian said.

Leah looked at her, and their eyes met in a moment of understanding.

Who can teach you about the times when the well of love seems to run almost dry and you just have to keep going on faith . . .

Who? Maybe her mother. She waited until the teakettle whistled, until her mother filled their mugs with boiling water, to say, "Can I ask you something?"

Her mother walked over, sliding the mug across the surface of the island. "Be careful—I let it get a little too hot. And yes, of course you can ask me something."

Typically, her mother tended to avoid difficult conversations. Aside from the recent crisis with the winery, Vivian preferred to keep conversation on the surface of things. Vivian liked things to look a certain way, to be a certain way. And if they weren't, well, better to just pretend than to bring any conflict or ugliness in the light where it could shine. But after hours of talking about the book, she felt things had loosened up.

"I was wondering," Leah said slowly, "if there was ever a time in your marriage when it felt like things had just . . . I don't know. Run out of gas."

Vivian stirred a small spoon in her teacup. When she finally spoke, it was looking down at her tea.

"You and Steven are having problems," her mother said.

"I don't know if 'problems' is the right word. It's more of a . . . disconnection."

Her mother moved her spoon with unnecessary vigor, making a loud clanking noise.

"Mom—please. You're going to break that thing," Leah said. Vivian stopped, startled, as if she hadn't realized what she'd been doing.

"There's a time in every relationship when one or the other person is dissatisfied," Vivian said. "The key to a lasting marriage is that the desire to end it never occurs to both parties at the same time."

"Wait—you thought about leaving Dad?" She tried to keep her tone even so Vivian didn't clam up, but she couldn't hide her surprise.

"That's not what I'm saying. And this is about *you*," she said. "I certainly hope your decision to stay here for so long isn't causing problems. As much as I love having you here, I wouldn't want it to be at the expense of your marriage."

"No, no. I mean, in all honesty, it's not helping. But the problems started before the summer. Steven and I . . . it's like we're roommates. Roommates who love each other, but . . ."

"I see." Vivian got up from the island and moved to the counter, looking out the window at the pool. When she turned around to face her, her expression was troubled. "You should return to the city. This week."

"Mom, it's okay. Now I'm sorry I said anything. Everything's fine. We're just going through a phase, I guess."

Vivian shook her head, her brow furrowed in consternation.

Leah reached out and touched her hand. "Really—it's fine. I didn't mean to worry you."

"It's not that. I need to tell you something, but please don't say a word to your father."

"Okay. I won't."

"There's another offer on the winery. I think this time it's for real."

She looked more distraught than the first time she told Leah they were selling.

"Mom, you can't roller coaster like this. It's not good for you. At some point, you might just have to accept that Dad's selling."

Vivian sipped her tea, her hands shaking. "It's not just that he's selling. It's who he's selling to. It's someone who partnered with him briefly in the eighties. Delphine's uncle."

"Didn't that business relationship end badly?"

"Yes. It did." Vivian pressed her hand to her forehead.

"Mom, it's going to be okay."

"I don't know about that, Leah," Vivian said, her expression pained.

Leah didn't know what to say. There was nothing *to* say. But maybe, just maybe, there was something she could do.

Thirty-nine

The past was the past. It was very important that Vivian hold on to that fact. On the day the baron was scheduled to arrive for an extended visit, the winery closed to the public so he could explore the property in private. His arrival was set for noon, and lunch was being prepared on the veranda.

Leonard took her hand as they descended the stairs. Midway down, the grand entrance hall in view, she nearly swooned from anxiety. She leaned into Leonard for support, and he squeezed her hand, thinking she was being affectionate.

Outside, she broke into a sweat even though it wasn't especially hot, her dress clinging to her back. Vivian had been uncharacteristically uncertain about what to wear. She decided on a navy shift dress, Chanel flats, and a vintage gold and mother-of-pearl necklace from Van Cleef.

They walked through the pergola in silence. The sun was bright, the moist air redolent of the late-blooming flowers lining their path. She glanced at Leonard, his jaw set in determination.

Leonard could be difficult sometimes, but he wasn't a hypocrite. He always told her and the kids it was important to do the right thing when it was hard, not just when it was easy. Now he was doing something he felt he had to do even though it felt nearly impossible. She knew he was struggling with this decision. He tossed and turned beside her all night long, every night. He wasn't eating. It was bad enough to have to sell Hollander Estates—but to sell to a man who'd broken a previous partnership, leaving him in the lurch? If she'd ever doubted that Leonard had any option other than to sell, she no longer did.

They crossed the veranda. The table was set in a color scheme of navy and yellow, with a patterned runner and sunflowers in silver vases. The menu: a kale salad with pine nuts and roasted chicken in a Grand Marnier sauce paired with their Chardonnay and Pinot Noir.

They reached the front of the winery just as a black Mercedes SUV pulled up. The driver stepped out and opened the rear passenger door.

The man who emerged was thicker than she remembered him to be, with slicked-back gray hair. The baron had aged, but his sharply cut suit, his oversize watch, his wingtip shoes . . . every inch of him broadcast his wealth and privilege. He might not be young and handsome any longer, but he carried himself like a man to be reckoned with.

His pale eyes went first to Leonard.

"Good to see you, old friend," he said, holding out his hand to Leonard. "What a pleasure to be back *chez* Hollander." He turned to her. "Vivian. It's been a long time."

The baron scanned her from head to toe in appraisal, not greeting. He nodded, a near imperceptible gesture that said, *I like what I see.* She shuddered.

"Welcome," Leonard said. "We thought we'd start with lunch, if you're amenable."

The baron smiled, baring his teeth. "Perfect. Lead the way."

Vivian let the two men walk ahead.

The sparkling, crisp beauty of the day made the meeting that much more agonizing: The sun was bright, not a cloud in the sky. The air was delightfully low in humidity, a gentle breeze blowing off the nearby shores. As they took seats around the table, Vivian kept her back to the vineyard; for once, the view would not bring her joy.

Peternelle cleared away the extra place settings; the baron hadn't told them ahead of time if he was bringing an entourage.

The tasting room manager filled their wineglasses. Before Leonard could raise a glass to their guest, the baron stood. He took a pointed look around, as if surveying his domain. She realized, with a start, that he *was*, in fact, surveying his domain.

Leonard paled. It was one thing to know you had to sell, to negotiate dollars and cents with lawyers and to plan a way forward. But it was quite another to see another man stand at the head of his own table.

"To old friends," the baron said, with a smile that didn't reach his eyes. "It was a disappointment that things didn't work out those many years ago. But here we are, together again." With this he looked at Vivian. "I look forward to an arrangement that will satisfy all of us this time."

Sadie stood in the doorway of the office, waiting for Mateo to look up and notice her. When he did, she felt the usual frisson upon eye contact. Would she ever get used to being near him, or would his very presence always set her off-kilter?

"Lock the door," he said. Just the words made her knees go weak.

He left his seat and sat on the edge of his desk. She moved to stand between his knees, and he kissed her.

"You're late today," he said. "I thought you weren't coming."

"My grandparents are having a meeting at the winery," she said, breathing in the scent of him. "We're in the clear."

She had visited the barn every morning before sunrise. They could barely wait to lock the door before shedding their clothes, their touch as perfectly choreographed as that of longtime lovers, but at the same time as raw and potent as the meeting of strangers. Sex with Mateo felt profound. It was life-changing, and it was beginning to feel as necessary as oxygen.

But unlike the night in the field when they were covered by darkness and in solitude, their morning meetings meant risking Leonard's discovery when he made his rounds in the vineyard. Typically, Sadie would dash off quickly, just as the first morning light peeked into the room around the edges of the drawn shade. But today, she knew Vivian and Leonard were hosting lunch on the veranda, so she and Mateo had time to luxuriate in each other's company for a few minutes. They lay side by side on the floor, holding hands, breathless.

"I think your mother knows about us," he said, turning to her.

"What? No way. Trust me—the only thing she's thinking about is the winery."

"I don't know. She definitely seemed to be looking at me in a weird way yesterday."

"In what way?"

"In an 'are you sleeping with my daughter' way."

Sadie laughed. She didn't care if her mother knew. She wanted the whole world to know. Mateo was the one who was into secrecy. He didn't want his father or her grandfather to find out, and she respected his wishes.

She asked him about his own mother, Maria Eugenia, whom she'd learned had left the winery after he went to college.

"She missed her mother and sisters back in Guatemala and was lonely here with my dad spending twelve hours a day in the field. It was frustrating for her, too, because she was from an agriculture family, but aside from your grandmother back in the day, all the workers here are men," he said. "Like I said, it was her idea to use noncommercial yeast. Back home, she really contributes."

"How often do you see her?" Sadie asked.

"We visit once a year, usually at Christmas. She used to come in August during fruit set, when the weather here is good, but we also have time before the intense workdays of harvest. But she hasn't come for the past few years. She's getting older, and I think she's just waiting for my father to retire and come 'home.'"

"Is that what he wants?"

"I don't think so. This has been his home for forty years. He's a citizen now. I never thought he'd actually leave. Leonard promised him Field House—that even after he retired, it would be his home. My father always believed he'd convince her to come back then. But with the sale of the winery, that's never going to happen."

"I feel terrible. My grandfather would never do this if it weren't his only option."

"He isn't thinking about my father's options. Or mine. If things are this bad, he's known about it for a long time. We deserved a warning."

Sadie's stomach churned with guilt, and the fact that it was just guilt by association didn't make it any less sickening.

"I think . . . I think they're still trying to turn it around."

"How? By meeting with the new buyer today?" She hadn't given him that detail, and the omission must have seemed like a betrayal—like she was colluding with her family while keeping Mateo and Javier in the dark.

He pulled away from her. "I should get to work."

She sat up, pulling on her T-shirt, trying not to feel rebuffed. She tried to get him to meet her eyes, but he busied himself getting dressed and then started arranging things on his desk.

"I'm not my grandfather, you know," she said.

He didn't look at her. "That's a ridiculous thing to say. I know that."

"So what, then? You just totally checked out."

He sighed impatiently.

"It's complicated, Sadie. That's what I was trying to tell you from that first day. Look, I like spending time with you. I do. You're smart and you care about things like art and you love your family and I know you think about things deeply. Not to mention the fact that I'm really, really attracted to you. But this . . ." He pointed back and forth between them. "It can't go anywhere. And I don't want you to get hurt. So let's just quit while we're ahead."

She stared at him, waiting for him to dial that back—to say that wasn't what he meant. She ached for him to look at her, to give her a sign that he was conflicted, that there was room for discussion. A terrible thought occurred to her: Was this a revenge thing? Her grandfather messed with his livelihood, so he was messing with her?

No. That wasn't possible. Still, she felt stupid. It wasn't a feeling she was used to.

She let herself out of the office and forced herself not to look back. He'd realize he was wrong about this.

Wouldn't he?

Forty

〜

Leah had preached the gospel of cheese for two decades, but it felt different doing so on her home turf. The indoor tasting room filled to capacity fifteen minutes before the official start time for her wine and cheese class. When she had posted a notice about the class across both the Bailey's Blue and Hollander Estates social media platforms and mailing lists, enough reservations had poured in that she asked her father if she could use the veranda instead.

"We can't disrupt the whole winery for this," he'd said irritably.

Her mother told her the real problem was that they were closing the winery the day before to give the new buyer a tour, so they couldn't disrupt the space two days in a row.

She could have sold double the tickets if he'd let her. *Baby steps*, she told herself. Even though she hadn't been able to use the largest spot at the winery, the tasting room still let her seat three times as many people as she was able to teach at Bailey's Blue.

Sadie helped her with the forty place settings; each spot had a small cheese board featuring Capri, Kunik, Stockinghall cheddar, and her favorite, Ewe's Blue, and the four glasses of wines she'd selected for the pairing: Sauvignon Blanc, Viognier, Merlot, and Malbec. In the center and at the end of each table, a basket of sliced crusty bread and bowls of dried cherries and chocolate-covered almonds.

Sadie had never shown any particular interest in cheese. She had always been a fussy eater, and there had been a time when Leah thought she might even become a vegan. But today, Sadie seemed as excited as Leah for the event. It was a relief because she'd been notably mopey at dinner the night before but wouldn't admit that anything was wrong. And this was a departure from the positive changes Leah had seen in her daughter this summer.

She'd never thought of Sadie as being in a shell; she'd been too busy admiring her intellectual rigor and academic accomplishments to consider that maybe she was, in some ways, limited in her approach to life. When Sadie, at age fifteen, got an internship in the herpetology department of the Museum of Natural History, Leah had asked her what her sudden interest in frogs was. "I'm not interested in frogs," Sadie had replied. "But it might make for a good short story one day." Leah never thought to tell her maybe she should be working behind the counter of the cheese shop instead—not for her fiction but for her real-life experience. But now she could see a different Sadie emerging; a Sadie who didn't mind a little sun on her face, getting her hands dirty.

If only her husband were capable of looking at the world a little differently.

In the few weeks since he'd visited, Steven made it clear that he had no interest in what was going on at the winery. Leah's decision to remain there was an issue on which they'd agreed to disagree. It was less than ideal, but she hadn't gotten through more than twenty years of marriage without a few of those. Besides, it was temporary. She knew she would have to go back to the city at some point, and in her mind that point was the end of the summer.

But as long as she was there, she was going to make the most of it.

Leah stepped to the front of the room and raised her glass of wine, waiting for the assembled group to notice and settle down. She started in with her welcome spiel, including the history of Hollander Estates. But she kept it brief, knowing from experience how eager people were to get to the good part: the drinking.

"Cheese and wine have so much in common. Both are made with

the philosophy of terroir," she said. "Terroir, loosely translated, means taste of a place. The wine that you are tasting today comes from grapes grown just a few steps away. Hollander wines are fermented with natural yeast that helps bring out the full terroir. Over the next hour, I look forward to exploring the tastes of this place. I'm Leah Hollander, and since I was born and raised here, I guess you could say this vineyard is my own personal terroir."

The women smiled, and yes—the room was completely full of only women. Again, the lack of rosé rankled her. If she'd had some at her disposal, she'd have paired it with a nice Pawlet. Or even a sparkling rosé would be delightful with Castelrosso.

Focus, she told herself. *You have all that you need for right now.*

"Our first wine today is the Sauvignon Blanc. This grape loves sea-side conditions, and that's exactly what we have here."

Nearly everyone reached for their glasses. People were always eager to drink. In some classes, the least ideal circumstance was when people arrived already half-drunk and the classes became more like a guided exercise in getting wasted. She didn't get that sense from this particular crowd, but she wanted to keep things in check.

"Before you taste the wine, let's first turn our attention to the Capri. Now, when it comes to pairing, there are two schools of thought: like with like, or 'what grows together goes together.' And then there's the 'opposites attract' approach. For the Sauvignon Blanc, we're going with the like-with-like: Capri, a pasteurized goat's milk cheese from Massachusetts. Notice the color: very white and no rind. Goat's milk is bright white, while cow's milk is more golden. And you see that in the cheese." She told the class to taste it, ideally first without the bread. "You'll note that the flavor is tangy and acidic. And cheese, like wine, is living in the sense that the way the cheese tastes today is different than the way it tasted in the spring."

She gave them the go-ahead to taste the Sauvignon Blanc and then suggested they try it along with the cheese. "You'll note that the wine is also acidic. What flavor notes do you detect?"

People raised their hands: Grapefruit. Lime. Grass. She nodded, encouraging them to also smell the wine. "Some of the lightest-colored wines are the most aromatic. The great wine critic and writer Lettie Teague has said that eighty percent of a wine's 'flavor' is actually its aroma. So it is not pretentious to sniff your wine. It's actually a shame not to."

She watched Sadie bring the glass to her nose with a smile, a smile that said, *I'm learning something.*

Leah, feeling in a groove, started to move on to the next pairing, then remembered to ask if anyone had any questions. A woman in the front row raised her hand.

"I'm just wondering: Could you pair this cheese with rosé? Or any of these cheeses? I mostly drink rosé in the summer, so . . ."

Leah swallowed hard. She felt like the press secretary for a president who'd just invaded a small defenseless country. How should she justify an obviously bad decision?

"You can absolutely pair the Capri with rosé. Hollander Estates is the North Fork's oldest winery, so the varietals we grow and the wines we sell tend to be on the more traditional end of the spectrum."

Another hand raised. She realized that at some point, a lone man had made his way into the room. He had slicked-back hair and watched her with sharp blue eyes.

Leah, trying not to look as confused as she felt, acted like he was just any other attendee. "Yes?"

"Is there any difference between wine produced out here and, say, wine produced in the venerable region of Bordeaux?"

He had a heavy French accent: it was the prospective buyer. What was he doing there? She knew he'd visited the day before, and she'd made herself scarce. No one told her he was returning today. But then, neither of her parents had said much of anything last night. Her mother didn't even make it to dinner, taking to her room with a headache.

Leah took a gulp from the glass of Sauvignon Blanc she'd intended only for display purposes.

"We have more in common with Bordeaux than, say, Napa. Both here and in Bordeaux wine growers can't take good weather for granted. They have to deal with rain during harvest just as we have the threat of hurricanes—obstacles we both overcome to make beautifully complex wine."

Great. Now her father wasn't the only one challenging her. She hoped that after she successfully lobbed his little missive back at him that he'd leave, but he stayed until the end of class. Mercifully, he stayed quiet for the rest of the hour. But as the last of the customers filed out of the room onto the veranda to continue enjoying their wine, he approached her.

"Henri de Villard," he said, extending his hand. She shook it, and the look in his eyes unnerved her. It was as if he knew something she didn't.

"Leah Hollander," she said.

"You don't look anything like your mother," he said.

"Pardon me?"

"Excellent class," he said. "I'm pleased I was able to make it. I do have one small request: for future events, please consult me first about the cheese and wine selections."

Leah could not believe what she was hearing. Was this guy for real?

"I hate to break it to you, but I answer to my father, Mr. de Villard."

"Baron," he said. "That's Baron de Villard. And I hate to break it to *you*, young lady: with the check I'm about to write, your father answers to me."

Forty-one

Vivian made her way through the crowd, greeting guests and stopping for selfies. Standing in the midst of dozens and dozens of people chatting, drinking, laughing, hearing the sound of corks popping against the backdrop of jazz music, she could almost forget what was happening behind the scenes.

"A little lower so I get you in the frame, Mrs. Hollander," said a woman adjusting the angle of her phone.

Vivian bent down to get into the shot with a knitting group visiting from Connecticut. Leah had been right to market more aggressively to women on their mailing list, and the outreach to her Bailey's Blue list had already gotten a twenty-person book club reservation for later in the week.

"Ladies, allow me to help so you can all be in the photo," a male voice said. A male voice with a French accent.

She whirled around. What was the baron doing there? Leonard hadn't told her he was coming back today. Was he going to be hovering over their shoulders every minute?

It was hard to believe she had once found him so compelling. Looking back on it, with the superpower of hindsight, she realized that the attraction had been more about what was wrong with herself at the time than what was right about him. Barely out of her teens, she had traded her ornamental existence in Manhattan for the promise of something more meaningful with Leonard on Long Island, only to be relegated to ornament once again. Yes, Leonard asked her opinion about some things and she oversaw a household. But she felt, by her thirties, that he took her for granted. And so, she'd let the immediate gratification of being the focal point of a strange man's attention distract her from what really mattered. She had thought, over the years, that she could not regret it more. The past couple days had proven her wrong.

Somehow, she forced a smile for the photo. When the baron handed the phone back to the guest, she tried to drift off, but he pulled her aside.

"You'll have to excuse me," she said stiffly. "I need to take care of something back at the house."

"I've seen the entire winery, but I'd like to see the house, too. That *is* part of the deal, is it not?"

Her stomach turned. The thought of him setting foot inside her home was bad enough. But the idea of him taking her home? Unthinkable. But she plastered a fake smile on her face.

"I'm sure Leonard can help you with that," she said.

"I'm sure *you* can help me with that," he said. "You did such an unforgettable job last time I visited. All those years ago, and still I remember it like it was yesterday."

Was he serious? She glanced around to make sure no one could overhear them and took a few steps away from the crowd.

"That's inappropriate," she hissed.

"I've never stopped thinking about you," he said, his hand on her arm. "When I heard that this winery was for sale, it brought back so much unfinished business. And you haven't changed one bit."

"Yes," she said, shaking off his hand, "I have."

"True," he acknowledged. "We are both older now. And so why not have some fun? At our age, what does it matter? And I would think you would want to show a little gratitude."

She pulled away from him and rushed to the nearest door, taking refuge inside the winery. Nervous that he might follow her, she slipped into the oak room to hide among the barrels until she regained her composure. But even there she wasn't alone: Leah stood in the middle of a row, writing on a notepad. Catching her breath, Vivian said, "What are you doing?"

"Trying to figure something out," Leah replied. "But I'm glad you're here. We need to talk."

"Not now, Leah," she said, still shaken.

Leah moved closer. Speaking quietly, so quietly that Vivian had to lean forward to hear her, she said, "It has to be now, Mom. We're running out of time. Dad can't sell to that guy. He just can't."

"Did something happen?" Vivian's chest seized in alarm. The baron wouldn't have dared cross the line with Leah—would he?

"Yes, something happened: he showed up at my wine and cheese class and told me that from now on I have to consult with him about my wine pairings."

Vivian exhaled. "I'm sorry. I don't know what to do."

"Well, I have some ideas to buy time. And it starts with producing a rosé. By the way, do you know half these barrels are empty? Chris told me, and I just can't believe it."

Vivian glanced to her right, at Leonard's closed office door just beyond the last row of barrels.

"Leah, it's done. Let it go."

"I can't! I don't understand how you keep missing opportunities. Producing rosé lets us put cash right back into the business."

"Yes, but your father can do the same fast turnaround with the whites."

"That's still delaying the profit on half the crop. And if you brought in more reds from an outside vineyard, there's even more to sell. If revenue has been flat for years—and that's what I'm hearing from Dad himself—this is a way to increase our margins immediately."

Vivian shook her head. "He doesn't trust the rosé market. It's going to bottom out, just like blush did when it was popular."

"You don't really believe that, do you?"

"I don't know." Vivian faltered. "It's easy for you to say because you didn't witness the damage after our investment in blush." Leah's question, the body language of her hands on her hips and her glare, made her feel defensive. The truth was, she didn't know what she believed anymore. She'd been deferring to Leonard for so long, her instinct for winemaking had atrophied like a paralyzed limb.

"So you won't help me?" Leah said.

"What exactly do you expect me to do?" Vivian said, exasperated. "Even if I think you're right, I can't force your father to do anything he doesn't want to do." She'd been trying to get Leonard to look at things differently, to take Leah seriously as part of the team. But now she was so rattled, it was all she could do to hold herself together.

"Mom, you helped build this winery. You took a chance when you moved out here with him fifty years ago. You helped plant the fields with your own hands. You have a right to your opinion about the business."

"What do you know about it, Leah? It was never my business. It was your father's idea, your father's know-how, your father's name and legacy. I married into it, but it was always his. Why don't you understand that?"

The door to Leonard's office opened.

"What's going on out here?" he said, annoyed.

"We're talking, Dad," Leah said.

Vivian reached out and squeezed her arm. "I'm tired. I'll see you at dinner."

She turned and walked into the office.

"Leah, can you find your brother?" Leonard said. "Tell him I need him at the office. He's not answering his phone."

With that, he closed the office door and Vivian collapsed into a chair.

Leonard crossed his arms. "Is Leah carrying on again?"

"She's not 'carrying on.' She's rightfully upset." Vivian covered her face with her hands. She took a deep breath before looking up at him.

"I'm trying hard to be supportive. To be on board with what you need to do to save us financially. But I just can't continue to go along with this. Don't sell to the baron. Stall. We'll borrow money somehow. Buy some time. We can run on a skeleton staff. I'll go back to doing the fieldwork myself . . ."

Leonard smacked his palm on his desk.

"Fieldwork at your age? Stop—just stop. You don't understand. I'm already behind in taxes. We owe a lot, and I need to start paying in the fall. The baron's money is the only way to make that payment."

"But—"

"It's done, Vivian. And I don't want to hear another word about it."

⁓

"Where have you *been*?" Leah asked Asher, finally locating him with Bridget sitting on a wrought iron bench in one of their mother's flower gardens behind the house. Bridget wore a strapless turquoise sundress, her red hair sun-bleached to a softer strawberry color. Asher was dressed like he was headed to a golf course. Both of them sported fluorescent-colored sunglasses with rubber frames.

"Dad said to make ourselves scarce while the new buyer is here," he said.

"And that's okay with you?"

Asher shrugged.

"He can help me with some video for social," Bridget said. "I'm a brand ambassador for these amazing sunglasses." She adjusted the pair of brightly colored frames on her face. "They're super lightweight and totally waterproof." She spoke like Leah had just walked into an info-mercial. "Do you want to try a pair?"

"Would you be filming me?" Leah said.

"Is that okay?" Bridget said.

"Um, maybe another time?" Leah turned to Asher. "We need to talk. Can you come out to the field with me for a few minutes?"

He followed her with surprising willingness.

"Thanks for rescuing me," he said, glancing back just once.

"Since when do you need rescuing from Bridget?"

"Since it became clear that I'm about to be unemployed and homeless."

Sometimes she forgot that Asher was suffering through all of this, too. That they had roamed these fields together as children, that he would sneak wine from the bottle room. They were the only two people in the world with those specific shared memories. She might be resentful of her father's favoritism, but it wasn't Asher's fault. The sale of the vineyard and the family home was a loss they shared equally.

"Asher, Bridget doesn't care about the money."

"But I do," he said, stopping in his tracks. "I know you think I'm lazy, but I have my pride. This isn't a situation I want to drag her into. And I certainly don't want to be living off her Instagram money."

"So what are you saying?"

"I think we need some time apart."

"Asher, don't push her away. Let's focus on saving the winery, okay?"

"How?" His eyes were hidden behind those ridiculous sunglasses, but the break in his voice betrayed the extent of his worry.

"I'm not sure, exactly. But we've both, in one way or another, been controlled—or, in my case, sidelined—by Dad our entire lives. For once, we need to push back. And we're going to start by talking to Mateo."

They resumed walking, Asher muttering something under his breath. Outside the barn, Javier piled equipment on the back of a truck. Leah called out, asking if Mateo was inside.

"He's in the reds," Javier said, pointing to the farthest outskirts of the vineyard.

Leah and Asher continued walking under the high morning sun. As bad as things were at the moment, it was hard to lose hope surrounded by the lush new life, the sugar-rich grapes. Veraison—the process of the grapes turning colors—never failed to amaze her; the Malbec was changing from green to red, the white grapes from dark green to golden yellow.

She spotted Mateo among the Malbec vines.

"Hey there," she said.

He looked up at the two of them and stopped what he was doing. The sun had burnished his complexion, making the chiseled angles of his face even more striking. She wondered what was going on between him and Sadie. She'd been waiting since the night of book club for another clue, or even for Sadie to confide in her. But nothing.

"Oh wow; this Merlot is still really green," she said, looking at the fruit. Beside her, Asher shifted impatiently.

"It's old," Mateo said. "The older plants go through veraison more slowly."

Leah knew that. She'd been thinking about it—and the fact that the older plants produced fewer fruit but the fruit they did produce was higher quality. Maybe she should take something from that. And so should her mother.

This was no time to give up.

"Mateo, I don't mean to interrupt your work, but I have some questions I'm hoping you can help me with. Chris said if we wanted to produce rosé this year we have enough reds. Do you agree?"

"Oh, come on, Leah," Asher said. Mateo looked at him, hesitating.

"Don't pay attention to him," Leah said with a wave.

"We have the grapes. The question is how your father allocates the use of the reds and the tank space."

"When does that have to be decided?" Leah said.

"Before Labor Day."

August was the calm before the harvest storm. It was a time of waiting, letting the vines do their work. It was also the window before decisions about production would be made, a window that would be closing quickly. In a month, her father would start pulling fruit to test sugar and pH to see when it was time to begin harvest. Leonard would be deciding what fruit was suitable for what wines.

As hard as she'd tried to leave the winery behind her, to start a new life in New York City, the rhythm of the vineyard was like muscle memory. It was a part of her. There was little Mateo could tell her that she didn't already know. She wasn't sure what she was searching for out in the field today.

"Mateo," she said, "I'm going to ask my father to earmark some of the reds for rosé. I don't know if he'll listen to me, but I'm going to try. I asked you once before, but now I need to know even more urgently: Is there anything else you would recommend?"

"There's a more efficient way to do the netting," Mateo said.

Putting protective netting around the grapes was a labor-intensive process that took weeks. Once the fruit hit a certain sugar level, it attracted predators. The vineyard was on a major migratory path for songbirds. Leah had seen blocks of starlings descend, and it was biblical. One year, her parents lost an entire Cabernet Franc crop to deer. Vivian had recounted seeing a wild turkey swallow an entire grape cluster, gulping it down like a pelican.

"Oh? What is it?"

"Instead of covering the entire tree and needing to be installed every August and then removed for harvest, there's a perennial netting that only covers the fruit. We wouldn't have to remove it. You just undo the ties and pull it down and it doesn't bother anything and you can hedge the crop—you can do anything."

"Why hasn't my father switched to this yet?" She glanced at Asher.

"It's too expensive," Asher said.

"Well, the initial investment is expensive," Mateo said. "But in the long run you save a lot of time and money. It's becoming industry standard."

"I hate to be the naysayer here, but are the two of you forgetting that this is all moot—the winery is selling. The buyer is here this week. Leah, don't get his hopes up"—Asher nodded toward Mateo—"and don't act like there's something I should be doing that I'm not. It's over."

With that, he trudged off toward the house. Leah turned back to Mateo, who looked impatient.

"Is that what you think, too?" she said.

Mateo began to speak, then stopped. He looked around at the vineyard.

"Leah, my concern is my father. I have to take care of him, and if that means accepting what's going on and moving forward, that's what I have to do. I know this is hard on you and your mom. But I'm afraid your brother's right. It's over."

Forty-two

In early August, wet conditions were the enemy of the grapes. And so, when the drops began to fall in the early afternoon, swelling into a full-blown downpour by dinnertime, Leonard's mood was a storm of its own.

"These grapes are the baron's problem now," Vivian said, trying to get him out of his funk. "The rain doesn't matter."

"It's Hollander Estates' final vintage. It matters to me," he said.

Vivian had asked Peternelle to serve dinner indoors, at the oak dining table that seated thirty. The grandeur of the dining room gave her comfort. Above their heads, a three-tiered, nineteenth-century English openwork chandelier. The side console table was inspired by a George III design from the 1700s. With the curtains drawn, they could perhaps forget the weather. A little togetherness would help brighten everyone's mood. She'd asked Peternelle to use her favorite dressage horse–themed custom china, as well as the Georgian silver. An extra place had been set by mistake; Asher said Bridget wasn't coming. That was a first, and Vivian didn't hide her surprise.

"She's in the city. Visiting friends," he said. But something about the obviously forced lightness of his tone made her wonder if there was more to the story. Were they not getting along? There had been a time when that would have given her relief. Now she took no pleasure in the thought.

Sadie was the first to arrive, wearing olive green cargo pants and a white V-neck T-shirt. Her curls were tucked behind her ears, her face free of makeup. She looked very young and more than a little melancholy. She chose the seat next to Vivian and kissed her on the cheek.

"Hi, Gran. You look nice."

Vivian had made an effort to dress in a way that might bring some cheer; she wore a short-sleeve Chanel dress, pink knit cotton with white piping.

"I can't believe how the weather turned," Leah said. "I was out in the field this morning and it was so beautiful."

The curtains were drawn, but the sound of rain pelting the windows echoed through the room. "Let's not talk about the rain," Vivian said. "Your father is in a foul mood because of it."

Leonard walked into the room practically vibrating with tension. Peternelle uncorked a bottle of Cabernet Franc, but he waved it away.

"Just water for me tonight," he said.

Vivian and Leah exchanged a glance.

"Peternelle, please clear this extra place setting," Vivian said.

"It's not extra," Leonard said. "The baron's joining us for dinner."

"What on earth for?" Vivian said, not even trying to hide her dismay.

"He asked to stay at the house for the next few weeks. The hotel is not to his liking."

"What? No. That's out of the question," she said.

"Don't give me grief, Vivian," Leonard said.

She leaned closer to him and whispered, "This is still our home—at least for the time being. Just let him sign the paperwork and write a check and keep some boundaries."

"He hasn't written the check yet," Leonard whispered back. "And until he does, whatever it takes to make him feel invested in this place, so be it."

She felt Leah looking at her but didn't dare return her glance. Who knew what her eyes would reveal: Shame? Fear? She felt trapped at the table, trapped in the situation. She'd never felt so out of control in her life.

Leah tried making small talk, but Vivian couldn't bring herself to contribute. She could barely breathe normally.

The baron arrived, sweeping into the room like a gust from the storm outside. He was dressed in a suit, a broad smile on his face. She saw his calculating eyes sweep over the room, homing in on Sadie.

"Young lady," he said to her, "would you mind switching places? I prefer this side of the table." Sadie glanced at Vivian like, *Is the guy for real?* but Leonard was already directing Peternelle to switch the place settings. The baron slid into the seat next to her, so close she could feel his body heat.

"What a beautiful family you have, Leonard," he said. "You must be very proud."

Vivian looked across the table at Leah, who had already made it clear how she felt about the baron—and this was without knowing the secret history between them. Oh, Vivian couldn't imagine the shame if she ever found out. As much as she wanted to hold on to her home and the vineyard, the sale couldn't happen soon enough. The baron's presence was putting her entire world at risk. The sooner her family was able to separate from him, the better.

Peternelle served the first course, and Vivian went through the motions of eating. This was why people arranged all sorts of things around dinner; it provided a distraction, props, an excuse not to talk.

Somehow, the baron engaged Sadie in a discussion about a French literary critic, and Vivian reached for her wine. *You can do this*, she told herself. *Just get through the meal.*

And then she felt his hand on her thigh.

Something was going on. First, her grandmother jumped up from the table like the house was on fire. Then her mother followed her. Sadie excused herself, too. By the time she caught up with her mother, she was halfway up the central staircase.

"Mom! What's wrong?"

She stopped and turned around. "I think selling this house is going to give Gran a nervous breakdown."

Sadie could understand that. She'd been having a hard time thinking about losing the library. She glanced behind her, taking in the grand entrance hall. When she was a child, the vantage point had made her almost dizzy. The stairs had seemed endlessly vast, the stuff of story-book castles. She used to pretend she was Rapunzel trapped in a tower. It was a house of whimsy, of romanticism, of fantasy. She didn't want to see it gone.

"There's so much history here," Sadie said. "I'm appreciating that now. You know what I found in the library? Grandpa's old wine logs. They're so intricate—like chemistry books."

Her mother perked up. "Really? I want to see them."

The library was hot and humid. It had absorbed all the heat of the day, the heavy curtains trapping it inside. The rain pattered against the large windows, but when Leah flipped on the air-conditioning, the gentle hum drowned out the sound of it.

"They're on the second level," Sadie said, leading the way up the stairs.

"My mother saves everything," Leah said when Sadie pulled the first ledger from the shelf and handed it to her.

Leah pulled a few of the books into her arms and flipped through the pages. "I wish I knew everything my father knew about wine-making. I feel like his expertise combined with my willingness to look at things differently could lead to a solution."

Sadie tried to think of anything she could offer, any insight she'd gleaned from her brief time with Mateo. And then she remembered something.

"Would it help to sell grapes to another vineyard? I was in Mateo's office—um, helping out—and someone called from another vineyard looking to buy from Grandpa." That day had been the first time she kissed Mateo, out in the field. It hurt to think about it. How could that have only been three weeks ago? It felt like a lifetime. With every day that passed, it became more and more clear he wasn't going to come around: she was part of the Hollander family, he was an employee. End of story.

"Selling grapes just leaves us less for production. There are already empty barrels in the oak room," her mother said. "But if we bring in outside grapes, we won't be an estates winery. I think at one point they wanted to acquire more land, but it didn't happen."

She slipped the notebooks into her handbag. "I'm keeping a few. Soon, there won't be much evidence of Hollander Estates. This time next year, someone else's name will be out front. On the bottles. All of this will be history. Like your great-great-grandfather's winery in Argentina."

"Oh, Mom. It'll be okay."

"I wonder where all of these books will end up," Leah said, reaching for a crowded shelf and pulling a few novels into her arms. One of the books, *Mistral's Daughter*, was by Judith Krantz—the same author who wrote *Scruples*. Sadie reached for it and opened to the description. When she looked up, her mother was studying her.

"Can I ask you something?" Leah said. "Where did you run off to the night of the book club?"

Sadie had wondered if her mother would ask her about that night, but after a few weeks passed, she felt like she was in the clear. It's not that she would have minded confiding in her mother—there had been moments when she wanted to shout her feelings for Mateo from the rooftop. But there was no point getting into it now.

If she should be talking to anyone, she realized, it should be Mateo. Yes, she felt rejected. But look at what the impending sale was doing to her grandmother—she couldn't even make it through a meal. It was keeping her parents apart since her mother refused to leave while her father had to work in the city. Bridget and Asher had to replan their wedding. Mateo was under the same stress.

"Sorry, Mom, I just remembered there's somewhere I need to be," she said, handing the book back to her.

"You're going out? It's pouring . . ."

Sadie was already rushing down the stairs.

When Leonard didn't come to bed, Vivian went looking for him. Failing to find him anywhere in the house, she pulled on a raincoat and boots and made her way to the dark winery. The rain pelted her so hard it made her heart beat fast. She found shelter under the veranda but didn't see Leonard until she walked halfway across it. He sat in a chair staring out at the vineyard with a drink in his hand—a whiskey tumbler, not a wineglass.

"Mind some company?" she said, pulling up a chair next to him.

He sipped his drink and said nothing. In the distance, an animal rustled in the grass.

When they first moved to the North Fork, the proximity to wildlife was surprising. Her childhood summers in East Hampton had not brought her many encounters with foxes, turkeys, brazen racoons, or feral cats. In the early days, there had been a few times when an animal crossed her path and she let out a startled yelp that brought Leonard running.

He had always been her protector. And whatever happened next, she knew he would protect her still.

"Leonard, it's going to be okay," she said.

He turned to her. "I don't blame you for being disappointed in me. I'm upset with myself."

"I'm not disappointed in you," she said. "You created this life for us. I wouldn't have wanted anything else."

He reached for her hand. "I love you. You know that, right?"

She looked into his eyes. "Of course. That's never been a question." She swallowed hard. "Leonard, I'm not upset with you. If anything, I blame myself . . ."

He nodded, but it was as if he were only half there.

She couldn't tell him the truth. It would shatter him. Whatever the burden of having the baron around, she could bear it for a few more weeks. No matter the ups and downs with their children, with money, with the winery, their marriage was the one thing she could hold on to. She took comfort in that. She hoped, when the sale was finalized and the shock of it all had eased, that Leonard would find comfort in it, too.

"I think the faster we move on, the better. Do you think the papers will be signed soon?" she said.

"Our attorneys are working on it. But it's a process."

"Still, it's just a matter of weeks, though. Right?"

He nodded. "Yes. But one of the conditions of the sale is that the baron asked me to stay on for a year. To help with the transition. But the good news is that he'll also keep most of the staff."

Vivian pulled her hand back. "What? He expects us to stay here after the sale?"

Leonard nodded. "For continuity."

"No. We're not doing that," she said.

"I'm afraid we are," he said. "I've already agreed."

Forty-three

The rain soaked through her clothes, plastering her hair to her face and neck. After texting Mateo to meet her at the barn, Sadie didn't wait for a response before dashing out into the night.

In the downpour, the scent of every flower, every plant, even the soil, seemed intensified. She inhaled deeply, her nerve endings perking up with each step. She'd tried to put Mateo out of her mind, but now that she'd allowed herself to reach out to him, admitted to herself how much she missed him, the physical longing that had been pent up for days felt excruciating. She would say her piece, telling him she understood the stress he was under—that despite what he might think, it was affecting her family, too. She understood what was at stake for all of them. And there, in the room where they'd shared such exquisite passion, he would take her in his arms and they would pick up right where they had left off.

One thing she hadn't factored into her impulsive non-plan was that the barn would be locked. Maybe she was spending too much time reading her grandmother's old books and was losing touch with reality.

The rain that had been a misty blanket earlier in the day had turned to a needlelike downpour. She pulled out her phone to text Mateo to bring the keys, but it was too wet, and besides, he had enough sense to do that. She was the one who climbed locked gates and fell into potted plants.

She inched closer to the building, trying to shelter herself under the narrow overhang of the roof. She waited and waited, shivering in the breeze that blew in off the bay. What if he was ignoring her text?

Finally, she saw a shadowy figure across the field. The rain and the wind were instantly forgotten. How could she have doubted that he would come meet her?

It took effort not to run up to him, to throw herself against him. When he reached her, she could barely see his eyes under the baseball hat pulled down low. She waited for him to reprimand her for not having a hat or an umbrella, the way he did out in the field under the hot sun—any hint of tenderness. But he just crossed his arms, the rain pelting him. He didn't even try to stand under the ledge.

"What's this about?" he said.

"Can we go inside?" she said, wiping the water away from her mouth.

"No. Whatever you have to say, just tell me."

He couldn't be serious.

"You want to stand out here talking in the rain?" she said. He just looked at her. "Okay . . . I wanted to clarify something. I think you think I don't understand the gravity of the situation here—that because my family is selling, I can't empathize with the situation it puts you and your family in. But I do. And I want you to know that my grandparents are suffering, too. No one is happy about this. But I don't see what this has to do with you and me as . . . people." She almost said "as a couple," but they hadn't gotten to that point. They hadn't had the time. But they could. She knew they could.

Mateo seemed unmoved. "My father had total faith in Leonard, and now everything is being pulled out from under him. It's not personal, but in the middle of all this, I don't want to be with you."

Not personal? It was the definition of personal! He'd known since before they started hooking up that her grandfather was selling. He told her as much that day she ran into him at the seafood restaurant.

Still, they'd found their way to each other. That first night in the vineyard he'd seemed as starved for her as she'd felt for him. What changed? Was it because the new buyer was walking around, getting in everyone's face? That was no excuse.

She now understood why Holden had broken up with her. He'd been completely justified: she held a part of herself back. She had put her work first, her time alone first. She didn't let him pull her out of her comfort zone in any way. But with Mateo, she couldn't hold back if she tried. She didn't even recognize the person she was becoming. And still, he had found a reason to end it.

"Fine," she said, wiping the rain from her mouth as she spoke. "I don't want to be involved with you, either. You think I have time to waste on this grape farm? I'm a writer. I've been published in *The New Yorker*!"

He shook his head, his expression not unkind. Wistful, even.

"Go back to school, Sadie. There's nothing for you here."

Leah sat on her bed, her window cracked just enough to let some fresh air in and keep the rain out. She pulled one of the wine logs onto her lap and flipped through it. Pages and pages of her father's tight, precise handwriting. It was so familiar to her. Oh, how she'd always looked up to him. It was too painful to read. Setting the log aside, she picked up the copy of *Mistral's Daughter* she'd taken from the library.

She glanced at her phone, silent next to her. Steven hadn't answered her call and text from before dinner. Sometimes it felt like he was punishing her for being out here. Did she have to beg him to talk?

Across the hall, Sadie's bedroom door slammed shut. She must be back from her "walk." Maybe after the visit with her new boyfriend she'd be more open to a conversation. Leah smiled, thinking of her girlhood crush on Mateo's father. Amazing how life could come full circle.

She remembered coming home from college one summer to find

Javier walking around with a dark-haired beauty by his side. When Leah learned the woman was his fiancée, she was jealous. It wasn't the fact that he was taken, but more that she felt so far from love in her own life. College dating had been a frustrating merry-go-round of casual hookups and short-lived relationships. Looking back on it, she wished her twenty-year-old self could have known that Steven Bailey was just around the corner.

With a pang, she looked again at her phone. She decided she'd say a quick goodnight to Sadie and then try calling Steven one more time.

As soon as she opened her bedroom door, she heard the sobs coming from Sadie's room. She rushed over and knocked with urgency.

"Sadie? Open up."

"I'm fine," her daughter called out.

"You're not fine."

Sadie must have known that of course Leah wouldn't leave, that she might as well let her in. Sure enough, she cracked the door, and Leah saw that her hair was soaking wet and her eyes were swollen. Moving into the room, she closed the door behind her and steered Sadie to the edge of the bed, where she put her arm around her shoulders. Her clothes were wet, too.

"What's wrong?"

"Earlier, when you asked me where I went the night of the book club? I think you know."

"I don't know anything. I just suspected maybe it was to see Mateo. I don't mean to pry, but I can't help but wonder. Is that what's wrong? Did something happen with him?"

Sadie nodded, sniffling into a crumpled tissue.

"We hooked up," she said. "And I really like him. I thought he felt the same way, but now he's mad about the sale, about what's happening to Javier. He doesn't want to see me anymore."

Leah hugged her, murmuring that she was sorry even as a part of her was relieved to see Sadie so emotionally invested in someone. She never seemed to take any of her relationships to heart. Leah and Steven had heard about the boy she was seeing at school for months, but then she showed up at the winery announcing it was over and hadn't seemed to miss a step. Better for her to experience strong feelings, both good and bad, than to do nothing but write all the time.

"I know you're hurting now," Leah said. "But you'll feel this way again. Maybe about someone at school. It won't be as complicated as things are here. And you have to go back next semester anyway. Try to see the positive in this: the good moments you had with him are something you will always remember. And the next time you experience this, it will hopefully last longer. I was only a few years older than you when I met your father."

Someone knocked on the door. Sadie jumped up.

"Do you think it's Gran?" she whispered. "I don't want to see her. I'm a mess."

"I'll handle it," Leah said, moving to the door. She opened it a hair. It wasn't her mother; it was Bridget.

"Oh, Leah—I was looking for you. Can you talk?"

"I thought you were in the city tonight."

"Yeah, well—I'm back. And I need to talk to you."

Leah had wondered if Asher had told her that they should take time apart after all. But she could only deal with one crisis of the heart at a time.

"Now's not a great time, Bridget. Tomorrow I'll be up early and we can—"

"Um, I think now is better."

Leah glanced back at Sadie, who was waving her hand like, *Not in here.* Leah stepped out into the hall. "Bridget, look—Asher is under a lot of stress. Don't take anything he says right now too seriously. He cares about you."

"Thanks, Leah. I appreciate that. But I didn't come back from the city tonight to talk about my relationship. I came to talk about yours."

Leah wasn't following. *Her* relationship?

"I saw Steven on my way to dinner," Bridget said.

"Really?" They hadn't spoken since earlier that day. It was odd that he hadn't at least texted her that he'd seen Bridget. "He didn't mention it."

"That's because he didn't notice me."

"And you didn't say hi?"

Bridget hesitated a beat—just long enough for Leah to sense that whatever was coming, it wasn't good.

"Leah, he wasn't alone. He was with a woman. A beautiful woman."

Forty-four

⁓

Leah was on the road by five in the morning to catch Steven before he opened the shop. She drove through the darkness with the line from *Scruples* running a loop in her mind: *Who can teach you about the times when the well of love seems to run almost dry and you just have to keep going on faith?*

The gut punch she felt when Bridget told her she'd seen Steven with another woman made it painfully clear that her well of love had *not* run dry. The threat of losing her husband instantly set her priorities straight: she was going home. If not for the few glasses of wine with dinner, she would have gotten into the car the night before. Instead, she packed her bag and lay awake for hours, mentally rehashing the past few months and wondering when, exactly, her marriage had gone off the rails. With every inch she combed over, she blamed herself more.

Now, as she drove on the Long Island Expressway, the "beautiful woman" Bridget had described took on more dimensions. She must be younger. She could have sex at the drop of a hat—and did. Leah tortured herself by imagining Steven touching this woman the way he touched her, kissing her the way her kissed her.

She could barely wait another moment to see Steven. But she arrived at rush hour, and she was stuck waiting on the street as precious minutes clicked by. By the time she reached the garage underneath their apartment building, her stomach was in knots.

Inside her building, she didn't bother with the elevator, walking the ten flights to their apartment. Turning the key in the door, she was in a sweat.

Steven, alerted by the sound of the door, met her in the foyer. And then she had a horrific thought: *What if he wasn't alone?*

"Leah! Why didn't you tell me you were coming home?"

Maybe she should have. As much as she wanted to know the truth, she didn't want to see it walking out of her bedroom.

He was dressed in khaki pants and a navy polo; he'd been so looking forward to not having to wear a suit every day. He'd worked for all these years at a job he didn't particularly like to provide for their family, and now all he wanted was to retire and spend his days building a business with his wife, and she was denying him that. Oh, and she'd chosen to spend the summer apart. And never wanted to have sex. So—shocker—the man had turned elsewhere.

He walked over to hug her, but she pulled back.

"Are we alone?" she whispered.

"What? Of course. Are you expecting someone?"

She felt a wave of exhaustion. She'd used up so much emotional energy to get to the apartment, and now that she'd arrived, the most difficult part was still ahead of her.

She walked past him into the kitchen, checking the sink for any lipstick-stained glasses. He took the bag from her shoulder.

"What's going on? Is something wrong with Sadie?"

She leaned against the counter. "Sadie's fine." Or, she would be. Heartbreak healed. At least for young people it did. She wasn't so sure how she herself was going to cope.

"Then what's wrong?"

"Bridget saw you yesterday afternoon."

"Really? Where? I didn't see her."

"I know," she said, hugging herself. "Apparently, you were occupied."

Steven looked at her quizzically, and then she saw the slow realization dawn on his face.

"She saw me with someone."

"Yes," Leah said, her voice breaking. She shook her head, trying to speak without crying. "I know things haven't been great between us, but how could you . . ."

He took her hands. She looked into his eyes, bracing herself.

"It was Anouk Jansen. From the cheese shop," Steven said.

"What?"

"That customer at Bailey's Blue who gave you her card. She's a real estate agent. I've been looking for a new space. I thought if I did all the legwork, if I found a great new spot for the store, you'd get excited about the idea."

"This is about the cheese shop?" She pressed her hand to her forehead, remembering now the brunette in the shop the day Mrs. Fryer made a fuss about the landlord selling the building.

"She works with a lot of food industry clients, so she understands the need for refrigeration and display space, the health department codes—"

"So you're not having an affair."

"Leah, I love you. I am *not* having an affair. I'm sorry you would ever, ever think that I would."

In an instant, the very idea that she'd accepted as fact just minutes earlier now seemed absurd. He wasn't cheating on her. Their marriage wasn't doomed.

She felt almost faint with relief. "But why didn't you call me back last night?"

"I was worn out after the day at the store, running around looking at spaces, and then teaching the cheese class at eight. And yeah, when I get really tired, I'm a little pissed off that you're not around. So that's part of it, sure."

The cheese class. She'd totally forgotten about it.

She reached for him, throwing her arms around his neck and inhaling the scent of him, fresh from the shower. The back of his hair was still damp. He kissed her.

"I've missed you," he murmured.

"I've missed you, too," she said, pressing her body against his. He slid his hands underneath the back of her T-shirt, and the simple motion gave her goose bumps. He kissed her and she could feel his arousal, and from somewhere deep inside, her own desire stirred.

If only they could stay like that, making out like teenagers. This, her body could do.

Steven took her by the hand and led her to the bedroom. She'd been away so long that she noticed the scents of home she didn't usually appreciate: the lavender sachets in her dresser drawers, the faint vanilla from her bedside candle.

"You're going to be late opening the shop," she said.

"I certainly am."

Side by side on the bed, he tugged off her T-shirt and she wriggled out of her shorts.

She felt, unlike other recent attempts at sex, that it was crucial she find a way to get her body to cooperate. This was their reunion. This was the moment that would set the tone moving forward. If she wanted a novel-worthy happy ending, she needed to do her part.

Panicked, she willed herself to feel passion. Surely there must be some way to accomplish mind-over-matter. She thought back to the last time she'd felt turned on: it had not been with Steven. She'd been reading *Scruples*. And so she replayed the sex scene in her mind of Billy ravaging the helicopter pilot. She felt her pulse quicken, a flutter in her belly—enough response to at least accept her husband's excitement, if not match it. When he stroked her thighs, his hands moving between her legs, she told herself that it didn't matter if she felt pleasure. Going through the motions was *okay*. As long as her body cooperated enough for him to move inside of her, and it did. Thank god it did! Steven, lost in pleasure, kissed her neck, his hands winding in her hair. All she felt was relief that at least he was happy. It didn't matter that she felt, well, a little robotic. Maybe she'd never experience physical ecstasy again— maybe it was simply something she had to let go of.

He moaned in a primal way that gave her a little chill, a shiver that told her she wasn't completely dead inside. Maybe this was the best she could hope for from now on. It was enough—it had to be enough. And it would be her little secret. Surely, what Steven didn't know wouldn't hurt him.

Surely, their marriage needed this one little lie.

The campus felt strange and familiar at the same time. It was like walking through a stage set of a place she had once known.

Sadie had two weeks before classes officially started at the end of August, and she needed that extra time to get her head on straight. She found herself wandering in a fog from task to task: Registering for classes. Meeting friends for coffee. Checking books out of the library. All the while, she thought about Mateo. It was irrational; they had had a brief summer fling. She thought for sure that once she was back on campus, back to reality and away from the insular world of the winery, she would forget all about him. But so far, that hadn't happened.

Mercifully, she had a big distraction that morning: her first academic meeting of the semester. On her way up the stairs to the English department offices, she considered yet another in endless variations of how to admit to her academic advisor, her academic *idol*, that she'd failed to get her thesis off the ground.

Dr. Moore wore one of her trademark colorful dresses, this one a green-and-blue pattern that looked like a Jackson Pollock painting. Her face was brightened by orange-red lipstick, her big dark eyes shining, lit from within. She couldn't help but feel happy at the sight of Dr. Moore, even though it was her moment of reckoning.

Sadie sat in the chair opposite her desk. Her palms were slick with perspiration despite the whirring table fan cooling the room.

"How was your summer?" Dr. Moore asked.

"It was good," Sadie said.

"I hope the time away helped get your creative juices flowing."

It would be a relief, really, to simply admit defeat. She'd been dreading this moment, but now that it was here, she was ready to just let go.

"Actually, it was just the opposite. I didn't get any writing done."

"I see," Dr. Moore said, steepling her fingers. "What did you do?"

"I helped out at my grandparents' winery."

"That sounds interesting. How long have they had the winery?"

"My whole life," Sadie said. "But this was the longest time I'd ever spent there."

Dr. Moore nodded. "Sometimes when you're engaged in the world, it's hard to make time to write. But then, when you get back to the page, these are the experiences that bring enrichment to your work."

Sadie nodded. Then she said, "I don't know. I think it was one big distraction."

"Did you do any reading?"

"No. Not really."

"Sadie. I find it hard to believe you didn't read any books all summer long."

"Well, I mean, I read some trashy novels. But just out of curiosity. I wasn't *reading* reading them." She would not mention the book club—no matter how far off the rails the meeting went.

"What novels?"

"Oh—nothing you've ever heard of. Books from the seventies and eighties. They were from my grandmother's book club."

"Try me," Dr. Moore said with a smile.

"Um, well, one was called *Lace*. Another was *Chances* . . ."

"By Jackie Collins."

"You know that book?"

"Of course."

"And also *Scruples* by Judith Krantz."

Dr. Moore nodded. "And what did you think of the books?"

"Oh, the writing is terrible," Sadie said.

"And yet the novels are classics in their own way."

"Classics? No. I mean, really—have you read them?"

"Yes," Dr. Moore said.

Sadie looked at her in surprise. "So then how can you call them classics?"

"Italo Calvino, in *The Uses of Literature*, said: 'A classic is a book that has never finished what it has to say.'"

If Sadie didn't know better, she would think Dr. Moore was mocking her. She couldn't possibly be suggesting that she take these books seriously. A book's merit was based on the words on the page.

Ever since she was a little girl, Sadie had thought a lot about the written word. She thought about words as she fell asleep at night; she thought about them when she dressed in the morning. She arranged them in her mind like colors on a painter's palette. In her mind, she could make them dance. Words conveyed meaning. Words had power. Words gave everything and asked nothing in return. Susan Sontag wielded words like a weapon. And yet the words she so admired failed to spark the creative velocity that she needed to get her thesis to the finish line.

"I don't know what these books were trying to say, if anything," Sadie said.

"People are still reading them forty years after they were published. Why do you think that is?"

"My grandmother has a big book collection. I don't know how many other people are still reading those books."

"Are they still in print?"

"Yes."

Dr. Moore leaned forward. "You read these books and nothing else all summer?"

Sadie swallowed hard. "Well, yes."

"I want you to think about why that might be. Actually, correction: I want you to *write* about why that might be."

Forty-five

"This could be the one," Steven said on their way to look at the space Anouk Jansen had shown him. It was exceedingly hot, even for mid-August in Manhattan. The two months on the North Fork had left her unprepared for the dog days of summer in the city.

In the forty-eight hours since she'd been home, they'd talked about what an expansion of Bailey's Blue would look like. They worked on their budget, their mailing list, ways to expand their offerings if they found a space.

All she could think about was the winery.

"Come on in, you two," Anouk said, unlocking the door to the vacant storefront on Lexington.

The woman who had sparked Leah's marital panic was, in reality, a warm and focused professional.

Inside, the air was stale, and Anouk propped the door open. In the heat and humidity it only made things worse. She pointed out the tin ceilings, the well-preserved moldings, and a rear area that was approved for commercial kitchen use.

"Look, Leah, a counter could go here, and all of this could be display space," Steven said. He seemed genuinely excited, and she wished she could muster a fraction of his enthusiasm.

"I don't know," she said.

Anouk consulted her phone. "There's a spot ten blocks south that I think you'll both fall in love with," she said. "But it's a bit pricier."

"Let's see it," Steven said, squeezing Leah's shoulder.

They hailed a cab to a pristine limestone building on the corner of Sixty-Fourth Street. Anouk unlocked an iron gate and then a glass door. Inside, the space had wide windows and filigree ceilings and charming exposed copper pipes. Leah could not deny its appeal, and Steven, sensing her approval, reached for her hand.

"This area here can be used for café tables," Anouk said, stopping in front of a space that dropped down a small step and leveled off in front of one of the windows. "I know you said you aren't planning on a dine-in area, but it's just too perfect not to consider here. Of course, if you're completely against it, this could all be for display."

Leah could see the shop come to life in her mind's eye: the countertops refinished in white marble, a wide refrigerated case alongside one wall, and, yes, a few small wooden tables near that window, maybe with a distressed paint that made them look like they'd been there forever. Upstairs, they could hold cheese tastings for up to twenty-five people.

It was the type of space she'd thought about over the years in the tight quarters of Bailey's Blue.

"Can we afford this?" she said to Steven.

"I'm going to run the numbers."

She felt a small bubble of optimism, of the sense that things might be back on track after all. Maybe she wouldn't feel relaxed until the winery was sold, and her parents resettled into whatever form their lives took next. But she was on solid footing with her husband. Sadie was back in school. It was time to move forward.

And yet after dinner, she felt herself mentally checking out again. She sat in bed and swirled a spoon in her cup of chamomile tea, wondering what was going on at the winery.

"Hello—earth to Leah," Steven said, putting down the TV remote and looking at her.

"I'm sorry," she said, placing her tea on the nightstand. "I missed that last part."

"I said, I don't want to lose the space. I've been looking for weeks now, and I'm telling you it's special."

"I know it's special," she said. "I just can't focus."

"You can't focus because you're only half here." He looked pointedly at her open suitcase in the corner of the room. "You haven't even fully unpacked."

"I *have* unpacked. That's just my dad's old wine journals in there. I'm not sure where to put them." She bent down and lifted the books out of the bag. A beetle scuttled from the edges. "A stowaway," she murmured, brushing out the bottom of the suitcase with her hand. She carried the notebooks to the window and opened them, looking for any other creatures who might have crawled between the pages. She pulled out the hardback of *Mistral's Daughter* and shook that out just to be sure. An envelope wafted to the floor.

The handwritten address was to her mother. The seal was broken, the postmark international. Curious, she reached into it and pulled out the thin slip of paper.

Mon chère Vivian, it read.

Leah looked up to find Steven, but he'd left the room.

She tucked the letter back inside the pages of the book and stood up. Some intuition deep inside of her told her she needed privacy. With the book in her hands, she headed to the bathroom and locked herself inside.

Leah leaned against the vanity and pulled the letter out from the book.

> *Mon chère Vivian:*
>
> *I cannot rest with our affaire inachevée. One afternoon of passion is not enough. It is, as you Americans would say, a tease. If you will not take my calls, at least respond via post. As I've said in my phone messages, I will meet you anywhere*

in the world. I hope you will consider this. If not, I'm afraid I
will have to reconsider my considerable investment in the
joint winery.
    Yours, Henri

Henri? Who was Henri? Leah checked the front of the envelope; it was postmarked December 1985. It was international, from France. Who did they know from France?

Henri de Villard. The letter had been written by the baron?

She reread the letter with growing disbelief. What on earth was he saying? Had her mother had an affair? She envisioned the bully of a man she had just recently met and tried to comprehend how beautiful, vivacious young Vivian could possibly have found him attractive. Worse, how could she have betrayed her father?

The bathroom felt airless, and she fumbled with the doorknob. Somehow, the bedroom was unchanged even though her entire world was upended. Steven sat on the bed eating ice cream from a takeout container, watching a ball game. The minutes still clicked forward on the cable box. Her cup of tea was cooling on the nightstand where she had left it.

She stepped in front of the television and turned it off.

"Are you okay?" Steven said.

She handed him the letter, trembling with anger. As infuriating as her father could be sometimes—a lot of the time—she never doubted his devotion to her mother. He didn't deserve this.

All summer, she'd viewed her mother as the victim of circumstance. Now it was clear that her father was the one with the most to lose: his vineyard, and also his pride. He couldn't possibly know about the affair if he'd agreed to sell to the baron. Leonard would sooner go down with the proverbial ship.

Was there any possibility they were still involved? No, absolutely not. Her mother could be dramatic at times, but she wasn't an actress. She was miserable about the sale, and miserable about who they were selling to. Her distress at the dinner table the other night had been genuine. And the night they'd talked in the kitchen after the book club. Leah could still imagine the tormented look on her face when she told Leah the news.

No. Regardless of what happened in the past, her mother did not want that man in her life now.

Leah started throwing clothes back in her suitcase.

"What are you doing?" Steven said, looking up from the piece of paper.

"I'm going to stop the sale of the winery."

Part Four

Crush

Losing your innocence has very little to do with
virginity, you know. Loss of innocence comes when you
have to deal with the real world by yourself, when you
learn that the first rule of life is kill or be killed.

—SHIRLEY CONRAN, *LACE*

Forty-six

The book club from Sag Harbor arrived in the late morning as scheduled. What had not been scheduled, however, was Leah's absence. Three days earlier, Vivian had awakened to a text from Leah reading: *Sorry—had to run back to the city.*

Vivian called her immediately, concerned, but all Leah said was something vague about the shop and Steven and needing to be more available—that she would try to make it out again soon. Vivian could hardly complain: Leah had done so much for them that summer; the group of over a dozen women arriving was just one example of the difference Leah made with her effort to breathe some life into Hollander Estates. And really, greeting the ladies, wearing her hostess hat, was something Vivian would have relished just weeks earlier. But now her days revolved around avoiding the baron.

He was getting more and more brazen with his advances and innuendo. It was just a matter of time before someone noticed, and if that someone was Leonard, she would be confronted with her secret of thirty-five years. If Leonard asked her point-blank what was going on, she'd lie. She would say she didn't know. She would say it was nothing. The alternative—confessing what happened that day in the barn—was unthinkable. For all of his faults, Leonard had cherished her since the day they met. She couldn't imagine looking into his eyes and not seeing that unconditional love. Worse, she couldn't stand the thought of him thinking that she didn't love him—that there had ever been a minute when she didn't love him. She just wanted it all to go away.

And so, she dressed the part of the carefree winery doyenne, in a yellow silk Chanel knit dress with a scoop neck, three-quarter sleeves, and Gripoix buttons. She layered ropes of costume pearls around her neck—real pearls did not like the heat—and a spritz of Bond No. 9 perfume. She applied red lipstick, covered her eyes with her sunglasses, and headed out to greet her guests.

The group's reservation had been made by a woman named Augustine Lout. Leah knew Augustine's daughter Roya, a regular at her cheese shop. Vivian greeted the small caravan in front of the winery. Augustine was a diminutive African-American woman who could have been fifty or seventy.

"I'm so sorry Leah couldn't be here today," Vivian said. "She had to run back to the city unexpectedly."

Augustine introduced Vivian to Roya, who in turn introduced every member of the flock. They all carried copies of the novel *LaRose* by Louise Erdrich. Vivian led them around to the veranda, asking how their book group came together.

"Our families all spent summers together at Ninevah Beach," Roya said, mentioning a spot in Sag Harbor just off Gardiners Bay. "It started with an annual reunion, and a few years ago we started talking about a book—what was it, Mom?"

"*Ruby* by Cynthia Bond."

"Right. So a lot of us happened to be reading that book—maybe it was an Oprah pick at the time—and we decided to start a club."

"How delightful," Vivian said. "Leah and I started our own club this summer. Just the two of us and Leah's daughter." Well, and Bridget.

"What book did you read?" Roya said.

Vivian hesitated for only a second. "*The Goldfinch* by Donna Tartt. Now, let's get you ladies settled in."

The group oohed and aahed their delight as the vineyard came into view. Vivian showed them up the veranda steps to the two long tables set with reservation placards and bottles of sparkling white wine on ice. The smaller surrounding tables were starting to fill up, and all around the sound of corks popping filled the air along with the chatter of birds and the music over the sound system, the gentle whir of standing fans to stave off the heat. Vivian inhaled, the air fresh with the scent of the jasmine and rose tabletop floral arrangements.

It was the idyll the winery promised in its brochures and newsletter, the time of year when nature shined above and beyond Vivian and Leonard's loftiest dreams for the place.

The ladies took their seats. Vivian launched into her standard brief introduction of the history of Hollander Estates—people were always surprised to learn there hadn't been a winery on the North Fork until 1971—but was distracted by the sight of a suit-clad figure cutting across the veranda toward them.

"Excuse me, everyone." She made a beeline for the steps back down to the lawn, but not quickly enough to escape the baron's notice. She could feel him behind her but didn't look back until he called out "Vivian!" so sharply she was certain they could hear it all the way in Mattituck.

"What?" she said, whirling around to face him. "What do you want from me?"

"I'd like to not be standing in the direct sun, for one thing. Let's find some shade."

"Absolutely not." She looked around, wondering where Leonard was. Or Javier. Or anyone. At least the lawn was in full view of the veranda—not that anyone was paying them any attention. Everyone was too busy enjoying themselves, as they should be. Vivian, alone, was suffering on the picture-perfect day. "We can talk here—or not at all, preferably."

"Take off your sunglasses," he said. "I hate that you hide your beautiful eyes."

She began walking away, and he grabbed hold of her arm. She shook off his hand.

286 · JAMIE BRENNER

"What's this about? Surely you can't be angry that I refused to be your mistress all those years ago. You can't possibly care after all this time."

"Successful people—truly successful—always care about the one that got away: The deal. The woman. Whatever it may be. That's what separates winners from losers."

She shook her head. "Fine. So you'll have your American vineyard after all. But I'm not part of the deal."

He smiled and reached for her sunglasses, pulling them off.

"For you to say that—it's *adorable*," he said, trilling the last syllable for the French pronunciation. "And naive. Do you forget what happened last time?"

Vivian snatched the glasses back from his hands. He reached for her arm, gripping it tightly at her elbow. Surprised by his force, she suddenly felt unsafe.

"Mother!" Leah called, rushing down the steps toward them.

The baron dropped his hold of her. Vivian, rattled and perspiring, tried to appear normal.

"What are you doing here?" she said. But Leah didn't look at her, focused instead on the baron.

"I need to speak to my mother," she said. "Alone."

~

Leah hadn't decided what she would say to her mother. The thought kept her up all night and preoccupied her the entire drive out from Manhattan. There was the measured, mature version: "I know life is complicated . . ." There was the business version: "Considering your history, is this really the best person to sell the winery to?" There was the aggrieved daughter version: "You betrayed Dad!" But as soon as she saw her with the baron, anything she'd planned was forgotten. The moment they were alone, sequestered in the flower garden behind the house, she burst out with a simple "How could you?"

Her mother's expression, no doubt telling, was hidden behind her damn sunglasses. The visible acknowledgment that she'd even heard her was the slightest twitch of her lower lip.

"What's going on?" Vivian said. "I thought you were staying in the city."

"I know about your affair," Leah said. Before Vivian could respond, she pulled the letter out of her handbag and waved it at her. "You saved this in one of your books. A memento, I guess."

Vivian reached for the letter, scanned it, then crumpled it into a ball.

"I wasn't saving it—I was *hiding* it. He was threatening me." She pressed her face into her hands, stifling a sob. "And now he's back." She sat down on a stone bench, trembling. She pulled off her sunglasses, dabbing at her eyes with the sleeve of her pretty yellow dress, smudging it with makeup.

Leah, confused and near tears herself, sat next to her, putting an arm around her. She couldn't remember the last time she saw her mother come undone.

"What happened?"

Her mother hesitated for a moment, and then the story came out in a rush: The visit to Bordeaux, the horseback riding. The tour of their own empty stables, and a fleeting moment of passion that was never fully consummated.

"And then he pulled out of the business partnership. I was relieved— the calls and letters stopped. He was out of our lives. But financially, it almost ruined us."

Vivian explained that they were left with huge losses after the investment in the joint venture didn't have time to pay off. Desperate to replace lost cash, Leonard saw only one way forward: he sold the development rights to all of their land back to the county in a deal that would prevent it from ever being sold for use other than for farmland—a move that brought them a windfall at the time, but limited how much they could sell their property for in the future.

"It was a decision that's left us vulnerable to the baron's buyout today." She dabbed at her nose with a tissue.

Leah noted that the creases around her mother's eyes looked deeper than just at the start of the summer. Or maybe she was imagining it. Either way, she knew she couldn't stay angry at her mother. What she'd done was wrong but not unforgivable.

"I'm not upset with you, Mom," she said. "But you have to tell Dad."

Vivian looked at her in surprise. "What? Leah—no. I can't."

"He has the right to know who he's handing his family business over to." She believed this completely. She also believed that once Leonard knew the truth, he'd never go through with the sale.

Vivian shook her head. "He'll never look at me the same again."

"I understand. But can you imagine how much worse it will be when he finds out after the sale?"

"What do you mean, when he finds out?"

"Once the papers are signed, once the check is cashed—what's to stop the baron from telling Dad? Then it will be too late for Dad to change his mind. And then, no, he probably won't forgive you. At least this way, there's a chance to salvage your relationship."

And maybe even the winery.

Forty-seven

Club Day on campus always took place the first week of classes. The grassy area behind the president's house, known as the quad, filled end to end with booths from the Environmental Coalition to the GSA Club to the theater group and beyond, offering information and email sign-ups to new would-be members or just the mildly curious.

Sadie, not a joiner, always took pains to avoid this particular display. But today, she was forced to cut through the crowd to reach Dr. Moore's office. She didn't even know if Dr. Moore would be holding office hours. It was that odd time of year when schedules were in flux—just like her academic future. But maybe—just maybe—she was on to something.

The idea had come to her in the middle of the night, and she hadn't had a moment's sleep since. It was close to ninety degrees and it wasn't yet noon. Sadie, overheated in her jeans and long-sleeved T-shirt, felt a little woozy making her way through the rows of fold-out tables: The Board Game Club. The Sketch Comedy Group. A few of her friends sat at a booth under a particularly colorful banner. One of them waved her over.

"Hey—I'm just passing through. I have to find my advisor," Sadie said.

"It'll just take a minute to sign up." Someone shoved an iPad in front of her.

"I don't have time for the . . ." She checked the banner. "Jane Austen Film Society. What do you guys do, anyway?"

"Talk about Jane Austen, of course. And watch film adaptations of her books . . ."

"Sadie Bailey," someone called from behind her.

It came from the direction of the Crew Team booth, where Holden sat flanked by his teammates, all tanned and golden from a summer at the beach. Sadie panicked. Of all places to run into Holden for the first time, did it have to be so public? She had no choice but to walk over to the table.

"Hey," Sadie said.

"Interested in rowing?" the guy next to him said.

"She's not into physical activity," Holden said. Someone snickered.

"Or maybe I just never found the right sport," she shot back.

For so long, she had thought something was wrong with her for not having strong romantic feelings. She'd explained it away as being too much in her head; her intellect got in the way of whimsy. She was too practical to experience true passion. She'd thought, if she didn't feel it with Holden—hot, smart, fun—who would she feel it with? She had been certain it wasn't a matter of meeting the right person; it was her emotional set point. But the way she'd gotten carried away with Mateo had disproven that. For the first time, her mind had been overcome by her body. She'd experienced the irrational thoughts and feelings that she'd believed to be part urban myth.

Now, missing Mateo, she was suffering just like everyone else. A mere mortal after all.

And then, across the lawn, a bright yellow dress caught her eye: Dr. Moore, crossing the field and headed away from the English offices. Sadie wedged between two tables to follow her.

"Hey, Sadie—I was just kidding. Come back . . . ," Holden called after her.

Sadie broke into a run. She was sweating now, light-headed from the encounter with Holden, lack of sleep, and a general sense of being overwhelmed. A Club Day volunteer stepped forward, handing her a bottle of water.

"Please recycle. The bottle easily flattens and can be mailed back to the company to be reused as fuel in a waste-to-energy plant . . ."

Sadie chugged the water and continued on, now facing Dr. Moore's back and trailing her by a yard.

"Dr. Moore!" she called out.

The professor turned, standing in place and shielding her eyes against the sun with her hand.

"Sadie, where are you running to in such a hurry?"

"To see you," Sadie said, trying to catch her breath.

"Oh. I have a meeting. Can you email me to set up an appointment for office hours?"

"It can't wait," she said. "Please—just let me get this out before I start doubting myself. I think I'm on to something. I've got a new thesis topic."

After Dr. Moore's prompt the week before, she found herself paging through *Lace*, *Chances*, and *Scruples*. She read through them all side by side, noting parallels between them: strong women finding their way in life, in love, in business. But beyond that, in a lightning-bolt moment of clarity, she recognized a connection to the writings of Susan Sontag.

Halfway through *Scruples*, she opened her copy of "Notes on 'Camp.'" She read it from beginning to end, doubting herself. But then it was clear—thrillingly clear—that the style of the novels, the merit of these books, could be explained by something Sontag wrote in "Notes on 'Camp'": "And one cheats oneself, as a human being, if one has respect only for the style of high culture, whatever else one may do or feel on the sly."

All summer long, she had told herself she couldn't take these novels seriously, of course she couldn't. The very idea was absurd. But then,

Sontag had written, "The whole point of Camp is to dethrone the serious." Oh, yes.

"It's still on Sontag. Still 'Notes on Camp,'" Sadie said. "But instead of writing about distance as methodology, I'm looking at three works by other authors filtered through Sontag's lens: it's my thesis that the novels of Jackie Collins, Shirley Conran, and Judith Krantz are the ultimate examples of literary Camp."

Dr. Moore smiled. "Now, that's the girl I met at Young Arts."

Vivian heard the bedroom door click open. The curtains had been closed against the sunlight for hours, and now she didn't know if it was light or dark outside. Leonard sat on the edge of the bed. Her back was to him, and she didn't turn around.

"Vivian," Leonard said. "Are you unwell?"

She felt his hand on her hair, stroking it away from her forehead.

"No," she whispered.

"I've been looking all over for you."

She blinked in the near darkness. When she didn't respond, Leonard got up and opened the curtains. Sunlight poured in. How could it still be the same day? It was like time had paused, waiting for her to make her confession, ready or not.

"Vivian!" he said, squinting at her.

"What?" She sat up.

"Your face . . ."

She pulled a hand mirror from her nightstand. Her cheeks were lined with streaks of mascara, the area around her mouth stained red from smeared lipstick. Only her hair was still in place, sprayed and bobby-pinned into submission.

"I just need to wash off my makeup," she said, walking to the bathroom. Her legs felt like lead. She dispensed the foaming cleanser into her hands, avoiding her own eyes in the mirror. She preferred to look her best for difficult conversations, but her skin was too blotchy, her eyes too swollen, to think about reapplying makeup. She would face her husband without armor, her skin as raw and vulnerable on the outside as she felt on the inside.

When she returned to the bedroom, Leonard was pacing.

"What's going on?" he said. "Did something happen with Leah? What's she doing back here?"

"It's not Leah," she said, not knowing whether to sit or stand. She decided to sit, but not on the bed. She chose one of the Georgian armchairs near the window. She and Leonard had bought the set while on vacation around the time they were renovating the house, both enthralled with the carved legs and pale green cotton jacquard upholstery. She ran her hand over it now, wishing she could go back to that time and tell her husband what had happened in the moment.

"You're being dramatic, Vivian," he said. "Out with it."

"Remember the day in your office when I asked you not to sell to the baron, if there was any way we could borrow or—"

"Oh, for heaven's sake, not this again."

"Please, Leonard. This is difficult for me, so just listen. I don't want to sell—you know that. But I especially don't want to sell to the baron."

Leonard sat in the chair next to hers.

"He was spiteful back in the day, and yes, pulling out of the deal like that hurt us. But it was a long time ago. And he's offering us good money now. You've got to let go of this, Vivian. All of it."

She nodded. "I want to. But first, there's something I need to tell you. The reason Leah is back here is that she found a letter. It was folded in one of the books she took from the library. The letter was from the baron to me. Thirty-five years ago."

"What do you mean, to you? To you about what?"

As difficult as it was, Vivian looked at her husband, wanted to imprint in her mind the way he looked at her before she lost all of his respect. Possibly his love. She gripped the arm of the chair.

"Remember when the baron came to visit after you fired Delphine, and I took him for a tour of the stables?"

"No," Leonard said.

"He wanted to see them even though I told him we didn't have any horses. While we were there . . . he kissed me. And I kissed him back."

"This is crazy talk, Vivian."

"I didn't sleep with him," she said quickly. "And it never happened again. It was a moment of insanity, and I put a halt to it the second I came to my senses. But he kept calling and writing me letters. He refused to take no for an answer. I know he told you he was ending the partnership because you fired Delphine. But I believe the real reason is that I spurned his advances. And now that he's back, he's made it clear his expectations haven't changed."

"No. That can't be." Leonard jumped up.

"I'm sorry. It was so long ago . . . I never meant to hurt you." He held up his hand to stop her from talking.

"I can't hear any more right now."

He paced back and forth for a minute while she watched him, feeling helpless. She just prayed he wouldn't leave. It felt like a long time before he looked at her. When he did, his eyes were cold.

"I can't go through with the sale. I'd sooner watch it all turn to dust than sell to him."

She nodded. "I understand. But maybe it's for the best. We can—"

"No sale. No money. A tax debt. We're in big trouble, Vivian." He stood and walked to the bedroom door, turning back one more time. "You might not have screwed him, but you screwed us."

With that, he walked out of the room.

Forty-eight

Leah stood in a secluded stretch of grass behind the barn, angling her phone to avoid the glare of the sun. Steven, on the other end of the video call, stood behind the counter at the cheese shop. She could see the shelves filled with jars of olives and packages of crackers.

"So your mother *didn't* have an affair?" he said.

"No. But enough of a line was crossed that my dad is going to have a real problem." She hadn't heard from Vivian since their conversation the day before and didn't know when—or if—she was going to talk to Leonard. Either way, Leah's conscience was clear now that she'd said her piece.

"So what's your plan?" Steven said, clearly impatient.

"You mean, as far as coming home?"

"Leah, I don't want to be the bad guy here. But one minute we're about to make an offer on a new space, and the next you're gone again."

"I know, I know. But this was a conversation I had to have in person."

"I understand that. And you did. So are you coming back now?"

"I mean, if there's nothing for me to do here, then yes, I'll leave . . ." Leah averted her eyes from the screen and saw her father a few yards away. It seemed he was just doing his routine inspection of the grapes, but then it became clear he was headed toward her. "Let me call you back. My dad's here."

Leonard's face was half-hidden by his black Hollander Estates baseball cap, but as he drew closer she could see the white stubble along his jaw. His gait was slow; it was as if he had aged overnight. She knew, in that moment, that her mother had told him about her history with the baron. Her heart ached for both of them.

"What are you doing all the way out here?" he asked, his breathing labored.

"Just taking a walk," she said, reaching into her bag for her water bottle. "Drink something, Dad. You look . . . tired."

He waved it away.

"Remember all the times I brought you out here as a little girl?" he said.

"Of course."

"When I used to thin the crops you'd insist on collecting all the fruit off the ground."

Leah smiled. As a girl, seeing the discarded grapes on the ground seemed unnatural. She'd gather them up and stick them in her pockets or in a straw basket she carried with her. It seemed sad to leave them in the grass like that, even though they were hard and inedible and, off the vine, would never ripen.

"You were always so enamored with the plants," he said.

"I still am." Their eyes met, the deep brown a mirror image of her own. Yes, she'd shared his passion for the vineyard, and whether it was by nature or by nurture, she would never know. And it never mattered— at least not to him. She had been cast aside in favor of his heir apparent, his only son. It was a story as old as time, but it felt uniquely theirs in light of how things were turning out.

"I know I haven't been . . . welcoming to your suggestions this summer," he said.

"Or ever," she said, crossing her arms.

He narrowed his eyes. "Do you see a way forward?"

"Are you saying you want my help?" she said, her pulse racing.

He didn't say anything for a moment, and they faced each other in a way that felt both intimate and adversarial. "I'm calling a production meeting for later in the week. I'd like for you to attend."

Leah felt breathless. It was the first acknowledgment, in her entire life, that he took her seriously. She was finally not the little girl at his knee, but a person who had something to offer in her own right.

At least, she hoped she did.

"I'll be there," she said.

Vivian cut through the water with sharp, determined strokes. It was impossible to cry while swimming. In the pool, she felt almost normal; the hammering of her heart was from exertion instead of despair. She had a set course in front of her: just back and forth. Move her arms, move her legs. That was all she had to think about. That was all she had to do.

But even the rhythmic laps couldn't quiet her mind. Leonard had slept in a guest room, and she hadn't seen him all morning. She didn't know what he was thinking about her; she didn't know what he was thinking at all.

Twenty minutes in, she switched to the breast stroke. During one of her laps toward the house, through the blur of her wet goggles, she saw what she thought was Leonard approaching the pool. She felt even more buoyant; he wanted to spend time with her. He would forgive her. But as he drew closer, she realized it was not, in fact, Leonard.

It was the baron.

Furious, she swam to the shallow end, keeping herself submerged in the water from the neck down and pushing up her goggles. The baron was dressed in a button-down shirt, slacks, and loafers without socks. His phone was in one hand, a bottle of mineral water in the other.

"I want some privacy," she said. "Please leave."

Possibly the only upside to making her confession to Leonard was that the baron no longer had anything over her. She didn't have to put up with his harassment.

"That's not very hospitable of you," he said, sitting on one of the lounge chairs.

"Fine. Then I'll leave."

She climbed out of the pool, rushing to grab a beach towel and cover herself. "You know what's been bothering me all these weeks?" she said, tightening the towel into a snug wrap. "I'm looking back and wondering why on earth I was interested in you for even a minute."

"Now, now, Vivian—nastiness isn't becoming on you. Perhaps you need a vacation. Where would you like to go?"

"I'll tell you where *you* can go . . ." Movement at the back of the deck near the house caught her eye, and she saw Leonard making his way toward them.

The baron followed her gaze and stood.

Vivian's pulse began to race. Leonard had seemed so weary lately, but she immediately saw the determined set of his jaw, a certain spark in his eyes.

"Leonard," the baron said, his face pulled into a tight smile. "Don't tell me you're done working for the day. I'm sure those grapes need your attention."

Leonard grabbed the baron by his collar and punched him squarely in the face. Stunned, the baron staggered, and Leonard stepped forward to shove him into the pool. Vivian instinctively jumped away from the splash of water.

She couldn't believe what she was witnessing, but after the initial moment of shock she felt a flood of relief. Leonard might be down, but he wasn't out. He was still a fighter.

"Are you out of your damn mind?" the baron sputtered.

"No. But you're out of a vineyard," Leonard said. "Get the hell off my property. Security will see you out."

The baron climbed up one of the side ladders, shaking water out of his eyes.

"You're ruined, Hollander," he said. "This place is finished."

Leonard's response was to summon their security team, waiting for his cue nearby. Two men took the baron by each arm. He shook one of them off, muttering something about assault charges.

When he was gone, Vivian turned to her husband.

"Fifty years together, and you can still surprise me," she said, smiling and hoping he might find some lightness in the moment.

That he might find it in his heart to continue loving her.

"You should have told me sooner, Vivian," he said.

And then, shoulders slumped, he walked back into the house.

Forty-nine

In August, the plants stopped producing. It was the calm before the harvest storm.

Leah walked through the field, the humid morning air like soup. All around her, unseen nature clicked and hummed and chirped. A woodpecker tapped out a code on a nearby tree. *Tell me your secrets,* she thought.

How big was the gap between what she knew and what she didn't know about the winery? This was the thought that kept Leah awake at night. It was a catch-22: her distance from the place was what let her see missed opportunities. But she also felt like the solution to saving it—if there was one—required deep operational understanding. The obvious solution would be to ask her father a ton of questions, but she didn't want him to get exasperated and throw up his hands and say, "Forget it! I'll do it myself."

The second-best option was talking to Javier, Mateo, and the senior winemaker, Chris Kessler. And so she called a meeting at the barn.

"Can we all fit in here?" she said as they squeezed into Mateo's office.

It was tight, but they made it work, with Mateo and Javier sitting on his desk while Leah and Chris used two folding chairs to face them.

Mateo turned on a standing fan and opened the window to try to catch the breeze.

"Thanks for taking the time to meet at such short notice," she said. "I have some questions about harvest planning."

The three men looked at one another. "Where's Leonard?" Chris said.

"We're all meeting in two days. I just want to ask a few things to get myself up to speed."

"Before we start," Chris said, "what's going on with the sale?"

It was a good question.

"The truth is, I can't really speak to that. But what I can say is that no one wants to sell. So what I'd like to do is figure out what's working and what's not working. Because I know you're a great team, and that's half the battle. So tell me, what comes next? Where are we in the production timeline?"

"Soon we'll put up the bird netting," Javier said. "Last year, we were picking fruit by September 20. But we didn't finish the reds until the end of October."

"This summer was hotter, so the reds are going to get extremely ripe. Our yields are going to be high," Mateo added.

She nodded, writing everything down in her notebook.

"The bottom line is, the window for production decision will be closing soon," Chris said. "Leonard is going to start pulling fruit to test sugar and pH. Then he'll decide what fruit to use for what wines and allocate tank space."

Leah looked up. "What if we wanted to produce a rosé this year?"

Chris looked at Javier, then said, "Leonard will never go for it."

"Let me worry about that," Leah said. "Just humor me: What grapes would you use?"

"We could use some of our Merlot and Cab Franc and Syrah grapes."

She nodded. "And just to clarify: What's the timeline for getting a rosé to market? I know that if we use those grapes for red wine, they'll be sitting in the barrels for at least a year, so we don't see profit on them for a while."

Chris thought for a minute. "The red grapes still have to ferment awhile for the rosé. But by December we could start blending trials to see what would make the best wine. Best-case scenario is we bottle in February and release March 1."

That was an even faster turnaround than she imagined. Still, she knew that revenue from the amount of rosé they could produce—even if they sold it all—wasn't enough to solve their problems. But with two days to go before the harvest production meeting, it was at least a start.

She had her father's ear. She had the beginning of an idea. Now she just had to find a way to tell her husband she wasn't coming home. Again.

Vivian wanted to take pleasure in the simple elegance of the dinner table, set with a yellow linen runner down the center and three bunches of sunflowers. But it did little to offset the tense mood. Leah looked deflated. She must be lonely without her husband—or, at the very least, aware of the fact that he had made the decision not to join her. She was quiet—the whole table was quiet. Except for Bridget. Vivian found herself actually welcoming Bridget's prattle for once.

"So this crochet bikini designer is paying me per views on my video. Everyone has to go onto Instagram and tell your friends."

Leonard rolled his eyes. "I'm supposed to tell people to go online to look at videos of my son's fiancée in a bathing suit?"

"Exactly! Thanks," Bridget said.

Leonard poured more wine into his glass, took a sip, and then stood as if to make a toast. But he didn't raise his glass.

"I have an announcement to make."

The kids looked at him expectantly. Vivian tried to make eye contact with him, but he avoided her.

"The deal is off. The sale of the winery is not happening. At least, not for now."

Vivian glanced at Leah, who gave a nearly imperceptible nod that she understood: the conversation had happened, and the outcome was as she'd predicted.

"What do you mean?" Asher said. "Don't tell me this guy backed out, too. What the hell? Maybe Harold needs to rethink how he's presenting the financials . . ."

Leonard held up his hand. "Enough. I'm the one who called off the deal. And I don't want to hear another word about it."

"When were you going to tell me?" Asher said, getting red in the face.

"I'm telling you now!"

"Okay, okay," Vivian said. "Can we all just . . . relax."

Leonard shot her an irritated look, and then it was back to silence. Leah, Asher, and Bridget clearly couldn't wait to finish eating and decamp back to the house. When Vivian was alone with Leonard, she said, "I know you're upset with me. But don't take it out on the kids."

Leonard pushed his plate away, looking around for Peternelle.

"I especially don't want you giving Leah a hard time," Vivian said. "It seems our marriage isn't the only one suffering in all of this."

"What are you talking about?"

"I don't like the fact that Leah's out here without Steven. It's not a good sign."

"Maybe not. I hope that isn't the case. But there's nothing we can do about it either way," he said, standing and dropping his napkin onto the table.

Vivian wasn't so sure about that. It was one thing for her marriage to be in jeopardy over all of this. But she wasn't going to sit by and watch her daughter's break apart.

Fifty

B ridget floated on a raft in the middle of the pool, wearing a skimpy black crochet bikini and a pair of the fluorescent rubber sunglasses covering her eyes. Her long red hair fanned out into the water. Leah stood for a minute, squinting against the sun. Was Bridget reading Vivian's copy of *Lace*?

"Bridget, hey—can I talk to you for a minute?"

She looked up, pushing her sunglasses on top of her head.

"Leah! Come on in. The water's amazing," she said.

All Leah could think about was the fact that her mother would go nuts if she saw her book in the pool.

"I'm afraid I can't right now. But can you come out for a minute? I want to ask you something."

"No one wants to have fun around here," she said, making no move to get out of the pool.

"It will just take a minute."

Bridget pulled her glasses down again, one hand drifting lazily into the water, paddling a small current to turn the raft in the other direction.

Oh, fine! Leah kicked off her sandals and stepped into the warm water of the shallow end, progressing only far enough that the water was above her knees but not soaking her shorts.

"I'm in the pool. Now can we talk?" Leah called out.

Bridget propelled the raft toward her. When she got close enough, Leah waded over.

"Isn't this better?" Bridget smiled.

"It's . . . fine." It was heavenly.

"Let me guess: you want to talk about Asher."

"No. What about him?"

"I dunno. He's been acting weird since dinner last night. Quiet. I thought maybe you knew."

As if she ever had a clue what was going on in that head of his. Her brother was only marginally less frustrating than her father.

"Sorry. Can't help you there. I actually wanted to talk about social media."

"You watched the video? This is the bathing suit," Bridget said, tugging on the string of her top.

"I did watch the video. And I was thinking we could really use your help amplifying Hollander Estates on Instagram."

Bridget's face lit up. "I thought you guys would never ask! There's so much more you could be doing."

Of course there was. That seemed to be the overriding theme around there.

Leah's idea for Instagram was to share not just photos of the wine but the story of life on a vineyard. Experiencing the seasons at the winery made every change sharper, more profound. It was a way of life she missed. It was a life she never stopped wanting to return to—not even when she moved on to her Manhattan world.

"Can we start taking some photos today?" Leah said.

"Absolutely! But you know, we should game-plan. Come up with a calendar of posts. I know my account probably looks spontaneous and random, but everything is planned out in advance."

Leah nodded, kicking herself for not having this conversation sooner. There was still some time to capture the summer, the plants bursting with fruit.

"You know what? We should get Vivian, too. Two generations of Hollander women on the family vineyard. Hashtag WomenInWine."

It was a good idea. But Leah hadn't seen her mother all morning. Where was she?

⁓

Vivian stared out the back seat window of the Escalade while her driver steered through the busy Manhattan streets.

"Please just let me out here," she said impatiently. What with all the double-parked delivery trucks, bike lanes, and traffic, she could get to the apartment building faster by walking.

Since the moment Leonard told her they were in financial trouble, she'd tried to come to terms with losing it all. She could never fully accept it. Now, thanks to Leah, she might not have to. But she didn't want Leah to lose what was most important to her in the process.

The sidewalk, mercifully, was not crowded. The last time she'd visited the city she'd barely been able to walk from Fifty-Third Street to Fifty-Ninth because of the hordes of pedestrians. But Yorkville was, if not a sleepy neighborhood, at the very least highly livable. She could see why Leah had chosen it as the place to make a home for herself and her family.

Vivian's childhood memories of Manhattan centered around visits to the Met. Ice skating in Central Park. Shopping with her mother on Fifth Avenue. She had loved the city, had assumed she would spend her entire life there. And then she married Leonard and never looked back.

Marriage was about compromise. Sacrifice. But not, she was finally realizing, only on the part of the wife. She might have failed as a partner in the winery, but she was not going to fail as a mother to her daughter. In her heart, she knew Steven loved Leah. The rest was just details. Steven just needed a little guidance seeing the details more clearly.

The building's doorman waved her along. Steven was expecting her; she'd called an hour earlier with the improbable story that she was going to "be in the neighborhood" and wanted to stop by.

"Vivian," he'd said. "Why don't you save yourself a trip and just say whatever you want to say on the phone."

"I'll see you soon."

He opened the door, and she shrugged off her light cashmere wrap and set her handbag down on the chair beside her. The room was small but filled with southern light. Whenever she visited Leah she had to adjust to the confining space. It was an average-size Manhattan apartment, but it felt like a closet to her. She'd been spoiled growing up in her family's sprawling Park Avenue home.

Steven put the coffee on—a traditional brewer, not automatic pods—and they sat at the scuffed dining room table. She could envision Sadie as a small child, coloring on the oversize drawing pads Vivian bought for her at State News on Eighty-Sixth Street. Leonard never joined her on her trips to the city. He didn't like Manhattan, and part of it was passive-aggressive punishment because Leah only visited them once or twice a year. Men could be so good at withholding. Steven was a prime example at the moment.

"You take your coffee black, right?" he called from the kitchen.

"Yes," she said. The fact that he knew that was indicative of the years they'd spent sitting across from each other at family meals. After all this time, they were family. And yet they'd never had a serious, intimate conversation.

He handed her a full mug and sat across from her.

"Thank you," she said. "I needed this."

"So what brings you here this morning, Vivian?"

"I'm concerned that you haven't been out to the winery to see Leah. Yes, I know the shop needs to be managed. But I'm sure you could find *some* time."

"With all due respect, Vivian, have you considered that this might not be any of your business?"

"Considered and dismissed," she said, smiling. "Now, what's going on?"

She saw him hesitate. He leaned back in his chair, focusing his blue eyes on her. They were unreadable, and for a moment she was afraid she wouldn't get a word out of him. But then . . .

"When I first met Leah, she'd just been cut out of the family business," he said.

Vivian winced to hear it put so bluntly. "Yes. It was not what I wanted, but Leonard had his mind set on how he wanted to run the winery."

Steven shrugged. "Whatever his rationale, or yours—it was unfair to Leah. But I told her then as I tell her now—we don't need the winery. We created something of our own. I had the 'day' job—a demanding, not terribly rewarding job—while Leah started a passion project. And I fell in love with it, too. Selfishly, I looked forward to retiring and then the two of us running a shop together. So no, I'm not thrilled that she's apparently chucking all that to fix Leonard's mess."

"I see. So the problem is that you're worried about the cheese shop."

"No, that's reductive, Vivian."

"So . . . talk to me. I'm listening."

He leaned back in his chair, running a hand through his hair. "I'm also worried about Leah. She's been a successful businesswoman for eighteen years. We're in a position to build on that success, and instead, she's setting herself up for failure. And I'm supposed to just pick up and move to the North Fork? None of this has been discussed in a rational, logical way. Leah just ran out of here the other day and shows no intention of coming back."

Vivian pressed her spine against the seatback, turning her mug in circles. The gold bangles around her wrist clinked together. Outside, a siren wailed.

Of all her life regrets, her biggest was failing to defend Leah's rightful place at the winery when she had expressed interest two decades earlier. Vivian hadn't asserted herself then, but she would not make the same mistake twice.

"It's true that this is a major decision," she said carefully. "One that should be made by you as a couple. In fact, I can't argue with anything you said. Except for one thing: the cheese shop was never Leah's passion project."

"Of course it was," he said, but there was a falter in his voice, a break in eye contact. This wasn't news to him.

"No. It was her consolation prize. The winery was always her dream. This is her chance to grab it. If you deny her this, you're no better than Leonard taking it away from her the first time around."

Fifty-one

There might have been no setting on earth more perfect for social media than a vineyard: In the twilight of summer, the jewel-toned fruit heavy on the vine. In the peak of harvest, giant bins full of grapes popping with color, conveyer belts carrying mounds of fruit past workers checking for quality, the bright red juice coming off the pressing machine. Even the winter was starkly beautiful, with its acres of plants lying still, in wait, with the promise of new life. It was a marketing gold mine—one Leah intended to take full advantage of. With Bridget's help.

"Do you think Sadie will come up again to visit?" Bridget said. "Then I can get all three of you."

"I'd settle for finding my mother at this point." Vivian had disappeared.

"Angle yourself a little lower so I get the grapes in this shot with you."

They had mapped out a social media calendar starting with harvest and going through next spring. The one idea Leah didn't share with Bridget was her thought about highlighting the rosé—if there was a rosé. She wanted to chronicle the creation of their first vintage from the minute the grapes were fermenting to the cork in the first bottle; people would feel an emotional investment in the journey from field to table.

In the winter, they would photograph the bare vines. The pruning process. Spring would bring the task of tying shoots to the trellis wire, taking new growth off the bottom of the existing vine. By the time the rosé was on the shelves, they would be posting about bud break, and then, bloom.

"Let's walk up to the veranda and do some photos with bottles of wine. We can come back to the grapes later when we find Vivian," Bridget said.

As flighty as Bridget might seem most of the time, the act of taking photos and videos gave her an intense focus. She was a woman with a vision; she kept talking about what would attract "engagement" and had clear opinions about staging the shots. Leah let herself relax, happy to have someone else making decisions for the moment. Speaking of engagement . . .

"So how's the wedding planning going?" Leah said.

"Um, let's just focus on the photos," Bridget said, clearly unhappy. "So this is the plan: we'll bank some video for later so we don't have to do this every day." She began arranging a dozen bottles of Sauvignon Blanc on a table.

"Every day?"

"Oh, *there's* your mother," Bridget said.

Leah turned around. Yes, there was her mother. And walking right alongside her, Steven.

The dozen or so friends crammed into Sadie's dorm room, waiting for her to tell them what this was all about.

Sadie didn't know exactly what it was all about, except she was searching for something. A feeling of incompleteness, of something left undone, nagged at Sadie day and night. This time, it wasn't her stalled thesis that kept her staring in the dark of her dorm room. If anything, that was the one thing in her life that had some momentum.

No, it was Mateo. Their time together played out in her mind like a romantic montage from a movie, a constant loop of sense memory and longing.

She should be happy that there was no one to pull her away from her writing, no pesky relationship demanding time and attention. Last semester with Holden, all she'd wanted was space. She'd thought the problem was that she wasn't cut out for intimacy, but now she knew differently. The strangest thing was that she had a six-month relationship with Holden, and when it ended she was able to move on, and she'd had only the tiniest fraction of that time with Mateo and she couldn't shake it. She kept telling herself that she was grown up, and she had to deal with the fact that it had been a fling and move on. But when someone comes into your life and changes your understanding of yourself, that person becomes a part of you.

She needed to keep her mind off him. And so, as she had always done in times of stress, she turned to books.

The book club with her mother and grandmother reminded her of what it was like to read just for pleasure. Most of her friends had grown up just picking popular books off the shelves for fun, while she'd always been too goal-oriented, focused on literary canons. Like the time she visited the Strand bookstore with her mother, refusing to read the YA novels.

Now that she was back to reading just for fun, she wanted company. She thought her friends in the Jane Austen Film Society would be a good place to start. After all, wasn't Austen the trashy novelist of her time?

The truth was, she didn't think of them as trashy novels anymore. At least, not in a bad way. "Trash" suggested something that no longer had value, while, as Dr. Moore pointed out, the books she'd been reading had found an audience for decades. Judith Krantz's and Jackie Collins's words were a part of her now, as surely as Susan Sontag's were.

If only, now that she was back on campus, she was able to get lost in them again.

"As promised, free wine," Sadie said, opening the bottles she'd brought back from the vineyard and pouring into Solo cups. She sat cross-legged on her bed, while the others took spots on the floor or leaned against her desk or stood by the door.

"I want to hear about the books you read for fun," Sadie said. "Your favorites. Like, you're reading and just forget about everything."

"Why?" one of the women said.

"Because I'm stressed out," said Sadie. The group nodded, a few women murmuring that they were also feeling pressure.

"That's what this is for," one of them said, holding up her cup.

"I'd like to get through this semester without a drinking problem," Sadie replied.

"Have you tried knitting?" someone suggested.

Exasperated, Sadie put down her cup and said, "Okay, let's do this. We're going to go around the room and everyone has to name one book. Fiction only."

At first, the responses were disappointing. *Pride and Prejudice*, *Little Women*, blah blah blah. But then, after a bottle or two was empty, the conversation took a turn. Someone mentioned, offhandedly, that she'd reread Anne Rice's *The Witching Hour* three times. "And it's a thousand pages."

The room erupted into chatter about everyone's favorite Anne Rice novel, interrupted only by someone bringing up *Outlander*. Someone declared her passion for J. R. Ward.

"When I was in high school I discovered my mother's stash of Nora Roberts and read all of them. I ordered her new one just last week."

Sadie typed the authors and titles into the notes section of her phone. She had a lot of catching up to do. She wondered if maybe it was time for this non-joiner to start a group of her own.

"What do you all think of starting a book club?"

The women looked at one another. "A book club? We don't have time to read more books on top of our class assignments. Are you crazy? That's why we just watch Jane Austen *movies*."

Sadie suddenly missed her mother and grandmother.

Fifty-two

Vivian's garden, like the vineyard, was in peak bloom. Leah and Steven sat on a stone bench among the giant purple Gladiator alliums. With their thick stalks and fluffy tops Leah always thought they looked like something out of a Dr. Seuss book. She had not chosen the spot by accident; surrounded by her favorite flowers and with the sight of her childhood home in the near distance, she felt buffered for the conversation.

My terroir, she thought.

Leah didn't know if Steven had showed up because he missed her or because he was giving her an ultimatum to come home or because he wanted to end their marriage. The way things had been between them lately, any one of those scenarios was possible. Okay, maybe not the end of their marriage. But it seemed like at the very least a temporary separation might be on the table. Their child was grown and out of the nest, their physical relationship was lagging, and they didn't agree about what their shared future should look like. Yes, they'd had a brief honeymoon moment when she showed up at the apartment that morning. But it had been more of a truce than a turning point: nothing fundamental had been solved.

She'd often wondered why marriages ended for people in their fifties. It had always seemed like things must get easier after child-rearing and careers. But now she saw the perilous, less-obvious pitfalls of midlife relationships.

"So I'm guessing you're here to tell me that you've lost your patience with all of this. And I understand. I do. I love you, and at the same time I—"

Steven reached for her hand.

"I'm here to support you," he said.

"You are?"

"Don't look so surprised."

"Well, I mean, you haven't been happy about this. We've been apart most of the summer. And I'm not blaming you—it's just an observation."

"I can't say I haven't felt a little pushed aside. And no, I don't fully understand what you're doing. But I understand *why* you're doing it."

She realized her hands had been clenched, and relaxed. "That means so much to me, Steven. I'm sorry if you felt . . . abandoned. But this place . . ." She looked around, searching for the words.

"I know," he said. "You've always wanted to be part of the family business. I know that better than anyone. Maybe I should have told you to fight for this twenty years ago."

She shook her head. "I wasn't ready." But she was now, and she knew that her confidence came from all the years of running Bailey's Blue. One of the most important decisions she'd made about the shop came early on: she specialized. "I was thinking about the shop, and what worked and what didn't. One thing we did really right was the way we opened with just blue cheese."

He nodded. "It was an instant brand identity. It even gave us direction for what the store should look like—those blue accents everywhere. And the hats and aprons . . ."

"Exactly. That's what Hollander Estates needs: rebranding. We need to build our identity around something, and I think it should be rosé."

He nodded in agreement but looked pensive. He rubbed his jaw for a minute.

"I hate to be a naysayer here, but how can you build around a type of wine Hollander doesn't even produce?"

"We have to start. Remember that first night we were here at the beginning of the summer? My dad asked us what wine we wanted with dinner, and we both wanted rosé. *Everyone* wants rosé."

"Except for Leonard."

"Yes, well, he's going to have to get used to the idea. For a long time, he stood out for being the first. But that doesn't matter anymore. These days, people want what they want. Or they want the new, shiny thing."

Steven seemed to consider this.

"I think you're on to something," he said. "And you know what? Your drive, your excitement over this, turns me on."

He kissed her, and she felt butterflies in her stomach. Apparently, working on a plan for the vineyard turned her on, too. Or maybe it was just Steven—it had always been Steven. Their passion for each other had been dormant, waiting to rise back to the surface. They just needed to give it room to breathe, like a decanted wine.

Their kiss deepened, the distinct scent of her husband mingled with that of the nearby honeysuckle blossoms, a heady combination.

"Maybe we should take this inside," Steven said.

He didn't have to ask her twice. They dashed into the house holding hands, Steven making a "shh" gesture so they didn't draw attention to themselves. She giggled, feeling like a teenager trying to evade her parents.

She locked the bedroom door, desire pulsing through her like adrenaline.

They fell onto the bed, their bodies entangled in a dance of touch and taste that was achingly familiar but at the same time edged with the thrill of discovery. For Leah, it was rediscovery—not just of her husband but of herself.

Steven paused for a moment, taking her face in his hands. They were both breathing fast, and she wondered why he'd slowed things down. But then he kissed her and said, "I've missed you."

"I've missed you, too," she said.

He traced the arc of her neck down to her breasts with one finger, sending a shiver through body. Then, leaning back against the pillows, he pulled her on top of him. She guided him with her hand, her body swaying with the universal rhythm of couples throughout time.

Afterward, they lay side by side, breathless and not speaking. She reached for his hand, and he squeezed tight. She had herself. She had her husband.

Now she just needed to hold on to the winery.

Fifty-three

Vivian watched her husband take his traditional spot at the front of the tasting room with their son by his side. It was the place where Leonard always held the first production meeting of the season. It was at this meeting every year, in a room where the very air molecules seemed permeated with wine, where thousands of guests flowed in and out, where the bar was as much a source of information as it was for recreation—it was here that Leonard announced his plans for the grapes as they headed into harvest.

All around her, their employees sat with their morning coffee. It was a familiar sight with one big difference: this time, Leah and Steven were in the group.

"As I say every year, this is as much a celebration as it is a meeting," Leonard said, looking around the room. "You've done your work this summer, and now we wait, the sugar accumulating in the grapes as we speak. Pretty soon we'll be tasting the literal fruit of our labor, and I think the exceptional weather this summer will result in one of the best vintages in Hollander Estates' long, esteemed history."

The room burst into applause. It was unthinkable that—if not for her confession—the baron would have been there to impose himself on the proceedings, contradicting Leonard's plans or, worse, not letting Leonard lead the meeting at all. Despite the fact that her husband was still being frosty and distant with her, she knew she'd done the right thing. Maybe things did happen for a reason. Maybe her transgression three decades earlier had planted the seed that would save the winery in the end. It was almost worth it—except for her growing fear that her marriage wasn't going to recover.

Leah caught her eye and gave a wink. Vivian nodded at her. Oh, how she wanted to believe that Leonard had invited their daughter because he was truly open to what she had to say. The production meeting wasn't just Leonard's opportunity to share his plans for the grapes; it was also the chance for everyone to take a breath before they dove into the busiest months of the year. It was the one time when Leonard at least made the pretense of being open to suggestions. It was at a production meeting one year that someone had suggested switching to screw-on caps instead of cork. ("Blasphemy!" Leonard had said.) Javier had suggested a more modern method of bird netting. ("Put a pin in that one," Leonard had said.) Even though he shut down ninety-nine percent of all new ideas, she at least gave him credit for trying to create a forum for discussion. She just hoped Leah didn't have high expectations for how this would play out. She might get her say, but that would be the end of it. She'd tried to warn her when Leah told her that Leonard invited her to the meeting.

"I'm glad he made the gesture," Vivian had said, cautious not to get Leah's hopes up.

"No, Mom," she had said, shaking her head, her eyes bright. "It's different this time."

Leonard tested his pen on the whiteboard set at the front of the room.

"If the weather holds, we'll have plenty of time to reach ideal ripeness. Isn't that right, Javier?" he said.

"Last year we picked at nineteen brix. This year I think we can get to twenty-two or twenty-three," Javier said, referring to the sugar levels of the grapes.

"We'll be able to hang our hat on some top-quality reds," Leonard said.

Leah stood, and Vivian knew what was coming. She just hoped Leonard wasn't too brutal in shutting her down.

"I'd like to designate some of the reds for rosé production," Leah said.

All eyes in the room turned to Leonard. Asher was already shaking his head like, *What a glutton for punishment.*

"A Hollander rosé," Leonard said, as if considering it. "What do you think of that, Chris?"

Chris glanced at Vivian, and she shrugged.

"We could do a combination of the Merlot and Cab Sauv . . . it will really depend on the actual ripeness levels."

Vivian couldn't believe what she was hearing. Leah beamed, triumphant.

"Great. I have some more ideas in this direction, but we can talk about that later," Leah said. *Yes*, Vivian thought. *Quit while you're ahead.* She looked at Leonard, a small smile forming on her lips. Change was possible; from near disaster to a new dawn.

Their eyes met, and what she saw gave her a chill: Leonard was checked out. His gaze was vacant. He might have the entire room fooled, but not her. She knew her husband: he wasn't really agreeing to a rosé, he was just going through the motions.

She wondered if they were going to have any harvest at all.

⌒

Leah followed Mateo back to his office, along with Javier. She was on a high from her father's receptivity to the rosé idea, but she also knew this battle was far from won.

She closed the door, and Javier pulled out folding chairs.

"I can't believe it," he said, shaking his head. "Leonard swore off those blush wines in the eighties. We made too much, people stopped buying . . ."

"We can't get bogged down in the past," she said, and this went for herself, too. She thought of Billy Ikehorn Orsini. It was something the character grappled with towards the end of *Scruples*: Nothing *heals old wounds. They were waiting there, inside, ready to incapacitate her, each and every time a situation came up that thrust her back into the emotional atmosphere of the past.*

Leah was not an eight-year-old girl learning about plants at her father's knee. She was not a twenty-two-year-old woman being turned away from the family business. She was a wife, a mother, a businesswoman—and the possessor of a birthright that needed saving.

She had to remember, because today's meeting was just the first small piece of a complicated puzzle. It would only get harder from that point on. "My father being open to a rosé is a step in the right direction. But to save this vineyard we have to go further."

"Like doing what?" Mateo said.

"I want to produce *only* rosé," she said.

Javier shook his head and muttered, *"Loca . . ."*

"What about all of our whites?" Mateo said.

It was the obvious issue, and she'd thought it through. The solution came from what Sadie mentioned the night before she left for school.

"Sadie mentioned you have a contact who's looking to buy." At the mention of Sadie's name, Mateo averted his eyes. He probably wondered if she knew about their little summer romance. Poor Sadie. Every time she called or texted, she couldn't help but ask if Leah had "seen" Mateo, which was really just fishing to see if Mateo had asked about her. He had not. And, despite this obvious opening to do so, clearly he would not.

"My buddy at a vineyard down the road wants whites. But Leonard's always made it clear that's not the business he's in," Mateo said.

"A week ago you would have sworn he'd never do a rosé," Leah said. "So humor me: check in with your friend and see if he's still in the market." She paused, wondering how best to deliver the kicker. "And I need to know who you both think would be best to approach about buying reds."

Javier said something in rapid-fire Spanish.

"We can't bring in reds without losing the estates designation," Mateo said.

"I know." But what good was a point-of-pride designation if they were out of business? She didn't say that, though. It was understood.

Again, father and son consulted in Spanish. Her high school knowledge of the language was failing her; she'd fully intended to be fluent when she planned on working at the vineyard, but over the decades she'd lost most of her vocabulary.

She looked around the office, admiring the framed photographs on the wall. It took her a minute to realize that one was a close-up of the glass container used during their annual Harvest Circle. The photo on the wall was visually stunning in its close-up capture of the colors: yellow and pink and deep violet. But the real beauty was in the sentiment behind the image.

"Javier, what gave you the idea to use the natural flora for fermentation?"

"That came from my wife. Her family is *agricultura*, too."

Leah thought how lucky she was that Steven was willing to be by her side when Javier's wife had left the vineyard years earlier. It wasn't for everyone, and even those who understood its rhythms and demands didn't necessarily want to make the compromises.

The ones who remained, the one who believed—they were worth fighting for.

Fifty-four

Vivian, alone in the bedroom, heard something loud thumping down the stairs.

In the days since she confessed to Leonard about the baron, he'd moved into one of the guest rooms on the third floor. She didn't know what to do about it. She wished she had someone to talk to, someone to offer some advice.

Her mother had been gone for twenty years, and before that, they'd had a distant relationship at best. Lillian had never forgiven her for running off to a "godforsaken potato farm." But for the first time in a long time, Vivian wished she could talk to her.

Maybe that was why she'd found such joy in the novels she read. The voices of women writers filled the hole in her life where her mother's used to be.

The thumping noise continued. She pulled on her robe and stepped into the hallway to find Bridget dragging a suitcase down the stairs.

"Bridget, for heaven's sake, don't let that bump into the side of the banister; it will damage the wood. Get Asher to help you."

Bridget turned around, and her face was red and puffy, her eyes teary.

"What's wrong?" Vivian said, taking the steps down to her.

"Asher broke off our engagement," she sniffed.

"Why?"

Bridget started sobbing. Oh, this wouldn't do at all.

"Bridget, leave that suitcase there and come with me." She led her back to her bedroom and closed the door. She handed her a box of tissues and had her take a seat in one of the Georgian armchairs while she folded herself onto the other, just as she'd sat with Leonard when she told him about her indiscretion. She wondered if Bridget had a similar story, if she'd betrayed Asher. Vivian couldn't imagine any other reason why he would break off the engagement.

"Now, what's going on?" Vivian said.

Bridget pulled a lock of hair loose from her ponytail holder and began twirling it. "He said he can't marry me . . . under the circumstances."

"*What* circumstances?" Vivian said impatiently.

"Losing the winery."

Apparently, Asher wasn't fooled by Leonard's show of bravado at the production meeting, either. He anticipated the worst. Only Leah was under the illusion that the winery could be saved, but how long could that last? More urgently, she wondered why Asher broke up with his fiancée over it.

"What does the winery have to do with your engagement?"

"He said, quote, he has nothing to offer me and it's not fair to drag me down into these problems."

Vivian was surprised that her spoiled, self-centered son would make such a selfless gesture. But she was upset thinking that Asher believed his only value was tied to the fortune—or misfortune—of his family. As if he had no inherent value and Bridget was just with him for money. Was his self-esteem that low? And if it was, did it explain why he seemed to not even try to keep up with Leonard in the business?

Vivian realized she was guilty of this thinking herself. She'd stewed for months over her belief that Bridget was just a gold digger until, well, until the night of the book club, when she saw another dimension to the young woman.

"I told him that I was totally supportive of him—like, literally supportive. I'm making money from my influencer sponsorships," Bridget said.

Vivian still didn't understand what that meant, but nonetheless she got the spirit of it.

"I'm sure he appreciates that," Vivian said.

"No, he doesn't. Just the opposite. He said he could never live with the idea of his wife making the money."

"*What?*"

Where would Asher get such an outdated, sexist, ridiculous attitude? Looking around the room as Bridget dabbed at her face with more tissues, she found her answer in the family photos arranged on the sideboard. In frame after frame, Leonard stared back at her. Leonard.

Vivian shook her head and turned to Bridget, whose pale eyes were shadowed with smudges of makeup.

"I'll talk to him," Vivian said.

She might not have her own mother to go to for advice, but she was a mother herself. And it was time to give it. She never imagined she would willingly be in a position to try to save Asher's relationship with Bridget Muldoon, but that was exactly what she was going to do.

⌒〜〜⌒

Leah sat propped up in bed, leafing through the pages of *Scruples*. She'd gone back to reread the part where Billy realized her store was failing and had to accept an entire new direction from an outsider. At first, Billy thought she'd rather just shutter the whole thing than change course. But ultimately, Billy was her father's daughter:

Billy began to exercise her father's Winthrop characteristics: total dedication to a cause, stern self-discipline, the willingness to struggle toward achievement at all costs . . .

Leah was nervous to tell her father her ultimate strategy for the winery. But while he might be determined to say no, she was just as determined to change his mind.

She would ease into her ideas. First, she'd get him used to the idea of producing a rosé. Then, only after he was totally on board with that, she'd drop the real bombshell: All rosé. Only rosé. A vineyard catering to women.

The only question was timing. When to drop the bombshell?

"Sooner is better than later," Steven said, climbing into bed next to her.

"How soon?"

Steven pulled the book from her hands and leaned in to kiss her on the cheek. "He seemed receptive at the meeting today. And you said he'll be making plans with Chris about tank space soon."

He was right. Any delay was just stalling. There was no room for fear in this situation. Or, rather, there was no room to act or not act out of fear.

"I'm going to find him right now," she said, getting out of bed.

"Now? I didn't mean *now* . . ."

Leah tied her robe around her waist as she headed down the hall. She reached her parents' bedroom only to hear her mother deep in conversation with Bridget. Ordinarily, that would have given her pause, but she was completely focused on finding Leonard.

She checked all around the house and only noticed the pool deck light was on when she walked through the kitchen and saw it through the window.

Leonard sat in a lounge chair, a blanket over his lap, staring out into the distance. He held a tumbler of amber liquid in his hand. He looked ten years older than the man who had held court at the production meeting that morning.

"Dad," Leah said quietly, so as not to startle him. He turned to her slowly, seeming dazed. "Got a minute?"

He made a sweeping gesture with his arm, either indicating endless time or infinite space—it was tough to tell. Either way, she took it as an opening.

"Good meeting today," she said, sitting in the chair next to him.

The pool water rippled in the breeze, the color taking on a silvery cast in the moonlight. Leonard didn't say anything. He just looked at her, his dark eyes sunken and shrouded by the deep creases in his face.

Her father had always seemed indomitable, and even as she prepared to seize the chance to change the direction of the vineyard, a part of her still wanted to believe that he was.

"Dad, I have to be honest with you: we need to make a bold move. And that move should be all-in on rosé." So much for easing into the idea!

"Is that right?" he said, rubbing his jaw. Her father was always meticulously clean-shaven, but the past few days she'd noticed stubble, his face in perpetual white shadow.

"Yes," she said. "And that means producing *only* rosé, catering directly to the women—and increasingly large groups of women—who have been our primary customers all summer."

"Is that all?" he said. She couldn't tell if he was amused or aggravated. He sat straighter in the lounge chair and placed his glass on the ground by his feet.

She took a breath. "We need to sell our whites to bring in cash—and, Dad, this is the hard part—we need to buy reds to increase our production. I know that means we won't be an estates winery, but what we gain—"

"Enough." Leonard held up his hand.

She sank back in her chair, her heart pounding. At least she'd said it. She'd put it out there. Of course he wasn't going to agree right away. But she believed in her position, and she was willing and able to defend it, no matter how many tense conversations it took.

"I appreciate your candor," Leonard said. "And your thoughts—as misguided as they are. But now I must be honest with *you*."

"Okay," she said, frustrated but not surprised that his immediate response was to tell her how wrong she was.

"Even if you have the right strategy, which I doubt, we can't make it to the spring to find out."

"What do you mean?"

"The soonest we can sell the new vintage is roughly March. There's not enough money to get us there. Even if I sell the house, it could take months and we have no operational funds. Or anything else we might sell, we can't put our last dollars into a winery that can't sustain itself. As they say, you can't throw good money after bad."

"But . . . the meeting . . ."

He nodded, a pained expression on his face. "I wanted to believe differently. Up until this morning I still thought there was a way out. But the numbers tell me otherwise. And so I put on a show. For the staff. Maybe for myself."

She couldn't believe it. She was too late.

Maybe Steven was right: she should have asserted herself twenty-five years earlier. But unlike in the books she'd been reading, in real life, women let themselves be pushed aside. They acted like good girls. They didn't make waves.

That was why she loved those old novels so much: the heroines had balls. They didn't ask permission, and they didn't beg forgiveness. They were bosses. Fine, it was fiction. But why couldn't it also be a playbook?

Leah knew she should be sad. A part of her wished she could cry.

But she was too angry.

Fifty-five

When Asher didn't show up for breakfast, not even at his typical late hour, Vivian went up to his room. There, she found another unhappy person wrestling with a suitcase. Asher was messily unpacking a bag that still had clothes in it from a previous trip. A different suitcase, empty, was open on the bed.

Bridget, she understood. But where on earth did he think he was going?

"What are you doing?" she said, closing the door behind her.

"Mother, I need some space," he said.

When Vivian gave birth to a son, her firstborn, she had assumed he would be just like his father. She had been twenty-two years old, without any grasp of the reality that children are their own people from the moment they take their first breath.

To be fair, she wasn't alone in this. Leonard had clearly believed that all he would need to do was set his son loose in the fields, and the winemaking that was in his blood would do the rest to ensure that he grew up to be Leonard's right hand and heir apparent. But Vivian realized early on that Asher was much more like herself; his beauty made it tempting to be more decorative than productive. He was capable of working hard, but at the same time he resented it. Plus, it wasn't unusual for the son of an accomplished man to struggle in his shadow.

If they'd had a second son, none of this would have mattered. Leonard could have put all of his time and energy into grooming him. But they had a little girl. And yes, Leonard did invest a lot of time and care in teaching her everything—the same as her brother. The only difference had been his intention. Only his son was presumed to be a worthy heir.

How ironic that as farmers, she and Leonard took so long to understand that nature was stronger than nurture.

Vivian picked up a T-shirt from the floor. "Is this all laundry?"

"Mother, I've got it."

She looked around the room, considering how best to ease into the conversation she intended to have. "Where's Bridget? I haven't seen her this morning." No, she hadn't seen Bridget since she gave her a ride last night to her apartment in town, eliciting a promise that she not run off too far.

"I asked her to leave. I broke off the engagement," he said. "Please don't do that."

Vivian continued to retrieve clothes from the floor. It gave her something to do, an excuse to linger in the room. "I'm sorry about your engagement. I thought you were happy with Bridget."

"I am. I was."

She looked up at him. "So then why?"

He ran his hand through his hair. "Because I have to figure out my life—something I should have done a long time ago. But Dad wanted me here and made me believe this place would always be something to count on."

"And that was an easy route for you to take," she said. "I think if we're being honest, that is part of the equation."

"Fine. It might have been easy at first. But I'm paying for that now."

"Why are you overreacting? You were at the meeting yesterday. Your father is optimistic." Had he, too, seen beneath Leonard's veneer? Or had Leonard told him something he wasn't telling her?

"Optimistic? If he's listening to Leah and her ideas about rosé, I'd say he's acting desperate."

"That's not fair. And regardless of what you think of Leah's strategy, why are you punishing Bridget over it?"

"I'm not punishing her. I'm letting her off the hook. When I asked her to marry me, I thought we'd live here and help out at the winery and it would be a comfortable life. Now I don't know where I'll be in a few months."

"So? That's what marriage is—being together through good times and difficult times. If Bridget left you because of this situation, I'd say fine—let her go. But if she isn't bothered by it, then I say that's all the more reason to marry her."

"I can't believe what I'm hearing. You've been side-eyeing her for a year now and suddenly *she's* the prize?"

"Oh, Asher. Stop being such a child. If you two love each other, *that* is the prize."

It was true. And it was true for her own marriage as well. Winery or no winery, mistakes had been made on both of their parts. She could forgive Leonard all of his faults—if only he could find it in his heart to forgive her.

"How long can that last when I'm unemployed and she's making money? Would your marriage to Dad have worked like that?"

"Don't you think I wish I could step in now and offer a financial contribution to this situation? Don't you think your father would be relieved if I could? Maybe our partnership would have been stronger if I hadn't been relegated to the sidelines."

Asher seemed to consider this. She moved to the bed, sitting down and patting the spot beside her. He rolled his eyes but sat down.

"Asher, it takes a strong man to let a woman shine—not a weak one. That's why Steven is out here for your sister. And why you should stick with Bridget. I wish your father made more room for me. In this way, you can outdo him. You can be the better man."

Leah faced a room filled with dozens of women looking to be inspired by the wonders of wine and cheese. The class, assembled in the tasting room, looked at her expectantly while she struggled to focus. The conversation the night before with her father played over and over in her mind. When she told Steven about it, he didn't seem surprised. She could tell he didn't want to push her, but at the same time, he was ready to pack up and leave. He didn't say this, but she could tell he was thinking it. And who could blame him? The roller coaster was getting to her, too.

"I'd like to start by telling you a little bit about Hollander Estates and the differences between our North Fork wines and the wines produced on the West Coast. North Fork wines are relatively new. While there are several dozen wineries out here now, Hollander Estates was the first, founded in 1971 by my father, Leonard Hollander. I come from a long line of winemakers, starting with my great-grandfather in Argentina."

The assembled women clapped. And then, incredibly, one more person joined the class: her father. Leonard took a seat in the back, an inscrutable expression on his face.

"Vintage is very important for East Coast wines. Vintage refers to the fall when the grapes are harvested. Out here on the North Fork, that means a lot. There's a greater difference from year to year for our wines than for our West Coast counterparts. This is also true for Europe. We are at the mercy of the weather. Cooler temperatures mean the grapes retain more acidity and are very aromatic."

Hands shaking, she poured herself a glass of Viognier and took a sip. Was Leonard there out of curiosity? To give feedback afterward?

"Our first pairing today is the Pawlet cheese and the Viognier. We'll sample the cheese first. You'll notice it's yellow and firm. This is a washed-rind cheese. Now slice a small piece and smell it. Light, slightly meaty. The rind, by the way, is edible, as are the rinds of all cheese made in the US."

She waited while everyone tasted the cheese, some eating it right off the small knife, others coupling it with bread.

"For our wine pairing, we have Viognier. We began planting these grapes in the mid-nineties and planted them again four years ago. Viognier does not have to age, and so these grapes were picked less than a year ago. You'll note this wine is very clear, crisp, acidic. It was actually more clear at the start of the summer, and the Pawlet was a paler yellow at one point. One of many parallels between cheese and wine."

The class sipped the wine.

"Any thoughts?"

A woman raised her hand. "It's a little like Sauvignon Blanc."

Leah nodded. "It's made in a similar way as Sauvignon Blanc. Our seaside conditions here on the North Fork are perfect for these wines. While I'm pairing the Pawlet with white wine today, another option is . . ." Did she dare say what she really wanted to say? What she'd planned on saying before her father showed up? "Another option is to pair it with a rosé. Next summer, we will have our very first vintage of rosé to share with you."

The women nodded appreciatively and clapped. Leonard jumped up from his seat and walked to the front of the room. Her stomach churned.

"Ladies," he said to the room. "I'm Leonard Hollander. Welcome to Hollander Estates." He consulted the printout in her hands. "I see your next cheese is the Capri. Why don't you sample that while I borrow my daughter for a moment."

She followed him into the oak room.

"Can't this wait?" she said. Fine, maybe she'd gotten ahead of herself. But he couldn't just interrupt the class.

"Leah, I'm fine with you carrying on business as usual as long as we're open. But don't make promises we can't keep. It's only going to make things worse when this inevitably hits the press."

"You told me last night that you put on a show at the production meeting. So let me put on a show now." She crossed her arms.

He narrowed his eyes. "I really bet on the wrong horse, didn't I?"

What was that supposed to mean? That she had tenacity and Asher didn't? It was gratifying to finally have her competence acknowledged, but not at Asher's expense. She sighed. Even when her father was complimenting her, he still found a way to be divisive!

"Dad, let's not go there."

But yes, he had bet on the wrong horse. She wasn't going to make the same mistake. She was absolutely willing to bet on herself. The question was, how? What to do?

She returned to her classroom, taking in the group. Mentally, she reached back into her earliest experiences of the winery, as a little girl watching her mother gather with her friends. In the past few weeks, with her wine and cheese classes, in reaching out to book clubs, she had taken steps to make Hollander a destination for women looking for a communal experience. But if Hollander was truly going to be for women like the ones filling the room that afternoon, if the *wine* was really for them, then she had to make them a part of it in a real way.

And she had an idea just how to do it.

Fifty-six

"Your daughter has lost her mind," Leonard said, bursting into the kitchen. "She's out there telling people to expect a Hollander rosé next spring."

Vivian and Peternelle were in the midst of trimming a bunch of bright pink ranunculus. The round, tightly petaled blossoms were one of her favorites, but they didn't seem to have much staying power. Peternelle had just been explaining to Vivian that the soft-stem flowers needed only a little bit of water in the vase, and that was why they weren't lasting as long when Vivian prepared them herself.

Peternelle, sensing the incoming storm, made a hasty retreat, mumbled about forgetting something from the herb garden.

"Oh, you've scared her off," Vivian said. "She was just explaining to me how I'm mistreating my poor ranunculus."

"Did you hear what I said?"

"Yes, I heard you," Vivian said. "And I have news for you: your son has also lost his mind; he broke off his engagement over all of this."

"I don't see what any of this has to do with his engagement. And frankly, it's not our business. It's bad enough you got involved dragging Steven out here."

As far as she could tell, that was one of the few things she'd done right. She saw the spark back in Leah's eyes with Steven by her side at the production meeting.

"Fine. It's not our business. But what about us? Is our relationship going to end over this, too?"

"Don't be dramatic, Vivian."

"Well, then please stop giving me the cold shoulder. Move back into the bedroom."

"You put me in a terrible position. You put *us* in a terrible position."

"What if I didn't put us in a terrible position? What if this prevented us from taking the easy way out, and although it's going to be tougher in the short term, we'll be thankful—"

"No," Leonard said.

She moved closer to him, looking into his eyes.

"What's one of the first things you taught me about the plants?"

"I'm in no mood for games, Vivian."

She held on to his arm, keeping him from moving away. "That the vines that have to struggle for resources ultimately produce the best grapes."

His eyes softened. "I remember the first time I brought you out here to see the property. Just the empty fields. It was fall, leaves covering the ground. You looked at me like I was crazy."

"No I did not."

He nodded sadly. "You did. And I told you, just you wait and see. You trusted me. You gave it a shot. And I let you down. We let each other down."

She began to protest, to tell him that no one let anyone down—that their struggle, like that of the vines, could make them stronger. But he walked out as abruptly as he had swept in, leaving her alone.

Vivian filled a vase one-third of the way with water, arranging it with flowers. She hoped this bunch would survive.

The English department offices hummed with the particular energy of the first week of classes. Office hours were populated by students wholly optimistic about the start of their new school year. No one had yet failed an exam, or run late on a paper, or doubted that they would correct any bad habits from the previous semester. No one, it seemed, except for Sadie.

She climbed the stairs to the second floor, gulping the dregs from her nearly empty coffee cup. Dr. Moore's office door was open.

A call came in from her mother before she settled into her seat. Sadie was already nervous and fumbling; she felt like her entire academic future rested on this meeting—which in a way it did. She sent the call to voicemail.

"Good morning, Sadie," Dr. Moore said, smiling. She looked stylish as usual, dressed a burnt-orange-colored linen suit with chocolate brown oversize beads around her neck and gold hoop earrings. Sadie, in her baggy jeans and wrinkled V-neck, her unkempt hair pulled back with a bandana, felt like a slob. But the past week had been twenty-four/seven work mode. She didn't have time to worry about what she looked like.

"So," Dr. Moore said, flipping through the pages in front of her. "'The Peak of Literary Camp: Judith Krantz, Jackie Collins, and the Blockbuster Novels of the 1980s.'"

Once Sadie had the idea, writing the paper had been like running downhill. For the first time since she'd begun this agonizing project a year earlier, it formulated in her mind faster than she could type it. But ultimately, all that mattered was Dr. Moore's opinion.

"I know you struggled to get this off the ground. It's counter-logical, but I do find that some of my most talented students hit a wall at some point as undergrads, whereas students who have always struggled have a more even-keeled academic experience when they get here."

Oh, that didn't sound good. Dr. Moore was trying to let her down easy—as if that were even remotely possible. The coffee churned in her stomach.

"You have a distinct voice, and that's something that can't be taught," Dr. Moore said.

Sadie braced herself for the "but."

"But with this paper," Dr. Moore said, "you've gone beyond intelli-gence and voice. You've found a point of view."

"Wait—you like it?"

"I think you've got an excellent thesis on your hands. Keep going."

They were the words she'd wanted to hear for months. She was back on track. She could throw herself into her schoolwork: No writer's block. No pesky relationship. Nothing but Susan Sontag, Jackie Collins, and Judith Krantz for the foreseeable future.

Her phone chirped with a text from her mother.

I'm calling you—please pick up. Need to talk.

She looked up at Dr. Moore. "Um, can you excuse me for a minute?"

She slipped out into the hall to answer.

"Mom, I'm in a meeting. What's wrong?"

"Nothing's wrong. But I do need some help. Can you come back to the winery?"

❧

The sun set before dinner for the first time all season. Just one of the many signs that fall was right around the corner despite the fact that it was still close to ninety degrees out. Leah pulled her hair off her neck, into a ponytail, walking with Steven to the veranda.

He put his arm around her shoulder. "For the record, I think you're on to something. And I'm behind you one hundred percent."

Leah squeezed his hand.

She'd told him the idea that had come to her during the wine and cheese class. Now she was going to spring it on her father over dinner. In this setting, she would at least have her mother's support, and maybe even Asher would chime in with some of his own. Leonard would be outnumbered—not that it had ever swayed him before. But at the same time, for too long, none of them had had the nerve to stand up for new ideas.

"Having you here has made all the difference," she said. And it had: she was freed up to consider all of her options with the winery. She was able to take professional risks because she didn't feel like she was taking a personal risk just being there. "So . . . thank you."

He kissed her, and as they hurried on, she had a moment of déjà vu, back to the first night they showed up at the house for their vacation and rushed to the veranda. She felt a pang, a sort of nostalgia, for her innocence in that moment. She'd believed her family home and the winery would always be there for her, something she could take for granted. Yes, ignorance was bliss. But at least now, under the threat of losing it all, she'd made room for herself. She was taking ownership in a way she never could have if things were running smoothly. For all the cracks, they did create an opening.

Her parents and brother were already seated. Leah was happily surprised to see Bridget back by Asher's side. Maybe that was at least one family issue resolved.

The table was dressed with a blue cotton runner and set with several vases of pink and blue ranunculus. Her mother wore a white sheath dress and pearls, a pink Hermès scarf perfectly picking up the accent of the flowers. If appearances were everything, her family wouldn't have a care in the world.

"I just opened the Viognier," Leonard said, filling glasses. "Would you like some?"

"Sure. Thanks, Dad," said Leah.

Peternelle set out Boston lettuce salad with blanched, salted Marcona almonds. Leah wouldn't be able to eat until she'd had her say. Leonard stood at the head of the table:

"Cheers, everyone."

"Cheers," Leah murmured in chorus with the rest of the family. Then she stood as well. "I've been thinking about the harvest . . ."

"Leah, it's been a long week. I'd like to relax over dinner. No work talk," Leonard said.

"Yes, let's enjoy just being together as a family," Vivian said.

Leah glanced at Steven, and he nodded her on. She took a sip of her wine, then continued. "You know, all these years of living in the city, one thing I still miss is the first day of harvest. The way the air smells. The way everything feels sort of electric—all that anticipation of the hard work ahead. And my favorite thing of all is the end of the first day, when it's almost dusk and everyone gathers to add things to the freshly pressed Chardonnay juice."

"Oh, we did that last year," Bridget said, turning to Asher. "Remember I added that pebble from the dock where we met?"

"It's a great tradition," Leah said. "And I want to share it more widely."

Leonard glared at her.

Vivian cleared her throat. "Leah, you heard what your father said."

Leah shot her mother a look. What happened to her wanting Leah to help save the winery? What happened to her belief in her ideas? Maybe her primary concern now was simply saving her marriage, and that meant being Team Leonard no matter what.

"Yeah, just chill for once," Asher said.

"'Chill'? Oh, babe, that expression is so nineties," Bridget said.

"Technically, it's probably from the eighties," Asher said.

Leah could see that there was no way anyone at the table was going to jump in to support her. She would have to switch gears.

"Well, as much as I'd love to 'just chill,' I wanted to make this suggestion while we're all together. Since it seems that we're in sort of uncharted territory here, I was wondering, Dad, if you'd let me host the Harvest Circle this year. I have some people I'd like to invite—just for the fun of it."

"What people?" Leonard said. "The whole point of the Harvest Circle is that our employees who spend the fall harvesting the wine are included in a ceremonial way. It gets them emotionally invested. That's the purpose."

Exactly, Leah thought. *So why not offer it to the people who will potentially be buying the wine?* She wanted to reach out to every group of women who had visited the winery over the summer and invite them to bring something from their home or garden to contribute to the starter yeast for their first vintage of Hollander rosé. The wine would be for them, and in this small way, also by them. It would be truly theirs—something they might even care enough about to preorder. It was something businesspeople called "proof of concept," and it might be just enough to convince her father not to give up. But that wasn't something she could explain to him. It was something she just had to make happen.

"Look, I'm asking if I can run with it this year. It's something I always dreamed of, and this is probably my last chance. It would mean a lot to me."

"Are you including the employees?"

"I want it to be only women," she said. "So no. Unless Peternelle wants to join in." The employees might be upset to miss out on what might be the final Harvest Circle. But this was what she needed to do to make sure it *wasn't* the last.

"This is crazy talk, Leah. The Harvest Circle isn't for entertainment," Leonard said.

"Leonard, with all due respect, she's never asked you for anything since the day she left this winery. Can you just consider this?" Steven said.

This seemed to give Leonard pause. He turned to her. "Just a few friends?"

"Absolutely," Leah said. "Just a few friends."

Fifty-seven

Leah converted the estate's unused stables into a makeshift office—a sort of war room for outreach and planning for the Harvest Circle. It was the one space that was large enough for the assembled team to get some work done while being out of the way enough that Leonard wasn't likely to intrude.

Steven helped her move a large folding table and chairs from the barn and bought portable chargers for their phones and laptops. She ordered a whiteboard, put it on a stand, and moved a bunch of fans from the house. At noon, heat was battling the whirring standing fans and winning.

The invite list was close to one hundred women, and Leah considered that number just the beginning. The more people who attended the event, the greater their chance of presales.

It was a lot to mobilize in a short amount of time. Still, calling Sadie to come help had been impulsive. Realistically, they could manage without her. Leah had just wanted her there for emotional reasons, but that wasn't a good enough reason to pull her away from school.

"I'm sorry—you really don't have to come," she'd said in another phone call, this one directly after the dinner when her father okayed the plan. But it was too late: Sadie was all in.

Now she was busy helping Steven sort out the Hollander Estates mailing list and the reservation log from the past few months.

"Any luck with that book club from Virginia?"

"I left a voicemail," Sadie said.

"So we have our book groups here." Leah made a circle on the whiteboard. "Our cheese class list, our email list from the guestbook they keep in the tasting room, and the emails from the newsletter list. When is the e-vite going to be ready to go out?"

"I'm almost finished with it," Bridget said from her corner. She was hunched over a laptop working in a graphic design application.

Leah still didn't have the full story of the reconciliation between her brother and Bridget, but she could see that Asher finally believed what Bridget had told Leah the day she was crying in the oak room: She didn't care about Asher's money. She didn't care about leaving the winery. She only cared about him.

"We're still missing a bunch of emails," Sadie said. "I'm working on the customers that only gave us phone numbers."

Hollander's weakness in maintaining a reliable mailing list was showing. Leah needed to act quickly; with just a few weeks to go before harvest, they had to give people enough time to plan if they wanted to attend the event. She and Steven had talked about how it was all very much a numbers game: realistically, only a fraction of the women they invited would actually show up, and only a fraction of *them* would preorder the rosé. So the more they started out with, the greater the odds of that final fraction generating enough sales to make an impact.

A flash of green entered Leah's field of vision.

"What's going on here?" Vivian strode into the stable, dressed in head-to-toe emerald: green blouse, green skirt, and a green straw hat.

"Gran, what's going on with *you*?" Sadie said. "That's a serious monochrome color commitment."

"This is camouflage," Vivian said. "I had to follow Steven here, slinking around the grounds like a criminal on my own property, since I've been excluded from . . . well, from whatever this is."

Leah sighed. "Mom, I was going to loop you in. But we wanted to get things started."

"Get what started?" She lifted her sunglasses and squinted at the whiteboard.

"We're getting our invitation list together for the Harvest Circle."

"I thought you were just inviting a few friends."

"It's a little . . . broader than that."

"What do you mean?" Vivian said.

Leah and Steven exchanged a look. "Do you really want to know? Because when Dad gave me a hard time over dinner the other night, you backed him up."

"I didn't back him up, Leah. I'm just trying to keep the peace. We've all been through enough."

Leah nodded. "Fair enough. But I don't want him involved. So if you feel caught in the middle you should probably leave."

"Well, I certainly can't leave now. Not without knowing what you're up to."

"Fine," Leah said. "If you really want to know, we're holding a 'preferred customer' Harvest Circle. Anyone who comes will get an exclusive chance to preorder our first vintage of Hollander rosé."

"How can they buy wine we don't have?"

"That's why I said *pre*order."

"Why would they do that?" Vivian crossed her arms.

"That's the second part of the idea: we're telling everyone to bring something from their home garden or other place that's meaningful to them. And we're going to hold a giant Harvest Circle, and everyone will get to contribute to our starter yeast. I'm hoping they'll find this unique and inspiring, and that they all want to make sure they get a bottle when it's available."

"Leah! It's a good thing your father hasn't caught wind of this. What happens when we aren't able to make the rosé that these customers paid for?"

"We can always refund money. But if we don't at least try something different, we'll definitely never get to next spring. This at least gives us a fighting chance."

Vivian turned to Steven. "And you support this idea?"

"I do," he said.

"I do, too," Bridget said from the corner.

Vivian removed her hat and began fanning herself. "Everyone's lost their senses."

Steven shook his head—her mother, dramatic as always.

"Mom, we need to reach out to as many women who've visited this place as possible—even ones who haven't. I'll show you our list, and you let me know if I've forgotten anyone."

Sadie looked up from her laptop. "I can think of one person we should invite. Not because she'll buy the wine but because she should be here."

"Who?" Leah said.

"Mateo's mother. This ceremony was her idea in the first place."

"Maria Eugenia? Oh, she left for Guatemala a long time ago," Vivian said. "She didn't like it here."

"She didn't like it here because there was no place for her. Just like there wasn't a place for *my* mother," Sadie said. "I think we should invite her and offer to fly her in for it. To thank her. If we're really truly looking to make female contribution a thing around here."

Leah knew Sadie was right. And from the look on Vivian's face, she did, too. For too long, they'd all been second-class citizens, going back to the day when Leonard fired their one female employee: Delphine. What had been her great sin? Hooking up with a wine buyer or two from their restaurant accounts? Her father never would have fired a man for that—at least, not back in the eighties. It had been the usual, old-fashioned double standard.

She didn't share this thought with the group. This invitation was one she would pursue privately; the connection to the baron would freak out Vivian, and understandably so. But the truth was, Delphine had also been a victim of Henri de Villard. He'd cast her out of her home just as Leonard had cast her out of Hollander Estates. All that was missing was the scarlet letter.

Sadie was right: if they were going to create a new era at Hollander Estates, it was time to correct the mistakes of the past.

⌒

The library was at its most majestic at night. When sun-filled, the room had a charm, an allure that suggested hours of reading curled up in a chair. But at night, the space beckoned discovery. It promised there was magic to be found among the stacks.

And there had been; Sadie's inspiration for her thesis had been discovered there. She tapped her pen on the table, looking up at the winding narrow stairs that led to the second-level shelves.

The room was also one of the few places at the vineyard that didn't remind her, with every rustling tree and warm breeze and sunset, of Mateo. It took all of her willpower and self-respect not to seek him out. She'd caught a few glimpses of him from afar, and every time she was useless for a solid few hours afterward.

She flipped through her dog-eared, Post-it-noted copy of *Scruples*, trailing her finger along the highlighted passages she was using as support text in her paper. She skimmed over a section she wasn't using but one that jumped off the page given her current state of mind: *She was no Emma Bovary, no Anna Karenina, no Camille—no spineless, adoring, passive creature who would let a man take away her reason for living by taking away his love.*

Damn right, Sadie thought. Still, the sooner she got back to campus, the better. Why torture herself? She gave her mother some help, now it was time to go. The thing was, she felt oddly torn between the two places. Before now, missing classes for any reason was unthinkable. But the vineyard felt more real and urgent than her life at school. She wanted to be a writer, and to be a writer she had to experience things. The creative juice she needed would not be found in the pages of a book—at least, not all of it.

"Sadie."

She jumped at the voice behind her. Mateo's voice. Incredulous, she turned around. He stood in the doorway, dressed in his usual jeans and a T-shirt, tan and achingly beautiful.

He walked toward her, and it seemed to happen in slow motion.

She stood up. "What are you doing here?"

"Your mother told me this was where I might find you."

Sadie processed this: He'd asked her mother about her? Did he specifically track Leah down, or did they just happen to run into each other? It didn't matter. Either way, she and Mateo were talking for the first time since the night she'd stood in the pouring rain, only to have him blame her for her grandfather's mistakes. And yes, she had made a slightly obnoxious comment about being published in *The New Yorker*. Clearly not the finest moment for either one of them.

"You spoke to my mother?" she said.

"I did. And your mother just spoke to *my* mother."

That didn't compute for a moment, but then she realized her mother had taken her suggestion to invite Maria Eugenia to the Harvest Circle. Mateo confirmed this. "And Leah offered to fly her in. She said it was all your idea."

Sadie nodded.

"What made you do that?" he said.

"I kept thinking about the photo in your office," Sadie said. "The one she took of the flowers in the wine. Also, what you said the day you told me about her."

"What did I say?"

"That she has a feminist heart." If there was one thing Sadie had learned that summer, it was that feminism took all different forms.

He smiled. "Well, I wanted to thank you. It was a really thoughtful gesture."

"I've missed you," she blurted out.

"Sadie . . ."

"I know, I know—my grandfather, your father, the sale of the winery. I'm just saying . . ." She crossed her arms, trying to stay measured even as her emotions bubbled up to the surface. Feelings she'd been trying to bury in schoolwork. In reading. In a campus book club that didn't get off the ground. "I thought being back at school would help me forget about you. But it hasn't. And what I said about *The New Yorker*? Writing isn't as important as what you're doing here. I create stories, but you create life."

He looked down at the ground, taking a long pause before responding. When he finally spoke, his voice was quiet. "For the record, I wasn't blaming you for what's happened with the winery. I was, in a clumsy way, trying to explain that it's complicated. Too complicated—especially since we have totally different lives."

She swallowed hard.

"I mean, our lives aren't that different. I'm here now, trying to help my mother save this place. And if things work out, I'll be back more often. I want to be here. Not just because it's where my family lives. Great writers are a part of something larger than themselves. That photo in your office of the man writing in chalk on the building to represent the lost of Guatemala—his art means something. It's not just academic or intellectual. I want my life and my work to mean something, too. So if we can keep this place in the family, I want to come back as much as possible. And even if that doesn't happen, well, I still want to open up my life more. And maybe, I don't know, you and I can hang out. I want to try. Don't you?"

It was hard to lay her feelings so bare in front of him, but it would be even harder to keep them unspoken and always wonder, what if? If he didn't feel the same way, at least she knew she had done all she could. She would know the ending would not be her fault.

He moved closer, touching a lock of her hair, his eyes searching her face. She held his gaze until he finally leaned forward to kiss her gently on the lips. She threw her arms around him, pulling him against her. Their kiss deepened. This was it, Sadie thought. This was love. This was her man. The rest of her life would have to fit around this.

"I guess I should have known I wasn't coming here just to thank you," he murmured. "I missed you, too. And yes, I want to spend more time together. We'll figure it out."

"No time like the present," she said.

"Oh, yeah?"

"I've always wanted to have sex in a library." And by "always," she meant suddenly—right in that moment.

"Very funny," he said.

"I'm serious."

"Someone could walk in," Mateo said.

"They won't," Sadie said. But just to be safe, she grabbed his hand and led him up the narrow winding stairs to the second level. Sadie's eyes immediately went to the shelf where she'd found the books, all now returned to their spots: *Lace. Scruples. Chances.* If she hadn't read those novels, would she be standing there with Mateo? Would she have figured out a thesis? She didn't know. But she suspected her life would look very different without the words written by those bold women so long ago.

"Here?" he said, looking at the floor space between the banister and the bookshelves.

"Yeah," she said.

"I've got a lot to learn about you, Sadie Bailey. I've never seen this side before." He started kissing her again. "But I like it."

They fell to the ground, and she laughed, feeling a thrill as if on the dip of a roller coaster. Mateo slipped his hand under her T-shirt, and her heart beat wildly.

Mateo kissed her neck, sighing with pleasure, pulled her T-shirt over her head. Sadie marveled at the curve of his jaw, his long dark lashes on his cheeks, the lock of hair falling across his forehead. As his hand moved between her thighs, she luxuriated in their surroundings, wondering if there had ever been a better use of a library. It was hot. It was forbidden.

It was just like something out of a trashy novel.

Fifty-eight

A winemaker's true genius reveals itself the moment he or she calls for harvest to begin.

Leah had grown up watching her father make that decision at the end of every summer, like a magician, reading the grapes for that moment. For the first time since her girlhood, she'd spent the past few weeks with him as he walked the vineyard acres, tasting the grapes, examining the skin thickness, the berry texture, all of his senses exquisitely tuned to the fruit.

If they picked too early, the tannins would be bitter. If they waited too long, the sugar levels could get too high, leaving them with "flabby" wine. While Leonard had made a few bad business decisions, mistiming a harvest had never been one of them.

He finally made the call in late September. They would begin, as always, with the Chardonnay.

Sadie arrived from school the night before and was up at dawn to work side by side with Mateo and Javier and the rest of the field crew picking the Chardonnay grapes. Harvesting the grapes was not a high-tech operation; everyone went to work with their handheld clippers and bins. They started as early in the day as possible, when it was still relatively cool. If skins accidentally broke on their way from the field to the winery, they could begin to ferment if conditions were too hot.

When the grapes were transported from the sorting table—where the team pulled out damaged grapes or leaves—to the crusher-destemmer machine, Leah and Vivian focused on final preparations for the Harvest Circle.

They'd lost count of the RSVPs, but it was somewhere between two hundred and three hundred women. Her parents' failure to maintain a consistent customer database led to their outreach being disjointed; some customers were reached by phone, some by email, some by snail mail. Regardless of how they managed to reach people, the message had been the same: *Come celebrate with us: this wine is for you.*

The biggest hurdle had been convincing her father to relinquish his usual place at the ceremony.

"You're asking me, the head winemaker, not to come to possibly the last Harvest Circle ceremony at my own vineyard? I know that you're still upset that I didn't welcome you into a position here when you were younger, but this is just petty . . ."

"Dad, I'm not upset. It's not that I don't want you there. But I need to offer a very specific experience to these customers in order to get the results we need. I'm asking you to trust me." He had agreed. Maybe it was because the grapes were looking like the best crop in a decade and he wanted desperately to get them to market, maybe it was because his damaged ego wanted to prove the baron wrong, or maybe it was because he actually did trust her. She didn't know, and it didn't matter. The important thing was that he wouldn't stand in the way of her putting the plan into action.

By dusk, the veranda was lit by candles and filled with the backdrop of her mother's favorite album, Carole King's *Tapestry*, playing over the sound system. It was as festive and lovely as Leah had ever seen it.

Peternelle's buffet included late-summer favorites: goat cheese tarts, Brussels sprout salad, corn on the cob, steak skewers, and lettuce wedges with blue cheese. White wine chilled in silver ice buckets, and the air smelled like the fresh-cut asters and chrysanthemums from Vivian's garden.

But appearances, as the saying went, could be deceiving. None of the guests arriving would ever guess that the entire winery was at stake. The truth was, Leah wouldn't know until the end of the evening if they had just celebrated a new beginning or bade Hollander Estates a grand farewell.

Vivian stood at the foot of the veranda steps, greeting each guest. Her mother, always elegant, had outdone herself for the occasion, wearing a billowing Alexander McQueen dress in pale pink organza with embroidered flowers. Bridget, off to the side, photographed all the arrivals. The women showed up in waves, in groups and alone, all carrying a little piece of home to contribute to the ceremony. Leah was touched to see many familiar faces: Roya Lout from the cheese shop with her mother and her mother's book club, women from the wine and cheese classes, Anouk the real estate agent, and many people she'd seen taking selfies with her mother on that very spot during the course of the summer. But one familiar face—both familiar and strange at the same time—stood out from the crowd: Delphine Fabron.

Leah had found her through social media, happily living in Boston with her husband—one of the restaurant wine reps she had gotten fired for sleeping with those many years earlier.

Delphine appeared on the steps of the veranda swathed in a black cashmere cape and wide-legged black pants. She wore high Louboutins, and her formerly gleaming dark hair, now a striking white silver, loose over her shoulders. The only blight on her otherworldly beauty was the creases around her mouth that signified her as a lifelong cigarette smoker. Leah remembered the days when her parents constantly admonished her not to smoke near the oak room, that the cigarettes would "blunt" the wine.

"It does not hurt us in France," she used to say. Delphine, the rebel. Delphine, the first woman to be cast out of the winery. She herself was the second. Now they were reunited.

"Thank you so much for coming," Leah said, leaning in to accept Delphine's double-cheek air kiss.

"Little Leah!" she said in the same lyrical accent that had so delighted Leah as a girl. "Hearing from you . . . life is just full of surprises."

Vivian stepped forward to embrace her. "I never stopped thinking about you," she said.

"Nor I you," Delphine said, still with a smile that hinted at mischief. "Read any good books lately?"

Leah and Vivian shared a look.

"Actually, we both have," Leah said. "And we'd love to talk to you about it later." She checked her phone. Sadie still hadn't returned from her trip to JFK to meet Maria Eugenia's flight. She couldn't start the ceremony without them. More important, she couldn't finish without them: Leah planned to have everyone take seats after the Harvest Circle ceremony. She would give a speech about offering them an exclusive chance to preorder a case of the rosé they would make from that night's starter yeast, and conduct a Q&A about harvest and winemaking. Sadie would go around with her digital credit card reader and process any orders they might get.

She checked her phone; Sadie texted that they were still twenty minutes away because of traffic on the Long Island Expressway.

"Let's get these bottles poured," Leah said to her mother and Peternelle, who was one step ahead as always and had a full tray of Cabernet Franc. The air filled with the sound of corks popping, the fizz of sparkling white filling flutes, and the buoyant laughter as people greeted one another.

"A toast," Leah said, climbing up to stand on a chair and raising her glass. "To friends, to harvest, to the next great vintage of Hollander Estates wine that will be in no small part possible because of all of you here tonight."

Everyone raised their glasses with big smiles, unaware of how literally she meant her words.

Fifty-nine

They formed a circle under a blanket of darkness, the only light coming from the star-filled sky, the full moon, and the flickering candles. The evening had cooled from the low eighties to the seventies, and a breeze blew in off the water.

The ring of women around the veranda was two-deep, and in the center, a table with a large glass jug filled with freshly pressed Chardonnay juice. It was the same carboy her father had been using every year since she was little, as the tiny chips around the rim and scuffs along the sides reminded her. Leah stepped forward, looking at the happy, expectant faces surrounding her. Only her mother looked tense.

"Promising a vintage of rosé is just going to make it that much more humiliating when we announce the closing," Vivian told Leah in the days leading up to the harvest. She was always so worried about surface appearances, she missed opportunities to make fundamental changes. There was no room for that kind of thinking anymore.

And it was up to Leah to prove that.

"I'm happy to see so many familiar faces here," she said. "Thank you for joining us to celebrate the most special time of year at the vineyard, the harvest. I'm always reminded at harvest that a fundamental element of wine is terroir, or taste of a place." Leah had spoken the words countless times over the years during her classes. But they had never meant more to her.

She'd read somewhere that a person could change everything about herself except her place of origin. And she'd seen this truth about the human condition play out in the book club novels: the heroines of each story managed to reinvent themselves, but they were always driven by their childhood experiences. Billy Ikehorn Orsini, no matter how rich and famous she became, was always a shy, overweight girl inside. Lucky Santangelo, no matter how powerful, was still the girl who lost her mother. And Leah, no matter how happy or successful in her life in Manhattan, was still the girl who had stood in that very spot, watching her glamorous mother with her friends, dreaming of the day when she would be a part of the winery herself.

She took a deep breath. "Hollander's very first vintage of rosé will have a terroir created in part by the places that mean the most to all of us. And since your contributions tonight will literally help create this vintage, we're offering exclusive presales of the Hollander rosé at the conclusion of the ceremony." The women nodded, a few murmurs in the crowd. "Now, before we get started I want to say that the tradition we're sharing tonight was started by our special guest, Maria Eugenia Argueta. Maria, along with her husband, Javier, began our practice of all contributing something to the starter yeast. And because of that, I'd like her to do the honors of adding the first item to the grape juice."

Maria Eugenia was no taller than five feet, with deep-set black eyes that were still bright and sharp. Her salt-and-pepper hair was thick and wavy, tied back in a loose knot. She looked reluctant to step forward. Of course—the woman had just flown in from another country. Leah hadn't meant to put her on the spot; she just wanted to give credit where credit was due.

Slowly, Maria Eugenia moved to stand beside Leah. Camera phone flashes went off, and Bridget climbed onto a bench to start shooting.

"Tonight, I give something from the garden outside my husband's house here, the home where we started our family." She placed a smooth white stone into the pot.

She returned to her place in the circle, and Vivian stepped forward. She was *not* reluctant to be the focus of attention. Her flawlessly tailored dress moved along with her like liquid, the gold necklace at her throat glinting in the candlelight. Surrounded by people on the veranda, her vast life's work on display everywhere Leah could possibly turn to look, Vivian was in her element. She looked every bit the matriarch, the Earth Mother as declared on the cover of *Town & Country* all those years earlier. She was finally back center stage at her winery, where she belonged.

"My husband and I moved out here nearly fifty years ago when this land was a potato farm," she said. "His family were vintners back in Argentina. Coming to the North Fork, I hoped we would build something that our children could continue. Something that could be shared for generations. Tonight, you've all become part of the future of Hollander Estates. And I thank you so much for being here."

The crowd applauded, and Vivian's lower lip trembled. Taking a breath, she said, "The first fruit we planted was our grape crop. But I had a real yearning for apple trees, and so we planted those next, knowing they would take years to bear fruit. And this apple I'm holding is the fruit of that tree."

Sadie helped her steady the apple to cut off a slice, and Vivian dropped it into the grape juice.

One by one, their guests stepped forward and shared their offerings. Sadie contributed a leaf from outside her dorm: "Bringing my two worlds together." Delphine brought a crust of bread from one of the restaurants she owned with her husband. Leah added a piece of rind from the English Wensleydale cheese she'd first spotted the day she told Steven she wasn't returning to New York City. The first day she admitted to herself that her heart had never left those green fields.

When the circle was complete, the contents of the glass jug resembled a bizarre sort of white sangria, the grape juice inside now mixed with flowers and fruit, small stones and twigs. The most interesting part would come over the next twenty-four hours, when fermentation would start. The juice would begin to look fizzy, with fine, tiny bubbles. Her father had taught her that this was not carbonation but "effervescence." After a few days they would remove all the things they'd added to the juice, strain it using a colander and cheesecloth, and then take a cup of that fermenting juice and add it to steel tanks. But for now, they just had a colorful concoction that held the promise of what was to come.

Vivian stepped forward one more time, clanging her glass until the buzz of the crowd quieted down.

"I want to thank you again for your contributions here tonight. A wise friend once told me, when women gather, there is power." She turned to look at Delphine, then back to the wider crowd. "And I've never felt that more strongly than I do standing here with all of you."

The women broke into applause, and then the circle closed in, its members gathering around Vivian and Leah, pulling wallets out of their handbags, happily snapping photos of the glass jug, and asking, "Is there a limit to how many cases we can order?"

With her adrenaline pumping, Leah waved Sadie forward to organize a line and start processing the sales. Suddenly, in the shadows of the veranda, she spotted Mateo and Javier. Of course—they couldn't wait to see Maria Eugenia. Leah beckoned them over, welcoming them. Mateo took quick, long strides to reach his mother, who laughed with delight at the sight of her husband and son. She hugged them both for a long minute, then turned excitedly to Vivian.

"Mrs. Hollander," she said to Vivian. "I left this winery years ago, thinking my work here was done. My son was grown. When I got the phone call inviting me back, well, I originally just wanted to come to see my son and husband. But standing now with all of you, I see the reason for being here. Just because our children are grown, we are not done. Just because we are older, we are not done. I look at what you and your daughter and granddaughter are doing, and I think: the best is ahead."

They embraced. Leah looked over at Mateo, but he was already heading over to help Sadie. He touched her shoulder, and the joy on her daughter's face when she turned around nearly brought tears to Leah's eyes.

That was when she noticed that Sadie wasn't the only one getting support from her man: Leonard headed across the veranda straight for Vivian. He put a tentative arm around her mother. Together, they watched the buying frenzy.

Leah felt a pang that Steven wasn't there to witness it. She pulled her phone out and texted him, *Can you come down to the veranda?* She waited while the dots appeared, and then:

Do you think I would miss your big moment?

He stepped out from the bushes just off the veranda steps. She hurried over to him.

"So you've been spying on me," she said, smiling.

"Of course. I never know what you'll get yourself into when we're apart." He hugged her. "I'm proud of you."

She leaned into him, experiencing a flash of memory. It was something he said to her back in the spring, standing behind the counter of the cheese shop.

Change can be a good thing.

⌒

The view from the bedroom window was, for the first time in months, a source of pleasure instead of worry. Vivian stared out into the darkness; although she couldn't see the fields, she was met by the bright half-moon. In the morning, she would open the curtains and look out at the vines, heavy with grapes, confident that the view would be hers for some time to come.

"Vivian, come to bed," Leonard said. She turned to find him already

tucked under the covers. It had only been a short time since he returned to her bed, and it was still a relief every time she saw him in his
rightful place.

"I'm too wound up to sleep," she said, well aware that it was close to
eleven. The Harvest Circle had turned into a party that lasted for hours.
Even the considerable amount of wine she'd consumed in celebration
wasn't enough to quell her energy.

"I feel the same," Leonard said.

She walked over to his side of the bed and reached for his hand.

"Come with me," she said.

"Where?"

"Night swimming," she said, fully anticipating his rebuff. To her
surprise, he climbed out of bed. "Really? You're coming?"

"As soon as I change into my trunks," he said.

"Don't change—let's just be spontaneous."

Again, he didn't protest. Vivian hurried them both down the stairs
and outside before he could change his mind.

The late-summer temperatures held in the seventies. In just two
days it would officially be fall, and pretty soon after that Leonard would
pull out the tarp for the season. It might be one of their last evenings
by the pool.

Usually, she wondered where the summer had gone. But this year,
she could account for every day, every hour of worry. Thanks to Leah,
she could put that behind her. Leah, and also Leonard—for being open
to change.

Untying her robe, she inhaled deeply. She felt a tremendous weight
off her shoulders, and she knew it wasn't just her newfound hope for
financial stability; it was being unburdened of her secret about the
baron.

Leonard pulled an upright chair to the edge of the pool. She pulled
off her peignoir and waded into the heated water up to her shoulders.

"You really are in a spontaneous mood tonight," he said.

"Come in—the water's heavenly."

Leonard hesitated. "I'm afraid I'm not as unconstrained as you, Vivian." He smiled. "I'm just here to keep you company."

She swam over to the side and held on to the ledge, looking up at him. He was more relaxed than she'd seen him in a long time. Deeply tanned, his white hair in need of a trim, he was as attractive to her as ever. What had led to her moment of betrayal all those years earlier? Maybe, like many women with young children, she'd felt her own needs become invisible. Maybe, because Leonard was consumed with the winery and shut her out of the decision-making, she'd felt neglected or bored or frustrated. Either way, it was one moment of weakness that she was just now able to put behind her.

"I'm sorry I didn't tell you sooner about what happened with the baron," she said. "I was afraid. And I didn't want to hurt you. And I didn't want you to hate me. I just hope you know . . . that nothing like that ever happened again. I love you, Leonard. And I have since the first night I saw you."

Leonard stood, and for a panicked second she thought he was leaving. But then he unbuttoned his pajama top and stripped down to his boxers before jumping into the pool with a splash. He surfaced, shaking his wet hair from his eyes.

"You're right—the water's perfect," he said, swimming over to her.

"So much for you not being spontaneous," she said, delighted. He touched her shoulder, his face turning serious.

The water rippled between them. She sensed her heart beating in her chest, her every breath feeling amplified like it always did in the pool.

"Vivian, I wish you'd told me sooner about the baron—not for my sake, but for yours. You didn't need to carry this alone all these years. I'd have ended the partnership back then myself if you'd told me the truth—not to punish him, but to keep you safe. And I certainly never would have allowed him back. My biggest regret is that you felt you couldn't confide in me, so I couldn't do my most important job: taking care of you."

Her eyes filled with tears. "I'm just thankful we didn't lose the winery to him."

Leonard leaned forward and kissed her. "You were right, what you said at the beginning of the summer: the vineyard is something we need to pass on to our family. To our children, and grandchildren, and their children, god willing."

"And you think you can make that happen?"

He pulled her into his arms and kissed her. "I think *we* can make that happen."

Vivian exhaled. Suddenly, it all made sense, every moment of struggle and doubt. It had all been leading to this moment, one of the happiest of her life, standing there above the fake stars. And looking up at the real ones she'd wished upon as a girl.

Sixty

Leah set her alarm for five in the morning, as she had been doing every day since harvest began. She dressed and made coffee in the dark kitchen, then made her way out to the vineyard, where she would inspect the fruit, on high alert for peak ripeness.

The morning was bright and crisp. Leah felt like she could crack the sky just by looking at it. It was the type of day that shamed her for missing fall on the North Fork for the past few decades.

She imagined what the day would be like in Manhattan, how the sidewalk along First Avenue would be filled with shoppers, the cheese shop bustling, maybe even a line at the counter. But the week before, as the first leaves fell from the trees, she and Steven began boxing up the store in preparation for their lease expiration. She was ready for it—had been ready, in a way, since the landlord gave her the news all those months earlier that he was selling the building. There had been two choices: find a new space, or move on. In her heart, she had known there was something else out there waiting for her.

They had already harvested the Malbec and the Syrah. That morning, she was tending to the Cabernet Sauvignon. The fruit color was peaking at vivid purple-blue. She pulled a berry and popped it into her mouth. She crunched into it and rolled the sweetness around on her tongue. She could pick the grapes today, or she could leave them on the vine and see if the sugar levels could get a little higher. Last year, after a rainy August, the grapes had only reached brix levels of 19. This year, she was picking at 23.

In the distance, her father approached. She waved. When he reached her, he pulled a grape from the vine and tasted it.

"I knew that this would be a banner crop," he said wistfully.

"I'm sure you did," Leah said. "Dad, I know you're not happy about the rosé. But we're doing what we have to do."

He sighed, looking out into the distance. "I worked very hard to uphold that estates designation," he said.

"I know. And I didn't make the decision lightly."

Part of leadership, of business, was making difficult decisions. Leonard recognized Leah was up to the task, because he'd appointed her CEO. He would cede the day-to-day business to her and focus on his true passion: winemaking. She hoped she could learn from watching him so that someday she would have his wide range of knowledge.

"So what will you be calling the vineyard?" he asked.

Leah swallowed hard. She'd considered this carefully, thinking not just about what the vineyard should be called for next year's vintage, but about a name that would take it into the future. And who would carry them into that future.

"I'm calling it Hollander Bailey Cellars," she said.

Steven was her partner. He was working by her side, helping her realize her dream. He deserved to have his name on the wine. And who knew—maybe someday Sadie might take the helm. A third-generation female winemaker.

Her father didn't answer. He turned, instead, to the grapes. "So what are you hitting with this fruit? Twenty-three?"

She nodded.

"You could make an outstanding Cab Sauv," he said.

"I know. It pains me, too." And it did. She truly respected the grapes. The winemaker in her would love to see what they could achieve leaving the red in the barrel for a few years. But the businesswoman in her wanted it on the shelves in five months. The juice would go into steel tanks for a few months of élevage—the time wine spent in the cellar after fermentation but before bottling.

"Have you considered, since you're bringing in fruit from the other vineyard, making a small batch of the Cab from these grapes? You have to do something with those oak barrels. Just to see what you get?"

It wasn't a bad idea. Just a tiny batch, just for them. She thought about it: while it aged in the barrel, she would rebuild the winery. And one day, hopefully in a moment of success, she could open one of the bottles for a celebratory toast.

"It was only a thought," he said. He put his hands on her shoulders. "Leah, for the record, you've got nothing to prove to me. I know you're a great winemaker. And it's got nothing to do with the weather or the decisions you make about what to do with these grapes." He pointed to her heart. "It's in there. It's always been in there."

It was what she'd wanted to hear from him since standing in that very spot all those decades earlier. But maybe, if he'd told her then, she wouldn't have believed it.

Maybe she had to figure it out for herself.

Epilogue

Cutchogue, New York
Bud Break

"Your middle button is undone," Steven said. She didn't have time to stop and look, instead keeping pace with him as they rushed from the house to the veranda. They were late.

After a day in the field, Leah showered and changed into a pin-striped shirtdress for dinner with the family, texting Steven, *Where are you?* Clearly, he'd lost track of time in his office at the winery—the space Asher used to occupy right next to Leonard's. His days were filled managing sales operations, and that meant keeping up with demand for their rosé.

When he finally returned to the house to do a quick change of clothes before dinner, he told her she looked beautiful, kissed her, and then, well, her dress came off just as quickly as she'd put it on. Lately, it was like they were newlyweds again. Something about working outdoors, working together, had ignited a physical hunger between them that surpassed even the earliest days of their courtship.

But some things never changed, and that included Vivian's intolerance for even a moment's lateness at the dinner table. So Leah and Steven dashed through the pergola, its flowers just starting to bloom, even as she was still straightening her clothes and fixing her hair.

"We were going to start without you," Leonard said from his spot at the head of the table, Vivian beside him. Everyone else was already seated: Asher and Bridget (her red hair now bleached a bohemian white-blond—she'd colored it just before her wedding to Asher, declaring that she wanted to be a blond bride for Instagram), Sadie (home for spring break), Mateo beside her, and Javier and Maria Eugenia. After the Harvest Circle last fall, Leah had urged her to consider moving back. "We don't just *want* you here, we *need* you," she said. And it was true. Maria Eugenia had left the vineyard because she didn't feel useful after her child was grown, and she wanted to work. Leah made it clear there was a true place for her at the winery. Women were now not only welcome, they had moved front and center.

Leonard, however, was still patriarch of the family. To that end, he stood at the head of the table, raising his glass filled with their signature rosé, a gorgeous, translucent, petal-pink wine. The flavor was a perfect balance between fruity and sweet, with notes of green apple and hibiscus balanced with the hint of fig. The bottle itself was a small work of art; Leah had chosen to go with the Burgundy bottle shape for the slightly wider base. She wanted the bottle to look generous, maybe a little decadent. The neck of the bottle was lightly frosted, making the pink color of the wine really pop. The cork was wrapped in silver, and the label was white parchment with *Hollander Bailey Cellars* in dove gray block letters and in small silver embossed lettering, the name of the wine: *Summer Blush.*

It was their calling card, their announcement to the world that a new era of Hollander winemaking had begun. It was a wine that Bridget had launched through social media in the months leading to its arrival on shelves, a campaign successful in building brand awareness and anticipation. Customers who visited Hollander looking for Summer Blush found that Hollander Bailey Cellars also produced a deeper-colored rosé, a pale ruby shade with a velvety mouth feel. The flavor had notes of almond and rose hips. They also offered a sparkling rosé that popped with citrus—her mother's favorite.

Leonard stood still for a moment, glancing out at the vineyard, then around the table. She knew what he was going to say: his traditional "To the start of the summer season." She was more than ready to drink to that.

"A toast," he said. "To my family."

By nightfall, only the women were left on the veranda. The table was cleared except for the wine. Instead of plates in front of them, they each had a copy of the same book.

They were only able to meet every few months, with Sadie at school and Bridget and Asher away in the winter. After their honeymoon, they'd started a catamaran charter business in the Caribbean. Starting next month, they planned to expand their business to Sag Harbor. Asher had gotten his wish to sail off into the sunset with Bridget after all.

Leah opened her copy of that month's book, *Mistral's Daughter* by Judith Krantz. Since October, they had read *The Thorn Birds* by Colleen McCullough, *Thurston House* by Danielle Steel, and—in the rare entry of a male author—*Master of the Game* by Sidney Sheldon ("He's so good, he's an honorary woman," Vivian had declared).

It had been Sadie's suggestion they return to Judith Krantz for their May book.

"I've been curious about it since I saw the title in your old journal, Gran," she'd said.

Sadie had started her own journal about the book club, recording the novels they read and their thoughts on them all. She told Leah that when it was finished, she would put it in the library.

"Who knows who might discover it one day," Sadie said.

"Yes. Your granddaughter will be scandalized," Vivian had teased.

Mistral's Daughter turned out to be Leah's favorite pick so far, an epic saga about three generations of women—Maggy, Teddy, and Fauve—set against the backdrops of New York City and war-torn France. It was everything a novel should be.

"Okay, thoughts?" Leah said, opening to the notes she'd jotted in the inside flap of her paperback.

"That first description of Maggy is just lovely," Vivian said. She opened her copy and began reading: *"Certain great beauties age gracefully; others hang on relentlessly to a particular period in their past and try to maintain themselves there, withering, nonetheless, just a little every year; and still others lose their beauty quite suddenly, so that it can only be fleetingly reconstructed in the imagination of those who meet them. Maggy Lunel had aged agelessly . . ."*

Leah listened, a movement out in the field catching her eye. It was hard to see, and she thought at first she had imagined it. But there was her father, wandering among the plants heavy with fruit, just on the cusp of ripeness, the second vintage of Summer Blush just waiting to be pressed. He stopped, as if sensing her gaze.

For a moment, they shared a smile.

Acknowledgments

Every book has its challenges, but weeks away from finishing this novel, Covid-19 shut down New York City. How could I keep my head in the imagined world of *Blush* when the real world was in crisis? My first call was to my aunt and uncle, Harriet and Paul Robinson, who immediately offered up their home in Philadelphia. My cousin Alison Anmuth sprang into action getting me settled. I love you all so much. Thank you for always being there for me.

Now, to the people who made *Blush* possible in the first place: A huge thank-you to Putnam's Sally Kim, SVP and publisher, who brought me into the PRH family. Sally, it's a privilege to work with you. Thank you for getting this story from day one, for your thoughtfulness and steady hand every step of the way. You are an author's dream. Thank you to Margot Lipschultz, who thoughtfully read the earliest drafts of this novel. Thank you to my editor, Gabriella Mongelli, who got me to the finish line during challenging times. I look forward to our work together! As I write these words, the journey of this book is just beginning, and I know there will be many more hardworking hands on deck in the coming months. So, Putnam team, thank you in advance!

I don't think you'd be holding *Blush* in your hands if it weren't for my agent, Adam Chromy. Thank you for being with me from the beginning and through every up and down. Our conversations about storytelling are my ballast. This book, in particular, gave me a moment of narrative crisis, and you solved it with a stroke of genius. Writing is solitary, but I never feel alone thanks to you.

Winemaking is an art and a craft and I knew absolutely nothing about it when I set out to write this novel. The person who changed that for me is Trent Preszler, author of the memoir *Little and Often*. Trent, as CEO of Bedell Cellars, brought me into the world of winemaking. He opened his home to me and shared his incredible breadth of knowledge and became a dear friend in the process. Thanks to the spectacular team at Bedell Cellars, in particular winemaker Rich Olsen-Harbich and vineyard manager Donna Rudolph, for taking the time to explain their complex and fascinating jobs. Thank you to Whitney Beaman for showing me a bit about how wine gets to the restaurant table. And, of course, what's wine without cheese? To that end, thank you to Lauren Toth of Murray's Cheese. Lauren, you got me addicted to Kunik!

Blush is a story about the transformative power of books. I can honestly say that reading Judith Krantz and Jackie Collins as a young teenager changed the course of my life. They opened my eyes to the world beyond my suburban upbringing. They shaped my ideas about living a passionate life chasing dreams. So the ultimate thank-you to both of them.

While I never got to meet the authors who captured my imagination in my youth, I have been incredibly fortunate to get to know the rock-star writers who inspire me in adulthood: Mary Kay Andrews, Elin Hilderbrand, Nancy Thayer, and Adriana Trigiani. Each of these powerhouse women has shown me incredible generosity. Despite their nonstop work, they've always found time to offer a blurb or a supportive email. Elin graciously included me in one of her own book events several years ago, and I will remember that night for the rest of my life. It's a true gift when people you admire professionally turn out to be more impressive as human beings than they are as artists.

Thank you to my pandemic Zoom crew: Susie Orman Schnall, Fiona Davis, Lynda Cohen Loigman, Amy Poeppel, Nicola Harrison, and Suzanne Leopold. I love you ladies.

To my daughter Bronwen: It's amazing when the teacher becomes the student. Your passion for Clarice Lispector, Susan Sontag, and Julia Kristeva gave me the idea for Sadie. As hard as I try, I could never capture the true joy of our conversations in fiction. You inspire me. To my daughter Georgia: I love you and I'm so proud of the young woman you've become this year. Thank you for being strong during our time apart.

Finally, to my husband: My stories of love and family on the page would ring hollow without you in my life. I love you.